**The Jake Mahegan Thrillers
by Anthony J. Tata**

Double Crossfire

Dark Winter

Direct Fire

Besieged

Three Minutes to Midnight

Foreign and Domestic

DOUBLE CROSSFIRE

ANTHONY J. TATA

PINNACLE BOOKS
Kensington Publishing Corp.
www.kensingtonbooks.com

PINNACLE BOOKS are published by

Kensington Publishing Corp.
119 West 40th Street
New York, NY 10018

All Kensington titles, imprints, and distributed lines are available at special quantity discounts for bulk purchases for sales promotions, premiums, fund-raising, educational, or institutional use. Special book excerpts or customized printings can also be created to fit specific needs. For details, write or phone the office of the Kensington sales manager: Kensington Publishing Corp., 119 West 40th Street, New York, NY 10018, attn: Sales Department; phone 1-800-221-2647.

This book is a work of fiction. Names, characters, businesses, organizations, places, events, and incidents either are the product of the author's imagination or are used fictitiously. Any resemblance to actual persons, living or dead, events, or locales is entirely coincidental.

PINNACLE BOOKS and the Pinnacle logo are Reg. U.S. Pat. & TM Off.

ISBN-13: 978-0-7860-4310-1
ISBN-10: 0-7860-4310-5

First Kensington hardcover printing: November 2019
First Pinnacle premium mass market paperback printing: May 2020

10 9 8 7 6 5 4

Printed in the United States of America

Electronic edition:

ISBN-13: 978-0-7860-4311-8 (e-book)
ISBN-10: 0-7860-4311-3 (e-book)

CHAPTER 1

Captain Cassie Bagwell's hand grasped Jake Mahegan's wrist as she said, "Jake."

There had been no expectation that she was alive. In fact, all of the reporting had indicated that there were no survivors from the furious combat action in the center of Yazd Province, Iran.

Mahegan and four fellow special operators with ties to the enigmatic Major General Bob Savage had disobeyed orders and conducted a static line jump into a hail of withering machine-gun fire from an MC-130J Combat Talon. They fought their way across a valley floor filled with the detritus of lethal combat. Burned-out tank hulls. Black smoke curling up from burning tires. The acrid smell of death hanging like smog, filling Mahegan's nostrils.

Their mission was to recover Cassie Bagwell's remains, or preferably rescue her from the clutches of brutal combat. Their only information was that it might have been possible to link up with the remnants of a Mossad and Jordanian Joint Special Operations team that had dismantled the Iranian nuclear arsenal. Through happenstance and the friction of combat, Cassie had found herself an integral part of that team.

Mahegan now looked at the peering eyes of tired and nearly defeated Mossad operatives, who had taken cover inside a deep cave near the drop zone Mahegan and team had used. On his way into the cave, Mahegan counted seven dead Jordanian and Mossad soldiers and six survivors, including Cassie. It was dark and difficult to discern who might be who. Nonetheless, he had found Cassie.

And she was alive, for now.

Cassie and her team had no water or food for the last forty-eight hours. How they had withheld the Iranian infantry onslaught, he didn't know. What he did know was that they were going to have to fight their way out. The cave smelled of sweat and urine and perhaps desperation. The boiling heat of August in the Iranian high mountain desert made everything stuffier, more pungent, and miserable.

On cue, O'Malley radioed, "Boss, got about twenty bogies moving to our ten o'clock. Two trucks with DShK machine guns, the rest walking."

The DShK machine gun was a Russian .50-caliber weapon that had a range of well over a kilometer. Its accuracy was dependent upon the stability of the firing platform. A moving pickup truck was not the most reliable, but Mahegan knew the enemy would park the truck in an overwatch position and use it to cover the infantry. These were reinforcements that the Iranian high command had sent in, the Combat Talon no doubt lighting up every radar screen between Afghanistan and Iran.

He whispered, "Roger. Stand by."

He didn't want to give anyone false hope. He had felt for a pulse and not received a report back from Cassie's carotid artery before she had weakly slid her hand over his.

He clasped Cassie's hand and said, "Cassie. I'm here."

She moved. He reached out with his large hand and slid it beneath her head, which had been resting on a rock.

"I'm wounded," she whispered.

"Where?"

He retrieved his Maglite and used it to sweep the length of her body. He brushed some matted hair away from the side of her head. A scalp laceration cut an angry path above her ear. A narrow graze from a bullet? Shrapnel? A fall? He checked her eyes. The pupils were dilated, a sure sign of concussion, maybe something worse. Farther down, he noticed she was wearing the U.S. Army combat uniform she had been wearing a week earlier when they had both jumped from an XB-2 bomber from forty thousand feet, using oxygen tanks. That jump had ultimately led to her position here. Two bullet holes as small as dimes peered at him from her upper thigh. After studying those, he moved the flashlight and found another near her left shoulder. A little lower and it would have pierced her heart.

Mahegan reached into his rucksack and produced two one-liter bags of intravenous fluid. He felt the presence of someone to his rear and without looking up, Mahegan said, "Hold this."

"Got it, boss," Patch Owens said. Owens was one of Mahegan's closest friends and most trusted advisors. Owens had been in charge of the North Korean portion of the mission and he and his three teammates, O'Malley, Hobart and Van Dreeves, had joined Mahegan in Kandahar, Afghanistan, where they had prepped for this rescue mission.

Mahegan put the flashlight between his teeth as he used both hands to clean the wound on her scalp. Not terrible, but bad enough. Dried blood painted a crusty black path along her neck, like a lava flow. He next rolled back Cassie's sleeve. There were two other puncture marks, and he noted the discarded IV bags he had passed on his way into the cave. He threaded the IV needle into her vein. Then he used the flashlight to inspect the gunshot wounds, starting with the one in her upper chest, near her clavicle. Someone had done a rudimentary, but effective, patch job with gauze and tape. Under the shining light, the gauze was stained a purplish red, Cassie's blood. Mahegan felt her back and a similar bandage was placed over the larger exit wound.

"Taken half a bag already," Owens said.

"Get the second one ready," Mahegan said.

The two leg wounds had fortunately been on the outside of her thigh, not the inner portion near the femoral artery. Each of the gashes had similar hasty gauze-and-tape patch jobs. Mahegan would clean the wounds when he had time. They were a day or two old, still tender but scabbing. The skin around the punctures was inflamed, a sign of infection. He didn't want to think about internal damage or bleeding.

"Second bag," Owens said.

Cassie was taking in IV fluids in record time. She had lost a lot of blood and was dehydrated. Mahegan removed his hydration system nozzle from his outer tactical vest and held it to her lips. Her eyes were open halfway, and she was on the verge of death. Mahegan had seen this look many times on dying soldiers. Often, they got better briefly, just to die with some dignity or awareness or to say good-bye. His throat tightened at the thought.

Was this Cassie's good-bye?

He pushed the nozzle between her dry lips and turned the valve wide open.

"Sip, Cassie," Mahegan said.

She pulled on the nozzle as if taking a drag on a cigarette. She swallowed the water and coughed.

"Take it slow," he said.

"Enemy firing on our position," O'Malley said from the cave mouth.

"Status of exfil?" Mahegan asked.

"Thirty minutes out. Two Chinooks, four Apaches, and two B-2 bombers overhead."

"Lase the target for the B-2s," Mahegan said. "They should be on station now." Then to Cassie, "We have to move you now."

She nodded, took another pull on the water nozzle, coughed again, and spit out the nozzle.

"Don't move, Cassie," Owens said. "I've got a needle in your arm."

"Almost two bags," Mahegan said. "I think we can move her."

"I feel . . . better," Cassie said.

Mahegan nodded. "Roger that."

A few seconds later, thunder erupted outside the cave mouth.

"Round up the Mossad. We're bringing everyone back. Dead, wounded, alive, it doesn't matter."

Mahegan and Owens gently lifted Cassie and moved her to the mouth of the cave. The Mossad had already organized and stacked the dead bodies of their team and those of the Jordanian Special Forces. Hobart and Van Dreeves snapped open a collapsible litter, upon which Mahegan and Owens laid, and secured Cassie with two-inch nylon webbed straps, like seat belts. Bullets sprayed wildly outside the cave, some within yards, others not even close.

"Tribal six, this is Night Stalker six one, inbound in ten minutes. Mark position," the pilot said.

"Roger. Marking with IR strobe," Mahegan said.

"Sean, where's that air support?"

"Thirty seconds," O'Malley said. He was kneeling at the mouth of the cave, holding a radio handset to his ear with one hand and a laser-signaling device on the advancing mass of infantry with the other.

The two pickup trucks advancing with the DShK machine guns had stopped and their fire was more accurate, causing O'Malley to duck behind a rock outcropping. He held the laser guidance system steady, painting the enemy mob that was about a quarter mile away. Bullets ricocheted inside the cave.

Mahegan shouted, "Everyone stay in the middle. Away from the sides!"

"Target," O'Malley said.

Following those words, the valley floor beneath them lit up with a series of explosions, which billowed high into the sky with orange fireballs mushrooming against the black night like miniature nuclear explosions.

"Night Stalkers five minutes out," Owens said.

"Roger, they're doing a ramp landing on the ledge," Mahegan said.

The cave mouth led to a twenty-five-meter ledge that looked out over the valley floor. Their only hope of making an egress with everyone was to have the pilots conduct a daring landing where they hovered with the ramp atop the ledge, and nothing beneath the wheels but two hundred meters of air. The speed with which they could load the aircraft would determine the success of the mission.

The B-2s made another run with one-minute remaining. The helicopters' blades echoed along the valley floor, a harbinger of hope. Mahegan suppressed those thoughts to focus on the mission at hand. The B-2s had done their job for the moment. The preassault fires had lessened, if not completely quieted, the enemy in the vicinity of the landing zone. The MH-47 Chinook helicopter flared to their front and pivoted in the air. The ramp dropped so that it was horizontal with the ledge. After two attempts, the pilots lowered the helicopter perfectly so that the ten-foot-wide metal ramp with nonslip traction strips was resting one foot over the rock ledge.

The crew chief tossed a rope from the back of the

helicopter, confusing Mahegan. He studied the rope, saw the snap hooks, thought he understood, and shouted, "Go!"

The rear rotor of the twin-bladed helicopter whirred overhead, narrowly avoiding the face of the mountain above the cave by less than twenty feet, well within the safety zone of the composite aluminum and steel blades. One minor adjustment by the pilots to avoid gunfire or an unexpected broadside of wind and the blade could nick the mountain wall and the rotor would disintegrate, negating the lift in the rear, causing the massive helicopter to flip, crash, and burn.

Hobart and Van Dreeves were the first ones on, with Cassie strapped to the litter. She was priority. The Apache gunships began making gun runs, to the north, perhaps cleaning up the remainder of what the B-2s didn't destroy or perhaps contending with a new threat.

Next on were the Mossad, ferrying their wounded, racing back and forth, shouting to one another in Arabic and Hebrew. Next were their dead, which they stacked like cordwood inside the helicopter.

Mahegan looked at O'Malley and Owens as the Chinook rocked, lifted off, and yawed about twenty meters away from the ledge. A rocket-propelled grenade slammed into the side of the mountain where the helicopter had just been.

Still on the rock ledge, the men who had led the mission to save Cassie were stranded for the moment. Mahegan looked at the uncoiled rope, a few feet of it still inside the cave.

"SPIES rope!"

Another RPG spit rock and shrapnel into their faces

as Mahegan, Owens, and O'Malley donned leather workman's gloves and snapped their specialized outer tactical vests into one of the five snap hooks affixed to the rope.

As soon as they were snapped in, the helicopter shot upward and outward from its position, flinging the three men into a near free fall as they were towed by the ascending helicopter. It banked to the east and picked up formation with Apache helicopters on either side. The rope was taut with the weight of three big men and their equipment.

Mahegan looked up. The loadmaster was monitoring them from the rear ramp that the pilots had now tilted upward at a forty-five-degree angle. The rope, though, was coming out of the middle of the helicopter, known as the hell hole, a three-foot by three-foot square in the middle of the floor of the helicopter. The loadmaster had routed the rope from beneath the helicopter to the ramp, prior to takeoff, using it as a safety in case something went wrong. Night Stalkers not only never quit—their motto—but they also always came prepared for the unexpected.

The second crew chief was operating the winch, which was slowly pulling them in. First it was O'Malley, then Owens, and finally Mahegan squeezed his massive frame through the awkward hole.

The Chinook sped at over 150 mph toward the Afghanistan border. As with the previous mission, they would have to stop and refuel somewhere, but Mahegan felt the first blossom of hope.

Medics hovered over Cassie. They had already hung an IV bag up and were cutting away her clothes, removing bandages and cleaning the wounds. Mahegan recognized one of the men as the combat surgeon for the Joint Special Operations Command. The doctors and medics of JSOC gladly took the same risks as the warfighters.

Mahegan asked the doctor, "Status?"

"Touch and go. Will let you know, Jake. I know that you've got a lot at stake here."

"Roger. I'll let you do your job."

After an hour, they landed, refueled without incident at a nameless point on the ground where an MC-130J had discreetly landed, and ran fuel hoses out of the back. With enough fuel to make the last leg to western Afghanistan, the MH-47 departed.

Mahegan took up residence next to Cassie's litter, sitting cross-legged on the floor. He clasped her hand as the medics continued to do their jobs above him.

"Need blood," the doctor said.

The medic pulled two bags of blood out of a cooler next to Mahegan. They had come prepared specifically to save Cassie, not only a soldier, but also the daughter of the former chairman of the Joint Chiefs of Staff.

"Hurry," the surgeon said.

The medics worked with unrivaled efficiency despite being in the back of the yawing, speeding helicopter.

Landing in Herat, Afghanistan, they taxied next to a large U.S. Air Force aircraft known as a C-9 Nightingale. Mahegan ran with the medics as they ferried Cassie to the aircraft.

He watched the one woman he loved disappear into the back of the plane, which then taxied and lifted into the sky.

"Next stop, Walter Reed," O'Malley said, placing his hand on Mahegan's shoulder.

Mahegan looked at his team, standing on the tarmac staring at him. He nodded and said, "Best damn team I've ever been on."

CHAPTER 2

Zara Perro stood on the deck of senator Jeff Hite's beach mansion and checked her phone again.

The text read: Cassie is alive.

That was the tripwire to set everything in motion. Zara had flown from the Blue Ridge Mountains to Figure Eight Island in a little over ninety minutes in the AugustaWestland 109 Trekker helicopter she had been calling home the last few months as she coordinated the Artemis assassins. After dropping her at Senator Hite's beachfront mansion, the helicopter repositioned north to New Bern, North Carolina. Given the time, nearly ten p.m., and the cumulative wealth of the inhabitants of the island, no one would bat an eye at a random helicopter making a random drop-off late at night.

She lifted her face to the night sky, closed her eyes, touched her hand to the hardware beneath her sarong, and watched Senator Jeff Hite switch on the deck light. The musty smell of the water reminded her of her time at the Valley Trauma Center, near Smith Mountain Lake in Virginia. They weren't pleasant memories, but they were there. She didn't consider herself a barbarian, just a true believer in the Resistance. The soft coup and the special prosecutor's investigation had failed to unseat the president she loathed, so it had come to this. There was no risking his reelection or the permanence of what would flow from a second term. By then, most of the Resistance members had been rooted out. She had a list of every single member of the movement. It was substantial, but their identities were being doxed every day at increasingly alarming rates. All the algorithms indicated the Resistance had reached a tipping point.

Billionaires, movie stars, media anchors, and their legions of followers that collectively pursued the dismantling of the President Smart's administration at all costs realized the time to cross the Rubicon was now. That Rubicon went from soft coup to hard coup.

From nonviolent to violent.

Smart had proven a worthy adversary against the most powerful conspiratorial efforts since Caesar's Roman Empire and Brutus. The president—rather to this group, the "Not My President"—had survived, so far. He was tough and frankly the scores of protesters and front men and women had underestimated him. Zara found herself at the nexus of the true believers in the illegitimacy of the Smart Administration and those that were positioned to continue the fight. While Smart had rooted out a fair number of moles from his administration, several remained. Between the big money, the promises of powerful positions, and the fame that some sought, there were enough people fully vested that they were receptive of Zara's plan. She was pragmatic and had discussed the entire operation with Smart's former opponent, ex-Senator Jamie Carter, two years ago after her loss. In typical fashion, Jamie had given an imperceptible nod to prepare, just in case the special counsel report didn't serve their purposes. They had no faith that a feckless Congress could successfully impeach Smart and relegate him to a footnote in American history, which to many was the only acceptable outcome.

And so, the images of fingernails scraping against rock walls, long hypodermic needles, classroom instruction, hand-to-hand combat, and target practice.

"All okay?" he asked, perhaps noticing the pensive look.

"Perfect," she replied.

Boats with running lights winking red and green plowed north and south along the Intracoastal Waterway, just beyond the long wooden pier, on this pleasant early November evening.

Tourist season was over, and Hite had invited her to his beach home for a quick weekend getaway. Zara knew that Hite's wife was in Charlotte and had declined the invitation to join him for such a brief visit. Truth be told, she most likely knew that he preferred a little random action at his exclusive retreat. Zara knew that she was this month's tasty treat. She had set up a meeting with the senator a few weeks before and could tell he was immediately smitten. She was not naïve enough to think it was because her Perro Policy Group lobbying firm was so powerful, or he had any glimpse of who she was. It was her looks. He'd already commented that she looked like an Eastern European swimsuit model. Men were always commenting on her tall, lean figure, full lips, and raven-black hair.

"Nice place," Zara said. She switched from leaning into the deck to leaning back against it. She was wearing four-inch Louboutin heels and a sarong wraparound, which Hite most likely knew was her only article of clothing. They hadn't fooled around yet, but she had seen the cameras placed in her bedroom. Because of the cameras, she had stripped down, taken a long shower, spent a lot of time naked so that he could get an eyeful.

She had then tied the sarong around her taut body. She handled everything with care, stepping softly and making sure she didn't leave a mess anywhere in the bathroom, wiping down surfaces she touched. She had turned away from the camera and fussed with her suitcase and sarong, so that Hite couldn't see her slip her Walther PPS M2 nine-millimeter pistol beneath the flimsy cloth. She even pinched the wineglass in her hand between two fingers. A perfect lady, she stood nearly six feet tall, the heels bringing her almost to his height.

"Thanks. Glad you could join me," Hite said. "I needed to take a break. Things are a bit crazy in DC right now. This president is insane."

"You've got that right," she said. Her accent was slight, but detectable. Of Spanish heritage, Zara had lived in the United States for twenty years, arriving as a teenager. Naturally, she knew that Hite's chief of staff had run a full background check on her. The only oddity that would show would be a few months in a trauma clinic in the Blue Ridge Mountains. Otherwise, there was nothing unusual about her background. Her parents were schoolteachers. She had an older brother and they had attended high school in northern Virginia. Then life took her to the University of Virginia for undergrad, George Mason University for a graduate degree in psychology, and Eastern Virginia Medical School for a medical degree in psychiatry. Married, divorced, no kids. Former psychiatrist, now a lobbyist, and a committed pussy-hat–wearing member of the Resistance.

"You're busy, too, I know," Hite said.

"I have twenty clients. They all expect me to deliver everything they ask for every day. They don't understand that I have no control over the outcome, because ultimately I have to convince you and others to vote a certain way."

"How many 'others' are there, Zara?" Hite asked. He turned away from the waterway, leaned against the teak rail of his deck, and stared her in the eyes. She knew what he was thinking. It was what they all saw. She was flawless. Perfect brown eyes, shoulder length black hair with straight-cut bangs, high cheekbones, full lips, the works. Her shoulders and collarbones accented her figure, and the coral sarong was snug around her firm breasts. She smiled with straight, whitened teeth and she actually saw Hite's jeans tighten in his crotch.

"For the moment, there is only you," she said. "Let's not pretend that you have not had other 'friends' on this very same deck, and I won't pretend that I haven't visited other clients."

"Fair enough," Hite said.

"You, with your Mitt Romney–looking hair." She

laughed playfully, attempting to change the mood from suspicious to fun. "Black on the top, gray on the sides. I love it."

"Everything about you is beautiful," he said. Taking a sip of his Lagavulin 24 Scotch, he squinted at her. "I mean everything."

"I'm glad you think so. I didn't come here to get your vote on any particular bill," she said. "I've enjoyed our texting the last few weeks ago. It's flirty and fun."

She could tell that Hite still enjoyed the rush of the element of danger. Would he get caught? Did anyone care nowadays, given the current environment?

"So, what's your kink, Senator?"

Hite grinned.

"Straight to the point. I like it." He paused. "I have a special room, actually. Would you like to see it?"

Her eyes caught a winking light in the Intracoastal and she smiled again, then looked at Hite. She lifted a hand to his shoulder.

"Beautiful out here," she said. "But, yes, I'd like to go to your special room."

She ran her tongue across her lips, not in a provocative way, but absentmindedly, perhaps in anticipation.

He stepped through the threshold into the spacious great room with a fireplace big enough to hold tree trunks. Elk, moose, mule deer, whitetail deer, zebra, lion, and water buffalo heads, even fully stuffed bodies hung from the walls or were perched in the corners. Literal baying animals cornered. A bobcat sat eternally embalmed atop a faux tree in the far corner of the room, opposite the fireplace. Having already navigated through this room, Zara felt no particular emotion. She understood killing and that people killed for different reasons.

Opening a heavy oak door, he stepped into the stairwell as she followed behind. Her heels clicked on the wooden steps, her calves tightening into ropey lengths as she guided her way behind him. The Walther was snug on her right hip, just below where she had tied off the sarong. As they turned the corner, Hite flipped on a switch, which lit a dim bank of lights around the periphery of the room. Pale circles of weak light shone down on the equipment. Most prominent was a whipping post, with iron shackles hanging down from crossing four-by-four poles, which appeared to be a modern version of public-humiliation stocks. A small padded ledge jutted outward, perhaps, she thought, for his face—or hers? Ropes fed through pulleys in each corner of the room and were secured to a swinging seat, with an open bottom about three feet above the floor. Handcuffs and shackles lined the walls, which were padded with Carolina blue velvet. A nice touch, she thought.

"Interesting tastes you have, Senator," she said.

Hite turned toward her and smiled sheepishly. He lifted his tumbler of Scotch toward her and said, "Yes, well, now you know my secrets."

"Actually, I don't." She ran her tongue across perfect teeth and pursed her lips. His eyes lowered to her lips, then her taut figure.

"I can show you," he said. His voice was a hoarse whisper.

She lifted a hand and placed it on the stock, nodding

her head toward it. "This turn you on? To be locked up? Humiliated?"

Hite coughed. "Yes, but I think I'm frankly aroused by you without any of this."

"That so?" She looked at his crotch and smirked.

He kicked off his shoes, unbuckled his belt, and slid his pants off, gathering his underwear as he did so. Pulling at the buttons on his shirt, he flung it into the corner and stood there completely naked. Zara barely suppressed a laugh and was only able to do so because she was calculating how much rope she would need.

Hite placed his face in the pad, like that on a massage table, and threaded his arms through the open wings of the stock. Removing a cloth from her purse, she covered her hand and pressed the open arms of the stock into place and snapped the metallic latch shut on each side. His hands dangled on the far side while his head was in the padded foam. There was a circular device above his head, which she pulled down, its edge pressing just beneath where his skull met his neck. With a click, she locked his head into place. The only freedom of maneuver that he still had were his feet and legs, which were splayed on either side of the sex swing, with his ass resting in the middle.

She considered that the seat was normally reserved for women, but everyone had their kink. The naked senator sat there, practically self-restrained, in full anticipation of something. A spanking? Pegging? Flogging? All of the above?

She thought about the signal she had seen in the Intracoastal Waterway behind Hite's estate and figured she needed to execute, literally.

Removing latex gloves from her purse, she snapped them on each hand and got to work. She removed a coiled red rope from a hook on the wall and looped it through a pulley hanging directly above the stock.

"Come on, baby," Hite said. His voice was muffled from the face pad, but understandable.

"Coming," she whispered. Finished with the noose, she reached up and looped the rope through the pulley groove. Cinching it down, until it was even with the noose, she ran the running end through a small hook on the far wall. Returning to the stock, she lifted the top lever, slid her hands along the contours of Hite's face, whispering in his ear, "This will be your best ever."

In a deft movement, she slid the noose over his head, around his neck, and then locked the top hold back in place. Hite struggled against the noose, perhaps realizing what was happening, but his head was locked down, along with his hands. His feet, however, kicked out and flailed on either side of the swing, which sashayed from left to right as he wrestled against the restraints.

Zara reached in her purse, popped a pill that would keep her focused, and then leaned over and pulled the rope taut. She placed one foot against the wall and, with a clean jerk, snapped the rope hard through the eyelet three times, like setting the hook on a fish. She felt Hite's neck break on the first pull, but added the extra two for insurance.

Tying off the rope with two half hitches, she checked Hite's pulse and waited a full minute. He was dead. She unlatched the stocks, removed his hands, and arranged one on the rope and the other on his crotch.

Reaching into her purse, she retrieved two thin dirty-blond hairs and dropped them on Hite's crotch.

Satisfied that she had accomplished the mission, she retraced her steps to the deck, followed the wooden pier into the Intracoastal Waterway, and retrieved her phone, upon which she flipped the flashlight function twice.

A few seconds later, an engine purred. A sleek speed-boat nosed up to the pier. Zara stepped onto the gunnel and into the vessel. Her boat captain was nameless to her. He had one job to do, which was to deliver her safely to New Bern, North Carolina, via the Intracoastal Waterway.

Soon the house and Hite were a distant memory.

She thought of what followed from Hite's death. The concept of operations was intricate and involved several moving parts.

I will kill again, she whispered to the wind as the sleek white vessel skimmed the glassy waters of the Intracoastal Waterway.

CHAPTER 3

Three months later in early November, Cassie Bagwell, now patient number 17, huddled in her "dorm room" with her roommate, Emma Tyndall.

She whispered, "It's got to be now. We've got to escape now."

Emma looked at Cassie with feral eyes. "I don't think I can do it."

"You've been riding bulls all your life and you can't run out of this building?" Cassie asked.

The room had two twin beds, a sink, latrine, and windowed door that locked from the outside. It was tantamount to a prison cell. At different intervals throughout the day, the "patients" would migrate to the cafeteria for their three squares; attend physical training class, which normally included hand-to-hand combat and other combative martial arts; and then shoot at least five hundred rounds on the known-distance range and close-quarters combat facility.

"I've seen the fences and the gates. Ain't no way we're getting out of here. And those guards, like Lucas, they'll hurt us real bad," Emma said. "Then Dr. Perro will come in and give us more shots. The only reason I don't go batshit crazy like the rest of you is because I've been on a pretty steady dose of opioids, which seems to counteract whatever the hell she's pumping in our veins."

"We can beat Lucas and the others. You're strong and fast. So am I," Cassie said.

Emma was sitting with her back to the cinder block wall, her arms wrapped around her knees. Her honey-brown hair hung across her face in ragged tendrils. Her face was all hard angles, not an ounce of fat, and her eyes looked at everything as if it might be a rattlesnake. For the past two weeks since Cassie had been transferred from Walter Reed Military Hospital to the Valley Trauma Center, their nightly conversations had started slow. Emma seemed suspicious that Cassie was somehow a plant or spy put in her room to monitor her activities. She hadn't exactly been participating, at least not willfully, in the training and sessions, she'd told Cassie.

"It's like they're training us for war or something," she had said.

When Cassie asked her why she had chosen VTC, Emma had said, "It chose me. I got kicked in the head by a bull and next thing I know, I'm here. Dr. Broome is supposedly advertised as the best at traumatic brain injury, and I told them there ain't nothing traumatic about my brain injury other than me not riding bulls and getting a paycheck. And I asked him why I can't be on the other side of the campus, but he just smiled and said this is where I fit in."

In two weeks of endless conversations, Cassie and Emma promised they would help each other.

Cassie now said, "Emma, I really need your help here. I want you to leave with me. That's all you've got to do."

"I just can't do it, Cassie. I'm sorry. My mama said she'd come get me, and that's what I'm counting on. These people will chase us down and put a hurtin' on us. Hell, they don't need a reason. They do it anyway."

The nurses doubled as guards, Cassie had figured out that much. They were universally large men who worked at the direction of Dr. Broome, the director of VTC.

"I have to go, Emma. I don't want to leave you. We have this creed: leave no soldier behind. I'm worried about you."

Emma smiled a slanted grin, lips closed, eyes knowing. "I can take care of myself, Cass. Been the only woman rider in the men's professional bull-riding circuit for a few years now. Most of them treat me real nice, but there's always a few. These yahoos ain't no different."

"When I leave, they might think you know where I went. They might ask you things."

"I don't know where you're going, and don't care, that's all I'll say. You were just another roomie," Emma said. "Easy come, easy go." Emma's eyes watered, a tear escaping her left eye.

"But that's not how you really feel, right?"

"You know how I feel. Every night for two weeks, we shared secrets. Stuff we want to do. Fought off those assholes," she said, throwing her chin toward the door and the malicious staff that lay beyond.

"And they'll see that. They'll be able to tell. They'll work you over, and while it's true you don't know where I'm going, they'll think you do."

Cassie had swept the room several times for fiber optic cameras and listening devices, finding a poorly concealed fiber optic cable sticking from the concrete block wall like the head of a small garden snake. There were two smoke alarms, one of which was obviously a camera. She removed it one night and disabled the audio portion, allowing the voyeurs to have their jollies while she and Emma talked in private.

"Hadn't really looked at it that way," Emma said in her Western twang. From Wyoming, she knew mostly about working on ranches and riding horses and bulls. Being distrustful by nature didn't provide her any particular skills or tradecraft; rather, it just made her skeptical of most everything and everyone.

Cassie stood and retrieved a small medical cooler from beneath her bunk. She unplugged it from an electrical outlet.

"You're taking that?"

"Collected as much as I could. I can't handle any more of the shots. I'm afraid it will make me like the others. I can't risk it," Cassie said. She stepped close to Emma and leaned in. "And neither can you."

"I'm between a rock and a hard place here, Cass. I really want to go, but there's no way. I'm not a soldier like you. I may be all hard and stuff, but on the inside, I'm soft. I avoid conflict, unless it doesn't avoid me."

"It's *not* avoiding you! It's right here in front of your face."

"Go, Cass. I'll catch you on the rebound. I can handle these rodeo clowns a few more days. I don't know if my brain feels any better, but I'm glad we became friends. Don't go getting yourself killed or any crazy shit like that, okay?"

Cassie smiled. "Yeah, no crazy shit. And you stay away from the training."

"I've asked five times to be transferred to the main ward. I don't know why they put me over here. It's like a military barracks and basic training or something."

"You like the president, right?" Cassie asked.

"Never really followed politics. I couldn't give a rat's ass about that kind of thing. But sure, I think he's hilarious and a straight shooter."

"Ever notice how all the other women are pretty liberal? You see what they're doing on the ranges and how they move around with almost military precision?"

"I see some of that," Emma said. "But avoid those stupid political discussions."

"Okay, girl, protect yourself. And if your mom doesn't come get you in the next couple of days, I will."

Emma nodded. "I know we just met a couple of weeks ago, but growing up with three big brothers and being in a man's world out there in Wyoming made me kind of look at you as a sister I never had."

They hugged. Cassie said, "I'm all that, and more. Keep that knife close."

"Always. Any of them sumbitches come at me, I'll filet 'em like a trout."

Cassie gathered her medical cooler and walked to the door.

"You're going like that?" Emma asked.

"You got a better option? If they see me in my civvies at this hour, they'll know something's up."

"I know, but once you're out, your ass will be hanging out of that thing," Emma said.

Cassie looked over her shoulder and winked. "Pretty nice ass, don't you think?"

Emma laughed. "Hey, hey, you know neither of us rolls that way."

"True that."

Cassie put her hand on the doorknob and was about to press SPEAKER to request the door be unlocked so she could go to the dining facility.

"Cass, just remember. Us bull riders, we've got a saying, 'The last ride is never the last ride, and the end is never the end.' Think about that if things get tough."

Cassie smiled softly. That was Emma's way of sending Cassie off with a piece of herself.

"Thanks, Emma. I'll see you in a few days."

"Maybe, maybe not. Regardless, let's plan on a rebound somewhere."

Cassie nodded, pressed the intercom button, and said, "Patient seventeen needs to go to dinner."

The door buzzed and Cassie stepped into the hallway with no intention of going to dinner.

Fighting the effects of Dr. Perro's injections, she willed herself forward. Thoughts of Jake served to

strengthen her resolve and reinforce the mental tough-
ness that had served her so well in Ranger school and
in combat. That same mettle that had allowed her to
forge ahead after the brutal murder of her parents.

Her next mission, though, was beyond anything she
thought possible. The Plan required her to escape,
today, right now, this minute.

Immediately.

CHAPTER 4

C assie walked in her hospital gown into the dining facility, where they were allowed to bring small coolers to take food back to the room. She continued walking along the edge of the open cafeteria and slid behind an auxiliary room that led to a hallway behind the kitchen. The other patients weren't paying attention to her because they most likely thought she was headed to the side of the kitchen where patients often bargained for extra food.

Looking over her shoulder with unrealistic hope that Emma would be behind her—she wasn't—Cassie leapt beyond the kitchen unseen and continued down the hallway, dodging collapsed dining tables, stacked chairs, and food tray racks. When she got to a little-used back door to Dr. Broome's office, she heard voices.

"Artemis teams are ready. Forty-eight hours. It's all happening now," Dr. Zara Perro said.

Zara was seated in a wooden chair that faced the

desk of Dr. Franklin Broome, the administrator of the
Valley Trauma Center. Cassie eased forward from the
dark crevice in which she hid. Through the thin vertical sliver between the closet door and its jamb, she listened to the conversation between Broome and Zara.
Zara had been Cassie's psychiatrist since her transfer
from Walter Reed National Military Medical Center in
Bethesda, Maryland, to this secluded rehabilitation
compound in the Blue Ridge Mountains.

Cassie held a syringe filled with water and crushed
Ambien—the best she could do—which she figured was
enough to knock out Broome or Zara, but not both. She
had not expected to see Zara, whom she had an oblique
profile of from her vantage. Dr. Perro, or Zara as she
preferred to be called, was the one who gave them the
shots that were supposed to be therapeutic for a healing brain.

Call me Zara, Cassie. I want you more comfortable.

Cassie was still working through the post-traumatic
stress of her captivity and near-death experiences in
Iran, just a few months removed. Zara had proven to
be an innovative psychiatrist, prescribing her medication that seemed to help lift her from her depression.

Broome was dressed in a white button-down shirt.
He wore wire-rimmed glasses and had thinning gray
hair. His suit coat hung on a wooden peg on the far wall.
Pictures of Broome with famous people—presidents,
senators, and actors—dotted the wall behind Zara, who
was wearing navy pants and a khaki blouse with matching blazer. Cassie could still smell the onions from the
kitchen some fifty yards behind her. She wondered if
the slightly ajar door was allowing the odor to drift
into the office.

Typically, everyone was gone by now, save the night shift staff. Cassie's previous scout missions revealed that Broome never worked late. The only real way out was through Broome's keypad-controlled, high-tech metal entry leading to the parking lot. It was nearly eight p.m., darkness had fallen on this fall evening in the Blue Ridge Mountains. The light whir of helicopter blades chopped in the distance.

"Okay. So it's happening," Broome said.

A man stepped into view. Tall and gangly, dressed in a dark business suit and white dress shirt with red tie, the man said, "We appreciate your services, Franklin, but you really don't have a need to know anything else."

His voice was cool, words clipped, to the point. There was no doubting what he was saying. *We are done with you.*

Cassie recognized the man as Syd Wise, a career FBI agent who now held one of the most powerful positions in the country. He was responsible for all counter-intelligence operations in the United States and overseas. The responsibility also came with a kit bag full of power tools for execution, such as e-mail and text message readers, cyber manipulation, and artificial-intelligence capabilities.

"I've been a full partner from the beginning. I'm networked across the country. It is my reputation as a traumatic brain injury specialist—especially one that has worked with some many . . . inmates—that has attracted most of your . . . *Artemis subjects*. I've recruited and prepared your teams tapping into my contacts from psych wards, prisons, you name it. All the criteria: no family, athletic, violent felony conviction, and female. Do you know how small that population is?" Broome said. He spat the words *Artemis subjects* out like rancid soup. His head swung back and forth from Zara to Wise, like he was watching a tennis match.

"Yes. I know there are about 35,000 women incarcerated for violent crimes in the U.S. About 12,000 of those are for murder and manslaughter. The remainder are violent felony offenders. Basically, we gave you a list of names. All you've done is *house* our teams," Zara corrected. "I identified and prepared every last one of them."

Wise nodded at her comment. "That's right. Anyway, I'm done here, Zara. I'll let you finish up with Mr. Broome here. Call me after when you get the chance," Wise said. He flicked some lint off his suit coat, pushed off the wall, and waved a fob in front of the card reader. The red light turned green and metallic plates retracted in circular motion. As soon as he passed through, the plates snapped shut, a diminishing circle, until the portal was locked.

Broome watched Wise depart and then turned his attention back to Zara. "How dare you diminish my contribution in front of this Johnny-come-lately. I've taken risks. And I've been promised . . . certain things," Broome said.

"What things?" Zara asked. She seemed amused.

"A cabinet position. Veterans Affairs," Broome said.

"Who promised you this?"

"You did! You said Jamie Carter would reward me. The day you delivered that Army Ranger captain lady here."

"I have no idea what you're talking about, and Jamie Carter has nothing to do with any of this."

Jamie Carter? Cassie thought. *My godmother? She was best friends with my deceased parents, and a former presidential candidate, too.*

Deceased. She wondered why she used that euphemism. Syrian terrorists had brutally slaughtered her parents.

"What are you talking about? She has everything to do with it!" Broome stood up from his chair, pushing it back against the wall toward Cassie.

"Sit down, Franklin. We are all saying the same thing," Zara said.

"Actually, it doesn't sound like it to me. I can blow the whistle on this entire thing. The training. The women. Everything," Broome replied.

"Actually, no, you won't be doing that, Franklin."

Zara effortlessly slipped on a pair of leather gloves and removed a Walther PK380 with muzzle suppressor from her satchel.

"What are you doing?"

"What? You think all of the hand-to-hand–combat training, the shooting, the knives, the ropes, were what? Make-believe? Artemis is real and it starts right now."

She aimed the pistol at Broome's heart and fired a double tap into the man's chest. Broome coughed, gagged up some blood, and fell back into his chair. His head slumped sideways as if he was taking a nap as a bright crimson rose was blossoming on his shirt. Zara wrapped the pistol in a plastic ziplock bag and placed it in her satchel.

Cassie remembered sitting in the exact chair from

which Zara had just risen. She had been in a meeting with Franklin Broome, discussing her potential exit from the program. She reported the things she had seen in the rooms on her ward. Women locked in their rooms. Men coming in and having their way. Premium athletes and wounded military women—no men—all going through "therapy," which included the handling of firearms, shooting them at ranges on the sprawling compound, hand-to-hand combat, knife work, and physical training rivaling anything she'd seen in the military.

And then there were the daily treatments of experimental drugs intended to erase or diminish the recall of the horrifying memories each patient harbored in the recesses of her mind. They all had been kept separate, though, for the most part, save carefully matched roommates. There was no ability to truly compare notes and commiserate. It had taken Cassie a few days to realize that she was not exactly in a trauma center, but some other kind of facility with a different purpose.

During her meeting with Broome, he had seemed disinterested, checking his phone frequently, even texting as she spoke. The smirks on his face made it obvious he wasn't listening to her, but rather sparring with a lover or friend. During one of his texting bouts, she had continued to talk evenly as she surveyed the room, gathering intelligence as she was trained to do. The door was the only way out. It was a spiraling series of blades that opened in circular fashion. She had noticed the keypad next to the door and the lanyard around Broome's neck. It appeared to lead to a chamber of sorts, then a door that opened to a parking lot.

Cassie's heart beat fast as she remembered her purpose now. To escape. She was done with the nightly wails of women locked in their rooms, the security guards taking their liberties, the mysterious drugs that amped up her and the others.

Zara walked to the door, waved her credentials across the keypad; the inner chamber spun open, metal jaws gaping. She stepped through the portal, opened the outer door, and then walked into the parking lot.

The doors snapped shut. Cassie moved quickly into Broome's office. She snatched the lanyard from Broome's neck, noticing the spatter of blood across the laminate. His head had lolled to one side, forcing her to touch his bloody forehead and lift it just enough to get the lanyard off his body. Bunching the cord in her hand, she put her back against the wall and snuck a peek into the parking lot through the window. The helicopter buzzed low over the roof of the compound, its rotor wash blowing debris in the parking lot.

Zara was gone, moving to her next appointment.

Artemis teams are ready.

Cassie waved the bloody credentials across the pad. The steel doors responded by retracting inside the walls. Then, as if the metal plates had a mind of their own—artificial intelligence?—they began to rapidly retract. Sirens wailed. Outside lights snapped on brighter than a night game at a high school football stadium. Her white hospital smock flowed behind her like gossamer angel wings as she darted through the narrowing gap in the closing electronic doors.

Clutching the needle-tipped syringe in one hand and a small medical cooler in the other, she did her best version of a baseball slide, still precisely executed as it had been during her college days as a shortstop for the University of Virginia softball team. With the feathered metal panels twisting to a close and looking like a kaleidoscope, Cassie popped upright, heard the exit snap shut behind her, pushed open the outer door, and continued running.

She ran through the bright lights, and for the first time saw the guard towers Emma had mentioned. Were the guards alerting on her or something external? Had Jake Mahegan decided to intervene? Instinctively racing toward the dark woods, she stumbled over branches and rocks. Cassie had a vague idea of where she might be and a firm idea of where she needed to go, but there might as well have been an ocean between those two locations.

To her distant front, spotlights buzzed alive, humming like a million volts of electricity in the sky. An exterior fence? She was feeling her way through the small copse of trees when she heard random gunfire, most likely shooting anything that might be Cassie Bagwell, patient number 17. Automatic weapons fire confirmed to Cassie that she had not been merely transferred from Walter Reed to a rehabilitation clinic in the Shenandoah Valley, but something far more nefarious.

The terrain was rising as she slipped in her bare feet up the muddy bank toward what she hoped was a road. Did she remember a road just a couple of weeks ago when they had increased her morphine drip and she had *voluntarily* admitted herself into this venue? A road, a gravel driveway, mountains in every direction, tall fences with razor wire. *More like a prison,* she remembered thinking.

She had been right.

As she clutched a root and pulled herself up with a

grunt, Cassie stood on freshly minted asphalt and stared at a shiny new eight-foot-tall chain-link fence with razor wire that gleamed in the dull moonlight, like small sickles, ready to reap.

She had waited a second too long. A camera buzzed and rotated from outward looking to scanning the interior fence line, like a robot that could sense her. In the near distance, a motorcycle fired up, sounding like a chain saw at full pitch. Spotlights crisscrossed like a big sale at a used-car parking lot.

Cassie was trapped.

Against every instinct she had, Cassie tossed the medical cooler on the side of the road, its reflective coating obvious bait for the motorcycle-riding guard. With her back to a tree, she held the syringe in her right hand. The dim running light from the motorcycle appeared to her left, behind her. The engine's high-pitched staccato whine was overwhelming, which was good enough to mask her movement. As the driver stopped to inspect the cooler, Cassie leapt from the tree line and covered the fifteen feet in record time, as if she was back running the bases in college.

She stabbed the needle beneath the driver's helmet into his neck and then pressed her thumb on the plunger, pumping her toxic brew into his neck. It was a week's worth of her supply that she had spirited from the pharmacy.

The driver initially resisted and fought back, reaching behind, grasping at Cassie's shoulder-length dirty-blond hair. Since her wounds in Iran, she had not trimmed her hair to military standards.

Cassie used that opportunity to repeatedly stab the man in the neck, eventually striking the carotid artery, causing a small spray of blood to stream out. Her white smock looked like something from a crime scene exhibit already: mud, blood, and sweat stains everywhere. The man's movements slowed as his artery acted like a garden hose with a pinprick puncture, blood fizzing out in a bubbly stream. The hole got bigger, the flow larger, the death quicker.

Cassie picked up the medical cooler, removed the man's helmet, fished for a cell phone, found one, pressed the man's thumb against the home button, kept it alive, used his knife to sever his thumb, and stuffed the knife, thumb, and phone in the outer pocket of the cooler. Another five seconds yielded an HK VP9 Tactical pistol. She used her thumb to pop the magazine from the pistol, inspected the nine-millimeter bullets, and slapped it back into the well. Tucking the pistol into her gown pocket, she yanked off his boots, jammed her feet in them—too big, but would do—and then straddled the Yamaha 450 cc motocross bike.

In addition to having a rifle arm from deep in the hole at shortstop, Cassie had been an amateur motocross racer in her youth on her parents' farm in Greene County, Virginia. Often coming home bruised and battered with an orange mud stripe up the back of her shirt, she had taken her share of risks and falls. While this bike had more power than she was accustomed to, it was all pretty much the same. Handle the power before it handled you.

Syrian terrorists had killed her father, the former chairman of the Joint Chiefs of Staff, and her mother. Holding General Bagwell responsible for the death of a wedding party, the terrorists executed her parents in a barren cabin near an Asheville, North Carolina, mine after kidnapping them to lure Jake Mahegan into an ambush.

Which had mostly worked, but then she had met Mahegan and together she saw that they had become an unstoppable force.

She gunned the engine, popping a slight wheelie, and sped along the fresh asphalt. She couldn't be certain, but the sounds of other motorcycles seemed to be vibrating through her helmet. Cassie scanned feverishly for any kind of opening or gate, but was coming up empty. Estimating her speed to be in the 50 mph range, she knew it wouldn't be long before Broome's lackeys, once they figured out what was happening, would corral her, perhaps even pinning his death on her. She had his credentials, after all, and was most likely video recorded leaving his office. This being her second escape attempt, Cassie knew that she carried a chip near her spine that could only be surgically removed.

She was on everyone's Find My Friends app—at least everyone in the lab.

Trees whipped past her like hundreds of indecisive soldiers, frozen in time, branches looking like outstretched arms, confused as to whether to help her or stop her. The shiny chain-link fence kept pushing her to her left, circular, back toward the facility from which she had escaped. To her left were the bright lights of the inner cordon, which now washed the first-perimeter fence in light brighter than day. She assumed the cordon to her right was the outer ring, the last barrier between her and freedom.

Two motorcycles from the opposite direction bore down on her from nearly two hundred yards away, the distance to a head-on collision closing fast. The head-lights cut through the trees like target lasers seeking aim on her body. A slight bend in the road was up ahead. She would maybe reach it a half second before the guards to her left.

Cassie gunned the engine. Death was better than what she would have to endure in the laboratory that masquer-aded as a trauma therapy clinic. Where the road bent, there was a slight depression to the right, as if the engi-neers had emplaced a culvert for drainage purposes. Out-side the fence, the land fell away sharply up ahead. Instead of seeing the bases of tree trunks, she was look-ing at the tops of the tree branches. The bend included a speed-calming bump. There was open air on the other side of the fence. Twisting the throttle to full, she popped a wheelie off the speed bump, stood from the seat, and lifted the bike into the air as she had done so many times before on so many tracks in Greene County. Two motor-cycles lay flat beneath her as she flew over them like an aircraft taking flight.

The razor wire hummed like a tuning fork as the rear wheel spun across it with barely enough clear-ance. It was also just enough friction to take the air out of her leap and force the motorcycle to nose over. There was a culvert to her right rear, high ground to her left, and a retention pond to her front. She double-wrapped the cooler strap around her wrist and pushed the bike away from her as she leapt in the opposite di-rection, toward the pond.

Landing with a splash, Cassie was up and running through the muck. Rifle fire echoed above her, the bul-lets plunking into the mud and water. High-powered spotlights homed in on her location as she fled toward the bank. Climbing out of the slime, she found the motor-cycle, which was damaged, but still operational. She climbed on, straightened out the handlebar, and sped into a thick forest, letting the flow of the steep terrain carry her down the hill . . . or was it a mountain? She couldn't be sure. While it had been just a few weeks since her admittance to the rehab clinic, it seemed like years. Her memory of arrival was painted over by the pain and anguish of what she and the other women had endured.

Branches scraped at her bleeding face, like sharp-nailed fingertips clawing for purchase on her soul. The air was crisp. Was it September? The drugs had mud-died her mind so much that she struggled with the ba-sics. Logs burned in a chimney not too far away, the acrid smoke giving her hope. The farther downhill she rode, the dimmer the lights became. Wouldn't they just meet her on the next switchback? She rode slowly, navigating between trees and deadfall. This was no trail. Eventually she found a red clay firebreak. She let the motorcycle idle; she feared if she shut it off, the en-gine would not restart. It sputtered in agreement. Straddling the bike, Cassie leaned against a pine tree and took deep breaths. An owl hooted overhead, per-haps sizing her up for the nightly kill. Another echoed, perhaps dismissing her as unattainable prey.

She unzipped the medical cooler's outer pouch and retrieved the cell phone. Beneath that pouch was a re-tractable electrical cord for keeping the cooler at the proper temperature for the concoction inside. Cassie looked at the phone and dialed the only number she knew from memory.

Two rings.

"Mahegan."

"Jake, it's Cassie."

She heard Mahegan pause, holding emotions in check, no doubt. It wasn't so long ago that he had found her near death in an Iranian high-mountain desert cave, surrounded by spent Mossad and Jordanian Special Forces soldiers.

"Status?" he said.

"I don't have time to do a back brief, Jake. I'm in a world of hurt," Cassie said.

"Roger. Where are you?"

"Not sure. Shenandoah Valley somewhere. Like, near Smith Mountain Lake, but not exactly that."

"I'll call Savage," Mahegan said.

"I'm sharing my location with you now," Cassie said.

After a moment, Mahegan said, "Rod Weston?"

"That must be the guy I killed."

"You're in between Lynchburg and Roanoke. Find a secure location and I'll send help. I'm on detail right now, but will break away ASAP." Mahegan spoke as if the thought of her killing someone was ordinary.

"Detail?"

"No time, Cassie. Go to ground."

"Jake, I've got a medical cooler," Cassie added, catching him before he could hang up.

Mahegan paused, no doubt processing. She hoped he understood what she was saying.

"How much time does the cooler have?"

She cursed herself for not having checked ahead of time. Unzipping the upper flap without opening the cooler, she saw the digital display flicker to life. An hour after being unplugged, the cooler began a countdown before it began using internal power to keep the contents at the proper temperature.

Dogs barked in the distance. She hadn't slept in days. Planning, plotting, and executing her escape had sapped her. Like with a soldier going to combat, often energy was depleted in the complex tasks of arriving at the battlefield. How was she supposed to fight, now that she was outside the wire? Could she keep running?

The red numbers winked at her, flashing like a warning.

"Seventy-one hours," she whispered into the phone.

"Ditch the phone. Stay alive, Cassie. I'll find you," Mahegan said.

Whining motorcycle engines sounded in the distance. Cassie looked over her shoulder and continued her flight downhill.

CHAPTER 5

Cassie sped along the winding trail that followed the mountain ridges until she saw a sign that read, TAYLOR'S MOUNTAIN. She slowed as she nosed over the eastern lip of the mountain and found a trail off the paved highway. Revving the throttle with her right hand, she winced at the number 17 tattooed on her right wrist, like a hip, modern-day tat. Her mind kept spinning with Zara's voice.

Artemis teams are ready.

Her relative isolation in Walter Reed and then in the Valley Trauma Center had shielded her from much of the political environment of the day. She knew it was nothing short of divisive, but had always believed the country could unite over common cause. There was nothing like a severe threat to the nation to bring people together. Yet, the Russia, Iran, and North Korea alliance had done little to sow unity. Rather, the identity politics and emphasis on uniqueness had led to hardened beliefs, tribal allegiances, and adherence to conspiracy theories.

Angry that the country she fought bravely to secure was so utterly divided, Cassie revved the engine again, and it whined like a chain saw.

She had done as Mahegan instructed and tossed the phone into a stream as soon as she'd sped from her temporary hide site outside the fence of the compound. Pulling up to the edge of the forest, she shut off the engine of the motorcycle and removed the helmet, giving herself some time for her ears to adjust to the sounds. The land sloped away from her at roughly a thirty-degree angle. Tall hardwood and pine trees towered above her. Cassie had used the motorcycle to hasten her egress to the southeast, away from the compound, but without a GPS, she had little idea where she was or where she might be going. Motorcycles screeched in the distance on the far side of the mountain, sounding like wailing banshees.

The wood frame cabin was maybe seventy yards from her position. It had a single smokestack on the right side. A footpath angled to her left from the back door into some lower ground. Cassie guessed there was a stream in that direction. A single cable hung low from two telephone poles and fed into the house opposite the chimney. A small satellite dish perched near the chimney and angled to the southwest, her right. The open land between her and the trees was worn, as if animals grazed, though she didn't immediately see anything moving. Maybe horses or cattle, she figured.

She stopped. To her far right, she saw the outline of a barn and considered that the animals might be in for the night, especially if they were horses. Another black cable fed into the barn, which was more than a hundred yards away. The evening sounds began to replace the muffled vibrations of the now-muted motorcycle engines. Crickets chimed their rhythmic buzz. Bears growled in the distance. A semitruck hit the rumble strips of a road somewhere in the distance, keeping it between the ditches. A horse whinnied from the barn.

And a pistol clicked to her right.

"Don't move," a voice said.

"Not moving," she responded quickly.

"A woman?"

"Yes. A woman." Her hand inched toward her gown pocket, heavy with the HK pistol, safety off, round chambered.

"This is my land," the man said. His voice had the tenor of an adult, but not an older man. It was solid, but not gruff. Deep, but not bass.

"No intention to trespass," Cassie said.

"Yet, here you are," the man countered.

"I was being chased," Cassie replied, wary of how much information to provide. More than likely the laboratory from which she had escaped paid retainers to people in the region to watch for escapees such as her. There were rumors. The infrequent interaction she had with the other "patients" had mainly consisted of sharing horror stories of treatment, plans to escape, and urban legends of those that had tried and failed.

"What's that box you're carrying?" the man asked. He spoke clearly with a country accent, but enunciated in such a way that she guessed he had some education.

"It's a medical cooler with vials of medicine that I have to keep chilled."

A long pause ensued. He was thinking. Her finger-tips touched the gown pocket, brushing the cotton and then sliding inside to touch the cool metal. She slipped the V of her hand into position and wrapped her three nonshooting fingers around the grip. Keeping her finger straight along the trigger housing, she began to slowly lift the pistol.

"Move that right hand another inch, this thirty-eight special will blow a hole in you the size of that helmet," the man said.

"Understand." He had given away what type of weapon he carried, which was useful. Or he had disclosed one of the types of weapons he might have on him.

Twigs broke and leaves rustled as the man closed the distance. She didn't have time to crank the motorcycle and speed away without risk of getting shot. On the other hand, he seemed to be considering all factors. He had every right to shoot her on the spot. She was likely on his property, as he'd said. Maybe the lab paid extra if he returned a live patient, she wasn't certain.

He was close now. She could smell the horses on him. He must have been in the barn earlier, probably prepping the horses for nighttime. Feed, water, and brush was the routine she remembered from her parents' farm.

His hand reached into her gown pocket and retrieved the pistol. He also removed the tactical knife. She was defenseless. Perhaps she should have provided more resistance, but instinct told her to not resist, despite the rage she was feeling. She fought the urge to attack and remained still.

"Step off the bike," he said. "Opposite side of me."

His voice was firm, but there was a thread of empathy hidden in the dialect. A voice carried the history of its owner, like a DNA marker. Pain, joy, anguish, happiness, discontent, contentment, stress, relief, all came through. As an intelligence officer and efficient linguist, Cassie listened for the crazy edge or the psychobabble, but found instead a humanitarian inflection. Not wanting to make too much of her two-second analysis, she remained on guard, as prepared as she could be, straddling the idle motorcycle.

She lifted her right leg and spun off the motorcycle slowly so that she was facing him. With her left hand holding the handlebar, and her right gripping the medical cooler strap and the padded racing seat, she stared at the figure standing less than five feet away. Night vision goggles protruded from his face like a robotic soldier. He held a pistol in one hand and had what looked like an M4 carbine—more likely an AR-15—strapped across his chest. He appeared to be a basic infantry soldier on patrol. A dark long-sleeved T-shirt covered his muscled upper body while he wore tan cargo pants above what appeared to be lightweight combat boots.

"What now?" Cassie asked.

"State your business," the man said.

State your business.

Words every infantryman who ever stood guard at a post knew by memory.

"I'm being chased by men that want to hurt me," Cassie said. Appealing to the inner knight in him seemed like the best move.

"Why did you come *here*?" he asked.

The question seemed loaded, as if his place might be a safe haven, maybe even a location others like her had found. She knew of no escapees from the compound, but she had only been there a few weeks.

"I followed Skyline Drive and took the turnoff onto this trail. Saw the clearing and wanted to proceed with caution. Not my property."

He nodded in the darkness. The goggles peered at her, then turned toward the house before returning to her.

"Walk the bike into the barn. I'll follow you," he said.

Cassie took some clumsy steps in her oversized boots.

Behind them two motorcycle engines whined loudly, maybe a half mile away, having just come over the ridge.

"Get on," he said, sweeping his arm around her torso. He straddled the bike behind her and pumped the START button. The engine roared to life and he stepped on the gearshift, propelling them forward. With his pistol wedged precariously between his hand and the throttle, he drove in serpentine fashion through the pasture, slowing as they approached the barn. Shutting the engine, he shifted into neutral and let the bike glide into one of the horse stalls. Three thoroughbreds looked up from their evening chow and studied the duo and went back to work on their oats.

"Close the doors," he directed. A pale light shone in the barn. He dimmed it. One of the stalls to her right was actually a small alcove with two rectangular tables and some equipment hanging from the wall. Like a workshop, but different, she thought. There were some electrical outlets at the end of the metal tubing snaking down from the rafters. The tubes were stapled to the two-by-four frame and carried the electrical cables.

Cassie jogged over and set the cooler on one of the tables, unwrapped the electrical cord, and plugged it in. Then she pushed the heavy oak doors shut and lowered the cantilevered arm through the holds on either door. She turned, and he was standing behind her.

"Know how to use this?" he asked. The AR-15 had a nightscope and PAQ-4C aiming light. This was advanced weaponry.

"Better than you think," she said. "But without goggles, it's useless."

"Here," he said, offering her a PVS-16 night vision monocle with head harness.

He guided her up to the loft, climbing a straight-up ladder, then leaned over and hefted her up onto the plywood flooring covered with hay. Bales of hay were stacked five high around the entire loft. Small windows were in the corner, like castle firing ports.

"I'll take the right and you take the left. Don't shoot unless I do. It's my property. If they trespass and have weapons, then we're good with hostile intent."

Hostile intent.

Another military maxim.

"Roger," she said.

"One question," he said. "If you lost them, how do they know you're here?"

"They injected an RFID tag in my back. I'm pinging live right now."

"Fuck. And you had to come here?"

"Sorry, but it looks like I came to the right place. Long rifles. Goggles. You got a Barrett or SR-25?"

Her question about the two sniper rifles was intended as a joke, but his face remained serious. "Just an SR. Barrett is expensive."

"If we're fighting together, what should I call you?"

"Doug," he said. "Doug Raxler. Or they just call me Rax."

"Rax it is," Cassie said.

"And you?"

"Cassie Bagwell," she said.

After a pause.

"I'm going to ask for proof of that after all this is done. If you're Captain Cassie Bagwell, we better keep you alive."

"I like that plan," she said.

He nodded and slid to the right about ten yards, while Cassie charged the AR-15, flipped off the safety, and crawled to the window. Donning the night vision goggle, she instantly saw the headlights of the two motorcycles bouncing along the same trail she had followed.

Using the scope, she tracked the trail rider as the two motorcycles fed single file into the clearing. It was a perfect ambush location. They paused, engines running, and then sped in their direction. Most likely using in-helmet communications systems, the riders wasted very little time. Strapped across their bodies were long rifles.

Rax must have taken that as a cue for hostile intent, because he squeezed two rounds into the chest of the lead rider. He flipped back, letting go of the handlebars, and spun off of his motorcycle, which popped a wheelie before spinning backward.

Cassie fired two rounds, clipping the rear rider in the shoulder, causing him to lay his bike flat as if trying to slide beneath a semitrailer. She shot twice more, both times aiming at the legs.

"Always shoot to kill, Bagwell," Rax said.

"Not when you want to take a prisoner. You've got overwatch," Cassie replied. She got up, moved down the ladder, lifted the bar from the barn doors, and shot out toward the attackers.

First she knelt next to the man whom she had shot and disarmed him of a knife and pistol, tossing them aside.

"Bitch," the man mumbled. He was bleeding from the upper right pectoral area. Two shots to the outer thigh had hamstrung him as well. The man threw a lame roundhouse at her, which Cassie avoided. She snatched his wrist, spun his arm, and yanked the flex-cuffs from his belt. She zip-tied his hands together and immediately checked the man Rax had shot.

He was dying. Two shots, center mass, sucking chest wounds aspirating blood into the air like small geysers. She removed the helmet from the man and, despite the weak moonlight, immediately recognized the ruddy, pockmarked face and slicked-back black hair. He was one of the guards at the facility. Ridley. The man was well known for taking liberties with the other women. He had only tried once with Cassie and she had successfully rebuffed him. Perhaps that was why he was so aggressively pursuing her tonight. Their eyes locked. Cassie grinned.

"Just accept it," she whispered, giving him back the phrase he used every time he showed up with the handcuffs and the K-Y. *Just accept it,* he would say as he violated the woman of his choice.

She pinched his nose and covered his mouth, hastening the irreversible arrival of death.

"You're a hard woman," Rax said. He was standing

to her left, watching the man she had cuffed, rifle aimed in his direction.

Cassie looked over her shoulder and nodded.

"You wouldn't say that if you knew what he did. I just avenged about ten women. Now, shut off both of those bikes, then help me drag him into the barn, but first pick up that knife over there," Cassie said.

"How is it all of a sudden you're giving me the orders?"

"Teamwork," she said.

Rax grabbed the knife that she had tossed to the side, pushed the kill switch on both dirt bikes, and then lifted the flex-cuffed man onto his shoulders. They jogged into the barn, Rax dumping the wounded man on a surgical table, where he immediately began to work on the more serious wound in the man's chest.

Cassie looked around the small alcove she had failed to assess earlier. Hanging from the wall were IV bags, scalpels, liquid petroleum, large work gloves, and other instruments.

"You're a vet?"

He turned toward her.

"Was a medic in the Army. Always liked dogs more than people. Went to vet school at Virginia Tech, using my GI Bill. Now I work mostly on farm animals, but here I am, doing the same shit I did in Iraq."

"Before you work on him, I need you to remove this tracker from my back or else they'll keep coming," Cassie said. She turned and parted her gown near her middle back.

"That red spot is the GPS tracker?" Rax asked.

"Has to be. They drugged me. Felt a pinch when I woke up later."

His fingers pressed lightly around the red welt she had seen in the mirror prior to her escape.

"Right by your spine. If I miss, I can kill you," he said.

"If you don't get it out, we can die, too," she snapped.

"Lean on the table," he said.

Cassie placed her forearms on the table as Rax swabbed her back with disinfectant. She felt a sharp tweak as he shot some anesthesia into her back. He quickly followed suit with a scalpel, digging into her back.

"Damn," he said.

He reached in with tweezers and removed a small silicon-encased beacon, which he showed to her. It was covered in blood.

"Great, thanks," she said. "Sew me up and destroy that thing."

The tugging on her skin told her that he had already begun the suture process. As he was finishing, he said, "I probably don't want to see what you're doing with this guy here, so I'm going to bring you some clothes."

He finished, wiped his hands on a towel, then retrieved a farrier's nailing hammer and smashed the tracking device with force, causing the chip to explode into multiple fragments. He added two more blows and swept the remnants into a small baggie, which he handed to Cassie.

"Don't want any of this on my property. They can make stuff so small now it's hard to completely destroy."

Cassie held the baggie full of splintered black plastic and frayed copper wires and said, "I'll take it with me and dump it somewhere."

"I'd appreciate it. Now I'm going to get those clothes I mentioned."

"Thanks," she said, turning her attention to the wounded man on the table behind her.

Rax walked through the barn doors as Cassie grabbed the scalpel he'd left there . . . on purpose?

"Nice ass, bitch," the man said.

"You'd like some of this, I know. What's your name? Sharpton, right?"

The look on his face told her she'd surprised him with her insight.

"You and your dead buddy out there have raped all the women several times, right?"

"How'd you get my name, bitch?"

She slapped the scalpel across her open palm and grimaced, shaking her head.

"I have to admire your hutzpah. You're going to die and yet you're getting in all the worthless verbal shots you can."

The man laughed. "Bitch, please. You're not going to last another minute."

Her mind cycled with all of the possibilities. Did he have a tracker also? Certainly Franklin Broome's security force at the compound had her last-known location. The motorcycles most likely had GPS devices as well. She listened. No motorcycle engines wailed, but there were other means of attack, via car or even airborne. The compound used helicopters often to ferry people and supplies into and out of the tight valley in the Blue Ridge Mountains.

"Who have you trained and released from the program?" she asked. The blade from the scalpel rested lightly in between his larynx and carotid artery. She turned her wrist and the scalpel's razor-edged point drew blood.

"There were twenty women when I got there," Cassie said. "There were eighteen when I escaped. I saw them training. I know what you're doing in there."

The man coughed, turned his head.

"You move, you die," she whispered. "I know your guys are coming for me. I've killed two already. You're next. You know it. You're a dead man. Make it right with your god. Tell me so I can stop what you've unleashed."

The man's face sagged with the realization that he would be dead soon. Did he have a god with whom to make anything right? Cassie didn't know. What she did know was that the security force was likely in a helicopter right now, smoothing along, nap-of-the-earth, staying off the radar, and keeping the noise signature as low as possible. She wondered what was taking Rax so long to bring her some decent fighting clothes.

"He drugs them. You. All of them. A little bit at first. It's rehab. Physical therapy. Hundreds of world-class athletes come there every year for treatment. Some are a bit . . . off. Into their personal bests and all of that. Not a stretch to get them hooked into the next level of . . . performance. But the others? The convicts? Those are new."

The man's words were rushed, jumbled, pained. He must have known one of two things: either he was giving away secrets for which Zara would have him killed, or Cassie was already amped up on the testosterone-booster shots and was hell-bent on killing him anyway. She believed she had escaped before the treatment took full effect, but couldn't deny that she was feeling a newfound primal rage.

Two muffled shots sounded outside. A thumping noise echoed from the barn roof. Cassie looked up to see a rifle poking through the hayloft window she had previously used to shoot the motorcyclists. Scooping up the pistol, she dropped the scalpel and fired suppressive shots, attempting to gain some time and space and to maneuver.

She was too late.

The first shot found the wounded man's head, which kicked sideways with a splash of blood on her robe. Between the mud stripes on her back and the blood splatter on her front, she looked like a piece of contemporary art, swirling and dashing as she avoided the succession of sniper fire from the window.

After another two muffled shots from outside, the sniper tumbled through the window onto the hayloft ledge. Cassie quickly closed the distance, climbed the ladder, and found a dark-haired man wearing a state-of-the-art night vision device and still rigged in his parachute harness, sans parachute. Skydivers.

Rax came in the barn door, checked the dead captive, and then locked eyes with her.

"He's dead. Others?"

"Two jumpers. Both dead, now."

"Thanks," Cassie said. "No identification here. Completely sanitized." She turned the man over, checking all of his cargo pockets and outer tactical vest. He carried an SR-25 sniper rifle and had two extra magazines of 7.62 mm ammunition in his OTV.

"I need to get you out of here, Cassie," Rax said.

"You need to stay with your animals," she said. "I can take care of myself. If you've got some gas, I can fill up the bike and head south."

She climbed down the ladder and snagged the folded clothes from Rax's hands. Stepping behind one of the stalls, she changed while talking to him.

"What's the quickest way to Raleigh, North Carolina?"

"I'll lead you," he said. There was something in his voice. Disappointment?

"That's mighty large of you, but if you just tell me, I'll be good to go."

"I'm going to the sheriff's office and your route is on the way," he said.

"Okay, good idea. Get backup. Promise me this," she said, stepping around the corner in dungarees, polypro shirt, and running shoes. "You'll never make fun of the way I look right now."

He smiled. "You got it. I'll also say I've never met you and that you weren't here."

"Might want to burn this, then," she said, pointing at the hospital gown on the dirt floor.

He bent over and picked it up. "Might make a good souvenir. Maybe I'll eBay this puppy someday. World-famous Cassie Bagwell. Muddy and bloody. Save me a role in the movie."

"You can't be the leading man, but you can be the great guy that the girl missed out on," she said.

Rax nodded in the weak light.

"Mahegan?"

"You know Jake?"

"Anyone who served in Afghanistan, Iraq, or Syria

knew of Jake. Very few know him. I read something about you guys in Iran."

Cassie nodded.

"Yeah, Mahegan."

"Total respect," he said.

"Back at you," she said. "Now we better get moving ASAP."

"Roger that."

After filling her motorcycle with gas, she secured the medical cooler to the back of the seat with a bungee cord. In the palm of her left hand, she held the wadded baggie with the bits of the demolished tracking device, which she presumed was inactive. Rax led her in his pickup truck along a winding, dark county road, which dumped onto a two-lane road that fed into the small town of Jasper, which Cassie guessed was the county seat. They passed several stores that seemed common on every main street in America: diners, boutique clothing shops, insurance and law offices, and a local pharmacy. After passing through the town, she saw the sign for Highway 29, which would take her south. He braked and she pulled even with him, lifted her helmet off, and said, "Thanks."

"I put some stuff under your seat. You might need it. Be safe and be in touch if you need me."

"You're pretty awesome, Rax."

"We both know that." He smiled.

Cassie nodded, tossed the baggie with the smashed tracker into a stream full of tumbling water that ran away from the mountains, to the east, shook her hair back, and slipped the helmet on. She revved the engine and sped onto Highway 29 South.

After two hours of winding along the road, she had passed three state troopers, none of whom had stopped her. She had no license plate on the motorcycle, nor did it appear to be street legal. Were they an escort? Had Rax or someone else called ahead to pave the way for her? She had just assumed he was going to get police help for the situation at the farm. Broome's commandos might still be pouring into the area.

She passed into North Carolina, skirted Martinsville, slid around Eden, and headed south of Greensboro toward High Point. She hadn't spent much time in this part of the state, but was familiar with the general layout.

As she was looking for a gas station, a police officer sped behind her, blue lights spinning like a strobe. Against her better judgment, Cassie slowed and stopped the motorcycle. Her heart pumped. Not sure where Mahegan was, she was heading to the only place she knew: General Savage's Southern Pines estate.

The bump of the pistol rubbed against her thigh from inside the oversized cargo pocket of the jeans. She was carrying an unlicensed gun in a state where she had spent much of her adult life. She knew the cops were tough on gun laws, though she was a soldier and sometimes that carried some weight with the locals.

"Hand me your license and registration," a deep voice said. "Slowly." The man stayed two steps to her left rear. The lights continued to bounce.

"Under the seat," she said.

"Step off the motorcycle and slowly retrieve the materials," the voice boomed. She sensed movement, and as she was dismounting, he drew his pistol and aimed it at her, using a respectable shooter's stance.

She lifted the seat, which opened toward her and away from the police officer, thankfully. Inside were a pistol, a passport, a license, and registration. She lifted the license and the registration, studied them briefly before handing them to the officer. She closed the seat lid and turned toward the officer.

Becky Raxler was the name on the license. Since Cassie was still wearing the helmet, there was a fifty-fifty chance she'd pass for the faded photo of either Raxler's ex-wife or sister. The officer was a big man in a gray state trooper uniform, complete with the wide black belt, pistol, baton, and ammunition pouches. In the darkness, the name was not legible. Always looking for a hook or an angle, Cassie thought she might be able to start a conversation. *Hey, I know a Sergeant Biggerstaff, any relation?*

"Doesn't look like you, ma'am," the officer said. "Do you have another form of identification?"

"It's a hair color thing, Officer," Cassie said.

The light blinded her briefly, then returned to the license.

"Wrong eyes. Good try, though. Yours are green, whoever you are. Becky Raxler's eyes are blue."

Cassie said nothing.

"There's an all points bulletin out from Virginia that someone escaped from a murder scene in Virginia. Cassie Bagwell. Like many law enforcement officials in North Carolina, I'm former military. If you're Captain Cassie Bagwell, it'd be wise to tell me sooner rather than later. We have a dead man who ran the Valley Trauma Center, where Captain Bagwell was going through treatment. Now, I'm sure a judge will be very understanding, given the post-traumatic stress, and all."

Cassie processed her options. Doubtful he would shoot her, she considered spinning on one foot, throwing her leg over the motorcycle seat, and kick-starting it with one fluid motion. She'd be gone before the cop could fire. Her heart was beating fast. Fight or flight. The treatments that Zara had been administering her had sometimes made emotion rule over reason. She had found herself more aggressive in the hand-to-hand training, kicking and slashing at her sparring partners with combat efficiency. The increased heart rate made the drugs cycle faster through her system, nudging emotion beyond reason.

"If you're the Cassie Bagwell we've all heard about, you're probably considering your options right now. Sticking with me is probably the best one. I've got three state troopers at different intersections about a mile away in each cardinal direction. Each direction you can go in any way. So I just need to know. Need to hear it from you. Are you Captain Cassie Bagwell?"

"I am," she said.

He handed her back the driver's license.

"If you are, and I believe that you are, then you've probably got at least one weapon, if not multiple weapons, on you. You understand that as an officer of the law, I have to ask you this, correct?"

"Actually, I don't. I've done nothing wrong. You have no reason to search," she replied. Her argument was weak. She was evidently reported by someone in connection with the firefight at Raxler's place.

"You've got an all-points bulletin out for your arrest. I may be your last best chance at avoiding some serious issues."

The state trooper smiled thinly and nodded, as if he'd checkmated her. His voice was even and steady. There was no detectable malice at all. Just a good cop doing his duty. She finally caught the nametag from the moonlight: DOBBINS.

Sirens wailed in the distance. The specter of emergency vehicle lights flashed on the horizon like distant lightning.

"I may be your last best chance," Dobbins emphasized. He glanced over her shoulder. "Get in the back of my car. I'll secure the items under your seat. First, though, I have to make sure you're unarmed."

"I'm armed, Officer," Cassie said.

"Okay. That right there is a good start. I noticed the bulge in your cargo pocket. Even money says you've got something under the seat of that bike."

Cassie slowly retrieved the pistol and handed it to the officer. The sirens grew louder. The lights more visible. She walked toward the back door of the cruiser. The cop watched and followed, opening the door for her with his right hand.

Cassie swept her right arm down with a quick, powerful blow to the trooper's left hand, which was carrying the pistol she had lifted from the guard at the compound after stabbing him in the neck with a syringe. A quick roundhouse from the oversized boot caught Officer Dobbins on the jaw, snapping his head to her left better than a Conor McGregor right cross. She pursued, punching him in the throat three times. When Dobbins came up with his hands to grab his throat, maybe rip it open so he could get some oxygen, she kneed him in the groin and then slammed his head into her knee, cracking his nose and for the second time tonight having a man's blood on her clothes.

The car was still running as she slid across the hood and into the driver's seat. She racked the seat forward and shifted into gear. Then stopped.

She saw an iPhone charging in the center console. Unplugging it, she raced around the front, found the deputy wallowing on the ground, and slammed her knee into his back. She wrenched his right arm behind him, causing him to wail with pain.

"Damnit, bitch!"

"Second time someone's called me a bitch tonight, Officer. I'm getting pissed off," Cassie said.

She pressed his thumb against the iPhone home button and the screen came to life. With her free hand, she slammed the deputy's face into the concrete for good measure, then grabbed the medical cooler and retraced her steps into the vehicle. It was a Dodge Charger Pursuit, with an oversized engine for the smaller frame. The engine roared as she raced south toward High Point and then, hopefully, Moore County, where she could link up with General Savage. Dobbins had left the lights on and the rack continued to spin. She sped past two oncoming cop cars, which were doing the same speed, only in the opposite direction. The closer she traveled to Moore County, the more familiar the terrain and transportation network. The police radio in the car migrated from frequent calls describing her attack on Dobbins and the direction in which she was last moving to the occasional "dummy" call to make her believe they had lost her trail. What Cassie knew was that the police had switched to an alternate form of communication and now had two men giving breathless updates. "We've lost her . . . No further sighting . . . Focus on Dobbins . . . She'll turn up somewhere . . ."

Then, as she sped south on Interstate 74, a police helicopter swooped across her field of view, closer than fifty yards from the cop car windshield. Blue lights appeared in all four cardinal directions as she approached Route 27, her key exit from the interstate. Knowing she needed to go east toward General Savage's Vass compound, she instead turned a sharp right onto Route 27, which paralleled Uwharrie National Forest, familiar terrain. She found a gravel road to the south and drove a half a mile into the dense terrain. She saw the land navigation sign, indiscernible to 99 percent of the people passing it, but something she knew Jake would recognize. It was a foot-wide piece of camouflaged wood nailed to a tree. The starting point for the orienteering phase of the Special Forces' selection course.

Towering hardwoods provided double and triple canopy, blocking any moonlight or starlight, but less so the invasive sensors of thermal and infrared cameras. Doubtless that the police had the equivalent of the Army's "blue force tracker," Cassie needed to get as far away from the police vehicle as she could.

The car spit gravel and fishtailed perpendicular to the road as she slammed on the brakes. Scooping up the medical cooler, the cop's iPhone, a shotgun, and pistol, she ensured the interior light was off and then bolted from the car. Helicopter blades chopped the air above the forest in the distance. Sirens wailed in surround sound from every direction. Counting her pace, Cassie darted into the brush.

And dogs barked.

They had been lying in wait, had known her destination. It was a fifty-fifty call whether to have trusted Dobbins or not. She had acted on instinct. Hyperventilating, she let her eyes adjust to the darkness as she crouched next to a large oak tree, listening to the sounds of the forest. Squirrels rustled in nests. A black bear growled in the distance. Owls synchronized their nightly kill.

She picked along a trail that led to the east. Branches slapped her in the face, as if punishing her for her decision to evade the police. But what else could she do? Whom could she trust? She found another large tree and leaned against it, took a few deep breaths and kicked at the tree. Her emotions raged unlike they had in a long time, if ever.

Cassie was 274 paces away from the police cruiser she had abandoned. She needed what was in the cooler, so she leaned the shotgun against the tree and removed the cooler from her torso. She slid her back down the base of the tree . . . and promptly fell backward into a hollow, landing in a soft pile of leaves and loose dirt and other things she didn't want to imagine. She scrambled to her feet and snared the shotgun, wild-eyed and feral, leaving the medical cooler in the peat for the moment.

A deep voice said, "We've got night vision goggles. We know exactly where you are. Lose the shotgun and the pistol. Now."

Every tree looked like a potential assailant. The leaves rustled as the man, no doubt, shifted his position to avoid a random shotgun blast. Nonetheless, she uncharacteristically fired, randomly and at will. Typically, she was precise and measured in her aim and fire. But something was coursing through her veins, pumping up her adrenaline, putting her on the border of rage.

Her heart was a war drum beating in her chest, pushing latent poison from her last shot at the Valley Trauma Center through her veins. Short, raspy breaths escaped her mouth. She reached into the medical cooler, releasing cool air, risking degrading the contents inside, changed her mind, and rezipped the cooler, her fingers trembling as she did so.

Then she retrieved the stolen mobile phone and texted Mahegan: Lane Charlie-274 paces-southeast firebreak.

Boom. Boom. Boom. The shotgun's loud report echoed through the night.

A different man's voice. This one from behind her said, "Now, Cassie, we don't want to hurt you, but we can."

The helicopter had not been chasing her, she guessed. It had dropped off a SWAT team to corral her. But these voices sounded . . . familiar. Not in the way that she might know them, but in their vernacular. They were military, or at least former military.

"You should have gone with Dobbins. Now you've got the entire state of North Carolina looking for you," a third voice said.

Her head whipped around. When she turned, her foot knocked the medical cooler into the hollow. Instinctively, she raised the shotgun, aiming at nothing in particular.

Boom. Boom.

A pistol fired, her back burned, and she fell to the ground, knowing one of the men had just fired Taser talons into her. The voltage was high, and she bucked, clutching the weapons, fired a couple of shots, heard the men scrambling, felt the men on her. She was unable to resist their removal of the weapons from her hands and the ultimate flex-cuffing. Absently, a voice in her mind was reminding her of the medical cooler with less than forty-eight hours of chill remaining. As she struggled and kicked, the deep recess of her mind, which only a short time ago controlled her thoughts and emotions, registered a number: *274.*

A large man lifted her over his shoulder as if carrying a bag of cement at a construction site.

"We've got her," the man said.

The helicopter landed on the firebreak, its blades barely clearing the trees on either side. Someone strapped her to the canvas bench seat of a Little Bird aircraft, which powered up, gained altitude, and sped away from the swirling blue lights.

At some point, she felt a needle prick her skin. Her mind continued to ping *274, 274, 274.* Then she blacked out.

CHAPTER 6

Jake Mahegan was in his own predicament after managing to field Cassie's earlier call.

"Stay alive. I'll find you," he had said. His eyes never left the window, where the shadow had crossed only moments before. He punched off the call and used his left hand to slide the new government-issued, encrypted smartphone in his back pocket. In his dominant right hand, he held his customary Sig Sauer Tribal 9 mm pistol. He was standing in the hallway of the nondescript brick rambler that sat on two hundred acres of premium horse country.

"Squirter toward the backyard," he said to Patch Owens, his best friend and teammate.

Mahegan was dressed in a long-sleeved dark shirt that stretched across his massive, cut torso, over black cargo pants and Doc Martens. He carried a night vision monocle on a lanyard around his neck, a clip-on holster for his overused Tribal pistol on his hip, and a Blackhawk special-operations knife on his ankle.

The only differing feature between Mahegan and Owens was that at six-two Owens was about four inches shorter than Mahegan. Otherwise, they dressed the same, carried the same equipment, and operated in the same professional manner. Eye contact, whispers, hand and arm signals. Like a basketball team that knew when to do the behind-the-back pass or the alley-oop.

"Roger that," Owens whispered. He slipped soundlessly toward the door off the den, which opened onto the deck, as Mahegan continued to close on the open bedroom door. The furnishings were sparse and Mahegan wondered what Biagatti truly did out here. There was a kitchen table, a sofa, an outdated large-screen television, and some partially filled bookcases.

Mahegan fired at a woman who stepped out from the master bathroom, catching the intruder with a double tap to the chest. A movement from beneath the bed preceded a random spray of bullets at ankle height. Mahegan dove and slid to the side of the bed, firing beneath it as a second woman attempted to crawl from the far side.

Two dead. Both women.

He stood in the middle of a dark bedroom, assessing the obvious signs of slaughter surrounding him. Blood was splattered on the wall across from the bed like an artist's contemporary painting. Rumpled sheets on the floor indicated an attempt at a quick escape or a struggle in the bed. He spun, holding his shooter's stance, breathing hard through his nose as he once did as a high school wrestling champion.

The floodlights outside hummed and painted the wooded backyard with prison yard–quality illumination. But whatever had happened in CIA Director Carmen Biagatti's Fauquier County hunting-and-fishing cabin near Hume, Virginia, couldn't be helped by lights. Two of the director's security detail were dead. The assailants had attempted to enter the safe room, but had proven unsuccessful at securing their ultimate objective. Mahegan and his team had been responsible for the Harmony Church safe house twenty miles from here when the call came that her compound had been compromised.

A faint shuffling whispered behind him. He spun, pistol ready. Curtains fluttered inward. The moon cast a dim glow through the open window. A haze of gunpowder hung in the air, but it drifted slowly toward the gap, a ghost fleeing the scene.

Five bodies now littered the floor, two personal security detail members for Director Biagatti and two attackers. One of the security detail had a bullet to the forehead; the other had a double tap to the heart, made evident by the blossoming crimson flower on his black tactical shirt. A third man was slumped against the vault door of the safe room. The two assailants, both women, were lying inert, dead, on the floor. Mahegan knew he had winged the fleeing assailant.

He spun the dial to the safe room vault door and found the steely-eyed director of the Central Intelligence Agency aiming a Glock 19 at him.

"It's me, don't shoot," he said, keeping the heavy metal door between him and Biagatti.

"How do I know there's not someone with a pistol to your head telling you what to do?"

"Director, does that make any sense at all?"

She sighed, lowered the weapon, and Mahegan entered the vault.

"We need to move, Director."

Biagatti deflated.

"Damn. Why would someone want to kill me?" she asked.

"I'm assuming that's a rhetorical question," Mahegan said.

She was a lean woman, with gray hair and ice-blue eyes. A career CIA employee, she had been an analyst and an operator. Married and divorced twice, she now lived alone and was simply dedicated to her work, all day, every day. The nation demanded it and she led the most able spy organization in the world, except perhaps for Mossad.

Wearing dark slacks atop New Balance running shoes, and a long-sleeved dress shirt, Biagatti appeared able to hold her own in a street fight. Her face was narrow, like a greyhound's, and she had an angular nose and thin lips. Her hair was stylishly cut to her shoulders. She holstered her weapon on her hip. Originally from Belleville, Illinois, a suburb of St. Louis, Missouri, Biagatti was the daughter of two schoolteachers. Her father had been a high school baseball coach. Of modest means, she had put herself through college at Ball State, where she dual-majored in criminal justice and international relations. She started early with the CIA with an internship that provided the hoped-for job interview follow-up. Mostly an analyst, she did have some field time as an operator, working the black sites in various countries surrounding Afghanistan and Iraq. Two years ago, her confirmation had passed by one vote.

"My intel has it that all CIA security teams are now considered suspect due to Resistance infiltration," Mahegan said.

"All? That's a stretch, don't you think?"

"If you're admitting that you believe some are, which shall we choose from then? I'll let you pick, but this is why Savage delivered me and my team here."

"I agreed with Bob to have you and your men provide my security until such time that it makes sense to switch back."

Mahegan nodded and said, "Need to move." Then to Owens, "Patch, anything?"

"Nothing. I'm monitoring." They were speaking through wireless encrypted earbuds.

"Meet us at the elevator now."

"Roger," Owens said.

"Okay. Where are we going?" Biagatti asked. She seemed unfazed by the recent attempt on her life.

"You know where."

As Owens jogged down the hallway in Mahegan's periphery, Biagatti drew her pistol like a Dodge City gunslinger. Mahegan swatted her arm as the Walther boomed in the hallway.

"He's friendly!"

"Damnit, Jake, tell me this shit, will you?" Biagatti said, stepping back.

Owens kept jogging and stopped next to Mahegan, saying, "No worries, she would have missed."

"Like hell," Biagatti said.

"Okay, Patch, you take our vehicle back to Harmony Church. I'm taking the director to CIA headquarters," Mahegan said.

"Roger," Owens said.

Owens sped back down the hallway while Mahegan and Biagatti stepped into the safe room, where Mahegan inserted a key into the wall and pressed a button on the back wall, which doubled as an elevator. They entered the small, enclosed space and the room lowered exactly as an elevator would, the length of descent taking a full thirty seconds. The doors opened with a snap. They stepped into a brightly lit tunnel complex, where an up-armored Porsche Panamera Turbo Sport Turismo, a car that cost just south of $500,000 with all of its passive and active protective features, waited.

Mahegan opened the rear door for the director, who said, "Fuck that, Jake. I'm riding up front with you."

She opened and closed her own door as Mahegan sped around to the driver's side and entered, pushing the electronic button all the way to the back to make room for his legs and large frame. He pushed some buttons on the touch screen. Three camera feeds showed them the three different exits from the hillside retreat. Guarding the primary exit was an appliance repair panel van that Mahegan and Owens had detected as they were en route to Biagatti's call for help.

The other two exits appeared clear, though they were rougher trails, not the most suitable for the Panamera, which was primarily a road vehicle.

"We'll take the back way and should be at Langley within forty-five minutes," Mahegan said.

"Whatever works, Jake," Biagatti said.

"Roger that."

Mahegan pressed some buttons on the touch screen, which opened the rear door. He spun the race car around and the wide tires boiled with smoke as the Porsche leapt onto the gravel trail. The first quarter mile was always the most dangerous when relocating from a known fixed location. The enemy had days, weeks, months, if not years, to recon the location. While off the grid, and not well known that the cabin belonged to Biagatti—it was held under a defense contractor limited-liability company—information today was readily available to someone who earnestly sought it.

The rear exit was concealed well enough, though. Vines and tree branches slapped at the Porsche as Mahegan navigated the winding road. The headlights cut a bright path into the black night. The canopy of the forest blocked any starlight or moonlight. A deer darted across the road at the last second, unsure what the light might mean. Mahegan loved all animals and jerked the steering wheel slightly to avoid the whitetail.

"Just a damn deer!" Biagatti shouted. The car narrowly missed a large oak on her side of the road.

"I've got it," Mahegan said.

He knew that if there was one ambush location, it was about two hundred meters ahead, a near U-turn that required him to slow considerably and turn back toward the east, climbing out of a small valley.

The Porsche splashed through a small stream, the nose scraping against the far side, but the powerful vehicle pushed through and began climbing. Mahegan shut off the lights and switched on the thermal sights, which allowed him to navigate through the green haze. And to see the two-person ambush team holding rocket-propelled grenade launchers to their shoulders.

Mahegan slipped a helmet on, popped the eye tracker in front of his right eye, and then pushed a button that caused the M230 chain gun, the same weapon on an Apache helicopter, to elevate from its well above the right wheel. Mahegan swiveled his head a couple of times and watched the weapon track with his movements.

Looking at the team of two, he thumbed a button on the steering wheel. The chain gun spat a large 30 mm round at over six hundred a minute. He kept his eye fixed on the ambush team's location, which was exploding under the fusillade of lethal ammunition. Mahegan kept the Porsche moving, hit the turn, and spun up the hill.

Biagatti held a set of night vision goggles up to her eyes, looking like a field commander staring through binoculars.

"Both dead," she said. "Good work."

A rare compliment from the taciturn director. Mahegan found an asphalt road, sped north, and gained access to I-66. He hit the blue grille lights and raced to 120 mph until he was on I-495 and finally at CIA headquarters in Langley.

Once inside and on the eighth floor, Biagatti told him to sit down. Mahegan sat in a chair at her conference room table. Biagatti walked over to a ballistic window and stared into the night.

"Why did two people try to kill me tonight, Jake?"

"Technically, it was five," Mahegan said. "One got away and two were in the ambush site at the hairpin turn."

"Bob did tell me you were a bit of a smart-ass," Biagatti said.

Bob. Major General Bob Savage. Mahegan's boss. To let Mahegan be near Cassie while she recuperated at Walter Reed Hospital in Bethesda, Savage had put Mahegan on loan to the director of the CIA, who was unclear as to whom she could trust.

"Just making sure you understand the severity of the threat, ma'am."

"I get it. Five people *at least*. But why? And all women? What is going on?"

Mahegan's phone buzzed with a text: Lane Charlie-274 paces-southeast firebreak.

He didn't recognize the number, but immediately knew that the message was from Cassie or one of his teammates, such as Owens, Sean O'Malley, Van Dreeves, or Hobart. But the latter four were at a nearby safe house positioned for whatever would happen next.

"Bet mine is better than yours," Biagatti said. Her phone had buzzed as well. Things were happening fast, Mahegan thought. The shit was going down.

Mahegan looked at Biagatti, who showed him her phone with a news alert: Newly elected Senator Jamie Carter wins praise of peers with selection as the Senate president pro tem.

"That was fast," Mahegan said.

Carter had famously run against President Jack Smart, a businessman with no political experience, and lost an election she was expected to easily win.

"Someone killed Hite three months ago. You were meant to be dead. And Carter is now a senator again . . . this time from North Carolina. Crazy time to be in politics."

"I'm not a politician, Jake. And Carter is in the opposite party. None of this is connected," Biagatti said, looking at her phone.

"Too much happening in twenty-four hours for it all to be one big coincidence," he said.

Mahegan stood and began walking to the door.

"Where are you going?" Biagatti asked.

"I need to go find something," he said over his shoulder.

"What about me? This job? I can get you intel. You can't just leave," she said.

Mahegan looked around the director's expansive office.

"You're in the safest place in the country at this moment. I'll be gone less than twenty-four hours," Mahegan said. "You've got Sean O'Malley and the rest of my team at the safe house in Loudoun County. They're on standby. Don't leave this building without me or one of them."

Typically, the CIA director had a full-time security team, but given the Resistance's penetration into the government, many senior officials were opting for private military contractors. As long as Biagatti didn't leave the building, she'd be fine.

He was out the door and into her Porsche with the flashers on as he sped toward I-95, plugged in his phone, and looked at the text again. He calculated the time it would take him to get to the Uwharrie National Forest in the middle of North Carolina. At 100 mph, he could make it in less than four hours.

Took him a shade over four hours. Twice he got caught in construction traffic and then had to wind his way around Raleigh and down US 1, which caused him to bump his speed down to 90 mph, sometimes 80 mph, but never less than that. Plus, he had pulled into a Kangaroo Gas Station, near Apex, which was a necessary pit stop. He navigated from memory past Camp Mackall, the Special Forces' training area, and onto the gravel roads he had memorized from his unit training. The Uwharrie was to Delta and Green Beret Special

Forces as the Farm was to CIA paramilitary operators. Soon, he was driving through a tunnel of trees along the control road, where the land navigation course began. Every couple of hundred meters, there were "lanes," meaning start points for long and nearly impossible land navigation and orienteering courses. He slowed the Porsche to a crawl, keeping the high beams on. He spotted the letter *B* nailed to a tree. Most people would have missed it in the dark. A green-and-black square of plywood with a faded letter on it, but Mahegan knew what he was looking for. He gunned the Porsche, saw the *C,* and immediately spotted the tire tracks and a blown-out area where a helicopter could have landed. This could have been from training, or it could be where Cassie had been.

He stopped, shut down the Porsche's turbo engine, then moved to the tree with the letter *C.* He remained motionless, letting his senses adjust from the ergonomics of the car to the familiar sounds of a wilderness training area. Owls hooted. Bears growled. Smaller animals rustled in the undergrowth. Mahegan knew this piece of land nearly as well as he knew his hometown in Frisco, North Carolina, maybe better. Days and weeks of training, surviving, evading, and winning the inevitable contests between trainee and trainer. He breathed deeply, inhaling the musty scent of the Uwharrie Forest.

The Uwharrie were an extinct Native American tribe, for which the oldest mountain range had been named. He thought about his native Croatan blood and how his ancestors were also extinct. Alone in the forest where his Native American brethren had hunted and gathered centuries before, he felt a peace wash over him. Disconnected from the erratic rhythms of today's connected lifestyle, Mahegan thought about tossing his mobile phone and walking into the darkness, never to return.

But this time, both duty and the woman he loved beckoned. Typically, he had to choose between the two, which usually led in polar opposite directions. Now he was in the atypical position of having alignment between his call to duty and helping Cassie. He retrieved his phone from his cargo pocket: Lane Charlie-274 paces-southeast firebreak.

He moved to the center of the firebreak, the ten-meter-wide gravel-and-dirt road intended to prevent fires from spreading and destroying the eighty-square-mile national forest filled with the first gold mines discovered in America.

Much of the land was as close to pristine as anyone could find in America, which made it the perfect place for training U.S. Army Special Forces.

Mahegan began walking, counting his paces, figuring one of his steps was one-third longer than one of Cassie's, but then again she might have been running, which would lengthen her stride. In the end, his gut told him that one of his walking paces would be about 10 percent longer than one of her running paces, which would make 274 of Cassie's steps equal to 300 of Mahegan's steps. He assumed she used the pace count method where she counted with every step of her left foot, not every step of both feet. He walked, counting his left footsteps, and put a rock in his pocket with each one hundred steps. He passed areas where the vegetation was thick on either side and noticed midway through his 280th step a disturbance on the fire-break. Footprints and shuffle marks toward the left side, to the east. Nonetheless, he continued walking and stopped when he had three rocks. He was standing in an area where the trees gave way to a more open area. Just behind him, there was enough room to land a small MH-6 helicopter, the type he had flown on many times.

He stopped and listened. Animal noises. Nothing out of the ordinary. The growling black bear sounded closer. The owls sounded farther away. There were smaller animals everywhere, making their rustling noises in the leaves. Most likely, whatever had happened to Cassie here had occurred as a onetime shot.

Unless people were looking for whatever she had.

Mahegan walked toward the thinning wood line at his three-hundred-pace mark. Stood and listened again. His hearing was in the top 1 percent of all U.S. Army personnel during his time of service, despite all of the combat and loud machinery. Sure, he had worn the earplugs some of the time, but mostly he hadn't. His hearing, like his sense of direction, was exceptional.

The slightest ting of metal on metal echoed from deep in the woods. There it was again. Facing the woods, he calculated the noise was coming from about fifty meters away at his ten o'clock. That azimuth and distance would put the trail near the 280-pace mark, where he had seen the footsteps.

There was a whisper, words he couldn't make out, but definitely a human voice. Mahegan took a knee and retrieved his night vision monocle from his pocket. He flipped the ON switch and held the goggle to his eye, scanning like a pirate searching for land. His goggle picked up the glint of a flashlight and the darkened forms of two men.

"Where the fuck is it?" a voice asked, louder this time.

Someone was looking for Cassie's medical cooler. The same people that had captured her? Someone else Cassie had asked to find it? That seemed unlikely. Cassie was not a trusting person, and she wouldn't play both ends against the middle to see who could find it first. Assuming he was confronting foes, he retrieved his Sig Sauer Tribal pistol.

Always preferring to remain on the offense, Mahegan scanned in the other cardinal directions, looking for accomplices and a vehicle. Certainly, these people hadn't walked into the Uwharrie National Forest. He saw the car parked about a hundred meters up the firebreak. They'd either missed their mark or had the sense not to park directly where they had entered the forest. Mahegan walked directly at the car. An object coincident with a person's line of sight was less likely to be detected than one moving laterally.

Head-on, directly at the vehicle, Mahegan walked. As he approached, he saw a head in the driver's seat. It was turned down with a light shining on his face. The man was on his cell phone, which was a bonus for Mahegan. The man's pupils would be constricted from the bright light of the phone. Mahegan continued walking straight toward the car until he was standing ten feet from the hood. They had not been there long, the engine's warmth radiated out from the grille. He stood motionless, watching the man smile as he was texting, head down.

Mahegan lifted his Tribal with its Maglite on the rail

underneath and took a large, slow step to the east, toward the passenger side of the car. If there had been a passenger, Mahegan would be looking directly at him. He watched. The man's head didn't move, so he took another soundless step to his left. Now he was beyond the car, eyeing a dark path between the undergrowth and the automobile, which was a black Dodge Charger. Its front end was solid and sleek, showing the heft he would expect of a muscle car. The side windows, he could see now, were tinted, which would further help him. The cant on the windshield was beyond forty-five degrees, which further strengthened his plan.

Mahegan slowly lowered himself and knelt. Stayed still. Waited. He was eye level with the man in the driver's seat, who was now laughing at some hilarious information on his brightly lit phone screen. After two lunge-type steps, Mahegan was even with the back door of the Charger. He briefly considered it for a return vehicle to Washington, DC, but the Porsche Panamera had performed well and had better options. Looking into the backseat, he only saw fast-food bags and drink cups.

Now Mahegan elevated and slowly walked around the vehicle, approaching from the rear. Positioned over the man's left shoulder, directly behind the driver's window, Mahegan studied the man. The texts were coming from someone named Patti. Pictures were being exchanged. Nudes. Sexual innuendo back and forth. Mahegan figured he could stand in front of the car and do jumping jacks and the guy wouldn't notice. He didn't do that, though. Instead, he spotted the man's pistol in the passenger seat and made a mental note as he refined his plan. Unsure if the doors were locked or not, Mahegan made sure his safety was in the ON position, grabbed his pistol by the barrel, rotated his right arm and upper torso to the left, and then stepped forward and slammed the pistol into the window, which shattered into a million pieces.

He quickly reached in with his left hand and grabbed the man's shirt, pulled him halfway through the window, and used the pistol to deliver a solid blow to the man's head.

A new text scrolled down on the man's phone.

What was that?

Mahegan grabbed the phone and looked at the thread, then mimicked a response.

Fuckin bear wanted our leftovers, dude

No shit?

Yeah I gave him yours

Haha ok

Any luck

All over it but can't find it

How's Patti?

Mahegan paused.

You know, the same

Come help us and fuck the opsec just shine us some light

Roger

Roger? When's a Navy guy say that?

Aye just fuckin w u

After a long pause, the next text read: K, just come on, Ben.

Mahegan reached into the unconscious man's pocket, retrieved his wallet, and saw his driver's license claimed he was Stanley Edgars. Mahegan figured Stan was the most likely name for Edgars, so he replied with:

Ben? WTF? This is Stan

Lol, k, just making sure you weren't the bear

Quit fuckin around . . . otw

K

Mahegan checked the unconscious man for weapons and found a Buck knife, then dragged him into the backseat. He put the man's knife and phone in his pocket, snagged his pistol, and cranked the engine. He drove until he was near the spot with the footprints and scuff marks. He Y-turned the vehicle so that its headlights were aimed in the general direction. He then turned on the high beams and showered the woods in penetrating light.

He exited the vehicle and jogged toward the noise, heard someone shout, "Stan!" and vectored in that direction. About a hundred meters in, he found a trail and saw two men staring in his direction. They were highlighted and he was backlighted. They were looking into the lights and he was looking at where the lights were shining. He was the rock star; they were the fawning fans, holding their hands up to block the high beams.

"Stan, what the fuck?"

Mahegan approached and flipped on the flashlight function on Stan's cell phone and the flashlight on his pistol rail.

He did his best neutral-toned voice, saying through panted breaths, "Hey, sorry."

He was ten feet from them. They were standing next to a large tree.

"Turn off the fuckin' lights and help us find this thing. The GPS shows us right on it."

Mahegan kept running, sizing up the two men. The

guy on the left was bigger than the one on the right, so he went after him first. He picked up speed and barreled into the one who had been talking. Raking the pistol butt against the man's head, Mahegan spun and landed a solid boot in the chest of the second man. He barreled into the stumbling second man and powered two right crosses against his chin.

He had no idea who these people were, but they were in between him and finding what Cassie needed. With both men unconscious, Mahegan found a handheld GPS device next to the big tree. It was an oak, towering high into the canopy. He checked the two men with the toe of his boot, nudging them. No response. He gathered two pistols, two wallets, two cell phones, and a knife. He used the thumbs of the two men on their phones' respective touch pads so that they were open. With his phone, he took pictures of the call and text screens to see who the contacts were, in case the phones closed again. To prevent that from happening, he silenced the phones and found the YouTube app on each, then turned on a repeating series of videos that would keep the phones open for him to later exploit. Then he pocketed the entire haul.

It took him less than five minutes to find the large opening at the base of the tree. The dark night and thick canopy concealed the gap, but it was there, easy enough to find. These guys had done most of the hard work, such as it was, but Mahegan shone the Maglite into the hole. A raccoon's shiny eyes peered back at him. He used the knife to slide the nocturnal scavenger out of the way as he reached in and grabbed the blue medical cooler.

Retracing his steps to the car, he approached carefully, saw the man in the back was still unconscious, slid him out onto the firebreak, and then drove the Charger to where his Porsche was parked. He slammed his knife into the four tires on the Charger and tossed the keys into the woods on the far side of the road. Emptying out his find onto the Porsche passenger seat, he sorted through the guns, wallets, knives, and phones. It was a substantial haul that could result in a significant connection to whatever had happened to Cassie, or it could lead to some hired amateurs.

Mahegan was betting on the amateur angle when he started the Porsche and began his return to DC.

Almost on cue, Biagatti called and said, "Get your ass back here now. We've got a coup."

CHAPTER 7

A rectangular beam of light cut across the room and burned through Cassie's eyelids. She struggled to open her eyes, slammed shut by fatigue or drugs, or both.

Someone was efficiently moving throughout the room, opening the heavy silk drapes on three sides of the bedroom. A woman in a black maid's outfit, with a white apron, was hefting back the last of the drapes, tying them off with a knotted silk cord the color of gold.

Cassie rolled over and stared at the woman, who glanced at her.

"Miss Bagwell, Senator Carter will be hosting you at eleven a.m. this morning. Your clothes are on the bench," she said.

Cassie's tongue was stuck to the roof of her mouth, her lips sticky with dehydration.

She tried to recall the events of the last, what,

twenty-four hours? She didn't know. The name Senator Carter bounced with familiarity in her mind: Images of growing up in Northern Virginia, near the Pentagon, found their way through the fog. Visits to a young congresswoman's house. Parties. Christmas caroling. Then, as she attended the University of Virginia, a woman hugging her as she received her diploma. The big grin, blond hair, and a steely voice saying, *Congratulations, Cass, so proud of you.*

A year ago she had seen the former senator at her parents' funeral. Syrian terrorists had kidnapped and held her parents captive in the Blue Ridge Mountains, near Asheville, North Carolina. Carter was fresh off a brutal presidential campaign, which she had lost. Gaining the majority of the popular vote, but losing the Electoral College vote, Carter had not taken her defeat either easily or lightly. The anguish on Carter's face hovered in Cassie's mind and her first coherent thought was that she had wondered whether the angry frown was in response to her parents' brutal slaying or left over from the election defeat. Jake had ushered her away in his large arms as she wept uncontrollably. Both parents. Both dead. Same day. Same killer.

"Do you understand, ma'am?" the woman asked. The maid's voice was high-pitched and accented. Something Hispanic.

"Where am I?"

"In Senator Carter's house."

Assuming the maid was using Carter's former title, Cassie shifted in the bed, trying to gain some altitude. She might as well have been looking through a dirty Coke bottle, though. The armoire across the room faded in and out. The woman leaned over and peered at her, looking like a bigmouthed Snapchat filter with oversized lips and funky glasses.

"You okay?" she asked, sounding distant and close at the same time.

Cassie took a few minutes to get her bearings, sitting up in the bed.

"Your name?"

"Mi nombre es Rosa," she said.

Cassie smiled. *"Gracias,* Rosa. I'm Cassie."

Rosa smiled and nodded. "Yes, we know you, Ms. Cassie."

"Where am I again?"

"Cassie, this is Jamie Carter, your godmother," said the commanding voice through the intercom. "Get cleaned up and come on down for some brunch, dear."

Four Sonos speakers were positioned in each corner of the room. There was no obvious camera and maybe one didn't exist, but "Jammie," as Cassie had once called her, seemed to be aware of what she was doing.

Rosa patted her knee, walked away, and stood by the door, turning her head to watch Cassie.

"I am leaving now. IV drip. Just disconnect like this," Rosa said. She showed Cassie how to remove the IV without removing the needle taped on the back of her hand. The plastic connector clicked and the line came from her hand, held up by a smiling Rosa. "See? Leave like this? Or put back in?"

"Leave it," Cassie said. "What's in the drip?" Her voice was terse, laced with anger at this stranger who hovered over her like an evil witch.

Rosa shrugged. "You were very dehydrated when

you came in this morning. But I watch over you. Like a hawk," she said with a big smile. Rosa made a claw with her hand and held it up in the air above Cassie. "Make sure you're okay."

"Get out!" Cassie swatted Rosa's hand away as best she could, disoriented. She tried to counterpunch the perceived attack. A momentary rage surged through her mind. She was disoriented and saw Rosa as an enemy. She visualized the hand-to-hand combat she had endured in Iran. Men coming at her from all directions. She had fired her Beretta pistol until it clicked hollow against an empty magazine. She had flipped it over in her hand and used it as a blunt-force instrument as men clawed at her. Shots rang out, echoing along the valley floor. Her Jordanian friend, Captain Hattab, tackled her and took three bullets to his torso, bleeding out all over her. She had snatched his pistol and continued to fire. But the men kept coming and coming and coming.

At some point, Rosa looped the IV drip tube on the metal stand next to the bed and stepped out of the room and closed the door.

After a few minutes, Cassie was able to focus, the haunting memories fading. Her mind searched for the energy of Zara's drugs. The needle? Where was the needle when she needed it? One minute, she was fine; the next, she was back on the desert floor or in the cave or in the fight of her life. Was this what post-traumatic stress was like? She looked at the floor from high upon the mattress on the poster bed. She managed to slide off, stumbling a bit. She grabbed the clothes that the maid had laid out for her.

Jeans, dark green sweater, socks, Converse tennis shoes, bra, and underwear. All new. All practical. She carried the clothes into the bathroom, ran the shower, took her time, checked her cuts and bruises in the mirror—not too bad, but not great—then dried herself, dressed—the clothes fit reasonably well—and walked downstairs. Still a bit foggy, still unsure exactly where she was, Cassie stood at the bottom of the oak landing, veins pulsing hot, feeling like fire under her skin.

Jamie Carter was reading a newspaper folded into one-eighth of its size, as if she were on the subway or train, and eating fruit from a white porcelain plate. The glassed-in sunroom shone brightly with the morning sun. Beyond the window was an expansive green lawn that sloped to a large lake or river. A wooden plank dock jutted into the dark water, a white speedboat moored to its side.

Without looking up, Jamie said, "Come, Cassie. Have a seat. You need to eat." She pointed at an open seat to her right. The newspaper was to her left.

Cassie walked carefully to the sunroom, passing through an expansive family room with high-end design furniture full of oak and walnut. A large-screen TV, about the size of a Jumbotron, hung above the stand-alone fireplace to her right. The back side of the fireplace poked onto the wraparound deck outside.

Sitting in the soft white leather dining-table chair, Cassie squinted at the harsh light blazing through every window, felt like lashing at it, resisted the urge. Jamie put down the newspaper and then her fork, which bore the cheesy remnants of eggs Benedict.

Jamie Carter was a graceful Southern lady with perfectly straight, razor-cut blond hair parted on the left side and hanging just off her shoulder. She wore a white silk long-sleeved blouse with an olive cashmere sweater draped around her shoulders. Khaki pants fell atop a pair of practical pumps. She had a pair of breakable readers hanging from her neck. Her eyes were narrow, showing a hint of blue, and her nose had been sculpted into a perfect little ski slope, straight down. Everything on her face was smooth and sanded.

"This doesn't look like your house in Virginia, Jammie," Cassie said. The hint of sarcasm was out of character, but there it was. Jamie eyed her for a moment and smirked as if to say, *Very well.*

"First of all, we're adults, so drop the 'Jammie,' Cassie. Jamie or Senator work just fine."

Cassie nodded. "Okay. *Senator?*" She said the word as if it didn't fit quite right, even though Jamie had been a senator from Virginia for nearly four terms, starting at the fresh age of thirty-five directly after her gubernatorial term.

"Yes, here. Catch up on the news. I saved these for you. It's November. You've been in the hospital for three months."

Jamie handed Cassie the *Washington Post,* which she unfolded to show two above-the-fold articles:

SENATOR HITE DIES IN BIZARRE SEX SCENE

JAMIE CARTER WINS SPECIAL ELECTION: NAMED SENATE PRO TEM BY PEERS

"Wow. I mean, I didn't know Hite, but congratulations, I guess."

"Thank you, I guess," Jamie said. She laughed. "That paper with Hite's death is from August." She tapped the folded *Post* on her left, then her finger flitted to the newspaper to her right. "This one is from yesterday. Cake walk, really."

"Wait," Cassie said. "Hite was from North Carolina. We're in North Carolina? I thought you lived in Virginia? What happened to your Middleburg place?"

Jamie placed a well-manicured hand on Cassie's wrist—a sign of affection or a shackle?—and said, "I've lived here since . . . your parents passed."

She snatched her wrist away, wrenching it free from her clutch.

"My parents didn't *pass,* Senator. They were slaughtered by Syrian terrorists," Cassie spat. Emotion wasn't her forte or her practice. Then she had a sudden recall of her harrowing escape from the facility, the medical cooler and its contents that had to be preserved at all costs, and a high-speed chase through North Carolina. The cooler. The tree. The men surrounding her. She needed the contents of the cooler, stat.

"I know they didn't *pass,* Cassie. Your mother was my best friend since college. Roommates. What do you want me to say? Since your parents were *brutally slain*? Is that better?"

Cassie looked outside, saw a woman walking toward them from the pier. She was tall, with shoulder-length black hair and a long stride. A black T-shirt read BADASS BITCH, written in big white letters. Tight yoga pants showed off her toned quadriceps and calf muscles. Most interesting was the pistol tucked into her right side.

"That's my new policy advisor, Zara Perro," Jamie said. "I believe you two know each other?"

Cassie's heart clutched. Zara. This is where she had flown after murdering Broome. Zara strode into the sunroom, sweat glistening off her brow, yoga mat tucked under her arm.

"Good morning," she said in a Hispanic-accented voice. As an intelligence officer, Cassie had studied languages in detail. From their previous sessions at the Valley Trauma Center, she had pegged Perro as being from the Basque region of Spain, most likely.

"Zara, I think you know Captain Bagwell here," Jamie said.

"Of course. She was my patient," Zara said. She reached out a hand and Cassie shook it, but all she could think is, *Artemis teams are ready.*

Rosa brought two plates of eggs Benedict and hash browns. Zara sat down opposite Jamie, their eyes locked for a moment, and then they both turned to Cassie, with Jamie saying, "Cassie, what do you remember about everything after Iran?"

"I've pretty much covered all of that with Zara in the lovely prison she was running with Broome. So let's start with some of my questions, Senator," Cassie said.

Jamie locked a steely gray-eyed gaze on Cassie. "This is my house. We play by my rules."

Zara smirked. "*In prison?* You were making great gains, Cassie. I'm disappointed to hear you call the trauma center a prison."

"Women locked in rooms. Guards doing what they wanted. What would you call that?"

"I never observed those conditions. That's a legitimate facility," Zara said.

"And that was a legitimate bullet you put in Dr. Broome's heart. Rather, two bullets?"

Zara nodded and smiled tightly. Her large brown eyes fixated on Cassie, unblinking.

"I see I've got your attention," Cassie said. "So let's start with my questions, my rules, shall we?"

Jamie and Zara exchanged furtive glances.

"Actually," Jamie said. "There is a video of you running from Dr. Broome's office near his time of death."

Cassie said, "Zara was about five minutes before me."

"The tapes don't show that. The police haven't mentioned that."

Cassie looked away. Of course, there would be no record of Zara departing the compound.

"So you're harboring a fugitive?" Cassie asked.

"I never said the police have this video," Jamie said.

She processed that information. Jamie and Zara sat comfortably across from her, shoveling information at her in heaps. A fantastic story about her arrival here in New Bern. Her implication in the murder of Dr. Broome.

"I get it. Either I work for you or you turn over the tape," Cassie said.

"You always were a direct one," Jamie said. "I never said any such thing. You're always free to do whatever you please."

The statement hung in the air as it was intended. A challenge. Defy Jamie and Zara and the cops would mysteriously find a tape. Comply and perhaps she was in the clear.

"Won't they make the connection that I went missing at exactly the same time as you shot Dr. Broome?" she said to Zara.

"Again, I had nothing to do with that, but if you must know, they already have one of the kitchen workers as a suspect. It seems that Dr. Broome had a nightly rendezvous with her, took some liberties she wasn't prepared to give, and she finally got her retribution."

"Then I'm in the clear," Cassie snapped.

"There's always exculpatory evidence that can be produced for her. Don't get full of yourself," Zara said. "I worry about you."

Cassie sighed, assessing her predicament. "Seriously? I have questions."

"Of course," Jamie said.

"Where am I?"

"New Bern, North Carolina. Craven County. You're on the Neuse River, which flooded last year with Hurricane Florence. I bought this property for pennies on a dollar from someone whose insurance had, unfortunately for them, lapsed. Next question?"

She knew New Bern. It was in between Raleigh and the coast, just upriver from Carteret County, Morehead City, Beaufort, and Atlantic Beach. Camp Lejeune was an hour or two away toward the coast.

"How did I get here?"

"Zara found you. You had been in a car accident in the middle of the state. Montgomery County, to be exact. Right next to your stomping grounds in Southern Pines. My guess is, you were headed to General Savage's place. Your new daddy? Anyway, the police were chasing you. I'm not sure what you did wrong, but I told the governor and the state bureau of investigation chief that you were with me and that they shouldn't pursue the matter any further."

Much of that rang true, but parts also did not. She remembered helicopters and men in tactical vests. She didn't recall a car accident. Maybe they had wrecked the car and Zara had happened upon the scene? That was too much of a coincidence.

To Zara, she asked, "Where did you find me?"

"In the woods, near the Uwharrie Forest," she said flatly.

That information rang true. Thick canopy above. Gravel road. Terrain with which she was familiar.

"What kind of car was I in when I wrecked?"

Her tenor was more like a prosecutor cross-examining a witness.

"You had stolen a police cruiser," Jamie said.

She remembered that, as well as Rax helping her in Virginia, her memory rushing back, like a flood.

"All coming together?" Jamie said.

"Yes, for the most part. Except the accident. I don't remember that," she said flatly.

"Here's a newspaper article about it from this morning," Jamie said. She reached to the floor and snagged a newspaper folded in half, then placed it on top of the one she had previously given to Cassie.

Cassie read the details. Police car stolen. Accident in Montgomery County. Unidentified female thrown from the vehicle into the woods. First responders arrived and called in a helicopter to life-flight her to the nearest hospital.

"When we learned it was you, Cassie, Zara inter-cepted you at the landing pad at WakeMed in Raleigh. She put you in an unmarked ambulance and brought you here."

Cassie looked at Zara, who nodded.

Could the helicopter have been a medical evacua-tion aircraft? Could the men in tactical vests have been EMS workers? What about the medical cooler? The drugs she had been given in the facility near Smith Moun-tain Lake in Virginia?

"How did you learn it was me?"

"Please. We have an operation that is scanning and gathering information every second. We knew the po-lice car had been stolen. Didn't know it was you. But we were tracking it, quite frankly, so I could put out a strong anticrime statement once the ordeal was over with. Then the dash cam flashed back a photo of you, which then went to the SBI, where I had Zara get in-volved. We made sure the photo was not distributed and that the 'chase' was intended to find you and get you out of trouble."

"Then why not life-flight me right here, if that was your goal?"

"And have every media van in the state parked out front of the newly appointed senator's house? You're smarter than that, Cassie. Zara's a medical doctor. She intervened at the exact right time, using her credentials to pose as your primary care physician. Then she whisked you away from the helipad."

Cassie had no memory of any of this. There were the four men, the needle, the pinch in her arm. She nodded.

"Coming together for you?" Jamie asked.

"Partially," Cassie said.

"Good, because I've notified the Army that you're in my care and on convalescent leave. And once you recover, you'll serve in the Office of Congressional Liaison on my staff, working with Zara."

Cassie thought of many fates she would prefer to face than being a staff weenie working for Congress, her latest predicament perhaps even preferable.

"After all, the new Senate president pro tem will need a crackerjack legislative team," Jamie said.

"President pro tem?" Cassie muttered.

"I know. You're thinking it's too soon for me to be named. With the president going off the rails the way he is, we need leadership now. With my election official last week, the majority leader called and told me my peers selected me as pro tem. I'm sure it was to keep me from moving on him as majority leader, but I'm fine with that. We face key votes *this week*. Climate change. Income equality. Infrastructure. Electoral College. All of this is coming due and we need Hite's vote, which is now *my* vote."

Cassie nodded. Jamie continued.

"My new-slash-former colleagues still see me as the leader of the party. Though my service was interrupted at twenty-two years, my peers have selected me to represent them. I've been on the phone all morning talking to the national committee and Senate leadership. Hite followed me when I stepped down to run for president, and now it only makes sense that I resume where I left off, pre-Hite."

"I wasn't wondering about any of that. I was trying to remember what the president pro tem does," Cassie said.

Jamie and Zara smiled in a patronizing way, no teeth, one-sided smirk, and eyes cast downward.

"The Senate president pro tempore, dear Cassie, is the leader of the Senate. The most powerful *unknown* person in the Senate. You've been to war. You understand power and chain of command. God knows your father and mother did. They were the ultimate power couple."

"When do you start?"

"Immediately. Because the seat was vacated by Hite's death, I now get to finish the remainder of the term. Two years."

Cassie nodded.

"I'll be wanting you with me, as part of my team," Jamie said.

"I have an apartment in Fayetteville. I have soldiers that I lead. I can't just move to DC," Cassie said.

"You can, and you will," Jamie responded. "Zara will help you. She's already secured a nice place on Capitol Hill for you. Your soldiers will be fine. They change commanders all the time."

Cassie leaned back in her chair, unsure what to make of the last few months. Combat and near death in Iran. Rehabilitation at Walter Reed National Military Medical Center. Then being transferred to the private facility the residents called "Psycho Central." The physical wounds had healed properly with time, as they typically do. Gunshot wound to the upper chest and two in the outer thigh.

It was the memory and trauma to her brain that had proven troublesome. On that thought, she asked Jamie, "What do you know about me being transferred from Walter Reed?"

"That was me, Cassie. I came to see you in Walter Reed—you probably don't even remember—and you said they were shit. That you weren't getting the psychological help you needed. So I asked what could be done."

"I'm not crazy, Jamie," Cassie protested. "I don't remember any of that."

"No, maybe not crazy, but you definitely asked me to help. You were pretty doped up at the time. Also, what you went through in Iran . . . changed something," Jamie said.

"It's true," Zara added.

"How would you even know?"

"We were there, Captain Bagwell," Zara said. "I was with your godmother when we talked to the doctors. They had no idea what they were doing."

"And you know this how?" Cassie snapped. The rage began boiling again. Her veins and arteries pumped wildly. She needed what was in the cooler, but she pushed the anxiety down, shoved it away. What she was really thinking, though, was: *Why were Jamie and her wingwoman, Zara, talking to my doctor?* She hadn't paid much attention to her parents' wills. Had there been some provision listing Jamie as her next of kin? She didn't think so, but she would have to check it soon.

"As you know, I'm a trained psychiatrist, Cassie. I can make several hundred thousand dollars a year evaluating a patient at a time, or I can make millions representing health care companies and making sure Americans have proper care," Zara said.

"Very noble," Cassie quipped. "I don't recall signing anything saying you could see my health care records." She turned toward Jamie and said, "Let me guess. My parents made you my NOK?"

"They did. And, frankly, I don't understand the hostility. We have helped you. You broke out of a trauma center, stole a police car, Cassie. Any other person would be in jail. You ran from a classified mental-health facility, where only patients with top secret clearances are allowed."

"What?"

"I had you transferred to the Valley Trauma Center. *You asked me!* There's a general-practice wing, and then there's the wing where we had you placed. Surely, you can understand the sensitivity the government might have with someone possessing a top secret clearance who is also struggling with severe post-traumatic stress disorder, Cassie."

Cassie nodded blankly. *Could Jamie be speaking the truth? Was I in a classified wing of the trauma clinic? Sure didn't seem like it.*

"I see you processing. Do you remember? They needed me to sign the papers. As much as you and this Indian fellow are dating and all, he doesn't count legally. I count legally when you're incapacitated."

"Jake saved my life," Cassie hissed. Her mind flashed white. Jake was sacrosanct. Sacred ground.

"Down, girl. I know exactly what happened. He left

you there, and then we made him go get you," Jamie said.

"How dare you!" Cassie shouted. She pushed away from the table, the metal legs of her chair protesting on the slate floor of the sunroom. She shot a toned, but bruised, arm at Jamie and then Zara, pointing a finger like a gun.

"Jake didn't *leave* me. I told him to go. It was combat, damnit. And it was his decision to come back and get me. He *fought*. Not you."

Jamie gave Cassie a sympathetic smile, dabbed her thin lips with a white cotton napkin, and placed it on her plate.

"Would you like to see?" she asked.

"See what? I saw! I was there." Cassie turned her hand and pointed her finger at her chest.

"Misdirected anger like this is common in PTSD patients," Zara said to Jamie, speaking as if Cassie wasn't sitting in the room.

Jamie frowned, looked at Cassie. "C'mon, girl. Let's go look at some stuff." She waved her hand in melodramatic, guffaw fashion, the cashmere sweater remaining perfectly in place. A tall woman—maybe pushing five-nine in stocking feet—Jamie stood and ushered Cassie from the kitchen into an oak-paneled study across the living area. Zara followed quietly behind. Cassie was an inch taller and more muscular, but the senator carried herself in a way that made her the dominant gene in the room.

In the study, Jamie picked up a remote and an HD TV blinked to life. It showed a grainy video, probably Apache helicopter gun tape, Cassie thought, of the landing zone where the extraction from Yazd Province, Iran, had taken place a few months ago. Beads of perspiration broke out on Cassie's brow, but she tried to remain focused.

Suddenly a voice bellowed, "We need to get Captain Bagwell."

It was impossible to determine who was talking through the sound of the helicopter blades. The radio static carried another voice.

"There's no time. She's dead. Leave her."

Cassie's heart stopped. She audibly caught her breath.

"Sir, we need to get the captain."

"Direct order to leave now."

That was Jake's voice. While the background noise obscured it some, Jake had a unique, deep monotone, especially when he was in command.

The video showed the helicopters departing, with Cassie in captivity on the ground. It was followed by a video of a meeting in a nameless conference room. She recognized the voice of Major General Bob Savage, the commander of Joint Special Operations Command at Fort Bragg, North Carolina. His voice was emanating from a speakerphone on the table while several four-star generals sat around, listening intently.

"Mahegan thinks she's dead. He doesn't think it's worth the effort."

Tears tumbled from Cassie's welling eyes.

"We have to go in to get her. She's the former chairman's daughter."

There was some conversation in the background of the phone speaker. It sounded like Jake's voice saying, "We'll just get more men killed. Not worth it."

"We're going in," the voice said.

"If you're ordering me to do it, I'll do it." Jake again.

Another voice crackled over the phone. It was Jamie Carter.

"Do it, General. I don't care what it takes. Get her back."

As soon as Jamie cut the video and audio link, Cassie sobbed. "Why? Why are you showing me this . . . this . . . fucked-up movie? I know it's not true," she challenged.

"It's all real," Jamie said.

"The mind tends to reject images and audibles that don't conform to its preconceived notions and patterns. You believed that Jake loved you above all else. Clearly, that's not true. You heard *his* voice say that you were not worth the life of any of his men," Zara said.

"Stop it!" Cassie held her hands in the air. "Just stop!"

"This is real, Cassie. Zara says the best way to heal your trauma is to confront the reality, not to live in some fictional universe."

This couldn't be real. She had seen the determination in Jake's eyes when he found her dying in that cave. She had heard his voice telling the Blackhawk pilot to turn around. That was her reality.

As if on cue, Zara said, "We have memories that play tricks on us. Hidden memories, suppressed memories, and even false memories—those we desperately want to believe we remember. Things our desires have shaped in our minds. Something we wish to be true."

Cassie was shaking her head. The two women stared at her sympathetically, but with a conviction that she likened to that of suicide bombers. She'd seen the look before. Zara persisted.

"False memories can only be undone by viewing the facts. You just saw the facts. We can leave you alone in here to watch them over and over again, Cassie. They won't change. The facts are the facts."

Cassie recalled a probability and statistics class she had taken where the professor had said, "You can always make the numbers support your conclusion if you've decided beforehand what result you want." Was the mind the same way? Did she so love Jake that she imagined what she had heard when he was ordering the pilots to turn around and go back to the landing zone? What about the struggle for him to get out of the aircraft and that others had held him back in? She believed her own ears. She had heard the shouts. The loadmaster had placed a snap hook on his tactical vest, keeping him in the aircraft.

Or had he told her that?

Stop it, she admonished herself. They were deliberately confusing her. Jake loved her and had come back for her.

But the words she had just heard. She knew Jake's voice. Had heard it up close, whispering in her ear. Commanded her to take cover. Consoled her when she was wounded. The soft echo of his commands to his team, the one that rescued her. She knew every octave. Every range-bound syllable of his controlled demeanor.

That was Jake's voice on the recording.

But how could it be? She had been there and heard it live.

Or had she? She had been in the clutches of Ian Gorham's Serbian henchman, Dax Stasovich, who had tricked two Army Rangers and avoided capture. Not only that, he had reversed the fortunes and yanked her from the ascending helicopter. She had been safe. Jake was on the other helicopter with the assault team. She had convinced him to go forward into the cave and gather intelligence. That was the entire purpose of the mission.

But did anyone really tell Jake what to do? He admittedly was a mission-driven man. But his touch. His words. He had told her he loved her. Shown her. His first vacation in forever had been with her at Bald Head Island.

"We need to get Captain Bagwell."

"There's no time. She's dead. Leave her."

"Sir, we need to get the captain."

"Direct order to leave now."

The video was playing again, the images flickering in her periphery.

Then she remembered something else.

Zara leaving the Valley Trauma Center. Her shooting Dr. Broome, saying she was a member of the Resistance.

"One memory that I'm sure about is you shooting Dr. Broome," Cassie said. Then, looking at Jamie Carter, she said, "Zara's part of a plot to overthrow the government."

Jamie chuckled. "Come now, Cassie. We're all familiar with the drugs Zara has prescribed for you. Hallucinations, daydreams, nightmares, overactive imagination. It's all there and you're showing all the signs."

"I was in the hallway. I watched you through the doorway. You shot Broome!" Cassie said.

Zara looked at Jamie and nodded.

"Okay. You want the truth?" Zara asked.

"That would be nice for a change," Cassie said.

"I've been running an investigation on the Valley Trauma Center for the Secret Service. Using my cover as a medical doctor, I was able to infiltrate and pretend to be a member of the Resistance. Broome was training suicide squads of assassins. All of the training you went through? That was to turn you into a stone-cold killer," Zara said.

"Ranger school pretty much did that," Cassie replied.

"I was a spy in that operation. I've learned that it is unfolding rapidly. And we have to move now to stop it."

Cassie ran her hands through her hair and shook her head.

"None of this makes sense," she said.

Zara was a bad actor, and now a noble actor. Jamie was a Virginia senator, and now a North Carolina senator. Jake loves me, but left me?

She stood from the table, confused. The sun was shining bright squares of light onto the table. Cassie always understood her mission, but this new information was shocking. How was she to square this with what she believed?

"Dear, are you okay?"

"Yes. I mean . . . no. Everything is upside down," she whispered.

Then Jake's words from the recording started replaying in her mind like one of those cheesy commercial jingles, the four-sentence refrain kept repeating as she absently ascended the stairs, found "her" room, and crawled into the soft cotton sheets.

We need to get Captain Bagwell.

There's no time. She's dead. Leave her.

Sir, we need to get the captain.

Direct order to leave now.

Jake Mahegan left her to die? Or already believed she wasn't even worth retrieving, if he thought she was dead?

It couldn't be true.

Or could it?

Jake had not found her. Zara had. Jake had said, "Stay alive. I'll find you."

He hadn't, had he?

What was real? Her mind swam with memories of her father shouting at her, being stern with her, saying hurtful things in public about her. Then the carnage of her parents being slaughtered by Syrian terrorists, left to die in their own blood, chained in separate but adjoining cages. The cruelty was unimaginable. Married for over forty years and her father had to watch her mother die, alone in the cage, and then the terrorist shot him, leaving him alone on the cold concrete floor.

Then there was Iran. The high-altitude jump into combat with Jake. He had been calm and reassuring. They had spoken through their communications devices on the descent. She had twisted her ankle on the landing. Jake had rushed toward her and protected her, helped her stabilize her leg. Then Stasovich had attacked her, and Jake had literally saved her life by wrestling Stasovich away and knocking him unconscious. He had flex-cuffed the big man and left her to complete the mission, all at her urging. She had told him to carry on with the plan, urged him forward. She *knew* that Jake was torn between protecting her and taking the small Ranger force into the tunnels. But it had proven successful. She couldn't fault Jake for what happened next. They were under fire. The Ranger support-by-fire team had helped her to the rear helicopter that was buzzing on the pickup zone. Jake was leading the Ranger assault force back up the narrow gorge to the landing zone. They had captured a high-value target and secured a wounded dog, which turned out to be the Russian president's animal and key to everything.

Then the helicopters were under fire. The Iranians were rushing the landing zone. Jake and the Ranger assault team loaded the lead helicopter. They were taking off. Stasovich broke free. Grabbed Cassie's legs. No one had secured her in the aircraft.

She was on the ground. Stasovich's stale breath poured over her as he hauled her away. The Iranian infantry provided him cover as she became a prisoner of war.

It was all too much to remember. The memories of what had ensued haunted her. So much trauma in her life. What was real? What was fake?

Had the combat changed her? She knew deep down that Jake loved her. That Zara was evil. And that Jamie Carter was devious.

But here she was. With them, not Jake.

Why?

She pulled the covers over her torso and turned to the side, lost in her thoughts. She ran a finger lightly across the scar above her left ear. Her hair felt silky and clean.

Shaking off the manipulation and mind games, Cassie breathed deep. She centered herself by lying perfectly still in the bed and shutting down her mind. She gave an imperceptible nod to Jamie and Zara and their manipulation efforts. Solid performance. All lies.

As her mind swooned, she thought of Jake and The Plan. While she didn't know what was going to happen next, Cassie was exactly where she needed to be.

Inside.

CHAPTER 8

Zara and Jamie sat at the sunroom table, the Neuse river in the background. Zara looked at Jamie and said, "That's a good start. I saw real confusion in her eyes."

"A seed of doubt has been planted. She's confused. If nothing else, it will make her hesitate when we get to the end game."

"Which is in less than two days, mind you," Zara said.

Jamie gave Zara the side eye and chuckled.

"I've been waiting for this day for three years," she said. "Just don't fuck it up, Zara."

Zara's stare was nondescript, but her thoughts wandered to the Valley Trauma Center, where she had "treated" patients, exploiting the trauma, making it worse, driving them crazy. She made them doubt themselves, their family, their loved ones; then she injected them with a steady diet of DHT, technically known as dihydrotestosterone, Flakka, a synthetic drug, and bath salts. The lethal combination made the men or women more aggressive, more prone to outrage, and capable of committing psychotic actions, like 'roid rage, but different and more lethal when also combined with effects of post-traumatic stress. The victims of Zara's home brew were the most vulnerable: veterans of combat or law enforcement trauma or victims of assault. They were the most pliable.

"You're a senator today, aren't you?" Zara said.

"Indeed. And if you want the prize at the end of the rainbow, then you only have to be successful three more times."

"Be careful what you wish for, Senator. We are beyond the point of no return," Zara said.

"You do your job, I'll do mine, Zara."

With that, Zara nodded and said, "As you wish. She's not ready, but she'll have to do. She's trapped, confused, and she's no dummy. We have a small window of opportunity."

"The tape from Broome's office was a good thing," Jamie said.

"A better thing was the chip in her back. I knew she was watching me."

"Well, get her a new one."

"No time, plus she'll be with me."

"Get moving."

"We need to check in with Wise. Make sure everything is on track," Zara said.

"Okay, let's do it from the secure line," Jamie replied.

They walked into the basement and sat at a table

with a small Cisco encrypted video conference camera. It was point to point, and as secure as anything could be today. Zara dialed the number and Wise answered. His face was large in the screen. Brown hair parted on the left. Acne scars visible. Red tie loosened and the spread collar on his white dress shirt open at the neck.

"What's the status?"

During the run-up to the uprising, Zara had completely vetted Wise. He was a former Navy SEAL, who had entered the service at eighteen and departed at twenty-one years old, used the GI Bill to attend George Mason University and graduate with a degree in criminal justice. Joining the FBI in his midtwenties, his stock had steadily risen until the American people had elected President Smart. Wise was two removed from an earlier FBI plot to derail the Smart presidency and had ultimately paid the price from flying too close to the sun. His rocketing career flamed out and he was lucky to keep his job.

A year ago, Zara and Wise had met through a high-end dating app that catered to professionals and weeded out the riffraff. What Zara had intended as a one-night stand turned into a political affiliation that had endured to this day. Having a seasoned veteran and political ally, coupled with the occasional good, solid fuck, was a bonus for her.

She and Wise had hatched a plan to put in motion the wheels of a coup. Half the country would consider their plan seditious, like John Wilkes Booth, Mary Surratt, and his other co-conspirators, while the other half would consider it patriotic, ridding the country of a polarizing political figure.

"Like most things in life, it's a fifty-fifty shot," Zara had said after sex one night. The postcoital discussion had hatched the plan that they were executing today.

Now, Zara said, "We've got Cassie with us. From an enemy point of view, Mahegan is guarding the CIA director. Savage is at Fort Bragg."

He had taught her to always lay out the enemy situation first, like a military operation. You had to know where the enemy was arrayed on the battlefield and what their intentions might be.

"And friendlies?" Wise asked.

"We lost four at the director's country house, but we expected that. We didn't think Mahegan or his team would be easy targets."

Wise nodded. "Four down and how many left?"

"We've got sixteen trainees remaining. We started with five teams of four. I can break them into teams of two, if necessary. That will give us eight teams, nine including Cassie and me. I've got them deployed in four different locations around the National Capital Region."

"Cassie?"

"Yes, I'm taking Cassie with me. I've got her confused enough with a drug regimen that she's pretty pliable."

"Be careful there. She is an Army Ranger."

"And I'm a psychiatrist who can change her brain," Zara said.

Jamie remained off screen and silent; should anyone be recording this, Zara presumed.

"Okay. It's your funeral, literally or figuratively."

"I know what I'm doing. There's no way the female body can fight the DHT, Flakka, and midazolam cocktail. It injects the supercharged testosterone into the body, makes them crazy with rage, and then swings them all the way down with the midazolam."

"Sounds awesome," Wise said. The sarcasm bit at Zara, who had worked hard on weaponizing the women.

"Thanks," she said. "What have you got?"

"The presidential schedule went black today, but my sources tell me that number one and number two will be at a safe house in Loudoun County, not far from her residence."

The president and vice president.

"And the Speaker?" she asked.

"He's on his boat. But you have to go to his house first. You'll be greeted there by a guide, who will take you where you need to go."

"A guide?"

"Just meet with the Speaker and he'll give you the rest of the plan."

"Okay, thanks."

"I know your friend is there listening. Nothing short of director works for me," Wise said.

"I understand," Zara said.

"We have a deal. I know what you did to Broome. To paraphrase Ben Franklin, either we all hang together, or we most assuredly will all hang separately."

"It's yours for the taking," she said.

"Okay, good luck."

Zara pressed the end button and the connection dropped.

"He filming that?" Jamie asked.

"Probably, but who cares? Like he said, we either have this in the bag or we don't. It's all or nothing. A video is the least of our worries, especially one that you're not on."

The two women climbed the stairs and sat at the kitchen table again, Jamie resting her head in her hands.

"This better work," Jamie said.

"It's all for you," Zara replied.

Jamie looked up at her, gave her a hard stare, and said, "It's for the country, Zara, and don't forget that."

Yeah, right, Zara thought. Her political alliance with Jamie was pragmatic, not ideological. Able to flip to either side of an issue, Zara was 51 to 49 percent on most policy matters of the day; however, she was 100 percent committed to power and money. She certainly believed in better health care, higher taxes on the rich, and protections for those historically discriminated against. Yet, she lacked the passion about those and other issues and focused on building wealth and positioning herself to pivot into power. Having made in the high six figures as a psychiatrist, Zara parlayed her feminism and Spanish heritage into an explosive lobbying and consulting business on K Street in Washington, DC. With each passing day of tasting the wealth and power of those she engaged, Zara became equally powerful, if not more so. Her business grew to eight figures in revenue, most of which she pocketed. With the money, came power. She transitioned from app dating to sleeping with some of the most powerful players in DC: a Federal Reserve Board member, senators, congressmen and congresswomen, generals and admirals. Over the last five years, she left no stone unturned in her drive to accumulate leverage and its resultant power.

That ascendancy had led her to the rare political affiliation with Jamie Carter, whom she had met during the early days of Jamie's presidential exploratory committee. One of Jamie's Senate staffers had reached out to Zara, asking if she could meet with Jamie to discuss opioid addiction and other health care–related issues. Zara seized on the opportunity to meet with the likely next president—all of the polls were showing her close to a double-digit lead over any of the candidates from the opposing party. Zara had the right look: ethnic, olive skin, black hair, slender body, the slightest hint of an accent when she wanted it, and large, seductive eyes. Her intelligence matched her beauty, and she believed that Jamie saw in her the rare strategic thinker and tactical operator that she was. After a lengthy discussion that led to a lengthy dinner, Jamie had called a week later and asked Zara to join her team. Zara had replied that she would do so, only for the right price and unfiltered access. After some debate, Jamie must have seen the promise that Zara held and had agreed to Zara's terms.

Then came the exhilarating primary win and campaign, touting health care as a major issue. The telegenic Zara Perro scoring near-daily segments with CNN and MSNBC. She migrated from being a niche health care advisor to the face of the campaign. She was inside the ropes, next to the future president. Well spoken and direct, Zara was the perfect advisor. Everyone wanted to either be her or next to her. Accustomed to influence and control, even Zara admitted to herself that the spotlight she was under had become intoxicating. She began to catch herself believing that she was *that* good, *that* smart, *that* beautiful.

But she knew better. Still, the current became stronger and harder to resist. Like a swimmer stuck in a riptide, she went with the flow, instead of wearing herself out fighting it. Then came the crushing, unpredicted defeat and accompanying fall from grace. She had landed a lucrative talking-head contract with CNN, but she found herself to be a bitter voice in the wilderness. Not her style. If she was anything, it wasn't ideological. The CNN money could not compensate for the damage to her brand and business that her proximity to the losing candidate had caused.

She had taken her eye off the ball. Eight figures rapidly dropped to seven and then to six. She fired most of her staff, because she didn't have the access she'd anticipated or was seen as being too closely aligned with a bitter loser. It had even taken her a few days to pull out of the riptide and get her head above water to see that she was too far from land to be rescued. Her presence in the Carter campaign had been so pervasive that when people thought of Zara Perro, they thought of Jamie Carter, and vice versa.

And so here she was, plotting the comeback. Hopes for a landslide in the Senate and House had provided meager returns, certainly nothing that would lead to eviction of the president through impeachment, no matter the special counsel's tepid product. While Jamie had saved money and was financially stable, Zara knew the absence of power and influence was a tangible hole in her being. She was outside looking in.

So Jamie saying that this conspiracy to dethrone Smart was about the country was utter bullshit. It was pure revenge and lust for power.

Which Zara was okay with, as long as it served her purposes. She missed the power, the access, and the money. She hated being associated with a losing cause, and if this was the only way to set it right, then so be it. She was a mercenary, not a true believer.

Zara looked at Jamie, her countenance blank, and said, "You're the boss."

"Don't forget that. We're almost there."

Jamie's phone chimed with a text. She picked it up, shielded it from Zara's view, and said, "Okay. Get rolling. Just remember. This thing goes south, I've got nothing to do with it. I'm Teflon."

Zara nodded and pushed away from the table. Climbing the stairs, she held a finger to her lips as Rosa padded along the hall. Rosa stopped and turned around, away from Cassie's bedroom in the northeast corner of the house.

Zara peeked in Cassie's room. She had fallen asleep. Hooking the IV drip back up, this time with Zara's chemical recipe for success, the DHT-and-Flakka mix, she clicked it into the catheter taped onto the back of Cassie's hand.

Cassie turned her head. "What the . . ."

"It's okay, Cassie. Just like in therapy. This will make you feel better. I could tell you were missing the treatment. So bipolar. There should be another medicine from the trauma center in the pack you took. You wouldn't happen to know where that is, would you?"

Sleepy-eyed, Cassie shook her head.

"Because if you hid it somewhere, you know it is unique to you. It is the only thing that can undo what we are doing here. If you ever want to return to normal, you need the medicine that is missing. If you took it and aren't taking proper precautions, then you will age very quickly with this treatment. It won't end well."

"Then why are you doing it," Cassie muttered.

"Because it makes you a better killer than you already are."

"Why do you want me to kill?"

The drug was already taking effect. Her eyes opened wide as she sat upright.

"I call this concoction Running Eagle, named after the female Native American warrior in honor of your fab boyfriend, Chayton Mahegan. He spells his name wrong, by the way. It should be Mohegan."

"Jake," Cassie said absently, as if she was dreaming about him. Perhaps she had been.

"Get dressed, Cassie, we've got some business to take care of. Do what I say and everything will be okay."

Cassie looked at her, seemed to understand, nodded, slid off the bed, grabbed her clothes, and walked into the bathroom, shutting the door behind her.

The NetJets airplane landed at Reagan National Airport in Arlington, Virginia. A car with a nameless driver took Zara and Cassie to a Georgetown M Street address, where they then walked three blocks north into the heart of the residential townhomes. Cassie watched Zara fish around a brick walkway, something she presumed Zara had done before.

"The Speaker and I have a thing," Zara said. The key was right there, under a loose brick on the side-walk in front of a town house. They continued walking and looped around the row of homes and circled to the back alley, where the garages were lined up behind their respective residences.

Cassie had been relatively subdued. She felt differ-ent, as if she had been given a sedative. She was tired of all the drugs, the ups and downs, and she really needed what was in the medical cooler. To her knowl-edge, she didn't know if the contents could be repli-cated ever again. As she was waking up, she caught Zara giving her what had to be a DHT cocktail shot, like she had received at the trauma clinic. She felt her eyes roll back into her head, dazed, confused.

"Where are we going?" Cassie asked.

"We're meeting with the Speaker of the House. He wants to discuss Senator Carter's new appointment."

"At night? In Georgetown? On a Sunday?"

"Yes, yes, and yes. What better time or location? He's in the opposite party and doesn't want to be seen talking to us. The political divide is so deep right now, he can't risk it."

"What's my role?"

"Listen and learn," Zara said.

They entered through the back door and were met by two men in ski masks holding pistols with silencer cans screwed on the muzzles. Cassie recognized the pistols as M17s, the new U.S. Army sidearm. The two men were dressed in black tactical cargo pants and stretch nylon shirts that showed off their considerable bulk.

"Hands out front," one man said.

"Do what he says," Zara said. Cassie's veins were on fire again. She was raging and ready to fight.

She lashed out with a high kick that went straight up into the left gunman's face. Simultaneously she swept the pistol from the man on the right, using a knuckle-fisted punch to the throat and a smooth sweep downward, grabbing the pistol from the man on the right. She shoved it under that man's chin as she spun and kicked the pistol out of the other man's hands. It skidded across the floor with a loud, scraping sound of metal on tile. Back to the other man, who now had drawn a knife.

She said, "You know that saying about gunfights and knives?"

The man smiled beneath the balaclava about the time his partner fired a stun gun at Cassie, sending enough voltage through her body to make her drop the pistol and slowly go to her knees, convulsing.

"Now that we have that out of the way," one of the men said. A man stepped forward with flex-cuffs, while the other man retrieved his pistol and kept it aimed at Zara's forehead. The man expertly tightened the plastic handcuffs on each woman and turned them around, placed sandbags over their heads and tightened them around the neck. A vehicle pulled into the alley. The motor idled roughly, as if it was turbocharged. The men marched Cassie and Zara to the middle seat. One man sat behind them and the other sat shotgun. The driver was similarly dressed and masked.

The SUV made sharp turns through the tight streets of Georgetown until it veered sharply and stopped. The musty smell of the Potomac River permeated the air even in the vehicle. Quickly the men were out of the car, dragging the women from their seats and shutting the doors. The vehicle sped away, leaving silence in its wake. A man grabbed Cassie by the arm and walked her toward the crisp sounds of tumbling water sloshing against a pier or berth. The freeway or bridge hissed in the distance.

The man helped Cassie stumble over a pier or gunnel onto a boat of some type. It rocked beneath her feet as she lowered herself onto a padded seat cushion. A large hand grabbed her and pulled her belowdecks. Someone untied the lines and the boat sped away, downriver as best Cassie could determine. After twenty minutes, the boat slowed and spent another ten minutes crawling through the water. Finally it stopped and nudged against something firm.

"Let's go," one of the men said, waving a pistol at them.

"Take these damn sandbags off," Zara demanded. For Cassie's part, everything was reminding her of Iran. Her capture, the torture, the escape. She had to escape.

"As you wish," one man said.

The men removed the sandbags and Cassie immediately began scanning, taking in her surroundings. She was trying to place the marina at which they were moored, but failed. She didn't know Washington, DC, all that well, despite the fact that her father had been chairman of the Joint Chiefs and she had grown up in nearby rural Greene County, Virginia.

There were over fifty boats parked at adjacent piers. A passenger jet flew overhead, low and slow, giving Cassie the idea that they were located either north or south of Reagan National Airport. They walked along the pier as the men guided them onto a large sailboat, which had the mainsail wrapped around a mast that stood at least fifty feet high. Cassie had run along the Potomac River trail many times when she'd trained for ROTC and triathlons. *This could be Daingerfield Island,* she thought. Her mind began rapidly processing escape routes away from the remote marina: *Swim to Maryland. Run onto the trail to Old Town. Jimmy a car in the parking lot. Steal a boat and head into the river. Stop a car on GW Parkway.*

"Into the galley," the man said.

Once they were standing in the small galley of the sailboat, Cassie immediately recognized the Speaker of the House.

"Hope you don't mind the extra security. They can be a bit rough, but with Hite dead, I can't be too careful," Speaker Josh Williams said.

"Well, I'd say you were careful enough," Zara replied.

Williams was a stout man, with thinning gray hair and a bulbous nose, riddled with veins from drinking too much. Not Tip O'Neill, but close. He had small, narrow eyes that seemed out of place on his large head. Perpetually unkempt, Williams was wearing an unzipped, oversized blue Windbreaker over a wrinkled blue sweatshirt that read, NITTANY LIONS, an ode to his alma mater, Penn State. The boat smelled of the dank, musty water in which it sat and of fried food, the McDonald's bag sitting on the galley table the most likely culprit.

"Who's this newbie?" Williams asked Zara.

"Cassie Bagwell, first female Army Ranger," Zara said.

Williams nodded. "I knew your father."

"He's dead," Cassie said.

After a pause, Williams smiled thinly and looked at Zara. "I see why you like her."

Cassie asked, "What are we doing here?"

"You've demonstrated some ample skills, young lady," Williams said. "Zara told me that you were good. My men here have already attested to that. You took them both down. I watched the video at the house. Impressive." He pointed at a small tablet that had Ring software programmed so that he could monitor his home with cameras.

"They were easy," Cassie said. "As would be the entire crew here." She gave a half shrug.

"Perhaps," Williams replied. "But Zara's the tough one."

Cassie wheeled and lashed out with a thin-bladed hand, going for Zara's throat behind her, but the Spaniard was too quick. Zara blocked the slicing movement and counterpunched, catching Cassie in the solar plexus. Not to be deterred, Cassie whipped a sharp elbow into Zara's jaw about the time two men stepped in and pushed them apart in the small confines of the sailboat.

Heavy breaths escaped Cassie's lungs as she recovered from having the wind knocked out of her.

"There's a plot to kill the president and vice president," Williams said.

The statement floated in the air like a football punt with maximum hang time.

"Tomorrow," Williams continued. "CIA Director Carmen Biagatti has called for an emergency meeting with both of them. As some of you may know, she's a member of the Resistance. They're going to meet in the SCIF in a Loudoun County safe house near one of the president's golf courses. She's going to lock the SCIF and commit suicide."

"How will she kill the president and veep, then?" Cassie asked.

"They'll die with her. Lethal hydrogen cyanide gas will pour through the circulation system killing anyone in the small room."

"Zyklon B?" Cassie asked. "Like the Nazis used?"

"Like that," Williams said.

"Where are you getting your intel from?" Cassie said.

"My intel is good. You don't need to worry about that. We need you and Zara to stop the attack. It's really a simple matter of changing out the tanks that feed the SCIF."

"Won't it be guarded?" Zara asked this time.

"It will, but your skills are good. Biagatti's inner circle is in on it. Not to the extent that they're going to be willing to be in the room, but if you recall, she brought in her team. She's kept her secret hidden well, but it's about to break. In three days, Breitbart and Project Veritas are going to run exposés on her allegiance to the soft revolution taking place in our country. People can no longer wait, apparently, for elections. The circumstances have become too dire—for them anyway."

The Speaker of the House was of the same political party as the president, yet Cassie knew he was no fan of the commander in chief. The Speaker, a traditional swamp rat DC politician used to brokering deals with the opposition, had little time for the histrionics or the populist wave of the president. Reports were that he was getting rich by cutting backroom deals and would prefer a new president as opposed to one who through his every action was shining a spotlight on the corruption in Washington, DC, whether he intended to or not.

Still, assassinating the president and vice president was a coup, plain and simple. But she had heard Zara's words.

Artemis teams are ready.

"We have to stop this," Cassie said.

"I agree," echoed Zara.

"That's why I asked Zara to come tonight," the Speaker said. "The cover was that we were going to discuss Carter's platform, whatever the fuck that might be, but the reality is that we need to protect the nation from Carmen Biagatti. As much as I dislike the current commander in chief, treason is treason. A coup is a coup. We can't allow it to happen. So now that we've decided this, here's the deal. You'll need to infiltrate this compound, kill these guards, and then change out the tanks."

"Why not just warn them off?" Cassie asked.

"Perfectly logical question, young lady. You're an intelligence officer, correct?"

"I am," she replied.

"Okay, then. Would you prefer to give up gobs of information you're collecting from a target by killing him or her, or would you prefer to keep that target alive and know precisely what's happening twenty-four/ seven?"

"The second one," Cassie replied. "But the president can just fire her if we let him know."

"And he would believe us, why?"

She didn't have a good response to that question. She didn't know anyone in the administration, despite her father having served as chairman of the Joint Chiefs prior to his death.

"I'm an intelligence officer in the United States Army," Cassie said.

"No. You're a damaged, traumatized woman who is a national security risk. You just escaped from a trauma clinic, for Christ's sake. Secret Service won't let you anywhere near the president."

"Biagatti knew my father," Cassie said. "I can get close to her. Warn her that we are on to her."

Williams seemed to mull this over, rubbing his meaty fingers over his chin.

"I know for a fact that Secret Service has been warned about you. Returning combat vet. PTSD. Danger to the nation. All that shit. You'd think it would be different, but the previous Homeland Security secretary still has some acolytes in the department. All part of this Resistance thing," Williams said, shaking his head sadly.

Cassie cast her eyes downward, thinking. The rage building, but somehow subdued. Her behavior had been erratic. No Secret Service officer in his or her right mind would let her near the president.

"A letter?" she asked.

"Anthrax," Williams countered.

"Okay, so we just what? Kill Secret Service and replace the tanks? That seems worse than me trying to talk to the president."

"I'm told the tanks are in there. If we replace them tonight, they've just got a few rent-a-cops out there. You could probably get away without having to kill anyone," Williams said.

The boat creaked and rocked. The claustrophobic galley was beginning to make her head spin. She just wanted out, and fast. She looked at Zara, who was eyeing Williams questioningly. Glad she wasn't the only one who thought this mission was bonkers.

"SCIFs are eight inches of concrete all around, minimum. The air ducts are sealed and monitored with alarms," Cassie said.

"Again, tonight you two do a recon and execute if you have enough time. If not, the Secret Service will be closing in, about nine a.m. It's almost midnight. An hour to get there. An hour to recon. An hour to execute. An hour to escape. That leaves five hours for the fog of combat, so to speak," Williams said.

"Where are the tanks?" Cassie asked. Her mind was racing. Execute mode. Normally, she would have been more circumspect, but her energy was high. She wanted to act, do something. Her sworn duty was to protect the nation against all enemies, foreign and domestic. Here was an enemy of the nation, a member of the Resistance, with a potentially easy way to catalyze the coup that so many desired.

"Right here," Williams said. He pointed at one of the beefy security guards who was holding two small green tanks, about half the size of a scuba tank, that read OXYGEN on the side. Fresh paint seemed to shine from the canisters, both the body and the letters.

Still unsure, Cassie said, "Let's do this."

"Do we have transportation?" Zara asked.

"Black Suburban. You're on Daingerfield Island, just south of Reagan National. GPS shows about an hour to the compound."

And with that, they loaded the Suburban with the oxygen tanks, pistols, long rifles, and a few knives. Zara drove while Cassie navigated. They wound their way through Alexandria and Arlington, finally hitting Interstate 66, where they made some decent time in the middle of the night. The conversation was muted. Cassie noticed that Zara seemed amped as well, focused on the mission. Save the president and vice president.

"I've got it figured out," Zara said. "I'm quicker than you. You're quick, but I'm quicker. So I'll watch and deter any threats. You handle the tanks. Get them switched out. We take the old ones and deliver them as proof to the FBI."

"Why don't we just call the FBI right now?" Cassie asked. Hamlet's phrase "The lady doth protest too much" briefly appeared in her mind. Still, she had to balance her natural inquisitiveness with a willingness to go along. Being her authentic self was the key to success. Zara had to know that Cassie didn't trust her, in which case the questions seemed perfectly logical. It seemed smart to feed into the patient-doctor relationship that Zara feigned.

"Focus. We went through all of that. Nobody will believe any of this shit. Plus, could be a member of the

Resistance that answers the phone. Ever think of that? People want the president dead."

"How solid is Williams's intel?" Cassie asked.

"One hundred percent," Zara said. "Hasn't failed me yet."

"Okay, then let's do this right," Cassie said. "No mistakes."

Emma's refrain from the hospital bed next to her rolled now through her mind.

The last ride is never the last ride, and the end is never the end.

CHAPTER 9

Upon Mahegan's return to CIA headquarters, director Biagatti was nowhere to be found. She had said there was a coup on hand. Where was she now?

While waiting, Mahegan plugged in the medical cooler, ate in the cafeteria, sorted through the treasure trove of intel he had collected from the Uwharrie, and then laid on the floor of his temporary office.

As soon as he was comfortable, Biagatti called, asking him to come to her office. He stood, ran a hand through his hair, hit the restroom on the way, knocked on the door, and entered her office.

It was expansive and filled with the usual *I-love-me* wall of pictures, showing Biagatti with recognizable political figures. Biagatti was sitting at a conference table at the far end of her office.

"Jake, sit."

Mahegan sat across from Biagatti and stared at her. Her face was furrowed with concern.

"You said we had a coup. I've been back an hour and you're nowhere to be found," Mahegan said.

Biagatti waved off his comment and said, "The president and vice president are coming to the compound to receive a briefing. Yes, we've got intel. The Resistance is everywhere and it appears they've gone operational."

"I've got intel, too. I need to see Cassie," Mahegan said.

"Jake, your place of duty is here, with me," Biagatti said. Her words were razor sharp, leaving no room for interpretation. "You understand duty, right?"

"To a fault," he muttered.

He had always avoided protection details because they were too restricting. He didn't like being tethered to another person, at least professionally. Cassie was a different story. Avoiding being tethered to a woman his entire life, he had finally found the balance he was seeking. Cassie grounded him in a way no one else could. Having lost his parents and best friend in the most unimaginable ways, Mahegan needed Cassie. Perhaps she needed him in the same way, having lost her parents to slaughter as well. He was unaccustomed to the notion of needing anything or anyone other than himself. Now, a life shared with Cassie seemed better than a life without her, unshared, alone, and barren.

"Bob Savage said you were reliable and wouldn't go off the reservation," she said.

Mahegan didn't take the bait on whether she intended the *reservation* word choice in relation to his Native American heritage.

In theory, Savage had moved him to the Biagatti

bodyguard detail in part so that he could be near Cassie as she was recuperating from her wounds. He had religiously visited Cassie every day in Walter Reed, spending several nights with her. While he was on an overnight protection detail with Biagatti, Cassie had been transferred to the Valley Trauma Center. Despite his attempts to see Cassie at the remote facility, he had been denied by Dr. Franklin Broome, the enigmatic leader of the VTC. Cassie had been experiencing severe nightmares, waking up in a full sweat, shivering. Once, she had leapt from the bed, intravenous needle stuck in the back of her hand, as she bent into a shooter's stance, spinning 360 degrees, her hand kicking backward as if the imaginary pistol were firing.

"Jake?"

Biagatti's voice pulled him from the searing memory and anguish.

"I'm here," he said.

"But you're not, are you?" she emphasized.

"I am, Director. What do you need me to do?"

"We need to head to the Harmony Church safe house ASAP," she said.

"Where's your intel coming from?"

"Syd Wise at FBI," Biagatti said.

As if on cue, the secure video-messaging system began its melodic ring. Biagatti pressed the green button and a man's face appeared on the screen.

"Syd, do we have an update?" Biagatti said.

Mahegan found it interesting that the director of the CIA was communicating directly with a subordinate figure in the FBI. Why was she not speaking with the director of the FBI? Maybe he was off camera in the room, but the office behind Syd Wise looked small and unable to house more than one person.

"Just wanted to follow up on our earlier conversation. I see you've got Mahegan there with you. We've got chatter of an imminent coup effort. I've briefed the Secret Service and they are placing extra personnel at the meet location. Some will be obvious, others might not be."

"I'll need to know who is friendly," Mahegan said.

"You'll know," Wise replied.

"Syd, what exactly is the threat?"

"There's talk of assassinating the president," Wise said.

"There's always talk of doing that, ever since he became a candidate," Biagatti said.

"With the media fanning the flames of these new political figures who are so openly hostile to the administration, they've started a fire that they can't put out."

"I need something more specific," Mahegan said.

"Sorry, soldier. I'm giving you what I've got now. I'll have more in a bit."

"No, you're not. You're giving us wave-top-level esoteric bullshit. My questions are: Who said what? What specifically is being planned? How is this threat different than the millions of previous ones?" Mahegan pressed Wise.

"Sources and methods, bro," Wise said. "I'm telling you to be on your A game tonight." He turned to his computer and typed a few commands. "I just sent you what I have at the moment."

Biagatti's MacBook was open on the conference

table and chimed with an arriving e-mail. She opened it and clicked on the PowerPoint slide. It showed more wave-top-level bullshit. Fat arrows and circles and threat warnings.

"What does this mean?" Biagatti asked.

"It's a threat assessment. You see we've moved it to red for imminent. Take all precautions."

"What am I briefing the president on? The intel I've got is thin," Biagatti said.

"You'll get that packet shortly. It will have all the details that Mr. Mahegan is looking for," Wise said.

"Can't you give us what you've got now?" Mahegan asked.

"The analysts are still creating the products of record," Wise said. "Patience, grasshopper." Wise smirked.

Mahegan cocked his head. Something was off about Wise. Over the video-conferencing display, body language was sometimes harder to interpret. Wise looked into the camera, which was easier than looking into someone's eyes. Even then, he averted his gaze from the camera at times, but there could be other distractions in his office. Something wasn't ringing true for Mahegan, and it was more than the Delta Force versus Navy SEAL rivalry. Wise had spent a couple of years as a SEAL, whereas Mahegan had nearly a decade behind the fence at Fort Bragg.

"Okay, we will wait on the detailed information, Syd. Make it quick. We've got to get out to the compound."

"Yes, ma'am," Wise said. He was smiling a closed-lip grin when he signed off. Biagatti pressed the red button and disconnected the call.

"What was that all about?" Mahegan asked.

"It was an intel dump," she scoffed.

"Lightest dump I've ever seen. More of a show," Mahegan said.

"What are you saying?"

"That was a pointless call. Are we any smarter now than ten minutes ago?"

Biagatti paused. "Well, the details are coming."

Mahegan didn't argue. He wondered if he should update the director on what he had learned from his short trip to North Carolina.

He had spent the last hour scouring cell phones, digging through wallets, and running serial numbers on pistols. He had discovered the three men he "encountered" were local hires from a security firm in Fayetteville. The only interesting connection was that there were some calls to a landline in New Bern, a town in the eastern part of North Carolina that sat astride the Neuse River. That landline showed it belonged to an eighty-two-year-old woman that lived on a family plantation along the Neuse River. That lead seemed to be promising, but he'd decided to follow up later. Believing his information to be incomplete, he chose not to share it with Biagatti. He'd prefer to be able to paint the whole picture, especially in light of the bogus conversation they just had with Wise.

"We should go," Biagatti said.

"Roger." Mahegan returned to his closet of an office, swept everything he had retrieved from North Carolina into a small duffel bag, unplugged the medical cooler, and holstered his weapon. He returned to Biagatti's office and she had changed clothes.

"I'm ready," he said. "We going to a funeral?"

Biagatti was dressed in black jeans and a black

sweater over a black T-shirt. She wore hiking boots and had a black Windbreaker.

"I think it's best we be tactical tonight," she said.

They left the building, jumped in the Panamera, and Mahegan found I-66. Using the emergency lights, he made good time on the interstate, but shut them off once he was off the highway. He navigated to US 234 and US 15, then turned onto Harmony Church Road, eased up the gravel driveway, and pulled up to the guard shack.

In the moonlight, the large home that doubled as a CIA safe house was visible on the hill. Its white frame and black roof harkened to a previous era, while Mahegan knew that the home was built with reinforced steel, blast-resistant ballistic windows, and full situational-awareness communications throughout. The garage led to a sensitive compartmented information facility, or SCIF, in the backyard.

"Mahegan," the guard said. He was a muscled man with a shaved head and goatee. He wore a Glock 19 on his hip and had a *Semper Fi* tattoo on his left forearm. The guard shack smelled of fried food, as if the guard had hit McDonald's before reporting to duty.

"Who are you?" Mahegan responded. "And where's your partner? No solos here."

"Secret Service. I'm Martin. Jackson is napping," the guard said, stone-faced. He turned his jaw toward the back of the guard shack. "What's your business here?"

Mahegan knew all of the guards and most of the Secret Service. He didn't like having a new team on the night that the commander in chief was going to be visiting. "Driving the director here. Just a layman."

"I see that. Have at it," Martin said, waving his hand behind him toward the house on the hill.

Mahegan paused, almost said something, but felt Biagatti's hand on his forearm, as if she was saying, *They're fine.*

"We good?" Martin asked.

"Just fine," Mahegan said. The tire shredders lowered, the gate lifted, and Mahegan wound his way through the dragon's-teeth roadblocks. The driveway was nearly a quarter-mile rise framed on either side by fields where cattle grazed. They were visible in the moonlight, motionless, staring at him as he parked the car in the driveway. A single light shone from the study.

"I know them, Jake. The president always has advance men," Biagatti said.

Mahegan said nothing. Something bothered him, but he would deal with that once he unloaded the director.

As they exited the car, two men closed on them from the dark corners of the house. They wore black pants and shirts with matching black Windbreakers. They were part of Mahegan's team.

"Jake," Patch Owens said. Sean O'Malley came from the opposite direction. Each man carried a pair of night vision goggles on a lanyard around their necks.

"Roger," Mahegan replied.

"Director," O'Malley said from over Mahegan's shoulder.

"Men," Biagatti said. Then to Mahegan: "Your men are quite efficient, Jake."

Mahegan ignored Biagatti's compliment and asked, "House clear?"

"Roger. Hobart and Van Dreeves are inside."

Mahegan had consolidated his team in Northern Virginia in part to review the Iran operation and in part so that they could all take turns visiting Cassie. The five men had been the core of the effort to retrieve her from the Yazd region.

Mahegan nodded and said, "Who are those guys in the guard shack?"

"They came in flashing Secret Service creds. We're still trying to get a fix on who they are," Owens said. "What VD and Hobart are doing right now. Running their info in the database."

Mahegan looked at the firmament, its blackness pinpricked by a billion stars. Then he looked at the guard shack again.

"'Let your plans be dark and impenetrable as night, and when you move, fall like a thunderbolt,'" Mahegan said.

"Heard that," Owens said.

"Didn't know you read Hemingway," O'Malley replied with a grin.

"That's Sun Tzu. Think about it," Mahegan said, and walked inside. The heavy oak door was unlocked. Inside, he took three steps and was met by Van Dreeves and Hobart.

"Guys," Mahegan said.

"Jake." Van Dreeves turned sideways to let Mahegan and Biagatti through. Hobart stared into the distance, always ready, searching for the enemy. Biagatti shook her head, muttered, "Men," and then made a beeline for her study, to the left.

"What do you know about the guards? Sean said you're checking them out."

"Got some calls into the White House. The deputy

over there said they're legit. I don't trust it, though, so we're running our own background. Should be done in fifteen."

"Get a sniper rifle aimed at that place," Mahegan said.

"Jake, you can't be serious. I know those men," Biagatti said from behind her desk twenty feet away.

"Let me do my job, Director, so that you can do yours. You've got an update to the president in less than two hours. Call Wise and get me the intel, then pretend we're not here."

"How can I do that, Jake? You've got Hobart there, aiming a sniper rifle at two Secret Service guys who are here to do their jobs."

"The Resistance has penetrated everywhere. You said so yourself. Wise has elevated everything to red, whatever that means to him. Could be that he's just covering his ass. The gate guards might be legit, but there's a chance they're not."

"There's a chance you're not," Biagatti countered.

"No, actually, there's not a chance of that," Mahegan said. He turned away from the study and peered through the bay window.

"Mission first, Jake," Biagatti said.

"Yes, ma'am," he replied. No one needed to tell Mahegan about placing mission first. He had placed the mission as primary in everything he'd done, including his recent combat action in Iran with Cassie. Placing the mission first had been both his hallmark and his cross to bear. Finding balance between his primary professional duty and his newfound love had not been easy, especially because he blamed himself for what had happened to Cassie in Iran. Her injured ankle, the captive that got free, the withering fire that prevented the pilots from turning around, the crew chief who had Snap-Linked him into the helicopter when he tried to jump from one hundred feet. His fault. Not his fault. It didn't matter.

"The president and vice president are coming here tonight in less than two hours, now. We're keeping a low footprint intentionally. Okay, you're right. With the Resistance in full operational mode, I can't trust any of my security guys. We busted two of them a month of ago using insider threat software. That's why you're here, Jake. Plus, this place isn't necessarily outfitted for presidential security. It's a safe house, not the White House. So I need you in charge of your team, plus whomever the president brings. Should be plenty to save the Alamo, if it ever comes to that."

"Any word from Wise?" Mahegan asked.

"None. The president is flying from Camp David straight to here, in a Task Force 160 MH-47, while Marine One is doing a head fake back to the White House. The vice president is riding out here in his car, with just a single chase car. Low footprint."

"A lot of risk right there," Mahegan said. "Where's the meeting?"

"The only place we can discuss the things we need to talk about is the SCIF."

"Makes sense."

Biagatti stared at him for a long minute. She removed her glasses, rubbed her eyes, and ran a hand through her silver hair. Mahegan stepped into the study.

"What aren't you telling me?" Mahegan asked.

"I'm concerned about Syd Wise. He's husbanding the information," she said.

"Explain."

"The Resistance has been communicating. Our intelligence shows us they've got a plan called Operation Critical Mass. Senator Hite's murder was phase one. That's what I wanted Wise to confirm for me, but anytime you involve the FBI, you're taking a big risk. Now they're acting like this is their deal and I still can't get anything on Hite from three months ago. All I've got is two blond hairs at the murder scene, which they're running DNA on right now."

"*Murder?* Word is that was an autoerotic jerk-off," Mahegan said.

Biagatti walked to her large mahogany desk and retrieved a picture. Behind her were bookshelves that rivaled the local library stacks. Whether the books were real or not, that was anyone's guess. Behind them might lie an assortment of weapons.

"Surely, you don't believe in coincidences like this, do you, Jake?"

She handed him a photo of an attractive woman with long black hair and dark eyes. High cheekbones and almond-shaped eyes. Plump lips. She was dressed in a black dress, with four-inch Louboutin stilettos, showing sharp-edged calf muscles. Someone had taken the photo with a professional camera from a distance, using a zoom lens.

"Taken two days ago. She's standing on the deck of Senator Jamie Carter's home. Where Cassie supposedly is. We had a photographer in a boat on the Neuse River snap these pictures."

Mahegan thought about the phone number he had traced to a landline in New Bern. There was the connection. Carter was either using a place there or had bought something. But why relocate from Virginia to North Carolina? Just to become a senator again? She wouldn't have been able to predict Hite's murder. Mahegan didn't know enough about Jamie Carter to speculate one way or the other. He decided to not say anything to Biagatti just yet. He had more dots to connect, but something was taking shape.

"Why did you have pictures taken? Isn't that the FBI's job? Wise and his yahoos?"

"You're kidding?"

"So the CIA spies on other Americans, too?"

"*Spying* is such a draconian word, Jake. I would say that's a flattering photo. She may want it for a scrapbook one day.

"Who is it?" Mahegan asked.

"Zara Perro. She's a lobbyist and a doctor. She has her MD in psychiatry. Close with Carter and has been seen at the Valley Trauma Center, where Carter had Cassie moved. Perro was the insider for Carter's campaign, three to four years ago. You don't remember?"

"I was up to my ass in Taliban alligators four years ago," Mahegan said. The fact was that he paid little attention to domestic politics other than the impact that policy decisions were having on national security. He believed in sticking with what he was good at, which was killing people that wanted to harm the nation or those he cared about.

"Carter moved Cassie?" He did his best to ask the right questions as he was piecing everything together. Chief among his curiosities was, why was the CIA so heavily involved in a domestic action?

"That's what the Walter Reed doctor said. Carter is Cassie's next of kin, now that her parents are dead."

Mahegan thought about their combat deployment. They had returned from the Blue Ridge Mountains, where they had stopped a nuclear device from detonating, and were relaxing on Bald Head Island. No time to update her will or next of kin documents. Owens and O'Malley snatched them off the beach and they were on the way to combat in less than a few hours. Now, wounded and recovering, Cassie and her strings were being pulled by Senator Carter. Mahegan shook his head.

Biagatti's computer chimed with another incoming e-mail from Wise. She opened it and a classified narrative filled about two-thirds of a Word document surrounded by the words *Top Secret* and *SPECAT*.

They both read the document that had been delivered from Wise's e-mail account. It outlined a plan to be executed in the next forty-eight hours to assassinate the line of succession so that the secretary of state, the fourth in line, would take control.

"Where's he getting this? Their plan is to kill the president, vice president, Speaker of the House, and pro tem all at once so that the secretary of state can be president? It doesn't make sense," Mahegan said.

"The secretary of state is out of the country in Vietnam at the moment," she said.

Mahegan processed what he had just read. What if this was about Carter becoming president?

"Could this be about Carter? She didn't win the election, so she kills her way to the top?" Mahegan asked. "Three months ago, someone assassinates Senator Hite, Carter wins a special election, and her peers hold an emergency caucus to establish her as the pro tem, not the majority leader. Now we have a plot to kill the line of succession?"

Biagatti shrugged. "I think from her party's point of view, there are so many critical votes coming up on health care, budget, and so on that one vote will make the difference. I think it's a smart move within her party."

"And if she is part of this, whatever is unfolding will be over. Done. She'll be president. So, it's important to figure out the source of the intelligence and the origin of the plot. If it's the secretary of state, which makes no sense, then that's an entirely different investigation path than, say, the much more logical choice of Jamie Carter."

"I don't disagree, Jake. Why would Wise tell us this if it's not their intel?"

"Two reasons. The intel could be bad and his analysts did their best, or he could be in on it and angling to be the next FBI director."

Biagatti turned from the computer display and looked at Mahegan.

"That would be a hell of a Machiavellian move," she said. "Regardless, let's say it is Carter. All of this would have to go down simultaneously for it to work."

"Like John Wilkes Booth planned with Lincoln and Seward," Mahegan said.

"Yes, like that. And what was the fallacy in their plan?"

"The others chickened out," Mahegan said. "Booth relied upon everyone being as crazy as he was. Turned out they were crazy, but not as psycho."

"Exactly," she said.

"If this is Carter, who does she have executing her plan?"

"That's a big leap to think that it is Carter, Jake, but for the sake of your line of thinking, she would have her pick of crazy loyalists. In this case, the executors may be crazier than the leader."

"The Globalist Resistance Force," Mahegan said. "It's all over the Internet, but the media basically attempts to portray it as a right-wing conspiracy theory."

"Which, of course, makes them complicit, in a way," Biagatti said.

Changing the line of discussion to the present and his task, which was to secure the compound, he said, "Wouldn't having the president and vice president in the same spot, at the same time, with that type of threat being discussed, or even planned, be an . . . unwise move?"

"Perhaps. The president will be headed back to Camp David, most likely. The vice president is relocating to West Virginia, where we have a continuity-of-operations center established. So he's passing by here anyway. We tried to talk the president into taking this remotely, but you know how he is."

"Actually, I don't, but I'm assuming he wanted to talk to you in person."

"Right. He's not a video-conferencing kind of guy. Neither of them are, actually. Anyway, our precautions are sufficient, especially seeing how we're only beginning to pick up on the chatter. And we're more concerned about members of the Resistance inside the administration, working in the White House. We're never sure when we walk into the situation room if there's not some genius who's fully vetted, but suddenly turns into a psycho suicide bomber, who has been sneaking bomb parts into a desk drawer, one nail at a time. Even you have suspicions about Syd Wise, and you've never met him."

That was true. Mahegan visualized what Biagatti was saying. Someone could be playing the long game. A day at a time, over nearly three years, would be a possible strategy. Easy to bring in a roll of tape one day, a couple of nails the next day, the right chemicals, little by little, and suddenly you had a suicide vest or bomb that could kill at least two, if not all three, of the chain of command at once.

"I see you understand," Biagatti said.

"Why not keep the vice president here? With us?"

"That has been discussed. We'll leave it up to him to decide. You and your team may deploy with him to West Virginia if he feels like he needs the extra security."

"Why are we special?" Mahegan asked, referring to himself and his four teammates.

Biagatti shrugged, then chinned toward the door. "You guys just saved the world. I think your stock is pretty high."

Mahegan said nothing for a moment, processing. He and his team were here, no one else except Biagatti and the two guards at the front gate, a quarter mile away from the compound.

Last year, terrorists had targeted General Savage, Mahegan, Owens, and O'Malley—the Tribe as they had come to be known—because of their ability to operate in the shadows. Were they all together because of their teamwork and capabilities, or had someone planned

for them to be here for some unstated, perhaps nefarious, purpose? A well-planned raid could potentially
eliminate multiple high-value targets at once.

Van Dreeves and Hobart were new additions to the
Tribe, Mahegan's loose-knit consultancy to General
Savage.

"Don't think too hard about this, Jake. Your mission
is to protect me and this compound until the president
and vice president get here," Biagatti said. "Then, with
the Secret Service's help, you protect them."

"When does everyone arrive?"

"They're preparing to leave. Hit time is one hour,"
she said. She spun a computer monitor toward him.
The screen showed the road network of Virginia and
Maryland. The vice president's nondescript motorcade
was at the Naval Observatory, while the president's
MH-47 helicopter was preparing at Camp David.

"Who is with the president?"

"Limited team. His Secret Service guy, a couple of
aides, and his doctor," Biagatti said.

"His doctor?"

"Evidently, he was getting his annual physical at
Camp David."

Mahegan said nothing, but he was glad to see that
his recommendation that the doctor be present was
well received. The Plan's riskiest point in time was the
next two hours. Everything hinged on the premise of a
low-footprint, clandestine operation involving the
president and vice president. If he showed up with a
bunch of Secret Service agents, some of which might
not be vetted against the Resistance data base, the operation could go tragically wrong.

"You okay?" Biagatti asked.

"Just fine. I'm going to take a walk around. Prep," Mahegan said.

"Why walk when you can sit in a chair?" Biagatti said. She pointed at an array of monitors on the far wall of the study. There were four rows of four video feeds. Each row represented a direction from the house. One series faced south onto the front acreage and Harmony Church Road. The next two showed the flanks of the compound. Cameras peered into the wilderness, showing little more than bony trees and late-autumn deadfall. The last row kept watch on the rear of the property. The forest crept uncomfortably close for Mahegan's taste. Additionally, there was dead space behind the garage extension. The camera was poorly mounted, he thought.

"Thanks. I'll walk around and then keep an eye on things from here."

"Suit yourself, but don't take too long. Once things are in motion, I'm going to want everyone tucked in real tight."

"Roger," Mahegan said. He walked onto the front porch, nodded at Hobart and Van Dreeves, said, "I'm taking a look," and stepped onto the property.

CHAPTER 10

About the same time that Mahegan arrived at Biagatti's compound in Loudoun County, Cassie was swatting away tree branches as she followed Zara through the thick woods from the north.

They had parked in a small turnout on Virginia Route 707 and walked into the woods. On her back in a rucksack, Cassie was carrying two oxygen regulators, which were shaped like scuba tanks, but about half the size.

Zara carried a portable cell phone jammer and mobile Wi-Fi jammer she called a Sledgehammer. Each of them wore night vision goggles held by head harnesses. The terrain slid by in shades of green and black. As they approached the clearing, infrared security-fence beams shone like the barriers they were. Invisible to the naked eye, these beams poked starkly through the night, white lasers etched against the blackness.

Cassie's veins burned with the latest shot that Zara

had given her. The night vision display hummed as if everything was crackling with static electricity. Her eyes alerted on every leaf blown by the wind, each sway of a branch. And a light that switched on in the distance, maybe two hundred yards away. It was a spec, but the thermal and infrared sensors glowed brightly, as if a spotlight was shining.

A large shadow crossed the path of the light. Body features were indistinguishable. Could have been Bigfoot, for all she knew. The porch light cast a brilliant, exploding glow that backlit the individual. There was something in the step that gave her pause. The professional stride. The long legs. The slow-turning head, like a raptor hunting prey. This person was a predator on a mission, dominating its environment. She didn't rule out male or female, given what she had seen at the trauma center.

Cassie grabbed Zara's shoulder and pulled her to the ground.

"Down," she whispered.

Cassie never lost sight of the predator. When she and Zara lowered to the ground, they made the faintest rustle. A squirrel in the bushes. A bird alighting from a branch. They could have been any chord or musical note from the forest's symphony.

But still, the predator's head turned in their direction, held its position for a moment, and then continued around the target facility. The figure then disappeared through the side yard toward the front of the compound.

"What was that?" Zara asked.

"A guard," Cassie replied. "Did you have any intel on this facility?"

"Yes. We watched patterns of life for days, once we got word of the meeting," Zara whispered. "There is one guard at the gate, always. We didn't see anything else."

"Security is here ahead of the meeting," Cassie said.

"Or it's Resistance members protecting Biagatti until she completes her task," Zara said.

Cassie thought about that. The Resistance inside the CIA. People so unhappy with the current president and his administration that they would be willing to die, killing him. It was nothing short of a coup. Chess moves made at every level. Was Biagatti a member of the Resistance? She had seen the speculation in the media, but was that part of a media plan to drive a wedge between the president and his senior staff? The media, after all, was an extension of the Resistance, its megaphone. So much to think about. She was a patriot. Had fought and nearly died for her country. Now, she was executing The Plan, the highest risk mission she had ever encountered. There had been little time to rest after the combat in Iran. She was nearly recovered—her physical wounds had healed just as they were supposed to, with barely a trace, save a few scars that Jake would ultimately find sexy.

She thought about Jake.

Then for some reason she thought about the Raptor in the backyard of the safe house.

Jake Mahegan was definitely an apex predator. Why was she thinking of Jake when she saw the guard patrolling the back of the compound? The stride was similar, but most military professionals had the same careful step as they patrolled and searched. She remembered Jake saying, *I'll find you.*

But he hadn't. Zara and Senator Carter had made that clear. Jake had turned on her, apparently. It wasn't possible, though. Jake loved her. Was by her side. Fought his way into Iran to rescue her. Did just that and brought her home, alive.

But still, that was his voice on the recordings. The sound was seared into her brain.

There's no time. She's dead. Leave her.

Then.

We'll just get more men killed. Not worth it.

She didn't disagree. Though more men had not been killed in her rescue effort, the risk had been beyond reasonable. A parachute jump into the middle of Iran after the war had been declared over, but before all of the forces had received the word to stop fighting. The mission was insane. By all rights, a suicide mission. Why would Mahegan oppose it? He had always placed his own life last in the line of priorities when it came to his team and especially her.

"Look," Zara said, distracting her from a line of reasoning that she desperately wanted—needed—to pursue.

Cassie looked, but didn't see anything.

"What?"

"There," Zara said. She pointed at the left rear of the house.

A light had come on and there were two bodies

standing inside the house beyond a sliding ballistic glass door. Their bodies were black outlines through the sheer curtain. They were big people, most likely men, built powerfully and wearing tactical gear.

"We need to move now. The guard has swept the backyard. We run the hundred meters to the SCIF, replace the tanks, and then retreat back here. If we get separated, the car is the rally point. I'll wait an hour for you. You wait an hour for me. After an hour, we are each on our own."

"We're not getting separated. But I have to say, this mission seems crazy," Cassie said.

"It is. But it must be done. The president and vice president are at risk. You heard the Speaker. We must do this now."

Zara retrieved her phone. She tried to hide the device inside the palm of her hand, but Cassie watched as she pressed on a new text message. There was a picture of Biagatti talking to David Patrino, a well-known attorney, who represented Resistance members pro bono. He had a shaved head and looked like a wiry cage fighter. A media darling of almost every mainstream channel, Patrino was everywhere, representing every client that the Capitol Hill Police dragged out of a hearing room. If there was any one person who represented the Resistance and everything it stood for—immigration rights for everyone, illegal-alien voting rights, threatening the Second Amendment, free college and free health care for all—it was David Patrino, Esquire.

The picture showed Biagatti and Patrino standing on a trail along the Potomac River. The view was a downward angle, as if taken from a bridge. There was very little light, but the zoom lens captured Biagatti handing a packet of papers to Patrino.

"What's this?" Cassie asked.

"Biagatti's last will and testament. Two days ago," Zara said. "She's all set for tonight."

Cassie processed the information. Logic was attempting to tell her something, but her veins burned white hot with Zara's poison. Even now, Cassie craved the needle. She badly needed what she had been carrying in the cooler, but knew that even Jake would not be able to deliver it soon enough, even if he wanted to. Biagatti was trying to kill the president and vice president? Did that make sense? Was it so the Speaker could become president? Was she capable of rational thought? All she understood was that she had to get the oxygen tanks into the SCIF circulation system. That much was clear.

Then they could warn off the president, which brought an idea into her head. Why wait?

"Why haven't we just gone to the Secret Service?"

"I told you. The Resistance is everywhere. If the director of the CIA is willing to die for the cause, don't you think the Secret Service has moles? Besides, how are we supposed to stop this fast-moving train other than making sure Biagatti doesn't gas them?"

The distant chop of helicopter blades sang through the night air. About a mile away, headlights from two vehicles turned onto Harmony Church Road. There was commotion in the house.

"Time to go," Zara said. She waited a few seconds, then pressed a button on the Sledgehammer Wi-Fi blocker. The infrared lasers remained in place, but the technology supposedly disabled communication between the sensors and the base station located inside the house. Likewise, the Sledgehammer was supposed to have the same effect on the security cameras positioned around the compound. They would soon find out the Sledgehammer's effectiveness, Cassie figured.

"Now," Zara said. She was up and moving. Cassie followed, stepping through the infrared beams, feeling nothing tangible but anxiety riding high. What if the Sledgehammer didn't work? They'd be shot dead by the Raptor and the remainder of the team. She knew how the highly trained professional guards worked. Jake was a member of a team that did precisely this type of security work.

She sprinted, feeling the weight of the oxygen tanks on her back. The SCIF building grew larger in her night vision goggle sight picture. Zara was behind her, running effortlessly, it seemed. Cassie's wounds bit at her. The shoulder and leg wounds had healed, but the scar tissue ripped with every stride. Tears streamed down her face from the pain, a release from so much pain and rehab effort. She missed Jake desperately, but knew he had been there by her side in Walter Reed. Had relocated to Northern Virginia to be near her. She remembered his last visit, prior to her middle-of-the-night relocation to the trauma center.

Jake had smuggled in a pint of Häagen-Dazs cookies-and-cream ice cream, which they shared. They had discussed Bald Head Island, the craziness that had occurred near Asheville, North Carolina, and, of course, the mission in Iran. Cassie had helped Mossad and Jordanian

Special Forces disable the Iranian nuclear capabilities, protecting Israel and much of Europe. On that night, he had mentioned something about their mentor, Major General Bob Savage, reassigning him to the area. It was all *double top secret* probation stuff, they had joked. Something to do with the intelligence community.

The SCIF was suddenly in front of her, interrupting her flashback to Jake's visit, but something hung in the back of her mind that she couldn't fully process. A connection between the predator and something Jake had said. But that was for another time.

Cassie slowed and then pressed her body into the back side of the SCIF. It was a structure about ten feet high and seemed to have a fair amount of belowground penetration as well. The windowless building had an external air filtration system with oxygen regulators lying horizontally on a rack. A Master Lock secured a hasp that locked the two tanks in place. Hoses fed from the valve in the tanks to a fixture, which very much looked like a faucet for a garden hose, located on the back of the building.

The pictures had proven reliable. Cassie released her rucksack and placed it on the ground. Zara pulled up next to her, breathing steadily as she retrieved her pistol and placed her shoulder against the wall, securing the corner of the SCIF nearest the house. She then quickly jogged to the far side and looked around that corner. Apparently satisfied, Zara said, "Clear. Let's go."

Her voice was mostly drowned out by the thunderous roar of the MH-47 rotor blades. Cassie used a set of bolt cutters to snap through the lock, which flipped off the hasp. She removed her night vision goggle and

placed a protective mask over her head. She didn't expect any of the poison to spray when she unscrewed
the fitting, but was prepared for that possibility. As she
lifted the first tank away from its curved hold, she noticed a tag that had a handwritten date of inspection,
which was a month earlier.

Clever, she thought.

She tightened the valve to the off position, then unscrewed the hose fitting, heard a slight hiss, was glad
she had the mask on, and then put the container on the
ground. She repeated the process with the second tank.
Looking up at Zara, Cassie nodded.

Zara said, "Less than one minute. The helicopter is
on the ground."

Cassie lifted the first oxygen tank from her rucksack
and laid it in the twelve-inch-wide groove. Then the
second. She pressed the valve connector into the re-
ceptacle on the regulator and tightened it. Repeated the
process on the second, then turned the knob to open the
valve for the first and the second.

Clean oxygen would now flow into the SCIF when
Biagatti led the president and vice president into the
classified chamber.

"We have to move!"

Two Little Bird MH-6 helicopters zipped over the
house and fanned in opposite directions, conducting
aerial reconnaissance, no doubt. Cassie placed the containers in her rucksack and fled to the north, Zara
sprinting along with her, keeping pace. The helicopters
sped a quarter mile ahead of them and then began to
circle back as Cassie and Zara entered the forest.

The woods were little comfort for Cassie. She had

been on enough operations with intelligence feeds from special-operations aircraft to know that the pilots and the avionics were the best in the world. The thermal and infrared sensors would cut through the foliage and find anything that had a pulse.

"We're no match for those Little Birds," Cassie said.

"The forest is thicker to the north. Keep running," Zara replied. They were now hurdling deadfall and logs as big as car tires. Cassie stepped into a stream, which she didn't recall crossing on the way down—perhaps they had veered off course.

"Wait," she said. Zara stepped into the stream. The water was cool, flowing from some unknown source in the mountains to the west. There had already been November snow in the Blue Ridge, followed by a warming trend for a couple of days. Cassie looked up. The forest canopy was thick, the leaves were turning but had yet to fall.

"Why? What? We have to get to the car," Zara said.

"Between the trees and cold water, we can cool our body temperature down. Maybe stay off the radar of the helicopters. We'll never outrun them."

To emphasize her point, the two Little Birds buzzed low, seemingly clipping the tops of the trees. They circled high into the air, their engines whining, straining against the forces of gravity.

Cassie tackled Zara and they fell into the stream, submerged fully except for the rucksack. They both held their breaths for as long as possible, maybe a minute, maybe a tad less. Zara began to struggle against Cassie's weight, so Cassie emerged from the water and lifted Zara.

"Bitch, are you trying to drown me?" Zara spat.

"Saving you. Now shut up," Cassie said.

She listened. The Little Birds had relocated to another area south of the compound, the opposite direction. Cassie held her palm over her phone, pulled up the map function, found their location, saw they had drifted to the northwest, which was okay because they had found the stream. She calculated the route in her mind, studied the terrain in the darkness, flipped down her night vision goggle, looked uphill, found a route, and waded through the water until she was climbing up the bank.

Zara followed her for twenty minutes as they picked their way through the forest. Approaching the vehicle they left in a gravel turnout, Cassie halted, took a knee, and pulled Zara down with her. To the right, about a quarter of a mile, there was a parked vehicle, and it had not been there before. The road was a long ribbon of blackness beneath the starlit sky. Trees framed the pavement and the ditches on either side like a tunnel.

"What?" Zara asked.

"Car. Quarter mile. Two o'clock."

Zara turned her head slowly, then looked at Cassie and said, "We have to move."

"We have to deal with this first," Cassie said. "I'll be right back."

She backed down the hill about twenty meters and then walked parallel to the road until her pace count approximated just beyond a quarter mile. She approached the road, known as a danger area in her Ranger training, and the car was now to her left by about ten meters. Two people sat in the front seat of the car. They wore ski masks and most likely weren't part of the presidential detail, but it was impossible to tell.

Should I kill them? Disable their vehicle? Ignore them and try to get away clean?

"Two bogies wearing ski masks," she whispered. The earbud radio was not secure, but she had to risk it.

"I'll get the car and pick you up a half mile down the road," Zara said. "If they start, shoot their tires. If you miss, shoot to kill."

"That only works in the movies. If I shoot, then they'll shoot. And we'll have a shit show on our hands." *How many innocents will I have to kill?* Her mission could not be more important and so she would do her duty, yet where she could, she would avoid random slaughter.

After a pause, Zara said, "Okay. Come back and we'll do it together. I've got a plan."

Cassie returned about the time she heard the Little Bird helicopters buzzing just north of the property and about a mile to their south. They had to move.

Linking back up with Zara, together they walked another hundred meters to the west, where there was a slight bend to the north. They low-crawled across the road and then backtracked toward the car. Entering through the passenger door, Cassie took the wheel and Zara sat shotgun. In her hand, Zara held two smoke grenades, safety pins pulled.

Cassie looked over her shoulder—still no car moving toward them—started the car, kept the lights off, slammed the gear into drive, and sped away. In the rearview mirror, she noticed the other car was now racing toward them. At the bend in the road where they had crossed, Cassie said, "Now!"

Zara tossed the two smoke grenades out of the window. Gray smoke boiled and quickly created a thick curtain screening their movement west. The car, nonetheless, barreled through, smoke twirling in its wake like airplane contrails.

But when it needed to turn about thirty degrees to the right, it continued straight. A wheel caught the edge of the drainage ditch and the car flipped toward the downhill side, rolling until it smashed into a tree.

Cassie sped away toward Route 7, fire dancing in the rearview mirror.

CHAPTER 11

Through the scope of an M24 bolt-action sniper rifle, Mahegan watched a woman, who looked just like Cassie. The crosshairs were on her back as she flitted into the woods with an accomplice. Cassie had a long-legged gait and recognizable way she carried her arms when she ran, forearms almost parallel with the ground. Though, without direct communication, and no control over her role, he guessed that Cassie was part of the team that Syd Wise had mentioned having on the grounds? Or was it something else?

"Not shooting?" Owens asked.

Mahegan breathed out and tightened his finger on the trigger, moving the scope to the other woman.

"Moving too fast," Mahegan said.

"Bullshit, boss," Owens replied. After a pause, he said, "Always a chance she'd go native, you know." Not a question, but a statement.

Mahegan shrugged.

"No chance Cassie goes native. Go check the back of the SCIF. It's a blind spot. No cameras," Mahegan said. "Take Sean with you."

"Roger," Owens said. He moved out quickly from the kitchen window, where Mahegan was seated, sighting the rifle through an open window.

Then into his portable earbud microphone, Mahegan said, "Hobart, VD, one of you meet me now in the kitchen. Keep eyes on the guard shack."

As he waited, Mahegan watched Owens and O'Malley jog to the rear of the SCIF about fifty meters to his ten o'clock. An automatic sensor light tripped and shone brightly, which had not happened when Cassie and her partner had infiltrated. *Jamming,* Mahegan thought. Both women had been carrying a rucksack, one of which probably contained a portable jamming system.

Mahegan wondered about Cassie's last several months. Wounded in Iran. Rescued. Patched up in Walter Reed Medical Center. Transferred to Valley Trauma Center. Escaped. Captured, or rescued again, allegedly by Senator Jamie Carter. And now on a mission in Northern Virginia. She was a busy woman.

Too bad he loved her. She was now in the game, on the hunt, doing things she shouldn't do. Mahegan's sense of right and wrong always revolved around what was best for the country and his teammates. His Ranger tab tattoo on his left shoulder and teammates tattoo on his right bicep attested to his twin, sometimes competing, loyalties.

Mission and men, to include women when they were part of the team.

Cassie was on the team. Now she was executing a mission that *appeared* to be in direct contravention of Mahegan's code and values. An Army Ranger, Cassie was tough, but Mahegan had seen others with more combat experience come home irretrievably broken. He believed that Cassie was not broken, but only she knew the depths she was plumbing. Not to mention that he had opened himself to her. For the first time in his life, he had viewed a woman through the lens of a potential long-term future.

Would their relationship be able to survive this gambit? Would either of them survive, period?

The nation was at a political crossroads: the divisions so deep and penetrating that the divide was wider than even the Grand Canyon. Evel Knievel wouldn't have been able to jump this chasm with a rocket-fueled motorcycle. Mahegan had visions of the French Revolution, the *chasseur des barrières en grande tenue* standing in lockstep against the ragtag students waving the tricolor and shouting, *"Liberté, egalité, fraternité!"* Would there be barricades in Washington, DC, as the coup unfolded? Burning tires. Helicopters swooping low through the streets of Washington, DC, spitting machine-gun rounds at the Resistance as they assaulted the White House?

Probably not. The peaceful protests, so far, had been interrupted only by a smattering of singleton violent attacks. A shooting here, a stabbing there. Nothing that would ring the alarm bell that a coup was imminent, but perhaps that was the idea. Just as Osama bin Laden had gone silent months before the 9/11 attacks, the Resistance could have been training their assassins, such as the women focused on the CIA Director. What was at play? They had some limited intelligence, but it was weak and difficult to cross-verify with a second source.

"Here's the deal, boss," Owens reported in, over the radio.

Owens talked and Mahegan listened. He thought about it and then gave his two men the instructions. They had ten minutes until the helicopters came. They had to move quickly, which they did.

Hobart knelt next to Mahegan, who gave Hobart instructions. When he was done, Mahegan said, "Got it?"

Hobart nodded and said, "No problem." He stood, spun, and jogged to get Van Dreeves. The side door to the garage opened and shut. Mahegan stood and walked to the window, saw Hobart and Van Dreeves snaking along the high shrub line down to the guard shack. They had to move quickly.

If they were wrong, they would all be shot for treason.

He walked into the study, where Biagatti was reviewing some paperwork. He turned her monitor toward him and studied the multiple camera feeds.

"Where's the guard shack?"

"That black one, right in the middle," she said, tapping her finger on the monitor, as if trying to make it work.

"You know these guys?" Mahegan asked, eyeing her.

"The guards? Enough to know they are not new," she said.

Moving back to the window, Mahegan watched his two men close on the small building. They stacked against the back.

Suddenly the MH-47 helicopter was shaking the windows of the safe house. Vice President Grainger's car was snaking along Harmony Church Road, approaching the guard shack.

"Status," Mahegan said.

"No change," Owens reported.

The soft pop of distant gunfire sounded about the time the two-car convoy turned onto the driveway. Hobart stepped from the guard shack, like he had been there all night. He lowered the tire shredder for the vice president's car, but raised it as the chase car followed.

"Sean, I need you or Patch on the front lawn," Mahegan said.

"Heading that way," O'Malley said.

"Roger." Then to Hobart, "What's happening with the chase car?"

"Stand by," Hobart replied.

The chase car, a Dodge Charger, stopped at the bared teeth of the tire shredder. Two men stepped out with pistols up. Van Dreeves fired two shots from the guardhouse window. He was using a twelve-gauge Beretta shotgun and beanbag rounds. Both shots caught the chase car detail in their heads, knocking them to the ground. Hobart was quickly on top of them, most likely flex-cuffing them. Mahegan nodded and thought, *Okay, this is a gamble, but everything's in place.*

Owens and O'Malley met him halfway between the helicopter, which was landing, and the house. The president and his security man walked down the back ramp toward them. The vice president stepped out of his car and walked with his security guy toward Mahegan.

Mahegan nodded at O'Malley and said, "Follow me." Biagatti stood from her chair and came to the front door and walked onto the lawn.

"Was that gunfire?" Biagatti asked Mahegan as they waited for the MH-47 to land. Its thunderous rotors washed over the house, scattering anything that wasn't tied down. It hovered briefly, then landed about fifty meters from the front porch. The ramp lowered as a crew chief was standing at the back with his flight helmet and Nomex suit on.

"Probably a deer hunter," Mahegan said.

What he was knew, though, was that he and his team were in zero-defects execute mode and they couldn't take the risk that the two secret service men would potentially disrupt The Plan.

"Two RPGs in the guard shack," Hobart radioed.

Mahegan stepped away, letting Biagatti speak privately with the vice president. Replying to Hobart, he said, "Roger. Charlie Mike."

"Just saying. You were right. There's a threat," Hobart said. "And now we have options with the two shack guys."

"Safer inside right now," Mahegan countered. Mahegan knew his options were to keep the president on the aircraft and have the trustworthy TF-160 pilots take him back to Camp David or to the White House or to gather them inside the compound. His gut told him he needed to play this out to shake out some of the moles. He wouldn't get all of them, but the only way to catch the big fish was to use big bait. They didn't come any bigger than the president and vice president.

"Watch your six with the Secret Service guys coming off the aircraft," Hobart said.

"Understand," Mahegan said. His mind raced with the endless possibilities that could evolve from this moment. By sending Van Dreeves and Hobart to the guardhouse, he quite possibly averted the shoot-down of the MH-47, saving the lives of the precious cargo and the six-soldier crew. Now he had to factor the president, vice president, two bodyguards, and the director of the CIA. Chances were, at least one of them was a member of the Resistance. His mind calculated the myriad scenarios and he settled on two or three that he thought might occur. Given the known infiltration of Cassie and what looked like Zara Perro, coupled with the two men at the guard shack, the Resistance plan was most likely to use the SCIF as the decisive point. The RPGs were probably a backup plan, in case whatever was supposed to happen at the SCIF didn't occur exactly as planned. A gas attack in the SCIF would be much more efficient than a fireball in the sky that could be seen for miles. It gave the Resistance all kinds of options of how to dispose of the bodies, change the story of what happened, create a false narrative, and certainly find a way to place the blame on the president himself.

Mahegan walked up the ramp and greeted the president, who was standing just inside the cargo bay next to a large African-American man, Secret Service Agent Tyrus Vance. Behind him was a tall white man, holding a duffel bag. The doctor. They were all dressed in casual attire. The president was wearing khaki slacks, a white leisure shirt, and a brown bomber jacket. The doctor had on the same attire, except for a blue Windbreaker instead of the bomber jacket. Vance was dressed in a dark blue shirt, which seemed to barely fit his massive frame.

"Sir, welcome. I'd appreciate it if just you and Vance came in initially. We're trying to keep access to the compound to a minimum."

"Where's the vice president?" President Smart asked.

"He's arrived and is with Director Biagatti. Perfect timing."

"Okay, let's get this show on the road," Smart said. They walked down the ramp, Mahegan leading. At the same time, the vice president and his bodyguard, a woman whom Mahegan didn't know, walked toward him up the sidewalk from a forty-five-degree angle.

Mahegan looked at the vice president and his bodyguard. Next to them was Biagatti, who clenched her fist and pumped her arm, the universal symbol for move quickly. Mahegan took long strides. Vance touched the president's elbow, urging him forward, and they moved quickly toward the porch. As they arrived, Biagatti said, "Welcome, Mr. President. We need to move inside now."

He led them into the house, through the kitchen, and down some steps that led to a long hallway, which connected to the SCIF. Biagatti stopped them and said, "Good evening, Mr. President and Vice President."

"Carmen. This better be good," the president said. "We're violating all kinds of protocols here."

"Being unpredictable right now is a good thing, Mr. President."

"Okay, we managed that. What's next?"

Biagatti had moved to the front of the column, but Mahegan crowded her away from the SCIF door. There was a little gaggle outside of the door, because everyone thought that Mahegan was going to lead them into the room immediately. Instead, he paused outside and said, "Let's take a moment."

"What is this, church? C'mon, Mahegan, let's go," Biagatti said.

Mahegan's hand rested on the door handle to the SCIF, then said, "No. But everyone needs to be aware of what's happening locally, tactically, right here, right now."

"Okay, explain," President Smart said.

"Director Biagatti led us here to the SCIF, but I think we can talk downstairs in the basement. It's probably just as secure."

"What we need to discuss can only be done in the SCIF," Biagatti said. "This house wasn't built for classified conversations, and it's not used enough to be a thousand percent certain that someone hasn't . . . tampered and emplaced listening devices."

The SCIF's closed door was metallic and looked like the opening to a walk-in freezer. A twenty-meter enclosed connecting walkway from the house kitchen led to this cube of a room. As Biagatti had said, it was never intended for presidential visits, but still, as a CIA safe house, it *was* intended for protection and security from those that wanted to find and kill them.

In Mahegan's ear, Hobart said, "I'm listening to this. This is an ambush. Execute conplan ASAP."

"Roger. Just a sec," Mahegan said. Hobart was recommending executing the contingency plan that they had only briefly discussed. It was complex and required precision.

"Who are you talking to?" Biagatti asked.

"My security team. We're fine," Mahegan said.

Biagatti, President Smart, Vice President Grainger, and the bodyguards looked at him. The two leaders of the Free World were dressed in identical khaki slacks, blue shirts, and bomber jackets. Smart was a tall, thin man, with thick graying hair and an angular nose. Grainger looked a bit like Dick Cheney, with his crooked glasses and bald head. He was short and disheveled and had a hard time keeping eye contact. A slight bulge on the left side of his bomber jacket could be the pouch of chewing tobacco he typically carried with him, or it could be something else, entirely. Outside of their tight circle were two bodyguards. Mahegan knew only one of them, though only remotely. Both bodyguards had slightly puffed-out chests, as if they might be wearing body armor underneath their shirts and jackets.

Tyrus Vance, the president's man, was a tall, thick African American. He was a former collegiate defensive end at Michigan. Vance's aura dominated a room, much the same as Mahegan's did. Both men had presence and naturally the testosterone was at maximum wattage. Mahegan sensed the tension. The perennial question "Who's in charge" was never really an issue for Mahegan. He took charge until someone else proved more capable or had a position of authority over him. Vance's job was singular in purpose: keep the president alive. Mahegan's mission was broader, but inclusive of Vance's.

Vance stared at Mahegan with suspicious eyes and stepped closer to his boss, who was opposite Mahegan. To Mahegan's right was the door to the SCIF. To his left was Biagatti. Across from him were the president, vice president, Vance, and the vice president's bodyguard, a woman named Twinkler, whose nickname was "Twinkie," which Mahegan assumed she didn't particularly care for. Twinkie was a stocky woman, perhaps a weight lifter, he didn't know, but she looked the part.

This is the moment of truth. Can everyone play their part? Mahegan steeled himself for the series of actions that were supposed to flow from this point when Biagatti interrupted his focus.

"Why can't we go in the SCIF, Jake?" Biagatti asked.

Patience was never your strong suit, Mahegan thought.

"There might be an issue," Mahegan said.

"What kind of an issue?" President Smart asked.

"Shouldn't it be enough that there's an issue, sir? You pay us well to determine these things. It's best if you don't go in the SCIF," Mahegan said.

"I pay Vance here. I barely know you," the president said. He looked over his shoulder and said, "Vance, what's your call?"

"I don't see a problem, sir. It's a SCIF. Jake here's a little jumpy after his girlfriend almost got killed in Iran. The advance team swept the place then relocated to the guard shack. They screened in the Vice President," Vance said.

The president shrugged. "See there, Mahegan. Vance says it's okay. He's my guy. You're not my guy."

"Technically, we're all your guys," Mahegan said.

"I get paid the same way Vance gets paid—by the U.S. Treasury. We all work for you."

"Do you? Vance here has been my guy for three years. He's busted up more plots against me than you can imagine."

"Sometimes people get overconfident when they have so much success. Vance looks entirely competent, but then again, he could be off his game a bit."

"You hear that, Vance? Are you *off your game,* as Mahegan here suggests?" The president smiled.

"Not a chance, sir. The SCIF is clean," Vance said.

"Vance says the SCIF is clean. I take him at his word. Let's quit wasting time," Smart said.

"If Vance is so confident, I suggest we let him go first and sweep the SCIF while we stay out here and watch."

The skin under Vance's right eye ticked briefly; then he smirked. He knew Mahegan was calling his bluff. Was he a member of the Resistance or not? Was he a mole in the best-possible place a mole could be?

"No problem," Vance said.

"What about you, Twinkie? Going to leave your wingman in there?"

"Twinkie stays with me," Vice President Grainger said.

Mahegan smiled. "You're safe with us, sir. I think both security personnel should go in the SCIF. After all, isn't Twinkie responsible for your safety? Are you willing to take Vance's word, and only Vance's word? If something were to happen, and the report that gets filed says that Twinkie didn't do her job, is that a legacy you want her to have?"

"Twinkie's only been with me a few weeks, I'm sure she'll be fine. Anyway, why are you making such a big deal out of going in the SCIF?" Vice President Grainger asked. "Three feet are separating us from that room. What danger is in there that isn't out here?"

"That's an excellent question. Twinkie is your gal. She should answer it," Mahegan said. "You may remember that Senator Hite is dead. That's open-source information, so we discuss it here. What's not open source, but most likely still not classified, is that Director Biagatti had an attempt on her life last night. The Senate pro tem is killed and a few months later the director of the CIA is attacked. Maybe I'm just paranoid, or maybe there's a connection."

What Owens had found at the back of the SCIF didn't necessarily surprise Mahegan, mainly because the world seemed to be getting crazier with each passing day. Since he left the military, all he had seen were secret plots, conspiracies, and threats against the nation, large and small. They had seen Cassie and another woman jogging toward the home, and then a few minutes later jogging away. Earlier, several female assassins had attacked Biagatti. Was the Resistance employing a new brand of assassin? Women only? If so, why?

Mahegan was unsure if Biagatti was a member of the Resistance. There was no guarantee, of course, because the entire attack might have been staged. The embeds were deep and high level. As the president's reelection numbers looked decent, the Resistance had moved into its Direct Action stage, which meant that they were closing in on the objective. No life was too special, too sacred, to spare. Like the final assault up the hill. Robert E. Lee ordering Pickett on the third day at Gettysburg. Or General Santa Anna ordering the final assault on the Alamo. Pick your history. The differences were that stark. Lose or win. Everything exposed. Three years of preparation and taking no chances at losing the next election.

The president shrugged his shoulders and said, "Alright, Vance and Twinkie, why don't the two of you go ahead and clear the room for your principals? Make Mahegan here happy," the president said.

"Sure thing," Vance said. He stepped forward. Twinkie didn't move. Vance's hand was on the door handle. It was a sleek latch with polished chrome. Vance's large hand pulled on the grip, which broke the seal of the metal and the rubber grommet that ran the length of the doorjamb. Mahegan stared at Twinkie and Vice President Grainger. Neither was moving.

"What's the matter, Twinkie?" Mahegan asked.

She stepped closer to the vice president. President Smart looked at them and said, "Twinkie, get in there with Vance. Be a wingwoman."

Twinkie shifted, shuffled her feet, and looked down at the floor. The vice president nudged her, saying, "Go ahead, Twinkie. Go with Vance."

Twinkie's head snapped up and she looked at the vice president. "But, sir . . ."

"Get in there!" the vice president roared.

Vance still was holding the door handle. Some air was slipping between the SCIF and hallway. The vice president eyed the minor gap nervously. "Go ahead," he said.

"What's going on?" Smart asked. He looked from Grainger to Twinkie to Mahegan.

President Smart didn't know him well, but Mahegan figured he knew of him. Mahegan's name had probably been in the president's briefing book on several occasions. Mahegan made problems disappear. A president had to like that. Though one could also assume that Mahegan might be a part of the problem and not the solution.

Mahegan looked at Vance's hand on the door, then caught Vance's eyes, which were staring back at Mahegan with a knowing look. Mahegan nodded. This was the moment that everything had to go right down to the very last detail, which almost never happened even on the best, most precisely executed operations.

"You open that door, one of two things will happen," Mahegan said.

"What's that?" Smart asked. Biagatti's stare burned holes in Mahegan's face, like lasers.

"Not to overstate the obvious, but you either live or die," Mahegan said.

"Are you threatening the president and vice president of the United States?" Grainger challenged, recovering from whatever was bothering him. Still, perspiration was beading on his shiny forehead. Twinkie was still shuffling her feet. "I'm happy to walk in there if Director Biagatti says it's okay," she said.

"No, sir. Just stating a fact," Mahegan said. "The Resistance is in direct attack mode. Earlier I walked into a raid on Director Biagatti's house. Even your Secret Service teams have been compromised. Embeds are everywhere. There's a coup happening. I'm what you've got. If Vance and Twinkie clear the room, then I'd say you're fine."

"A coup?" the vice president protested. "That's just insane."

"Perhaps," Mahegan said. "It's hard to tell, but Director Biagatti here probably could tell you best." As Biagatti began to talk, a thought lodged in Mahegan's mind. Something he had cycled through only moments earlier. Something about the Resistance and women attacking Biagatti's house. He listened to Biagatti as he grappled to synthesize the complete idea.

"There has been chatter, but you know we are limited in our ability to collect on U.S. citizens in the United States—the whole purpose behind meeting here. As far as embeds, or moles, or whatever you want to call them, they're real, no doubt about that. The problem is smoking them out. You have those that remained from the previous administration that were downgraded into protected federal bureaucrat positions. Nothing you can do about them. They start out as political hires, and then when the previous administration sees its party has lost, they execute a plan that embeds holdovers in every agency. The Resistance has access to top secret, comparted information every day, all day. They have members in the Secret Service and they have members in my organization. D-day has arrived for them and they are executing."

"What kind of chatter?" the vice president asked. Maybe it was Mahegan, but the man appeared to be unreasonably nervous.

"If we're not going in the SCIF, I'd recommend we walk toward the front of the house as we continue this conversation," Mahegan said. "Based on what Director Biagatti is saying, that twenty percent of the administration might be Resistance, out of the six of us, there's a probability that one is a member of the Resistance."

"I'd say you're being insubordinate, Mahegan," President Smart said.

"Maybe, but I'd rather ruffle a few feathers and call it as I see it, to do my job, which is protecting you, primarily," Mahegan said. He nodded at the president. The president gauged him for a moment.

"Okay. Seems like we're not going in the SCIF. We're already discussing classified information. Wouldn't be the first time we didn't do so in a SCIF. Mahegan, you're in charge of this gaggle. Let's go," Smart said.

As the president was turning to follow Mahegan, Grainger retrieved a pistol from a holster beneath the left side of his jacket.

Mahegan didn't move with the momentum of the group. He watched the vice president level his pistol at Twinkie at the same time Mahegan had his Tribal Sig Sauer out and up and aimed at the vice president. Vance shut the SCIF door and tackled the president to get him out of the line of fire and leveled his pistol at Mahegan.

"Don't do it, Jake," Biagatti said. "You'll be killing the vice president of the United States."

"Shut up!" Grainger said. "Nobody's killing me. Twinkler here is a Resistance member. She's got two assassins at my home right now, ready to kill my wife and children. I've been suspecting her for a few weeks. She's been sneaking off for private conversations. I started carrying my own pistol, in case she made a move against me in the next forty-eight hours. And now she's wired with a suicide vest."

That's why she looks so blocky, Mahegan thought. His mind raced. The scene was insane. Vance was now up and running through the hallway toward the kitchen as he shielded the president with his considerable mass. Biagatti was frozen in place, looking at the vice president with a pistol to the head of his bodyguard.

"So, is it true, Twinkie? Are you in on the Resistance?" Mahegan asked.

Twinkie didn't respond. She was catatonic, probably wondering how the evening had gone so wrong. Her lips then spread into a thin smile as she slowly moved her fingers toward her wrist. The movement was almost imperceptible, but Mahegan had seen that façade on suicide bombers before. The look was one of serene commitment—a woman at peace with what she was less than a second from doing. The vice president wasn't positioned to see the distant stare or the nearly imperceptible movement of Twinkie's hand. Director Biagatti was too busy staring at the pistol Grainger held to Twinkie's head to notice the guard's intent.

Vance shouted over his shoulder as he pushed the president and ran, "Bomb! Come with me, Vice President!"

Mahegan quickly snapped off two rounds into Twinkie's forehead, then opened the door, tackled Biagatti and fell into the SCIF, pulling the door shut behind him. Grainger had tripped backward as Twinkler's body fell into him.

Mahegan and Biagatti lay on the SCIF floor, keeping low to avoid any penetrating shrapnel. There was a pregnant pause, extended and drawn out. Was the bomb going to explode?

"What the hell is going on, Jake? We can't be in here!" Biagatti said.

Her eyes were wide, a frightened animal. But Mahegan registered no apparent concern about Biagatti. She looked over her shoulder at the back wall, like a smaller animal fearing a predator. Noises in the hallway caused her to look back toward the door.

No way is Twinkler still alive, Mahegan thought. *That better be Hobart and Van Dreeves. Is 60 seconds enough time to do what they need to do?*

What was probably a minute, maybe slightly more seemed like five minutes. After a few more noises in the hallway, an explosion rocked the SCIF, shrapnel piercing the walls and whizzing above their heads. Fire licked inward like a serpent's tongue, quickly receding. Smoke filled the SCIF with the acrid chemical stench of spent urea nitrate.

Mahegan was quickly up, pulling at Biagatti, who appeared okay.

"What the hell?" She looked up at the vents in the SCIF ceiling. "We have to get out of here!"

Mahegan nodded. "Just a few more seconds. Make sure there are no secondaries."

"Now, Jake! We can't stay in here!" Then after a

pause, she gathered herself, calmed her emotions. "We have to find the president and vice president."

Mahegan said nothing, kept his arm over Biagatti, pinning her to the floor. She was wriggling to escape his clutch, fearful of something, perhaps because Mahegan had said it was unsafe in the SCIF. After another minute, he stood and assisted her, but she stayed in a low, crouching position, covering her mouth against the smoke filling the SCIF and the hallway connecting the kitchen and the SCIF.

"Follow me," Mahegan said. The door had buckled inward and it took Mahegan placing his foot against the frame of the SCIF wall to pry it open against its seared hinges. Smoke continued to suck into the SCIF, pulled by the HVAC filter system Mahegan had turned on after being debriefed by Owens.

Stepping into the hall, he looked to his right and saw the mangled remains of Twinkler and what appeared to be Vice President Grainger. Smoke boiled in the hallway, obscuring everything. The scene was such that Grainger had never reached Vance, Twinkler somehow blocking his egress in her death. Not much was left intact of either body. Being that close to a bomb blast shredded body parts, leaving a leg here, an arm there, faces completely unrecognizable. Pieces of the vice president's bomber jacket littered the hallway like confetti. Anyone looking at the scene would assume the vice president died next to his secret service agent.

"You let the vice president be killed!" Biagatti shouted.

"No. I saved you. Whether you're worth saving, now there's a real question."

"Savage warned me about you, Mahegan."

"Good. Glad there weren't any false expectations."

They raced along the hallway, where Vance was kneeling over another unrecognizable body, whose face he had already covered. The bomber jacket was shredded in the back and the scene gave the appearance that when Vance had stepped forward to open the door for the president, the bomb exploded, and shrapnel cut into the president.

Vance was staring at the dead man, pressing his hand against the mangled neck.

"I was supposed to protect the president," Vance muttered. "I'm just . . . lost, man."

"Call an ambulance," Biagatti said. "Now!"

"We can't do that," Mahegan said. "We'll have to put them all on the helicopter. It will be more discreet and much faster."

Smoke hung in the hallway like a lingering ghost, leering at the destruction. Biagatti was oddly sanguine, now that she was out of the SCIF and in the smoky hallway, though she cast a skittish glance over her shoulder.

"Dead?" she asked.

Vance looked up and nodded, eyes moist.

"Director, why don't you link up with the team in the study. We will move out from there," Mahegan said.

Biagatti nodded, coughed, and said, "Okay." She stepped past Mahegan, over what appeared to be the president's body, and beyond Vance as she navigated the steps.

When she had shut the door, Mahegan said, "We have to execute now."

Vance nodded. The safe house had stretchers. They placed one set of remains on one stretcher and combined the two nearest the bomb blast on the other. There wasn't much left of Twinkler, and the body parts fit easily on one. Handling the burnt flesh reminded Mahegan of losing his best friend, Sergeant Wesley Colgate, to a bombmaker using a Siri voice command a few years back. He had killed the bombmaker, who was attempting to flee, and then raced toward Colgate's vehicle, which was demolished and on fire. The haunting memories of combat were never far from the surface, and this scene brought those images barreling to the fore.

"You okay?" Vance asked.

They were carrying the litter with the body parts through the side door and onto the lawn as the helicopter landed again. They retraced their steps and snagged the second litter. Hobart and Van Dreeves were securing the guard shack, as if they had never departed. Owens and O'Malley carried two more stretchers onto the helicopter.

Mahegan walked up the ramp beneath the whipping rear rotor of the MH-47 and grabbed the loadmaster by the outer tactical vest.

"Let me talk to the pilot!" he shouted.

The loadmaster removed his helmet and handed it to Mahegan, who donned it, then pressed the PUSH TO TALK button on the communications intercom. "Night Stalker six, this is Tribal six," Mahegan said.

"Damn, Mahegan, you're everywhere, man."

"Putting some precious cargo on here. Will send you encrypted message to the cockpit, but I wanted you to know it's legit. It's going to sound strange, but it's accurate. I've got O'Malley working up the message right now. Four litters on the back. Vance is going to ride with you. He'll explain the rest."

"Roger that. Coming from you, Jake. No issues. We've got your precious cargo and will deliver it where the customer wants it."

"I'm the customer," Mahegan said.

During the pilot's pause, Mahegan watched Vance and one of the crew members ferry the two other litters into the belly of the aircraft.

"No doubt," the pilot said.

"Be safe," Mahegan said, and handed the helmet to the crew chief.

Mahegan walked off the ramp where Vance met him.

"You have the controls," Mahegan said to Vance.

"I've got this. You watch that woman in there . . . and your back," Vance shouted above the roaring rotors.

Mahegan gave the crew chief a circular motion with his hand, meaning *lift the ramp and get going.*

He jogged back into the house and found O'Malley, who had returned already and was prepared to hit SEND on the secure-text communications to the pilot.

Mahegan nodded. They had nearly precisely executed the first part of The Plan. That sense of perfection, though, always gave him pause.

What was he missing? There was always something.

He thought about Cassie. The drugs concerned him and maybe that was the issue. He had no control over Cassie's role in all of this.

Would she be able to complete The Plan?

Biagatti was there, hugging herself and staring distantly out the window.

"The president and vice president are dead," she said. Her voice was flat, without affect.

"You better call the Speaker of the House," Mahegan said.

Biagatti turned and looked at him. "Yes, I better."

CHAPTER 12

Cassie sat in a stylish blue velvet chair made somewhere in Scandinavia. Its curves were sleek and angular. Her arms and legs were crossed as she looked through the darkness at the Potomac River from the penthouse apartment of Zara Perro. The rucksack was beside her. Somehow, it seemed smarter to keep it with them than to leave it in the car.

Zara was drinking a glass of vodka, neat from the freezer. The tumbler had been two-thirds full and now was nearly empty. She sat in a similar modern chair that faced outward, overlooking the Potomac River as the wide body of water angled southeast, splitting Virginia and Maryland.

"The Wharf?" Cassie asked. "When I was a kid, this place was a fish market. My dad would bring me here. It smelled like a trash heap, but we would always buy the stripers. Dad loved his stripers."

She thought of her father, the former chairman of the Joint Chiefs of Staff. A U.S. Army four-star general. Their relationship had waxed and waned. When she was a young girl, he had doted on her, embodying the proud family man. As she became an athlete and wished to follow in his footsteps, he resisted. Law school, med school, anything other than the military, he had urged. His words strengthened her resolve to pursue a military path. The more he resisted, the more she had forged ahead, all the way to becoming the first female graduate of Ranger school. Instead of being proud of her, though, he had made a mockery of her by publicly stating women should not be Rangers. Didn't have the abilities. Might fail their comrades in battle. Too weak.

While she missed her father, she was glad to have proven him wrong.

"Yeah? Well, now it's a billion-dollar development. The fish people made some money and never set up shop again, as far as I know."

Cassie swallowed and stuffed the memories away. To the south was Reagan National Airport. Flights between ten p.m. and seven a.m. were limited due to noise restrictions, so the early-morning hours were quiet. Zara had opened the sliding glass door, allowing cool air to drift in from her terrace. They had narrowly escaped the imaging sensors of the MH-47, the MH-6 helicopters, the infrared beams, the security cameras, and whoever was lying in wait for them near their car. It all seemed pretty incredible to Cassie, and perhaps it was. She wondered what Zara thought, so she asked her.

"Go as expected?"

"We will only know that, once we hear that the president and vice president are okay," she said.

"Seems to me that we should be plugged into some kind of communications network. We should know the results of our work right away. In the Army we call it battle damage assessment," Cassie said.

"We're not in the Army, though we did do a daring raid to save the commander in chief. No news is good news, as the saying goes."

"Still, we should have some confirmation that we were successful."

"What? You want a medal?" Zara asked.

"Just the opposite. I simply want to know that our effort was worth it. The mission was high risk."

Cassie looked at the rucksack with the two tanks of Zyklon B, which they had removed from the premises of the CIA safe house. She wondered why Zara was nonchalant about having the poison gas in her home. There was no *Hey, we better turn these over to the police, so they can fingerprint them,* or *Let's ditch these so we don't suffer the intended fate of the president and vice president.*

"What's the plan for these?" Cassie asked. She used her foot to nudge the rucksack sitting inertly on the floor.

Perro paused, looked away, then stared at the river. "We will dump them in the river at first chance."

"Why not turn them over to authorities? People tried to kill the president and vice president. Why hide what we've done?"

"We were not supposed to be there. There are people that will be very unhappy with our actions. They will come after us if they learn what we did. Going to the authorities is like hanging a bull's-eye on our backs," Perro said.

"You seem pretty comfortable with two containers of cyanide in your living room," Cassie said.

Zara smirked. "What are you implying?"

"Nothing more than I said. I barely know you. Perhaps you've got nerves of steel. Maybe your PhD also gives you special knowledge about the seams and fittings of these regulators. Your skills could be vast and deep. Me? I'm a little nervous sitting here, wondering if, in all of the hustle, we didn't pop a leak somewhere."

"I'm surprised, Cassie, that anything makes you nervous. You've been shot in combat. You've been stabbed. You fought off notorious Serbian martial-arts specialist Dax Stasovich . . . and won. You fought side by side with Mossad and Jordanian Special Forces, some of the most hardened and elite commandos in the world." She paused and leveled her eyes on Cassie, who returned the stare. "So, why do two containers scare you? Like a snake, they leave you alone if you leave them alone."

"Fair enough. I said I was nervous, not scared. Nervous is smart. And just because I've been there, done that doesn't make me immune to fear. Just the opposite, it helps me recognize a threat that much more acutely."

"And do you see a threat?"

Their eyes remained locked.

"I think the containers are, as you say, inert until made active. It's not as if you're going to open the valve of one if I were to fall asleep. So there's nothing to be concerned about. Let's move along, as they say," Cassie replied.

"No, but you're giving me interesting ideas. Perhaps the containers are excellent motivation for you to follow my lead, instead of going rogue."

"Why would I go rogue? What is my incentive in that? I am here of my own free will, am I not?"

"I don't know, are you?"

"It's all about trust, Zara. Through our actions just now, we are connected, whether we want to be or not. We have to trust each other."

Zara smiled again.

"You're feeling better, I see," she said.

Cassie rubbed her arm. "Going to give me another shot?"

"You're my patient and I have a duty to help you heal. The medicine I've been giving you counteracts your depression and post-traumatic stress disorder."

"I don't really look at it as a disorder, Zara," Cassie said.

Zara's phone rang. As she retrieved it, Cassie saw that it was Senator Carter calling.

"Perro," she said.

Carter's voice was loud enough for Cassie to hear through the iPhone speaker. "Status?" Jamie asked.

"We are waiting on the intelligence," Zara replied.

"What does the Speaker have to say?"

"He's who we're waiting on," Zara said.

"Okay, keep me up to date," Jamie demanded.

"Nothing has changed. I know who I work for," Zara said.

She hung up and looked at Cassie. "Our boss wants

us to keep her informed." She tossed the phone on the sofa next to her and picked up a remote to switch on the television. CNN filled the screen with BREAKING NEWS ALERT.

The screen faded to CNN anchor Wolf Blitzer, who was standing in the middle of his *The Situation Room* set at a little past four in the morning.

"As many of you know, this is not my usual time for being on television, but extraordinary events have brought me and the entire CNN news team into the studio, yes, at four a.m." He did his signature pause, stared into the camera, and said, "Our sources tell us that White House doctor Benjamin White confirms for us this morning that the president and vice president have been killed in an alleged terrorist attack on a CIA safe house in Loudoun County. These are initial reports, but Dr. White issued this release just minutes ago. It says, 'I am saddened to confirm the deaths of the president and vice president. Cause of death for each man was shrapnel from an improvised explosive device detonated from the secret facility, known as the SCIF.' This is a startling development at a time when the nation is under siege both domestically and internationally. Regardless of what you think of the administration, whether you are for or against this president and what he stands for, you have to take pause at what is being reported. Again, we have confirmation from the White House physician, Dr. Colin White, that the president and vice president were killed by an explosion at a safe house in Loudoun County. Information is incomplete at this time, but we at least have the statement from the doctor confirming that our president and vice president have been killed. It is impossible to confirm whether this was an accidental mishap or a terrorist attack, but given the doctor's statement, it sounds like a terrorist attack of some type. A bomb intended to kill the two leaders of the Free World."

Blitzer held his hand to his ear for a moment, listening.

Cassie said, "Oh my God."

"Reports are coming in rapidly now. CNN has been able to obtain video footage of two people who appear to be women retreating from the safe house into the woods just minutes before the explosion. There is confirmation from area residents that helicopters and vehicles perhaps chased these two people from the scene. Of course, no one understood the president and vice president were in the vicinity, but as the news is breaking, we are getting confirmation of high-speed chases both in the air and on the ground. We're going to play video that even I haven't seen yet. Here it is."

Cassie and Zara leaned forward, staring at the large-screen television, watching the grainy security camera footage replay their jogging retreat into the woods. Cassie immediately recognized her gait. Anyone who knew her would realize that was Cassie Bagwell.

"This image clearly shows two people, presumed to be women, running from the back of the house directly prior to the explosion."

"Where the hell did they get that footage?" Zara asked.

It was a rhetorical question, Cassie knew, but the Little Bird helicopters had the capability to film. She decided to change the topic.

"What exactly was in those tanks, Zara?"

Cassie watched the dark water of the Potomac slide massively and powerfully to the south. The floor-to-ceiling windows of Zara's penthouse apartment provided expansive 360-degree views of Washington, DC, and Northern Virginia. To her left was the Capitol dome, to her right the Jefferson Memorial. Light traffic buzzed along the Fourteenth Street Bridge, steadily increasing with the leading edge of rush hour approaching.

Cassie shook her head as if to clear the fog. At times, she felt whole and normal, as if she hadn't nearly bled out on a dank cave floor in Iran just three months earlier. At others, she felt almost bipolar. She struggled with the mood swings ranging from near normalcy to hyperaggression. She had become reliant upon the elixir that Zara had pumped into her veins.

She licked her lips. She yearned for the needle. That feeling of adrenaline rushing through her body. The drugs gave new meaning to the term *adrenaline junkie*. Here, at just past four a.m., she was feeling the ebb of the surge, a wave receding out to sea. The excitement of the swell lifting and cresting and curling along the beach was gone. Crashed and washed up onto the shore, the resultant descent from the high was a sucking riptide that funneled into the ocean.

Cassie rubbed her arm. Zara noticed.

"Oxygen, Cassie. The tanks had exactly what I said was in them. Something else must have caused that explosion. Our mission was to replace the tanks. That's it. We aren't responsible for what the Secret Service did or failed to do."

She kept rubbing her arm, looked at Zara, who nodded.

"I've got more in the bathroom, but I'm concerned you're becoming hooked."

"Isn't that what you wanted with me? Addicted to your drug?"

Cassie had seen Zara murder Dr. Broome. Had heard her tell him about the Resistance and the immediate plans for what amounted to a coup. How could she pretend even now not to be the architect of this coup? Watching Zara, Cassie was even more convinced that the dramatic plan—The Plan—was more necessary than ever. Still, without being able to communicate with Jake, she was operating in an information deficit that diminished her situational awareness.

"I want you well. I have a Hippocratic oath to do no harm."

"You give me these treatments at alternating intervals, as if you want me confused sometimes. I believe I know what I've seen. My memory is fine sometimes, and at other times, I question it."

Keep playing the role, Cass. Can't afford any cracks in the legend.

"*Believing you know* is the operative term, Cassie. The brain reformats itself, like a hard drive. You want to believe Jake was there for you, so your mind creates those conditions, forces you to believe it, as if it is second nature. You've heard the term *fake news,* I'm sure. Well, about half the people in the country believe whatever the other half is calling fake. So, what is real? The very origins of our belief systems are being challenged by information overload. It is all so complicated and we are learning more about the brain every day."

"Yes, it's complicated," Cassie whispered. She watched a lone scull crew rhythmically dip their oars in the water and stroke, lift, and repeat the process, navigating the dark waters and predawn blackness.

"We are counting on your patriotism here. I'm trying to help you remember. Navigate you back toward a healthy mind, Cassie. Just as your physical wounds need time to heal, so do your mental wounds. Those perhaps need more time. The memories don't really go away. Every nightmare tears away the stitches, so to speak, and we have to start all over again."

"Yes," Cassie said, lifting her head. "It's like that. I want to be helpful, but sometimes I find myself resisting, believing the other narrative. The other fifty percent. What is real anymore, as you said?"

Zara's phone rang with the soft tones of a spa, a subtle gong followed by chimes blowing in the wind.

"Zara here," she said. She pressed her thumb down to lower the volume so that Cassie couldn't hear the conversation on the other end.

After a minute of silence, Zara hung up and said, "We have to go. The Speaker of the House needs protection. His team has been infiltrated and he needs us to help him get to the swearing-in ceremony."

"What happened to all those guys we dealt with?"

"They're still there, but believe me, I have a special relationship with the Speaker. He trusts me more than anyone."

Cassie thought about those words, remembered how

all of this started, with the cold-blooded execution of Dr. Broome.

Without talking to Jake, Cassie had to rely on her own intuition, which admittedly was not as honed and refined as it was pre-Iran. While she had signed up for The Plan, Cassie still found herself oscillating, like now. Was Zara a member of the Resistance leading the charge? Or was she a counteragent inside the Resistance, attempting to prevent the pending coup? Was her murder of Dr. Broome a legitimate anti-Resistance act, as she claimed? Or was it a part of the grand plan, as his task was done? Wasn't that why she was here? To figure that out? And the only way to confirm or deny Zara's status was to be right here, right now, with her.

She stood, weary, and followed Zara to the closet in her master bedroom. There was a circular king-sized bed with a pulley countersunk into the ceiling. Ropes angled off the pulley and were tied off on hitches along the baseboard, like a sailor would find on the pier for the lines to secure a boat. At the apex near the pulley, a small two-slatted seat hung three feet below the ceiling.

Zara saw Cassie staring and said, "Everybody has their kink, Cassie. You should try it sometime."

"I'm good," Cassie said. Her eyes drifted from the ropes to the bed, which was covered in mauve satin sheets and had pillows stacked high on the headboard. They stepped into a substantial walk-in closet with dresses, blouses, pants, and coats all hung perfectly by color, size, and formality. Above the hanging bars were glassed-in displays filled with Louboutin, Jimmy Choo, Manolo Blahnik, Gucci, and Chanel shoes.

"Little high end for Washington, DC, don't you think?"

"Ever since a supermodel moved into the White House, the standards are different now," Zara said.

Cassie nodded.

"We're not in here to marvel at my wardrobe, Cassie," Zara said, handing her an M4 rifle, fully kitted out with a rail mount system, infrared aiming light, Maglite, muzzle suppressor, and red-dot scope.

"Goes with the Chanel gown over there," Cassie said, gripping the rifle.

Zara actually smiled. "That's more like it, girl."

"This is the real deal. How did you get this, much less have it here in the gun-free zone of DC?"

"I'm resourceful," she said. Her long arm produced another M4, tricked out with the same equipment. She retrieved four magazines, closed the gun case, spun the dial, and brushed past Cassie.

"All this for a simple meet and greet with the Speaker?"

"Shit's breaking loose, Cassie. The Resistance is at full throttle. Obviously, if the president and vice president are dead, then the coup is under way."

"Obviously. Do you think the Speaker woke up this morning thinking he'd be president?"

"I think the Speaker just went to sleep trashed out of his mind with four hookers passed out around him."

Cassie stared at Zara, then said, "Huh. I didn't see that, but maybe now I can."

"Seems you're thinking more clearly," Zara said.

Cassie lifted the rifle. "Always when you give me one of these. Universal language."

"One more thing before we go," Zara said.

In a small anteroom off the master, there were two IV drips positioned next to two wooden chairs. The entire condo was appointed with the finest in Scandinavian space-saving, sleek furniture, but these two chairs looked like she might have borrowed them from a schoolhouse.

"Juice up before we go," Zara said. "Shit might get real."

"Roger that," Cassie said.

Cassie poked Zara's arm with the IV and Zara returned the favor. They both took on about five minutes' worth of fluids, which were laced with Zara's concoction. Cassie could feel the burn in her arms and throughout her body. More important, she felt the rage building within. It was the same fire that had burned when she was on the run. The "juice," as Zara nicknamed it, didn't cloud her judgment as much as make her hyperaggressive. She never had any issues in that department, anyway, being the first female graduate of the U.S. Army Ranger School. Yet, this concoction took her to her primal core. Like a T. rex, she began scanning the room, looking for targets. She could feel her decisiveness blur a bit, bringing her back to the basic question of the morality of what she was doing. She had to stay in control, at least as much as possible, while also trying to govern what Zara was ultimately going to do. As Zara said, "The shit is getting real." Cassie had to maintain control while also remaining believable as a confused and recovering soldier.

"You seem . . . focused," Zara said.

With a slow turn of her head, Cassie said, "I am." She spread an evil grin on her face that prompted a wary look from Zara.

"Have I created a monster?"

"You've given me more focus. I was already a monster."

They both removed their IV needles, cleaned up briefly, and then grabbed their gear as they walked to the elevator. Zara produced two guitar cases, just another girl band heading to a gig, then stepped into the elevator car. They rode it down to Zara's Range Rover. They slid the gear into the back and Zara jumped into the driver's seat.

"I'll ride back here. Prep the gear," Cassie said. She sat in the backseat and retrieved the weapons from the cases. The magazines were filled with shiny 5.56 mm ammunition. She saw an ammunition can filled with smoke grenades and removed a few of those. Outer tactical vests were laid out on the opposing backseat. Cassie donned one, stuffing the pockets with magazines and smoke grenades. She filled Zara's outer tactical vest and passed it forward. As she was driving, Zara snaked her arms through the vest. They still had their night vision goggles from the safe house Zyklon B mission.

Cassie was feeling the thrum of excitement. A new mission. A new purpose. She was focused. Clear. Except for one thing.

"I'm not going in this time without knowing the chain of command and the threat. At least give me a two sentence mission statement."

"We're protecting the Speaker of the House. Going to meet him at his boat. He texted me a distress signal. People with guns are closing in on his position"

Zara wound her way across the Fourteenth Street Bridge, looped onto the George Washington Parkway, heading south, and was quickly turning into the parking lot for Daingerfield Island. She pulled as close to the marina as she could. They exited the vehicle, and by now, Cassie's veins were pumping pure adrenaline. She walked quickly with her rifle held at eye level, as if she were crossing a danger area. The parking lot had cars, but there were no people visible in the darkness. The George Washington Parkway hissed behind them by fifty yards. They were shielded by trees and a high hedge row. Inside the sleepy marina, there should not be anyone moving at five a.m. Zara pointed out the Speaker's boat.

"There," she said. Cassie recognized it from their visit last night. It seemed like days ago, so much had happened.

They stepped onto the creaky wooden pier, their footfalls light but not totally silent. Cassie flipped her night vision goggle over her right eye and scanned. The water smelled musty and the temperature was that perfect mission coolness. No humidity, clear skies, and just a little fall bite in the air.

She immediately saw two individuals at the far end of the pier walking toward the Speaker's vessel.

"Bogies at eleven o'clock," Cassie said. "Two people. Looks like they're holding pistols."

"See them. We've also got another two coming from across the parking lot," Zara said. "Stay here and cover me. I'm going to run. Shoot them if they make a move on me."

Cassie felt the dilemma. Let Zara go in and possibly kill the Speaker of the House or stay and fight off the attackers? Was the Speaker a part of the Resistance? Jake's intelligence on him had been unclear. Rooting out Resistance members was nearly an impossible task. The people providing the intelligence had tried a soft coup already. That failure inspired this full bore junta. The Plan called for her to monitor Zara. Her tactical acumen kicked in, however, and convinced her that self-preservation was the first order of business.

"Roger."

Zara darted forward along the pier as Cassie knelt behind one of the pylons and found relative cover and good fields of fire. She had the two approaching, almost head-on, and the other two that were at her three o'clock. All four appeared to be relatively average height, if not on the smaller side. They were slender and quick, moving in synchronized effort, apparently. Cassie considered herself lucky to have beaten them— potentially two Resistance members—to the Speaker's boat.

The two coming head-on saw Zara and bolted into a sprint, lifting something in their hands that looked like pistols. *That's hostile intent,* Cassie thought. She knew her rules of engagement. Using the PAQ-4C infrared aiming light, she zeroed in on the faster of the two, led the body just a bit, and squeezed the trigger.

The person fell, tumbling head over heels, causing the teammate to slow, stop, look down, and then look up, scanning. That was when Cassie fired a double tap into the face of the would-be assailant.

Her silencer wasn't completely silent on this still night. The traffic was light enough that the ambient noise did not envelop the ratcheting of the bolt, the miniature explosion in the chamber, nor the exit of the bullet from the muzzle.

The two attackers at her three o'clock had taken cover and were scanning in her direction. Her opponents were wearing night vision goggles, eliminating her night vision advantage. Two shots snapped off above her head, spraying splinters into her face. The cover was thin gruel. She pressed her shoulder into the narrow pylon and kept her angle coincident with the axis of their movement. To her right was a hedgerow filled with thick boxwoods that would provide better concealment, but less cover. The bullets would easily blow through sticks and leaves, but her current position was untenable.

Especially since the two had split up in order to gain an angle on her. Two more shots sang overhead. Cassie rolled to her front and low-crawled twenty meters to the hedge. The shooters were spraying and praying now, and as happens with that technique, their fire was inaccurate. There was a small gap in the hedgerow where Cassie was able to slither through, observe her attackers' movements, and then pop out on the opposite side as they closed to her rear.

They had reversed positions. Confused, they stood there for a moment too long, wondering where Cassie had gone. She used that opportunity to rise to one knee and fire to her left, knocking that target down, then to her right, missing at first, but then winging the person.

Cassie jogged around to the right and was upon who

she assumed was a wounded Resistance member, who was a woman. She had been hit in the upper left chest area, above her heart and just below her clavicle.

"Who are you?" Cassie asked, baring her knife at the throat of the woman.

"You know me, Cassie," the woman said.

Cassie's breath caught. She *did* recognize the woman from the Valley Trauma Center. Her name was Sally something. A world-class pentathlete, Sally had been injured in a motorcycle crash and had been directed to the Valley Trauma Center for rehab. Cassie had seen Sally only on brief occasions. Sometimes in the cafeteria, other times doing physical training.

"Sally?"

"Yes. Sally Bergeron. Don't kill me, please."

"What are you doing here?"

"Probably the same thing you're doing," Sally said.

"What's that?"

"Killing whoever you're told," Sally said. She coughed up some blood.

Sally had a hard edge to her. For the first time she noticed an amateur tattoo crawling out from under her sleeve. There was nothing about Sally that gave off the world class athlete vibe now that Cassie studied her.

"What was your crime?" Cassie asked. It was a wild guess, but Sally, if that was her real name, appeared more San Quentin than Quintana Roo, the renowned triathlon bike.

"What?" Sally spat.

"Leavenworth? Folsom?"

"Fuck you," Sally coughed.

Cassie lifted her eyes, cast a glance toward the pier

where Zara had turned. Three dead bodies and Sally Bergeron hanging by a thread. She now expected all of them to be women, perhaps from the Valley Trauma Center. *Perhaps convicts?*

Broome and Zara had been training assassin squads for the Resistance revolution, that much was obvious now. The physical training and marksmanship, all explained to her as rehabilitation. Easing her from combat to something less traumatic, a rifle range. She assumed the others were in similar situations. There had been no group sessions. The staff and doctors told her that each individual's rehab plan was highly specialized, and too much interaction with other patients, who were equally or more psychologically damaged, might alter each person's recovery. She had been a newbie, though. Some of the women had been there for nearly a year. The Valley Trauma Center was tantamount to a remote jihadi training center in the Blue Ridge Mountains. But the question was a good one. Where would the Resistance recruit enough hard killers to do this bidding? With Syd Wise from the FBI involved, the federal prison system was certainly a possibility.

A series of gunshots, muffled but loud enough, sounded from the direction of the Speaker's boat.

Cassie reacted swiftly to a quick movement beneath her. Sally's knife sparked off hers as she blocked the wounded woman's thrust. A fighter to the end. Cassie drove her knife deep into Sally's neck. The carotid artery sprayed into the hedgerow like a water sprinkler. Cassie wasted no time as she ran toward Sally's partner, saw her on the ground, and placed a hand against her neck to confirm. No pulse. She believed she recognized this woman also.

What is happening?

She jogged along the pier and knelt next to the two women she had shot as Zara ran to the Speaker's boat. This was nothing short of a combat operation. Zara had known what they were about to face and had prepared them well. She reached into the ammunition pouch of her outer tactical vest and switched magazines.

Her head turning, the night vision goggle catching every flicker of light, every movement, Cassie rose and walked to the boat aptly named *Two,* which she presumed was his position on the depth chart for ascendancy to the presidency.

Is the Speaker behind all of this? she wondered.

She approached the boat, its stern abutting the pier. Stepping onto the ladder, Cassie surveyed the deck and saw two guards dead on the floor. Her head swept left, then right as her foot found the deck, and she walked toward the galley stairs. She cocked the night vision goggle and locked it into place on her head harness, switching to the flashlight beneath the rail of her M4.

As she descended into the galley, the flashlight beam caught the reflection of something slick on the floor. Dark and red, the blood pooled at the bottom of the ladder. She crouched, using one hand to press against the sidewall, another to hold her weapon and shine the flashlight into the dim bowel of the galley. Two more guards were dead on the floor, both of whom she recognized from their visit last night to this very boat.

Speaker Josh Williams was slumped, face-first, onto the navigational map of the world lacquered atop the dining table. Sitting with her back to the wall, Zara was clutching her shoulder. Blood oozed between her fingers. In the harsh beam of the flashlight, Zara appeared to be a theater actor onstage. Tight grimace on her face, pistol in her right hand, wounded shoulder clutched in her left. Her M4 rifle was lying in a pool of blood next to her.

Sirens wailed in the distance. Could be random, could be for them—she didn't know. Coming down a bit from the testosterone high, Cassie felt an ebb in her energy and an inverse surge in her empathy. Everything was connected. The top three elected officials in the country. Killed in one night. And somehow she was in the middle of it.

She did her best to step over the blood and cross the galley to retrieve Zara. The sirens grew louder, not far away at all now. Zara lifted her pistol and aimed it at Cassie.

"Zara, no," Cassie said. "You're hurt."

"I couldn't save him," she said. "They got him."

"Who got him?"

"The women. The Resistance."

"Let's get out of here," Cassie said. "We can figure it out later. There are sirens. The police are coming."

Cassie was talking to a woman who had either failed in her mission of protecting the Speaker of the House or succeeded in her mission of killing him. What stood out to Cassie was that the four bodyguards were the same four men who had been on the boat last night when they had arrived here. Either there was an insider threat or Zara had been the trigger puller.

Which is it?

Zara's hand wavered as she pulled the trigger, the bullet blowing past Cassie's head. Cassie charged Zara and kicked the pistol out of her hand. She used the butt of her M4 to place a solid stroke across Zara's head, knocking her unconscious. As the sirens wailed in her ears, she retrieved Zara's set of keys from her pocket.

The footsteps on the pier grew louder. Escape through the stern was unlikely. She stepped over Zara's unconscious body into the bedroom. She shone the flashlight up and saw the square hatch. She fumbled with the latch as footsteps thundered closer. Harsh voices fired through the night like gunshots.

"Cover me . . ."

"Alpha team going in . . ."

The hatch was open. Cassie slid her weapon through the gap. Someone was on the boat. Two people, maybe three.

She pulled herself through the hatch, straining from pull-up motion to dip motion, like a gymnast performing. The mainsail was wadded and tied around the mast, providing momentary cover for her. Sliding her butt onto the deck, Cassie lifted her legs out of the hole. She carefully closed the hatch and inched her way toward the bow.

"We have dead bodies!" a voice shouted from the galley.

"Secure the area. Bravo team, face outward, look for movement."

Cassie slipped the two-point sling over her neck and let the M4 hang diagonally across her back. She slid over the lip of the bow beneath the stanchion and suspended her weight from her two hands holding on to the lip of the bow. She was staring at the anchor, held in place by its chain and the winch inside the boat. Her shoes were touching the water. She didn't know how deep the marina basin was, but did know this was her only slim chance of evading the authorities. Retrieving her M4 from the deck caused more noise than she had anticipated, but she was able to slide off the bow and enter the water amidst the shouting.

Her feet touched bottom after her head was about three feet under water. She turned north and swam, the only way out of the marina. She swam awkwardly underwater, fumbling with her gear, not gaining the traction she needed. She counted the hulls of five boats she had passed. At the sixth, she had to risk gaining a breath, but decided no, go for the seventh. She pulled and slid beneath the V-shaped hull of a large sport boat. Using her hands along the hull, she pulled herself up for oxygen, letting her face barely break the meniscus of the water. Her nose and mouth were above the surface. The dank water dribbled into her mouth, interrupting her attempt to breathe silently. The cold water stung the incision Rax had made to remove the tracker that had been placed in her back at the Valley Trauma Center.

Muffled voices penetrated the water covering her ears.

"Hatch is open! We've got a runner! Check all of the boats!"

Cassie took a deep breath and sank vertically before pulling toward the shore nearly one hundred meters away. She stroked until she couldn't pull anymore, felt like her brain was going to explode from lack of oxygen, and slowly surfaced. Her nose and mouth crested again, the rest of her body and face hovering just below the surface. The stars were brilliant tonight. She shifted her eyes and tried to look in the direction of the marina, but only caught a glimpse. Besides, she wasn't sightseeing; she needed to escape.

As she was preparing to surface, a wild exchange of gunfire reminded her of combat in Iran. The sounds were muted, like a mattress falling several times. Shots were coming from inside a boat. Some were more distinct with cracking noises, fired from the pier, most likely.

She slid back under the water as a boat engine revved in the distance. *Is it coming after me? Searching the marina?*

She pulled through the black water, not being able to see her hands in front of her as she reached out. There was just a brief glimpse of her white hands, like baitfish, darting in front of her. With every stroke, she felt the anxiety lessen by a degree, but cautioned herself not to get too hopeful. She'd been disappointed before, like the time she was sitting on the Blackhawk cargo bay in Iran, only to be snatched away by Stasovich.

When Jake couldn't save me. Or wouldn't?

Stop it! she admonished herself. Her mind kept swinging between two different realities: one where Jake was the perfect man for her, and one where he had abandoned her on the battlefield.

Another forty meters or so and she had to surface. Same process. Float to the top, tilt her head upward, break the surface, and suck in air. The boat engine was puttering in the harbor, definitely searching. She took a few deep breaths and repeated the process, submerging, pulling through the dark water, the baitfish flying in front of her eyes with every stroke. Soon she was on the far bank when her hand struck rock. She pulled herself up through two giant riprap boulders.

One of the approach lights for Reagan National Airport was directly to her front. She was on airport property. Exhausted from swimming nearly two hundred meters, she sat on the cusp between the rocks and the hardpan of the runway. The curtain of gray was beginning to push up in the east, meaning flights would be landing in earnest soon. Her adrenaline ebbed and her body began to shiver from the cold water.

The lights flicked on, as if on cue. She needed to move away from the airport, but was trapped on two sides by water and two sides by airport security. She stood and ran under the cover of darkness to the west, the only chance of getting away from those searching for her and the Transportation Security Administration. While TSA were mostly guys eating doughnuts and checking shoes, Reagan National had a quick response team, given their proximity to the Capitol and the clientele that normally flew to and from DC.

As she ran, the fencing dove into the water directly before someone could gain access to the airport, or leave it, from the solid land near the George Washington Parkway. Going back in the water was an option, but it didn't seem to be a good one.

A bright spotlight snapped on twenty yards to her front and began scanning the fence. She saw men jogging. One was holding a snarling German shepherd. They were maybe three hundred meters away and working the fence line that she had planned on pursuing.

She retraced her steps and walked back onto the riprap, sliding into the water. She was maybe fifty meters from a large culvert that ran under the GW Parkway. The only problem was that this was a natural collection point for trash and logs that flowed downstream from upper Virginia and Maryland. She fought her way through debris and thought maybe she could walk on the logs, but didn't try. The dog was barking loudly, perhaps sensing her. The flashlights crisscrossed in the dense foliage along the fence, their penetrating beams not reaching her . . . yet.

The culvert loomed large and dark ahead. She pushed sticks and detritus out of the way and gained enough leverage to pull herself up onto the lip of the culvert. The water level was even with the lower part of the concrete pipe, which was large enough for her to stand in, which she did. The shepherd was going crazy, barking and sniffing where Cassie had entered the water.

"We've got a runner in the water," a voice said coolly into a megaphone.

Right about that, she thought.

She splashed through ankle-deep water in the culvert, trying to find a higher line so that she could run along the drier portions, but the slimy mud caused her to slip and fall. Undeterred, she pushed up and sprinted forward, wiping the mud from her face. She didn't dare think about what kind of crap, literally, she was wading through.

Reaching the far end, she saw a maintenance path that took her up to the far side of the GW Parkway. She was near some apartment buildings that she recognized. Cassie needed desperately to hide the long gun and get back to Zara's apartment. She needed to confirm that what was in the oxygen tanks was not cyanide gas, otherwise an entire condo full of people were at risk. She ran back down the maintenance trail to the culvert and studied the west side. It was nothing but muck and marsh for over two hundred meters.

Cassie removed her rifle from her back and did her best version of a javelin toss, watching it dive into the muck and disappear—she hoped for forever.

In her boots and wet clothes, she ran along the road, and sprinted until she was in the Crystal City underground. She leapt over the Metro turnstile and raced onto the platform as a Yellow Line train was approaching. The few commuters at this hour barely gave her a glance. She boarded and rode five tense minutes to L'Enfant Plaza, where she exited and hurdled the turnstile on her way out, some man shouting, "Hey!" but not bothering to pursue her.

She raced up the steps, popped out onto the street, and darted to Zara's new apartment building on the waterfront at the Wharf. Retrieving Zara's keys, she fumbled with the fob, waved it in front of the reader; the light turned green and she pressed the PENTHOUSE button.

On the ride up, Cassie thought about Zara and the potential for a double cross. Who was she working for? Good or evil? They were important questions. As obvious as something may seem, intentions were always the most difficult motivations to discern. Plus, Cassie's personal code had matured in Iran. She had learned from Jake—yes, Jake—that the mission came first, and that you could accomplish the mission while also taking care of your people. No matter what Zara and Jamie told her, Jake was good to the core. He loved her and came back for her. The word from the Rangers was that he had tried to leap from his helicopter at one hundred feet above ground level, a fall that would have most likely killed him.

Now that the president, vice president, and Speaker of the House were reported as dead, the newly appointed Senate pro tem was next in line for the presidency.

Senator Carter, the same woman who had lost the presidency during the most recent election. Coincidence? Cassie didn't believe in those types of coincidences, which would confirm the foundational intelligence that Jake had provided her weeks ago as they developed The Plan. Neither, though, did she fully trust her mind and everything that she was processing. She had been at the scenes of the deaths of the top three figures in government. Her fingerprints were on this . . . everywhere.

The world went to sleep last night with a duly elected president and vice president and would awake this morning to the news that Senator Jamie Carter is now the president. She had achieved more popular votes than President Smart, but Smart, of course, had run the table on the Electoral College, winning where he needed to win.

And what about the women who were trained assassins? Was she one of them? Had she avoided similar brainwashing and directed lethality because she had escaped? Or had she been allowed to escape? Set up? Had Jake thought through all of these possibilities? Or was she on her own?

She needed Jake now more than ever, but now that she was involved and most likely a suspect, he might steer clear or even have orders to capture her. Did he trust her? Could he? She was unsure of whether she should try to reach out to him. With no means of communication, and fully into her undercover legend, was that even a possibility? He had been such a grounding force for her ever since her parents had been slain: then, in Iran, and after. Now, though, she didn't know. But there was The Plan. She was doing her part and wondered if Jake had done his. She would press on for now, because she sensed there was safety with Senator Carter . . . until her purpose was done. With the Speaker of the House dead, perhaps that time had come. She would find out soon enough.

The elevator doors snapped open.

Staring at her was Senator Jamie Carter.

"We need to get to the swearing in ASAP," Jamie said.

CHAPTER 13

"You can't be serious," Cassie said.

She stepped from the elevator, looking like a paramilitary operative fresh off the battlefield. The mirror in the foyer reflected back at her matted shoulder-length dark blond hair, bloodshot eyes, muddy clothes, and outer tactical vest. Maybe fifty people had seen her, but without the M4, she could pass for an off-duty cop or a chick into popular street grunge wear, like Grunt Style clothing, who just finished a mud run for physical training.

"Yes, there's no time," Jamie said. "It's all happening so fast."

Jamie was dressed in a fashionable navy blue skirt and blazer, silk white blouse, and black heels. Stuck to the lapel of the blazer was an American flag pin, required ever since 9/11 and a brooch fashioned into a cardinal, crested tuft and all. Jamie's blond hair was swept straight back, coifed perfectly. Around her neck hung a

David Yurman necklace, with a gold-and-diamond cluster at the bottom that looked like a supernova bursting in the sky. A faint whiff of citrusy perfume hung in the air. Zara's ninety-five-inch HD television was showing CNN having a panel discussion with possible succession of the presidency. One lawyer was showing a flow chart from the president to the vice president to the Speaker to the Senate pro tem.

"But how did you even know to be here in DC?" Cassie asked. She stepped into the living room, saw the floor-to-ceiling windows with the automatic blinds raised, giving her an expansive view of precisely the location where she had just been. Maybe two miles straight-line distance.

"I was coming up anyway. Session is about to start back up after the holiday weekend," Jamie said.

Yes, it all made sense. Newly elected senator. She had to be here anyway. Cassie wondered if she was becoming delusional.

"You don't seem concerned about Zara?" Cassie asked.

"Why should she be?" Zara said, stepping from the master bedroom. Her hair was up in a towel, wrapped like a turban. She wore a bathrobe and was applying some cream to her face. She showed no evidence of the wound someone had inflicted on her, but there was swelling around her left temple, where Cassie had whacked her with the butt of her M4 rifle.

There was Jamie directly in front of her. Zara coming from her left. The rucksack with the Zyklon B was still sitting where she left it. What was happening? How did Zara get back before her? How did she get back at all? The police. The shots. True, her swim had taken some time. Plus, her circuitous route had consumed precious minutes. But she had left Zara among four dead guards, the dead Speaker of the House, and the bum-rush of police.

"What's on your mind, Cassie?" Zara asked. She phrased the question as if she was asking her how her day had been. Nonchalant.

"You seem . . . troubled," Jamie said. "Here, girl, have a seat."

Jamie reached out and gently tugged at her.

"This can't be happening," Cassie said.

"She's coming down off her medication," Zara said, toweling her black hair. Then to Jamie: "I'll get her enough to get through the next couple of hours."

Cassie walked into the living area and stood by the sofa, eyed the rucksack she had worn, and lifted it.

"I'm tired of your games," Cassie said. She removed one of the oxygen tanks and grabbed the valve release.

"Cassie, what are you doing? Those tanks are filled with poisonous gas," Zara said.

"Are they?" Cassie palmed the circular valve release, which looked like the average garden hose spigot. She lifted the tank and walked over to Jamie, who backed up.

"What? You're part of the Resistance? Trying to kill the third in line to the presidency? It's not enough that you were at the scenes of the other three murders? You have to potentially kill me, too? When all I've done is try to help you. Nurse you back to health after your trauma in Iran. Is this what you really believe? Is this what I deserve after all I've done for you?" Jamie said.

Jamie seemed nervous. Perhaps she didn't know, or perhaps Cassie was wrong? Maybe there was cyanide in these tanks. The report was that the president and vice president had been killed by an explosion, not cyanide gas. As if to emphasize this point, Zara said, "Cassie, we've discussed this. You don't trust well, right now. Think about it. Think about everything you've seen."

Cassie paused, the tank feeling heavier by the moment. "I know I saw four women I recognized from the Valley Trauma Center. Four women that I presume had sessions with you," Cassie said. She nodded at Zara.

"Yes. Our intelligence is showing us that Broome was running the trauma center as a secret training camp for the Resistance. Former athletes and military personnel who had traumatic brain injury. Easier to manipulate, I presume."

"Who's in charge?" Her comment was more of an accusation than a question.

"Carmen Biagatti, the director of the Central Intelligence Agency," Jamie said. "We've known this about her for several weeks. Our intelligence sources have pictures of her conversing with known Resistance leaders and operatives. She's got spies everywhere. It's pervasive."

"But I heard you! I heard you tell Broome he was no longer needed. I saw you shoot him! And Syd Wise from the FBI was there. I saw Sally Bergeron and she's not a pentathlete, is she? She's a convict from somewhere. Wise made all that happen, right?" Cassie shouted. She pushed the tank toward Zara, emphasizing her point.

Zara cocked her head and said, "We've been over this, Cassie. You think you saw a lot of things, which weren't real. Convicts? Syd Wise? You even think Jake loves you and wanted to save you." She walked back to her bedroom, was gone a second, and came back out with a syringe. She tapped it with her finger, expelling any air trapped inside as she applied force to the plunger.

"Let's get you some of your medicine. Then we can talk," Zara said.

"No. I don't want any more of that crazy-making shit," Cassie replied. She lifted the tank across her chest, as if to defend herself.

"This isn't going to make you crazy. Quite the opposite. It's what was in the medical cooler you took from the pharmacy. It is what brings you down from your controlled rage," Zara said. She cocked her head. "I know you enjoy the hunt. You're a warrior, after all. First female Army Ranger, and all of that."

"Then why? Why give me drugs that make me more aggressive, more hyped up?" Cassie asked. She could feel her resolve soften. Jamie stared at her disapprovingly, as she had done when Cassie was a child. Zara had recovered nicely and looked like she had a full night's sleep.

"The medicine I've been giving you, Cassie, has been to give you a soft landing. Your mind became conditioned to violence, expected the worst. You told me you even believed you were going to die in that cold cave surrounded by strangers. Jamie ordered General Savage and his team to go in and retrieve you, dead or alive. Thank God you're standing here alive. Your brain was conditioned to believe you had to do two things: first was to fight, and always fight. The second was to prepare to die and always be prepared. It's as if your fight-or-flight syndrome was stuck in high gear. The testosterone mix I've been giving you taps into that chemical imbalance and alters those perceptions, rewires your thinking, bit by bit. It can't be done overnight. It takes months. And I've also been giving you midazolam, which is a drug I rarely prescribe, but it is effective in helping separate your current thought processes from your agony."

"In other words, it helps me forget?"

"It does. When coupled with the other treatment, this seesawing effect taps into your fight instinct and the midazolam pulls you away from it. It's trial and error, but I've seen it work before. And it has been working on you."

"You're changing the topic," Cassie said.

"From what? You think you saw certain things tonight. Women from the trauma center. The Speaker of the House dead. Me, wounded in the boat. Police coming for you, so you ran, instead of staying to help me. I forgive you, by the way, because I understand that a heavy dose of flight comes with the fight, so that you can live to fight another day. It's primal and core to who you are."

"Listen to her, Cassie. You abandoned Zara in that boat. Left her to die, when all we've done is try to help you recover. My friends from the Secret Service had to pull her out of there," Jamie said. Zara walked up to

Cassie and placed her hands on the tank, pulling at it. She released it and let Zara carry it back to the center of the living room.

"We are not the Resistance, Cassie," Zara said. She turned and looked at Cassie, who was processing everything she was hearing.

"Then why not go to the police right now?"

"And say what?" Zara replied.

"That we've been at the crime scenes. We know," Cassie said. The words, when spoken, sounded ridiculous. Zara was right. What would they say? To that end, if Zara and Jamie were part of the Resistance, how could she even prove it? All the evidence seemed to point at the Valley Trauma Center and, more precisely, to the one former resident who had escaped and been at every critical juncture in the coup: Captain Cassie Bagwell.

"I see even you realize how crazy that sounds," Zara said.

"But that doesn't mean we can't benefit from what has transpired," Jamie said. Then, looking at Cassie, she said, "Do you believe that I am a good leader? A good person? The candidate that received the most popular votes in the last election?"

After a moment, Cassie said, "I honestly don't know what I believe anymore. My world is upside down. Here you and Zara are telling me there hasn't been a coup, when, in fact, that's exactly what has happened."

"We never said any such thing," Jamie said. "Just the opposite. It appears there has been one, indeed. Does that mean we can't seize the opportunity? You know the old saying 'Never let a good crisis go to waste,' correct?"

Cassie shrugged.

Jamie clucked and shook her head. Out of patience.

"We've wasted enough time, Cassie. We can't keep explaining everything to you. You either trust us or you don't. If you want to be the special assistant to the president, then you can be so. If you want to go back to your troops at Fort Bragg, I won't get in your way. Don't think that for a second anything you've seen has anything to do with me or Zara. We have been furiously trying to work behind the scenes to protect this country and its institutions, not overthrow the administration! Because the Resistance has metastasized, and because they view me as somewhat of an unofficial figurehead, we get intelligence fed to us daily. I ignore most of it. We tried to get in front of all of this. Zara's got those stupid canisters of poison gas in here. Both of you nearly got killed last night, but you were too late to help the Speaker, a dear friend. We either make the most of a bad situation or we let history pass us by. This has been thrust upon me. I will not let the nation down," Jamie said.

To Cassie, it sounded a bit as if she was practicing her acceptance speech there at the end.

"Let's get cleaned up," Zara said. She had slipped behind Cassie and pinched the needle into her neck, sending the fluid into her system.

"What the hell?" Cassie flinched, but Zara had placed her left arm around Cassie and held her. She had her tunnel vision on Jamie and she had lost sight of Zara.

"This is the midazolam. It will help you come down from the DHT. You need to get in the shower, get cleaned up, and be ready. We've got to get Jamie to the Capitol in twenty minutes. You've wasted a lot of time, but I understand. You're central to all of this, so we need to have you on board."

Cassie felt the effect of the concentrated antianxiety drug immediately. She stumbled, held on to Zara's shoulder. The doctor walked her to the shower in the guest bedroom. Jamie's hanging bag full of clothes was on the bed. Zara helped her strip her nasty clothes off and turned on the shower for Cassie.

"Might as well burn these putrid things," Zara said, holding up Cassie's clothes. She tossed them into the fireplace in the bedroom and torched them immediately. The outer tactical vest hung on a hook on the back of the bathroom door. "We'll clean up the rest afterward. Your clothes are in the closet. Put on something reasonable, but tactically practical also. You know the drill."

Cassie showered, picked out sensible black pants and a navy blouse, with a black Windbreaker. She walked into the living room and noticed the two tanks were on the balcony. Better to spray the neighborhood than just the inside of her apartment, Cassie figured. Jamie and Zara were sitting at the dining table, adjacent to the kitchen. An elaborate gold-and-silver chandelier hung above the granite table. They were both staring at the screen of a MacBook.

"Cassie, you need to see this," Jamie said.

Cassie walked around the table and looked over their shoulders. They were viewing a camera feed from a dark house somewhere. She saw two bodies, one holding a weapon, another holding a spotter's scope. She immediately recognized Jake as the one holding the weapon. The second man had to be Sean O'Malley. She recognized his tuft of curly hair and his Boston accent as the recorded conversation between the two men began.

"You've got the shot," O'Malley said.

"Be good to put this bitch down," Jake said.

"That's Cassie, you know," O'Malley said.

"Roger that," Jake said.

Her breath caught in her throat. She was seeing a different Jake Mahegan than she ever thought possible. One she never believed could exist.

"We need to ask you, Cassie. Has Jake ever said anything to make you believe he is a member of the Resistance? Here you and Zara are on a sanctioned mission to save the president and vice president without blowing the fact that we know Carmen Biagatti is the Resistance leader inside the administration. Is it just a coincidence that Jake winds up on Biagatti's team at this very time? This month, this week, when the revolution is happening?"

Cassie thought back. Jake had never uttered anything political in his life, as far as she could remember. He was 100 percent mission driven.

"He was angry about a lack of resources for the Russian, Iran, and North Korea fights we just had, but that's it," Cassie said.

"That's a pretty big thing right there," Jamie said.

"There's a chance we might see him if he's got the bodyguard mission on Biagatti. Can you handle that?"

"Seeing Jake?" Her voice was excited. She desperately wanted to see him, talk to him, straighten her head out.

"You wouldn't be socializing. And given the pace of everything, there might be gunshots. Can you kill Jake, Cassie? To protect the president?"

"What?!"

"Yes. That's the commitment I need from you," Jamie said. "It's either me or Jake. At the end of the day, it might come down to that. If he's in this with Biagatti, and we believe that he is, then he's got to be put down."

Cassie's mind whirled with memories of Jake and visualizations of their future, none of which included shooting him. She braced herself and said, "I'm a patriot and will always do the right thing."

"Okay, that's going to have to be good enough for now, because we have to get moving," Zara said. The elevator chimed and two Secret Service men stepped out. Both were wearing sunglasses, black coats, dark suits with blue ties, and black shoes. The bulk under their coats hinted that they were carrying significant hardware, plus wearing body armor. The lead man had a buzz cut, not unlike a Russian hit man. The second man's black hair was gelled back, Gordon Gekko style.

"Madam Senator, we have to get you to the Capitol for the swearing-in ceremony immediately," the lead man said.

Zara had her pistol on her hip, while Cassie's was beneath her blazer for a quick draw across her chest. They would have to be head shots, though, because the body mass of the two big men was covered with something that would stop a nine-millimeter bullet, she was certain.

"Who are you guys?" Jamie said, stepping back.

"We're Secret Service, ma'am. And we need to go now," the lead man said.

"How did you get into my apartment?" Zara asked.

Cassie continued to slide to her left, toward the kitchen, gaining the flank, grasping her personal rucksack as she did so.

"We don't have time for these questions. There has been a coup, and, Senator, you are next in line. Our mission is to protect you," Buzz Cut said.

Cassie snapped her pistol out of her holster and shouted, "On the floor now!"

Zara moved in front of Jamie as both men drew their weapons. Cassie wasted no time in capping Gordon Gekko in the head. Buzz Cut's pistol was up, but Zara fired two rounds into his face.

"Search them for credentials immediately," Jamie said.

Cassie was already kneeling next to Gekko and found nothing but a Secret Service Special Agent shield, which looked authentic enough, but could easily be purchased at the Spy Store up the road.

"Just shields," Cassie said. "Why would these men be sanitized? They used the shields to get into the building, gain access, and do what?"

"Kill me," Jamie said. "See? This is as serious as it gets. No one knew I was here. I have a phone that the NSA probably tracked. The Resistance is everywhere. If they're going three down on the depth chart, they're trying to clean house big-time."

"But you said yourself that the Resistance wanted you," Cassie said.

"What the fuck am I going to do with two dead bodies and two tanks of cyanide gas? This apartment is becoming a biohazard," Zara quipped.

"We have to get going. Straight to the garage and then straight to the Capitol, correct?" Jamie asked.

"Yes. Media is going batshit crazy," Zara said.

"Any of them onto me being here?"

"No. I'm not sure how these two figured it out," Zara replied. "Unless Jake told them."

"First, Jake doesn't know where I am. Second, if Jake wanted you dead, you'd both be dead," Cassie said.

"I think you overestimate your crush there, girl," Zara said.

"Are you with me or against me, Cassie? We've got to get moving now."

Cassie nodded. "I'm coming."

"Don't piss on my leg and tell me it's raining, Cassie, but I'll take that for now. Let's go," Jamie said.

The elevator chimed; they stepped over the two dead men and gathered into the elevator. The doors opened into the lower garage. Zara had positioned her car so that it was directly in front of the elevator. Zara entered the driver's compartment, with Cassie riding shotgun, her rucksack between her legs. Jamie sat in the customary VIP position of the back right seat.

As they pulled onto the M Street Southwest, Cassie said, "I've got three women dressed in black running along the river. They've spotted the car and are heading directly at us from our two o'clock."

"Damnit," Zara muttered. "Where is our OpSec?"

"Just make a turn and haul ass. Get off this road!" Jamie shouted.

Zara pulled a Rockford 180 and was driving in the opposite direction, which was when the first bullet struck the rear window.

CHAPTER 14

Jake Mahegan looked at director Biagatti and said, "the Speaker's dead, which leaves us with Jamie Carter."

"Lord help us with that bitch," Biagatti said.

"I don't know the woman, but a very coordinated effort began with Senator Hite, which put Carter in place. Then, just like that, we have the top three elected officials in the country killed," Mahegan said.

They were in the Porsche Panamera doing 100 mph on I-66 as the sun was cresting the horizon. Mahegan had switched the flashers on and they had already passed four cops, with Biagatti saying the same thing she always said, "We should have taken the helicopter."

To which, Mahegan said each time, "It's got more important stuff to do right now."

They crossed the Potomac into DC, and Mahegan kept the Porsche cruising past the White House, along Constitution, until he found a parking spot near the

Russell Senate Office Building, where he parked the car at the curb. They jumped out and immediately a member of the Capitol Police was on them, pistols raised, shouting, "Stop!"

"Director of the CIA here. We need to be at the swearing-in ceremony," Biagatti said, holding up her credentials. The Russell Building loomed to their front, Constitution Avenue to their rear. The cop was tall and stocky, with a shaved head and wraparound sunglasses. His blue uniform was crisp and sharp. His biceps strained the material of his uniform. He carried a Glock 19, which hadn't wavered since Biagatti had spoken. His nametag read: JENSEN, and Mahegan thought that he looked like a big Swede from Minnesota.

"Seriously? You're drawing down on the director of the CIA?" Mahegan said. "You might as well go inside and sign your own dismissal papers. I've never worked with the Capitol Police, but I imagine it isn't too different than the military, where I served and maybe you did, too. If this were the Army and you were aiming your pistol at the chief of staff, a four-star general, whom you clearly either recognize or should recognize, then I'd say your career would be over. Either way, you're derelict. You either recognize Director Biagatti here, and are still choosing to aim a loaded pistol in her face, or you don't recognize her, which makes you derelict in your duties, because you're supposed to know all of the key players here in DC. And now would be a good time to brush up on that depth chart, because there are some changes happening. So, what's it going to be? You going to shoot the director of the CIA?"

"How about I just shoot you?" Jensen said.

"You'd better shoot to kill, Jensen. That's all I've got to say," Mahegan said.

The two men stared at each other, and Mahegan took a step closer to Jensen.

"You part of the Resistance? That was this is all about? You patrolling for them?" Jensen asked.

Mahegan had his earbud in, and O'Malley could hear everything that was transpiring.

"Sergeant Olaf Jensen from St. Paul, Minnesota. Heavyweight wrestler in high school and college. Social media shows him as a supporter of the president and his political party. Dad was a cop. Mom was a schoolteacher. Has a younger sister, Helen, at the University of Minnesota studying engineering. Pictures on social media indicate they're close. There's nothing that would indicate he's a Resister. A few bar fights on his record, so I'm guessing he's got a bad temper, that's all," O'Malley said.

"Voices in your head talking to you?" Jensen said.

"Something like that, Olaf. Would your sister, Helen, be proud of you for aiming a weapon at a woman? She's studying hard to be an engineer and here she's got a hothead brother holding up the show. Going to make the front page. Dad's a cop. Mom's a teacher. This what you learned from them? Headline, St. Paul Man Shoots Director of the CIA."

Jensen's stone face melted. "How the fuck you know about my family?"

"I'm standing next to the director of the CIA. That info just flows out of her brain. Now get out of the way, Jensen, before I . . . disarm you in a way that will embarrass you," Mahegan said.

Mahegan nudged Biagatti's arm and they walked past Jensen, who didn't move. Mahegan's considerable mass bumped into Jensen's, causing the police officer to take a step to maintain his balance. They came through the private back entrance and rode the elevator to the main hallway, checked the directory, and began jogging to Senator Hite's former office. As they turned the corner, a gaggle of reporters was huddled around the main door. A tall, dark-haired woman pushed through, created an alley, and Senator Jamie Carter followed, with Cassie on her heels.

Cassie?

Mahegan stopped, Biagatti's forward momentum carrying her into the throng of reporters. She turned and said, "Jake, come on!"

Cassie's eyes were focused on the crowd of reporters, any of which could be Resistance members ready to complete the kill of the top four—unless, of course, installing Carter was the plan all along. Mahegan shoved through with the director. He was eyes down, looking at hands one minute, and eyes up, looking at eyes the next. All he saw was a rabid press corps trying to make sense of everything that had happened. The fact was that no one could completely understand the last three years. The country had been splitting apart, forcing people to choose sides. You either hated or loved the president. Mahegan kept his politics to himself, to the extent that he had any. He was an operator, but that didn't mean he didn't see the damage being done to a country he loved and served.

Never one to place blame, Mahegan had tired of the media wars, picking apart everything the current administration did or failed to do. If he was tired of it, he knew that most of the country had to be over it. None-theless, the Resistance that had begun with the president's election, and continued to this day, had manifested itself in a revolution. First it was classic James Madison's "Violence of Factions" venting through government channels and semipeaceful protests. The semipeaceful transitioned to semiviolent at some unidentifiable tipping point, which then led to all-out violence, one year before the next election. Assassination was apparently a better option than voting. Certainly, it gave a more identifiable outcome for both sides.

Once in Jamie Carter's office, they pushed past the dark-haired woman, who, Mahegan believed, had been with Cassie last night when they changed out the tanks to the SCIF.

"Who are you?" she asked.

"I'm security for the director of the CIA, Carmen Biagatti. She needs to brief the incoming president on the intelligence and chaos happening right now."

Mahegan stared at the back of Cassie's head as she spoke with Carter, who was gesturing with her hands, emphasizing point after point. He only had an oblique view of Cassie's face, but even that gave him pause. *What have I done?*

The throng of reporters grew by the second, pushing against the thin line of security. Why was Carter still standing in line of sight of the doorway?

The mob parted as the chief justice of the Supreme Court barreled through with his security, two guys as big as Mahegan. It seemed that every public figure was upping their security game after what had happened in the last twelve hours.

"We need to brief Senator Carter, Ms. Perro," Biagatti said.

"Zara, please," she replied.

Zara Perro. *She's at the heart of this thing.*

"Now," Biagatti insisted.

Zara looked at Biagatti, then Mahegan, and said, "Let's do this in proper order. Chief Justice Walters is here. This will only take a minute. Then we can do the briefing. Your hunk of beef will have to stay out here, though."

"He's cleared to hear everything I have to say," Biagatti said.

"But perhaps not everything our new president will have to say. It's her call, after all," Zara said.

"That's right, so let her make it. Jake has been inside this thing from Jump Street and knows more than anyone else about what's happening."

"I go where the director goes," Mahegan said. "Right now, it's hard to tell who's on the right side of this thing."

"Indeed," Zara said. She smiled slightly. "I can see why Cassie likes you. Glad she's working for us."

"Working for you?"

"Just a sec," Zara said. She intercepted the chief justice and said to him, "Right this way." Guiding him through the doorway into an open conference room, the chief justice and Jamie Carter squared off. They were in full view of the press. Cassie was between them, holding the Bible in her hand.

Cassie. A million thoughts ran through his mind. The waves crashing on the beach just over the dunes from their Bald Head Island retreat. Riding flying suits and parachuting into a steep valley to rescue their boss,

General Savage. The intense firefight in Yazd, Iran. Her emerald eyes, like jade stones. Her smile, intelligent and humorous.

After the last 48 hours, was she still Cassie Bagwell, the woman he loved?

The doorway to the outer office was filled with heads and cameras and boom mikes, all trying to get the scoop, capture the moment. Mahegan understood. Carter wanted proof that she was being sworn in as the president after the "Coup Assassinations," as the *New York Post* had already labeled it.

Next through the throng was the president's doctor, who brushed past Mahegan, paused, leaned in, and whispered something; then he continued on to the small lectern set up with a microphone. With the doctor was the White House spokeswoman, Maggie Myers, known affectionately by the press pool as "M-Squared." Maggie was wearing a white blouse, navy suit, and low heels. She had pulled her brunette hair back into a ponytail, baring her grim facial features. Somehow, she had to explain the last twenty-four hours to the nation. Instead of doing it from the White House, someone had deferred to Senator Carter's desires to perform the ceremony from her Senate office.

Maggie stood before the podium and coughed. The gathering hushed as she began speaking.

"It is with the deepest sadness imaginable that I have to report the deaths of the president, vice president, and Speaker of the House. White House physician Dr. Colin White has confirmed everything I am telling you."

Dr. White stepped forward, nodded, and then returned to his position behind Maggie.

"Consistent with Article Twenty-five of the United States Constitution, Dr. White has declared the president unable to serve, which then transfers the acting presidency to the vice president, who Dr. White has also declared unable to serve. The next in the line of succession is the Speaker, who Dr. White has likewise confirmed is unable to serve. Terrorist attacks were effected at an undisclosed location in Northern Virginia against the president and vice president, and nearly simultaneously, terrorists attacked the Speaker of the House. This was a coordinated effort to overthrow the government. We have our director of the Central Intelligence Agency here to answer questions, to the extent she may have any answers, given the fluid situation. We also have Chief Justice Harrison Walters here to swear in the Senate pro tem, newly elected senator Jamie Carter, as the acting president."

Mahegan detected the slightest emphasis on the word *acting*.

"Consistent with an unprecedented and perhaps unforeseen evolution of events, we are acting out of an abundance of caution and rapidly designating Senator Carter as the president until further notice. Chief Justice Walters will conduct the swearing in."

Maggie left no time for questions, quickly pivoting to Chief Justice Walters, who somberly approached the microphone, turned to a ninety-degree angle, and motioned for Jamie to join him, which she did.

A hush fell over the journalists, even the gaggle behind the gaggle. They all seemed to get the message. This was history in the making, and no one wanted to be recorded as forever destroying the moment.

Mahegan thought about the grainy videos he had

seen of Lyndon Johnson taking the oath aboard Air Force One after John F. Kennedy's assassination. His wife, Lady Bird Johnson, and Jackie Kennedy flanked him then, as Cassie and Zara Perro joined Senator Jamie Carter today.

Cassie had not yet acknowledged him. Her eyes were downcast, focused on the task at hand. She didn't appear to be particularly pleased to be there. If anyone could see inside Cassie's mind, it was Mahegan. She was torn. Jamie was Cassie's godmother, and the only family Jamie had left in the world. That connection had allowed Cassie to get inside Senator, shortly to be President, Jamie Carter's inner circle less than forty-eight hours after calling him and asking for his help. Mahegan followed Director Biagatti into the conference room. They had counted on Zara's pursuit, and even though Jake had only the one communication with Cassie, it appeared to have worked.

Chief Justice Walters began speaking in a booming voice: "Unfortunate events have brought us to this point. Raise your right hand and repeat after me."

To Mahegan, Jamie Carter appeared to be suppressing a smile. Tragedy had struck the nation and she was . . . amused? Satisfied? Jamie was unmarried and without children. There was no family she could call her own except a few distant relatives. The full vetting of her had shown her parents passed much earlier than either of them should have. Her mother to a bad case of the flu that led to sepsis, and her father had a blood clot in his left anterior descending artery, often nicknamed the "widowmaker heart attack." He died instantly one morning after a jog at their Charlottesville Farmington Golf Course home. Her mother had died a slow, painful death; her father, a quick merciful one. With no other siblings, Jamie had inherited an eight-figure sum while attending the University of Virginia Law School. She graduated, worked in a prestigious firm, made partner, and very quickly ran for governor, won that, and then four years later ran for Senate, won that, kept winning, and expected the train to keep on rolling, until Jack Smart upended her run of luck.

A progressive politician who had the luxury of saying what she believed, but not having to live with the consequences of her decisions or legislation, Jamie was known for three things: her natural youthful good looks, her intellect, and her ambition. There was no denying that she was impatient as well. After winning the popular vote, but losing the Electoral College to Smart, she had asked for recounts in key states and districts, refusing to go away. Smart's brash style, coupled with Jamie's progressive policy positions, had ignited massive protests around the country by liberals who could not fathom that Jamie was not going to be the president.

Smart was a tough Las Vegas real estate developer used to dealing with the Mob, hucksters, and Hollywood. He had parlayed an investment from his family into a multibillion-dollar global real estate empire. That he had emerged out of political thin air and beaten Jamie Carter was out of the question for 50 percent of the population. Not only was it unacceptable that a political neophyte had beaten both party establishments, but that he had beaten the heretofore-unbeatable Jamie Carter and her wildly progressive agenda was heresy. It wasn't supposed to happen, all the polls had told everyone that.

And so, Mahegan figured, whatever was happening today, directly in front of him, would be seen by at least half the population as simply the world setting itself right, like a body rejecting a bad organ transplant and welcoming its healthy original back into the fold. While Jamie's image had been one of shiny perfection, Mahegan's work with Biagatti's intelligence team had uncovered byzantine connections domestically and internationally. Extensive travel to Europe and Canada had strengthened her progressive impulses. She had embraced the socialist economies and the cultural intersectionality of many European nations in particular. The rising tide of Islam in Europe had seeped into the historically secular governments, and their collective media now forbade any speech against Islamic crimes. Jamie had been a staunch supporter of the United Kingdom government's response to reporter and activist Tommy Robinson, who had published stories about the Islamic "grooming," which was a rite of passage for young Muslim men in Great Britain. Jamie's support for "these oppressed young men" and outrage at Tommy Robinson for "expressing xenophobic views" had made her a media darling in Europe and to liberals in the United States. She had walked back those comments, once she learned that the oppressed young men were gang-raping white British women as part of their transition to manhood. But by then, the story had passed and the monolithic mainstream media in the United States gave no airtime to Jamie's faux pas in supporting rape.

President Smart, though, had taken to Twitter, Facebook, and Instagram and had made sure that at least his 56 million followers knew that his likely foe in the next election had wholly supported Islamic gang rape in Great Britain. Jamie's odds were looking good, according to all polling, until this tweet:

> @realjacksmart: Why is the FakeNews not talking about Jamie Carter's love of Islam and hatred of women?? She supports Islamic "grooming" which is GANG RAPE by Muslims of white British teenagers! Carter supports rape and Islamic Jihad. Is that what we want, America?

That short statement last year from the sitting president had exposed one of Jamie Carter's few mistakes. There was no way to *un*ring the bell. The intelligence trail on Carter had subsequently shown she had spent ample time traveling throughout the country, shoring up her base, denying she supported rape, and walking the fine line between denouncing "all violence," while not alienating whatever Muslim support she perceived she might have. It had been a difficult time for Jamie, as she had gone from shoo-in to loser to an even bigger shoo-in to now potentially snatching defeat from the jaws of victory.

Had she engineered certain victory? Mahegan wondered.

Jamie raised her right hand, placed her left hand on the Bible, which Cassie held for her, and repeated after the chief justice's booming voice: "I, Jamie Elizabeth Carter, do solemnly swear that I will faithfully execute the office of the president of the United States, and will, to the best of my ability, preserve, protect, and defend the Constitution of the United States."

When she was finished, there was no ovation or

congratulations. The weight of the moment seemed to be settling over everyone. During the brief silent moment, Cassie's eyes lifted from the Bible to Mahegan, as if recognizing him being there for the first time. She held a steady gaze, unflinching, unmoving, and uncertain.

He didn't dare signal anything to her, understanding that she might be in over her head with Jamie Carter and Zara Perro.

"Madam President, I need to provide you an intelligence update on the attacks," Biagatti said.

"Let me first address the media," Jamie replied. She nudged Biagatti to the side and stepped to the microphone. The scene was claustrophobic inside the conference room. Reporters had piled in. Word had traveled fast as people were racing to the Russell Office Building. The Capitol Police had strengthened their numbers and established a solid cordon outside of the office. The fallacy in Jamie's thinking had been that she had only one exit. Her departure would be through the masses, layer by layer, but perhaps that was what she wanted.

She leaned into the microphone, appearing poised and in command as she had done so many times on the campaign trail three years earlier.

"To those in this room, and to all Americans watching at this moment, it is with deep sorrow that I find myself standing at this podium. The criminal activities that have led to this point are reprehensible and I promise to get to the bottom of these crimes. With so much happening around the world, it is imperative that we move swiftly to assure our citizens, our allies, and the world that we are a stable nation with a steady hand on the rudder of our global responsibilities. I need to be briefed by Director Biagatti before I answer any questions, which I will do in the next twenty-four hours."

As Jamie stepped away from the microphone, the press corps erupted in a thunderous round of questions.

"Who killed the president?"

"What is your plan for domestic policy?"

"Was this a coup?"

"Polls show fifty percent of the country are happy the president is dead. How do you feel about that?"

The words became an indistinguishable mash as Mahegan led Biagatti to the senator's office. He closed the heavy oak doors and turned to find Cassie staring at him. The office was huge, forty feet in both directions. Biagatti and Carter had already huddled by her desk at the far end from the door. Zara Perro was standing off to the side. And two Secret Service agents were walking toward them.

"Jake, what are you doing here?"

"You know. My detail is Director Biagatti. And it appears yours is now . . . President Carter?"

"I had no idea you would be here. This isn't easy for me," she said.

"Me neither. But we both have jobs to do," Mahegan said.

"I understand that. I'm learning the ropes, as I'm sure you are as well."

"Your wound is healing nicely," Mahegan said, pointing at the side of her head. Her hair was tucked behind her ears and he could see the tip of a bandage.

"Yes. Part of the job. I'm out of Band-Aids. Have a spare?"

Mahegan palmed what he had retrieved from the

medical cooler and shook Cassie's hand. She closed
her fist around the device and quickly pocketed it.

"Be careful with those blows to the head. You've
been through enough, Cassie."

"Tell me about it. Things are crazy right now."

"We should see what they're talking about," Mahegan said. He chinned in the direction of Biagatti and
Carter.

They walked toward the two new Secret Service
agents, who were presumably guarding the door. Cassie
walked past them, but then they closed ranks in front
of Mahegan.

"Not invited," the man on the left said. They looked
like identical twins. Both were about six and a half feet
tall, with block bodies, dark suits, earpieces, and bulges
under their jackets. Cassie stopped, turned, and said,
"He's with me."

The two men nodded and parted for Mahegan to
pass as they exited the senator's office and took up
their posts outside the door.

As Mahegan approached the conversation, Biagatti
said, "We should all sit down."

The four of them sat in two facing sofas, with Jamie
sitting in a chair in between, like the head of the table.
Jamie was wearing a ruby-red-and-gold brooch of a
cardinal perched on a flowering dogwood branch, the
cardinal's tufted hair in its distinctive angular point. It
fit nicely with her navy blue suit and white silk blouse,
blending into a patriotic red, white, and blue and com-
plimenting the smaller American flag pin on her lapel.

"I've got a lot on my plate, Carmen, but I guess
there's nothing more important than what you know.
Why isn't the FBI here also?"

"Can't be trusted," Biagatti said.

"And you can?" Jamie replied.

It's game on, Mahegan thought. He watched Zara Perro, whose eyes bore into Biagatti as she squared off with Jamie.

"Yes. After Operation Crossfire Hurricane, the FBI's reputation is still in shambles. Nobody trusts them. All the texts and insurance policies to protect against a Smart presidency."

"Yes, but it seems the president and vice president were killed in your presence. How do I know all of this isn't your doing?"

"You don't, but I can assure you it isn't. I was attacked this morning by four women. Another six were found at the Speaker's murder site. Two women are on video departing the safe house where the president and vice president were killed. We've traced some of the DNA already and we've got indicators that lead back to the Valley Trauma Center, where it appears Dr. Perro worked as a psychiatrist and Cassie Bagwell was a patient." Biagatti let that statement hang in the air a moment.

"What are you implying?" Jamie said.

"Nothing. Just stating facts. Jake here has done most of the analysis. I'll let him take over from here," Biagatti said.

Mahegan shifted forward, leaning his elbows on his knees.

"We think it's a coincidence and don't see any connection between Cassie, Dr. Perro, and the other events. We know they are part of your inner circle now and would like an opportunity to discuss the activities at the Valley Trauma Center with Cassie and Dr. Perro.

The CIA is handling this because of the foreign implications, and as Director Biagatti said, in addition to their incompetence, the FBI is seen as being complicit with the coup. Local law enforcement in North Carolina has turned up some interesting leads on Hite's death. There's some evidence he wasn't alone, that someone may have either been partnering with him or intentionally murdered him. When you look at the events, including Hite's death, the president and vice president, and now the Speaker's death, it's a very unlikely and unusual chain of events that led to your being president."

"Sounds like you're accusing me of something, Mr. Mahegan," Jamie snapped.

"Joe Six-Pack will be able to see the linkages and we want to clear things up for you to serve as the president. Our mission is to find those that led this coup, prosecute them, and clear the way for you to serve out your term."

Mahegan felt Cassie's eyes on him, steady and firm. Always a good listener, Cassie was processing and synthesizing. The lack of communications for the last day and a half had been tough on both of them. Her eyes were drawn, lacking their usual ferocity, dimmed from either the drugs or the pressure of maintaining her legend. Like him, she was most likely assessing threats and the path forward, the exit strategy from this predicament. Zara was a lethal killer and could lash out at any moment. Jamie was no slouch herself. The intel on her was that she was an expert marksman. Mahegan had to do everything he could to convey a sense of equanimity to Jamie so that the new president would see him as evenhanded. The truth was that he wasn't sure who had initiated the coup or who was involved. There was only one way to find out and that was to give Jamie all the rope and freedom she desired.

"Go on," Jamie said.

"I just need time with Cassie and Dr. Perro this morning. I know it has been nonstop and that it is hard to wrap your head around everything happening right now," Mahegan said.

"It's not difficult at all, Mr. Mahegan," Jamie said. "I have a single-minded purpose of leading this country. I didn't kill anyone and didn't ask for anyone to be killed. I moved to North Carolina almost a year ago. It was impossible to foresee the events that have unfolded in the last three months, much less twenty-four hours. Women being trained as assassins? I know that you have been involved in many plots around the world to protect this country, but something as nefarious as a conspiracy to establish a training camp to stage a coup on the Smart administration strains credulity."

"It's no secret that high-profile celebrities have threatened this president with death and dismemberment," Mahegan said. "And it's also no secret that chief among those most upset about the Smart victory was you. And so again, to properly protect you and your new team as you begin your duties, we need to get out in front of possible perceptions. At the moment, the nation is stunned, reeling from the loss of a president that half the country voted for."

"Less than half," Jamie snapped. "By a few million votes."

"My point," Mahegan said. "You're in a room of five people and you can't control your kneejerk hatred of the man."

"I'm among friends, aren't I?"

Cassie leaned forward and said, "I think what Jake is saying is that you're among people who want this country to succeed. All of us will do everything possible to stabilize the country and make sure that the conspiracy theories, which will surely arise, are put to rest as quickly as possible. The best way to do that is to look at the worst-case theories and work backward from there."

Mahegan couldn't deny the rush of emotion he felt for Cassie, something he had held in check ever since the day before she was transferred and he had visited her, held her hand, told her about what was going to transpire, asked her if she was up for it, and then assured her that all would be okay. He didn't dare lock eyes with her. The electricity would be visible to everyone, like lightning before the thunder.

"I agree," Mahegan said.

"You would, wouldn't you?" Jamie countered. "Given your feigned love for my goddaughter."

Mahegan said nothing.

"You're here now," Jamie continued. "But where were you when Cassie needed you in Iran?"

Mahegan said nothing.

Zara chimed in: "Your presence in this room creates trauma for Cassie, Mahegan. It's probably best you leave."

"I get a vote here," Cassie said.

"Actually, you don't," Jamie countered. "I've had enough of this 'briefing.' Director, this meeting is adjourned."

Biagatti nodded. "Very well, Madam President."

They stood, Mahegan staring at Jamie, whose eyes had never left his.

"Good luck," Mahegan said. He then walked to Cassie and shook hands with her, saying. "Stay strong."

Cassie nodded and said, "You, too, Jake."

He turned and walked out the door, picking up the lead as he shouldered his way through the throng of reporters, Biagatti holding his arm. They ricocheted through the crowd until they were outside, found the Panamera, and were heading back to a new CIA safe house in southeast D.C.

"What did you make of that?" Biagatti asked.

"Lots to sort through. Sitting in Hite's former office instead of the White House was a big middle finger to all of us. My guess is Carter had him killed, maybe even by Perro. She's lethal. But sitting in that room confirmed in my mind that we need to go back to the beginning. Everything that has happened since Hite's death is like a fast-burning lit fuse. It all started with lighting the fuse—killing Hite."

They pulled into the driveway and entered the garage, where Mahegan parked the car. As they got out, O'Malley, Owens, Van Dreeves, and Hobart came out to meet them, having repositioned during the swearing in ceremony.

"Shit show," Hobart said.

"About right," Mahegan replied.

"I've got something to show all you geniuses," O'Malley said. O'Malley was the computer expert in the group, and given the CIA resources, he had been a kid in a candy store for the past twenty-four hours.

They walked into a small study turned conference room, where O'Malley had set up shop. He had three

MacBooks linked together by LAN cables, which were connected to the CIA server farm, giving him full access to CIA algorithms and programs. He pointed at the fifty-five-inch monitor on the wall, which was connected to the computer array. Blown up on the screen was a grainy picture of Zara Perro sitting in a helicopter that was landing at night on a helipad near a body of water.

O'Malley said, "Pursued your theory and did some research. The video footage from Hite's security cameras had been erased by the time New Hanover County Sheriff's team got there, but some neighbors had posted a short video on Instagram of an inbound helicopter, probably thinking it was a high-level politician. I loaded Zara Perro's face into the CIA's database and ran some Carnivore-like programs. This picture is of Zara Perro landing on Hite's helipad within an hour of his murder."

"Any shot of a helicopter leaving?" Mahegan asked.

"No. And no other video."

"I know Figure Eight. It has a gate guard to get onto the island. She wouldn't have wanted to risk that," Mahegan said.

"No. But check this out," O'Malley said. He pointed his finger at a spec of light behind the helicopter. "It's a pier and there are boats in the water."

"Okay. Any idea on the flight path of the helicopter?"

"I did a tail number check and it's registered with the Lynchburg, Raleigh-Durham, and Wilmington air traffic controllers for the evening of the murder."

"How far is Lynchburg from the Valley Trauma Center?"

"Maybe twenty-five miles," O'Malley said.

"She kills Dr. Broome, flies to Figure Eight, kills Hite, jumps on a boat, and goes where?"

"Carter lives about a two-hour boat ride from there," Biagatti said.

"Okay. So fast forward this thing three months. When did Cassie show up at Carter's?"

"Yesterday morning, as best we know. She escaped from the Valley Trauma Center around the time of Broome's murder, then was tracked in the Greensboro area, where she stole a cop car. The GPS on the car put her in Uwharrie National Forest. After that, she disappeared and showed up the next morning at Jamie Carter's house."

"Okay. This is solid. Now we just have to wait and see what Carter does—who she fires and who she hires," Mahegan said.

"She'll fire some people. Name new cabinet secretaries. Bring in some aides. All the normal transition bullshit."

"No. Outside the normal stuff. If she's been calling the shots here, she still has loose ends to clean up. The Twitter conspiracy people are going to have a field day with this. Make sure we're tapping into that. A lot might be bullshit, but there's always a kernel of the truth in there, somewhere."

"Roger," O'Malley said, taking the task to write an algorithm to scroll through the traditional conspiracy feeds.

"What about forensics on the three crime scenes?" Mahegan asked.

"Two blond hairs found at the Hite crime scene that match Cassie's DNA. Cassie's fingerprints all over the cyanide tanks they placed behind the SCIF. Several eyewitness reports of someone matching Cassie's description at the scene of the Speaker's murder, not to mention some blood that matches her DNA. Pretty solid evidence that she is the connective tissue."

"What about Zara Perro?"

"Not a whisper," O'Malley said.

Then, from Owens, who was staring at the intelligence significant activities scrolling across the display monitor: "Oh, man. That's her next move right there."

Mahegan turned and stared at the screen. A picture of Cassie was staring back at him; an intelligence nugget scrolling beneath: FORMER CHAIRMAN OF JOINT CHIEF'S DAUGHTER LEAD SUSPECT IN COUP ASSASSINATIONS.

CHAPTER 15

"Here is a list of people that I want to bring into the administration immediately. And we need to create a Committee of Public Safety. Give me some names for that, too," Jamie said. "I'd like to meet with them today. I'd also like the first lady out of the White House by tomorrow."

"That seems a bit . . . extreme," Zara said.

"These are extreme times. I'm not going to the White House filled with people who don't agree with me."

Jamie handed the lists of names to Zara, who studied them briefly and kept them in her hand, absently holding the lists facing outward by her thigh. Zara looked at Cassie and stood, nodding to Jamie. They walked to the far side of the office and engaged in a whispering conversation.

All three phones in the office pinged with an alert. Retrieving her iPhone, Cassie fumbled the device when she saw the intel alert pop on her home screen. With a sharp, silent breath, she thumbed up the home screen, selected the camera function, placed the phone on video, turned it outward, and began walking toward the women. Cassie palmed her phone and spread her fingers so that the camera had a clear line of sight. She shouldered her rucksack as she approached Zara and Jamie, her heart beating like a war drum, both from the news she had just seen and from the feat she was about to attempt.

Jamie pulled up from the whispered conversation and looked at Cassie, who slowed, juxtaposed to Zara's back.

"Cassie?"

"Just going to use the restroom," Cassie said.

"Okay, quickly then. We have a lot to do, so let's get to it," Jamie said. "Zara, you're in charge of getting my team together. Cassie, you need to be by my side at all times. I'll work from here until we get everything situated at the White House."

"Okay. I'll just clean up in the bathroom. Been a long night," Cassie said. She brushed past Zara, who glanced over her shoulder at her, and then slid past the two security guards who were looking down at their phones. In fact, just about everyone was looking at the alert that had just been sent across all media networks.

Cassie was the number one "person of interest" in the "Coup Assassinations," as the media now called what had transpired.

Given the seniority of the pro tem position, the office was on the corner of the building, with windows in every room, including the bathroom.

Zara had looked at her phone at the same time, registering something Cassie couldn't quite place. Concern? Task checked off? She wasn't hanging around to find out, so she was up and out of the office before anyone could stop her. Seeing Jake had given her renewed confidence that what she was doing was the right thing, that her path was true.

She closed and locked the bathroom door, feeling the presence of the guards moving toward her. One of them began knocking on the door. Studying the Band-Aid Jake had placed in her hand, she opened it and placed it behind her ear ensuring the pad was centered on the mastoid bone. They had experimented with these micro communications devices previously, but before she could test it, she was interrupted.

"Captain Bagwell, we need you to come out."

"Just a sec," she said. "Can't a lady use the restroom?"

Using the heel of her hand to press up on the window that probably hadn't been opened in twenty years, she broke the seal of the paint. The gap was a reasonable size for her to slide through, though she wasn't sure about how she might climb down the three stories of sheer brick facing. She squeezed through the opening, her back scraping along the bottom of the window frame. She lowered herself until her hands were straining, her shoulders were nearly out of socket, and the bathroom door opened with a loud cracking noise.

Her feet found a small three-inch ledge, which allowed her to relax her arms and pivot her back to the wall. Constitution Avenue hummed with morning traffic. She was maybe forty feet above the sidewalk. Two dogwood trees were about ten feet to her left, growing out of a small rectangular patch of grass, maybe forty feet wide and ten feet deep. The only hope she had of not seriously injuring herself was to jump from the ledge into the dogwood, grasp a branch, and hope that it lowered her somewhat gently to the ground.

Visualizing the leap was very different than execution. She leapt, her rib cage bounced off a thick branch, causing her to roll toward thin branches, which gave way quickly as she plummeted into the grassy area. The only saving grace was that the rain had been heavy and softened the ground.

She had no time to waste on feeling sorry for herself, though, as the two Secret Service agents were at the window. One was climbing down, and the other was aiming his service pistol at her. Her mind fuzzy, like swimming through cotton, she knelt and then ran, like a sprinter out of the starting blocks. With no safe haven nearby, she had to disappear fast. Amtrak was two blocks away, but out of the question, as was using the Metro. Cameras everywhere.

She ran east, then south behind the Supreme Court. While she had been injured, her training regimen had been significant, including heavy cardio work. The Secret Service agent who had been chasing her either gave up or had taken another route to attempt to cut her off. She continued to wind her way into Southeast Washington, DC. From the halls of power on Capitol Hill to the projects along the Anacostia River. Helicopters now buzzed the skies in ever-expanding circles along the general azimuth she had run.

She found herself pressed up against a small boathouse, which had stacks of plastic kayaks leaning against the side. She pulled a Leatherman from her belt and used it to cut the thin wire looped through the carrying handles. She slid one of the kayaks into the water and grabbed one of the loose oars. Shoving quietly along the Anacostia, she realized that she was in full view of several major freeways, an easy target from the air, and particularly susceptible to sniper fire from any number of SWAT teams, which were most likely hustling to find her trail.

The surrounding highways were jammed with traffic, very little moving in any direction. The helicopters buzzed overhead about a mile behind her. She dug the paddle into the murky river and gained speed, skimming along the surface of the water. She covered the quarter mile in minutes. She was conspicuous and at the same time invisible: just another millennial out on a lunchtime kayak across the river. She made landfall in Anacostia Park, where some children were playing on swings. A parent or babysitter, it was tough to tell, was buried in her smartphone. The kids waved at Cassie as she tugged the kayak onto the shore and pulled it under a willow tree.

She kept the momentum by jogging into the dilapidated neighborhood behind the park. Crossing Martin Luther King Jr. Avenue, she ran along Good Hope Road and then turned onto W Street. Sprinting past the Frederick Douglass National Historic Site, she found the ramshackle row of homes she remembered from a childhood visit there.

Not much had changed in fifteen years. The red-brick buildings were in worse condition. They didn't appear inhabited. If they were, she would find out soon enough. Her lungs burned from the high-speed sprint across Washington, DC, but it was imperative she not be caught. A few hands pulled down window blinds, eyes peering out. People mostly kept to themselves here, she figured, but they would also be territorial. A blond white girl in the heart of Ward 8, Washington, DC, was a rare find. She moved swiftly inside the dank open doorway. There were blankets on the wood floors and the deeper she walked into the bowel of the building, the more decrepit it became. This place was inhabited on a daily basis.

A floorboard creaked on the other side of the wall, where she presumed whatever passed as the kitchen might be. She retrieved her pistol from her holster and pressed her back against the wall, keeping an eye on the doorway. Another footfall, another squeaky floorboard. A head poked around the door.

It was a child.

The kid stepped into the room, saw Cassie, and held his hands up. He was wearing a T-shirt that had a big star on it with a silk-screened image of Malcolm X over dirty, worn dungarees, and old PRO-Keds that were missing the laces.

"I ain't done nothing," he said. "Are you here from the school?"

"No," Cassie said. She shook her head, awaking to the fact that a boy who looked about ten was standing in front of her while she held a pistol at him. She had been through a lot in the last year and was still recovering, but she had never lost her moral compass. She didn't shoot kids. She didn't scare kids.

Lowering the pistol, she said, "No. I'm not from the school. I just need a place to hide from some bad people."

"You mean like principals and teachers?"

Cassie coughed out a laugh. "I wish," she said. "Mean people are chasing me."

"Principals are mean," the kid said, sticking with his main fear.

"Yeah, I guess they can be. What's your name? I'm Cassie."

"Jermaine," he said.

"Why are you hiding out in here, Jermaine?"

"My moms is at work. Teacher all mad at me, all the time. So I come here when I can and do my work."

"What work?"

"Schoolwork," he said.

Cassie sighed. "Want to show me?"

"Why?" Jermaine squinted at her with narrow eyes, suspicious, perhaps thinking that maybe she was a principal or a teacher.

"No reason. Got nothing else to do. I feel pretty safe in here. So might as well kill some time."

"Safe?" Jermaine shrugged. "If you say so, Miss, but you might not want to stay 'til night."

"I'll take my chances with you, Jermaine."

Jermaine disappeared into the next room. Cassie followed him and Jermaine sat cross-legged on the floor, papers stacked neatly on one side, books arranged similarly on the other. He had an old dingy brown clipboard fraying on the sides, with a rusty metal clip at the top. He was writing on a piece of paper, pressing the pencil firmly, his brow furrowed. The pencil moved quickly across the paper. He glanced down at an algebra 2 textbook.

Cassie walked over, dropped her rucksack on the floor, and slid her back down the wall. She watched him do what, to her, looked like a probability and statistics problem.

"How old are you, Jermaine?"

"Be ten next month," he said.

"And you're taking algebra two?"

"No, I ain't *taking* algebra two. They won't let me *take* algebra two. So I do it on my own."

"The school can't keep up with you," she whispered to herself. She was transformed from worrying about the tragedy unfolding across the nation to a microcosm tragedy exactly the size of one nine-year-old little boy.

"I keep telling everyone I'm done with everything they're teaching, but no one listens. So I robbed some textbooks and downloaded the flipped classrooms from Khan Academy. It's free and I can do it fast."

"An app?" Cassie asked.

"Something like that." He removed his phone and showed her a video of a young man teaching algebra. "Like that."

"You can do all your classes like this?"

"All that I want to do," he said. "English. Math. Chemistry. I want to be a doctor. Go to Howard or Harvard. As long as it starts with an *H,* I don't care." Jermaine cackled at his own joke. Cassie smiled.

"I was pretty good at math," Cassie said.

"I'm kind of like that guy on *Good Will Hunting*," Jermaine said.

"Good movie. I imagine you are like him." After a pause, Cassie asked, "What kind of doctor?"

"Like Ben Carson. Brain surgeon. I figure I'm ahead of where he was when he was a kid. Only problem is it's easy to get lost in this city. I'm just another dumb black kid to most people."

"Not to me," Cassie said. She picked up his pencil and wrote her phone number on a loose-leaf sheet of paper in his folder. "Call me in a few days. I'll come back and help if I can."

Jermaine nodded at her but didn't speak.

"I'll let you get back to your studies, then," she said. "I have some of my own homework to do." She held up her phone, knowing that if the FBI really wanted to find her, they could trace her by pinging her location, which was why she had switched off the cell and Wi-Fi functions. She only needed the video footage to see if she could decipher the list.

"You still in school?" Jermaine asked.

"No, but you never quit learning." Cassie sighed, then pulled up the photo reel and played back the video she had downloaded to her photo app. Jermaine seemed more interested in her phone than his studies.

"What's that?"

"Just a work thing," Cassie said. She felt exhaustion creeping through her body, but knew that she needed to see the list, which might contain the names of the key conspirators in the coup. Her mind fought for clarity. Through the haze of the drugs, she remembered The Plan. It had always been there in her mind. The challenge was fending off the influence efforts of Zara. Now that the façade had fallen, it was all clear. Rather than being an accomplice, all along she was an asset. Jake's temporary post protecting the CIA director had been a deliberate move by General Savage. The posting had allowed him to mine the CIA intelligence feeds and discover that Jamie Carter had been communicating with Zara Perro and Franklin Broome in code.

Just as President Smart's predecessor had unmasked

him and his transition team, President Smart had returned the favor, providing access not to the FBI, but to Joint Special Operations Command by using Jake as a cut out in the CIA. Knowing that her parents had left Jamie as her next of kin, Jake sent a U.S. Army casualty assistance officer to Jamie's home in New Bern two months ago. The officer had suggested she visit Cassie, which Jamie had done, dragging Zara Perro along.

Because this was a compartmented operation, labeled Double Crossfire, not even CIA Director Carmen Biagatti knew about this mission, mainly because it was unclear if Biagatti was involved in the Resistance or not. The media portrayal of the Globalist Resistance Force, or GRF, was that of deep and wide national, even international, support. In reality, Jake had discovered the leadership was nine people, including four holdovers in the FBI, Jamie Carter, Zara Perro, and three unknowns.

Is Biagatti one of the unknowns?

Cassie scrolled through her video; Jermaine rolled his eyes and said, "Boring," before going back to his flipped algebra. The video showed two separate documents. The facing-outward one was the only legible opportunity. She paused the video when she thought she could make out the list of names.

She took a screenshot of the most legible frame of the video. After a minute of adjusting lighting and black point compensation, she was able to read the names.

"Oh my God," she muttered.

She stood and walked into the front room of the house and pressed the Band-Aid behind her ear, which was actually a miniaturized transmitter and receiver developed by Nuvotronics in the Research Triangle Park of North Carolina.

After a few seconds of static, Jake's voice emanated through her mastoid bone into her ear canal. The microradio was mostly secure, operating on a fully encrypted signal within a discreet bandwidth of the radio spectrum. Ever since Bulgarian hackers had cracked the Zebra communications system used by Mahegan and his team, General Savage and the JSOC communications engineers had experimented with a variety of technologies.

"Go," Mahegan said.

"You need to move out now. You, me, Savage, and the team are all on Jamie's list."

"Roger. Thought we had a deal with her. Any other names?"

"Need to check that. Biagatti's *not* on it," Cassie said.

"Okay. If you see or hear the name Syd Wise, let me know."

"He's bad, I think."

"Understand," Mahegan said. "Status?"

"On the go. It's tight."

"Rally point?"

"Will get there eventually," she said. "Wait, one more thing."

"Send it."

"Jamie talked about setting up a Committee of Public Safety. Any clues?"

After a pause, Mahegan said, "Yes. They were the henchmen during the French Revolution who quelled rebellion. They had absolute power and authority and were savage."

"Makes sense. She'll probably go after all Smart supporters with martial law. She's double crossing any deal you've got in place with her."

"No politics, Cass, just tactics. Be safe."

"You too."

She pressed the tab in the center of the Band-Aid and the link evaporated.

"Who you talking to?" Jermaine was standing in the doorway, eyes wide.

Cassie rubbed her left arm, needing Zara's boost. She grimaced, hating herself for the loss of control, but it had been a necessary part of The Plan. She was all in, subjecting herself to Zara's abuses. Secretly watching the injections on the other women had bothered her most. The *pop, pop, pop* sounds of the Valley Trauma Center firing range echoed in her memory. One by one, the women were marched to the range, the gym, the weight room. They were trained to defend and attack, as much as to capture and kill. Their physical conditioning was superb, as she had seen at the marina. Was Zara controlling them? It couldn't be Jamie. She didn't have the skill sets. But Zara was a different story. Zara had come to her room at the VTC three times a day, hooked up the meds, wired her system. When she felt herself at the tipping point, near completely losing control, she fled.

The mission had required full immersion. The only way her legend would work was if she played the role 100 percent. All of the best deceptions were built around a sliver of the truth. Cassie did have a traumatic brain injury. She did struggle with post-traumatic stress. She did require extensive rehab and recuperation. Even the memory loss was real, she realized as she struggled to conjure the memory of Jamie's visit to her in Walter Reed Hospital and her gentle nudge for a transfer.

"Help me," she says to Jamie, who is standing above her.

"How, dear?"

"There's a better place."

"What place?"

"The Trauma Center in the Valley, I think."

"Who told you about this place?"

"I'm not sure. People talk."

"I'll check into it."

With that, Cassie's half-lidded eyes close. She feels her mind swoon, part act, part real. Through the thin sliver of daylight between her eyelids, she sees Zara Perro and remembers the list Jake gave her on his daily visit. The "visits" have become planning sessions. Mahegan's briefings are alarming.

"The only way to get inside the decision cycle of the GRF . . . the fever pitch of the Resistance is boiling over . . . investigations of the administration are still not yielding what they had hoped for . . . moving from outrage to planning to execution . . ."

"Cassie!"

Jermaine had been trying to get her attention, but she had been deep in the hole of a memory that had chosen to present itself.

"Yes? What is it?" She struggled to remember where she was. The DHT-and-Flakka cocktail had rewired her system to expect the elixir at specific times. Fighting through the void was, she imagined, like going cold turkey from heroin or opioids.

"We've got to go! There's people outside with guns!" Jermaine whispered with excitement and fear. "This way."

He led her through a back room, stepping through open studs that led to another home in the series of row houses. They seesawed through the complex like this, Jermaine leading and reaching back for her hand, until they slipped into a tunnel. Jermaine closed the door and said, "It smells real bad down here, but it's how we can get to another part of town. They thought about doing a Metro train or something down here, but it didn't go nowhere."

Cassie nodded, wondering how the Resistance forces had so quickly pinged her location. The Band-Aid communications had not been penetrated, she was certain. The galloping footsteps above prevented her from inspecting Jermaine's phone, but she had an idea that maybe he had communicated with someone. Any text from this area mentioning a woman on the run would easily reveal her position, or at least provide a clue as to her whereabouts. From that point, she would have been an easy find for the FBI's secret program operatives from the Valley Trauma Center.

"You better wait until it's dark out, if you got someone chasing you. I can walk out and nobody will pay me any mind. Just another black kid skipping school. Then I can come back and help you," Jermaine said.

"Why? Why would you do that? You don't know me," Cassie said.

"You talked to me more in the last hour than any of

my teachers have all year. You at least showed interest in what I'm doing," Jermaine said.

Cassie nodded, took a deep breath, and sighed. "I understand, but I can't involve you in this. If it is what I think it is, these people will kill you, Jermaine, if they think you know anything about me. They'll make it look like a gang shooting, if that."

"This is my turf," Jermaine said. He puffed his chest confidently. That's all Cassie needed was a nine-year-old kid helping her accomplish her mission. *Is this what it's come down to?*

Jermaine turned and ran through a door that led to a stairwell filled with debris. Ten minutes later, he returned, breathing heavily, his backpack slung over his shoulder.

"Four women walking the streets. White women, like you," he said.

Cassie nodded. "Did they see you?"

"Like I said, this is my hood, not theirs."

"Don't underestimate them," Cassie said. There was movement in her periphery. She instinctively reached for Jermaine and her pistol. *Protect the boy, kill the attackers.*

"That's right," a voice called out.

She pulled Jermaine behind her and snapped off two rounds at the figure moving through the doorway. The woman coming down the steps fell back, but not before firing her pistol. The bullet whizzed past her and pocked through the moldy drywall behind her. Tugging Jermaine with her, she moved toward the entrance, eyes focused on the fallen attacker. The woman's face was cocked sideways in the daylight spilling through the stairwell.

One down, three to go.

Hard breaths pumped from her lungs. She was subconsciously reaching for the juice. Images of needles, Zara, Jamie, and Jake, all swam through her mind, confusing her. She shook her head, clearing the confusion away.

"Is there another way out?" Cassie whispered.

Jermaine was staring at the dead woman, speechless.

"Jermaine!"

"Yes. Yes. Follow me." He snapped from his trance and tugged at Cassie. They ran to the far wall beyond the stairwell.

"This is a dead end," Cassie said. There was a solid wall of dirt, a stalled construction project.

Jermaine lifted a gray tarp that matched the excavated wall of dirt. On all fours, he scurried through a small tunnel. Cassie followed and found herself having to low-crawl through the muck. There were voices in the room they had just departed.

"Where'd they go?" a woman asked.

"Had to be that way," another said.

Footsteps pattered into the distance. Running. Athletes. Trained shooters. Killers. Jermaine crawled into the darkness as Cassie followed.

Had Zara set loose these assassins on her?

CHAPTER 16

Zara Perro sat in her blue velvet ergonomic chair, staring at the Potomac River, thinking about the mayhem they had unleashed on the country.

"Thanks for dumping those bodies," Zara said to Special Agent Syd Wise who was sitting across from her.

"It's what cargo elevators are made for," he replied.

Zara chuckled. "Not sure how those guys found us."

"It's crazy right now. It's wide open rebellion within the government. We were right to use convicts for this thing, you know."

"Well, it was the only way to really get their commitment. Some people pretend to be all in on our agenda, but they're just Twitter warriors, talking tough. If you can't kill someone, then what good are you? If your government tells you to fight, it's a war. If you choose to fight, it's a rebellion. This is a rebellion against tyranny."

"About right," Wise replied. "Anyway, so it worked?"

He was sitting on the low-slung gray sofa, drinking a beer. In front of him was a MacBook with blue dots on it, each one representing one of the Artemis team members. He and Zara had handpicked convicts from around the country to be at the Valley Trauma Center and then for ultimate selection onto the Artemis team. The trade was that Wise had the records of each of the women expunged. Once they had the team assembled, Wise had thought Artemis was a clever spin-off of Greek mythology, Artemis being the goddess of the hunt and twin sister of Apollo. NASA had the Artemis Project in the early 1990s, and Wise thought that if anyone intercepted their communications, they perhaps would think it was related to the NASA effort.

"*It's working* is a better way to put it," Zara said. "We just had sex and napped for thirty minutes, two things I know I needed."

"I'm always up for nailing you," Wise said.

"You say the sweetest things," Zara mocked.

"You've never appeared to me as someone who appreciates sweet things," Wise said. "I can lie, if you want me to?"

"About me or something else?" Zara pressed.

"Anything you wish," he replied.

"Why don't we focus on the facts in front of us," Zara said. She stood and moved next to him on the sofa. Leaning forward, she studied the array of images of Artemis assassins on his screen. Like a chessboard, the dead ones were square facial pictures with a red X through them. She saw the four from the action at the CIA director's home. Another two from the ambush effort that Mahegan had managed to detect and destroy. Then the six from the pier at the Daingerfield Island marina. Her force was down to fourteen.

"Another one," Wise said.

In Southeast DC, one of the chips went cold. If the chip detected a five-degree drop in body temperature, it registered a dead agent.

"Sandy McLemore," Zara said. "She was a good one."

"Not the best with a pistol, but an excellent athlete. Tennessee Prison for Women. Superb intramural program there," Wise said. Then he pointed at the screen and said, "There are three more close by. Must be the direction Cassie ran."

"They've all been on their own now for nearly forty-eight hours," she said. "You deployed each with a satchel of medication, correct?"

"The exact satchels you packed," Wise said. "This was always the tenuous part of the plan. Will they self-medicate?"

"We did enough testing before we deployed them. Of course, each one is different, but most got to the point where they relied upon medication enough."

"They have a two-day supply. The ones who are not killed, we will have to dispose of. You know that, right?"

"Yes. We discussed this," Zara said.

Looking at the screen, Wise said, "Those three are moving toward the military base, Bolling Air Force Base."

"DIA headquarters?"

"If they've got Cassie under pursuit, she's not getting in there."

"And there's a Catholic School across the street. She's got morals. Doubt she'll put at risk any teachers or staff that might still be there. We have to trap her."

"Two Metro stations. Anacostia and Congress Heights," Wise said.

"I've got another team headed there now. Two on each stop. She'd be crazy to get on a Metro. Too many cameras in the stations," Zara said. She leaned over and typed in some commands until a split screen showed the two Metro stop entrances. The signature lit *M* shone brightly in both displays. Night was falling. The escalators churned upward and downward, occasionally spilling passengers out and taking them in. Nothing remarkable was happening.

Wise pointed out of the window to the southeast, along the channel. "All of that is right there. Isn't it odd that we're watching it unfold digitally and it's all a mile or two away as the crow flies?"

"I'm typing in some algorithms that will project where she will most likely turn up," Zara said. "It doesn't strike me either way. I just want the job done so we can get on with it."

"Me too," Wise said.

She picked up the remote and said, "Might as well check in on the chaos."

CNN's Anderson Cooper was interviewing their political analyst, who was commenting.

"Anderson, I think what we are witnessing here is 'hybrid warfare.' Whether these attacks are in support or opposed to a particular person, we've seen a deterioration of our institutions under the current administration to the point that this is not unexpected. Protest has migrated to revolution in the form of armed conflict."

Cooper responded, "But don't you think this is a bit extreme?"

"Look, conservatives took pride in the Barry Goldwater saying 'Extremism in the defense of liberty is no vice. And moderation in the pursuit of justice is no virtue.' I think what we're seeing here is extremism, for sure, but is it wrongheaded if it is in defense of liberty and pursuit of justice?"

"I guess my question would be, who gets to define that? We have laws that make murder a crime. Assassinating the president, if that's what happened, and it appears that is the case, is tantamount to treason. U.S. Code makes it illegal to simply threaten to harm the president, much less kill him or her."

"I think again we are talking about the deterioration of our norms and institutions to the point where even U.S. Code may not apply. It will really be up to the Jamie Carter administration."

Cooper braced. "The Carter Administration. I haven't really heard that phrase in three years since she lost the election. What do you think a Carter administration will do in this time of utter national crisis?"

"Carter will come in and quickly take the mantle. She had an excellent, proper swearing-in ceremony. It was respectful and reminded me of Johnson being sworn in on the airplane. It happened as swiftly as possible and in an appropriate—"

"I'm sorry," Cooper said. "But I have to stop you there. We've got breaking news that the FBI is claiming that Senator, I guess now President, Jamie Carter is on a supposed 'hit list.' So the killing may not be intended to stop with the Speaker. This is a truly startling development. Next in line, of course, would be the secretary of state, General Lloyd Kinnear, who could not be reached for comment. He is on an airplane returning from Southeast Asia. The secretary of state is the fourth in line of succession for the presidency. Many of us remember the Alexander Haig statement 'I'm in charge,' when President Reagan was shot. Of course, he wasn't, but could we be looking at something inspired by that type of sentiment from a secretary with a similar background? Secretary Kinnear is a retired four star general, who certainly has gravitas and command presence. There have been, though, public squabbles between the president and General Kinnear. Also, importantly, Captain Cassie Bagwell and General Kinnear served together at Fort Bragg, North Carolina. So the plot thickens, as they say."

"Well done," Zara said.

"I try." Wise grinned.

She supposed that feeding the false narrative to his CNN contact had been easy enough.

Cooper continued with another breaking news banner flashing beneath him. "And as if there isn't enough information to sort through, there's this. A lead suspect in the case has been leaked to CNN. Her name is Cassie Bagwell. She is a captain in the U.S. Army and a Ranger who was recently wounded in combat in Iran. She had been recovering at Walter Reed Hospital in Bethesda and then at the Valley Trauma Center in Virginia. Two days ago, she apparently fled from the Valley Trauma Center, and now her DNA or fingerprints have been found at three different crime scenes, including the murder of Senator Hite. We don't have any details on how the three highest-elected officials were assassinated, other than to say that the White House doctor has confirmed the deaths of the president and vice president, and that the FBI has confirmed the death of the Speaker. Of course, Senator Hite was found dead three months ago in his North Carolina beach house. That investigation has picked up in light of recent developments, we are told by a North Carolina Special Bureau of Investigation spokesperson. Putting all of this together, we are certainly in the middle of a national crisis. Our democracy is reeling. Could it be at the hands of a disgruntled veteran?"

A CNN military analyst came on the television, saying, "This is troublesome news, Anderson. Captain Bagwell was the first female graduate of the U.S. Army Ranger School, so she definitely has the skill sets to kill people. A connection that many of your viewers have not made is that Captain Bagwell's father was the chairman of the Joint Chiefs of Staff when he and his wife, Bagwell's mother, were slaughtered in a cage by Syrian terrorists in the Blue Ridge Mountains a year ago. So not only does this veteran have post-traumatic stress disorder, traumatic brain injury, but she also has cause to blame the institutions of government for failing to stop terrorists from killing her parents."

A picture of Cassie appeared on the screen. It was her Ranger school graduation picture. She was thin with short, stringy dirty blond hair. Her cheeks appeared hollowed out from lack of food during the rigorous two-month training course. The rolled-up sleeves on her army combat uniform hung loosely around her muscled arms. The smile was disarming, and Cooper commented on that.

"Here is Captain Bagwell. Nobody knows where she is right now. Is this the face of a murderous traitor or a gleeful graduate of notoriously tough military training? More to follow on that," Cooper said.

"Wish they had used a different picture. Let's see what Faux News is having to say," Zara said. She pressed some buttons on the remote and Bret Baier's face filled the screen.

"An unbelievable development of events in the last twenty-four hours. The president, vice president, and Speaker of the House all assassinated. Former presidential candidate Senator Jamie Carter, now president, seems to be the benefactor of all of this bloodshed. Is this a coup staged on behalf of the Resistance or a foreign terrorist attack? Already the Russian and Chinese governments have made public denouncements of the bloodshed, but what does this upheaval in American politics mean for the safety and security of the country? And to add to the confusion, we have a leaked document that claims to be a credible intelligence report asserting that Jamie Carter's name is on some alleged 'hit list,' meaning she was supposed to go down in the carnage. Is it real or fake intel? Is it possible that this was a coup orchestrated to benefit one of two people, Jamie Carter or General Kinnear?"

"Good use of passive voice. Note, he doesn't accuse Jamie of anything," Zara said.

"I'm more concerned about his description of the document," Wise said.

"Surely, you know that these people are going to assume the worst. You *did* leak it."

"I do know that and yes I did. It's just unnerving to hear it laid bare like that."

"Well, better steel up for what is surely to come. There's a lot more coming at us," she said.

On cue, Baier continued: "We are just receiving reports that the goddaughter of Jamie Carter is the lead suspect in the assassinations that have rocked the nation. Recently returned from combat in Iran, Captain Cassie Bagwell was being treated at Walter Reed Military Hospital in Bethesda for gunshot and shrapnel wounds, traumatic brain injury and post-traumatic stress. The Army has made no statement yet regarding Captain Bagwell. Most striking, though, is her connection to the now-president Jamie Carter. Is this a major coincidence, or could Captain Bagwell have led what would be tantamount to a military coup? An active-duty member of the military killing the three highest-elected officials in the country is nothing short of a conspiracy on the level we haven't seen since Confederate sympathizer John Wilkes Booth assassinated President Lincoln, believing that his co-conspirators were executing their part of the plan. Captain Bagwell's fingerprints are allegedly at both crime scenes. Did she take matters into her own hands, as Booth wished he had done nearly one hundred and sixty years ago?"

Fox News showed a different image of Cassie. It was a picture of her as a lieutenant at her father's promotion to four-star general. She was smiling, but it was not the same generous grin that she was offering post–Ranger school. The picture also showed then-Senator Jamie Carter standing next to Cassie's mother.

"In this picture, we clearly see the closeness of then-Senator Carter to the Bagwell family. Our sources tell us that Captain Bagwell's mother and Senator Carter were college roommates. That relationship led to the

Bagwells asking Jamie Carter to be the godmother to Cassie Bagwell thirty years ago."

"This has a spin I don't like," Zara said.

"What do you expect. It's Fox?"

"Still, the undertone is that Cassie killed for her godmother. That's counterproductive."

"Jamie was nowhere near anything that was happening. She's clean. There are no communications between her and Cassie. There's no trace of how she got to DC," Wise said.

"I'm sure we stayed as much off the radar as possible, but still," Zara said.

Zara's mind spun. Who might have seen her with Cassie? There was the driver that picked Cassie and her up at the airport. Then there was whoever might have seen two dark figures in the night near the CIA compound where the president and vice president were killed. Had anyone seen them in the elevator to her place, coming or going? She had intentionally left Cassie behind at Daingerfield Island so that she could kill the Speaker with the signature of Team Artemis. Had anyone connected that Cassie was the drowned rat coming into the condo building and heading up to her place?

"Okay then. No spinning our wheels on this. Who else should be on the Committee of Public Safety?" Zara asked.

"Well, just you and me now. I'm not sure we need to broaden the aperture too much. We've got a lot of borderline stuff going on."

"Please, the media will eat this up and put stiff winds behind our sails."

"Maybe. That's actually a good thought. Which of the mainstream-media personalities would you like to pull in? An established figure or give some newcomer a break?" Wise pondered.

"I'm thinking that hot, new chick on CNN would be good. Who did you give the tip to?"

"Great minds think alike. You're talking about Rae Lantini, who was more than happy to run with my story," Wise said.

"Okay, good. She's always bashing Smart, getting thrown out of the press pool trying to be the new Acosta, and just emotional enough to work inside for us, I think. I used to leak to her during the campaign. Trial balloon info. Jamie Carter is thinking about lowering taxes on middle class, for example, and then we'd watch the reaction on Twitter and other social media," Zara explained.

"Add her to the list. She trusts me. But being on the committee means making decisions to kill people. Think she'll be okay with that?" Wise asked.

"More than okay. She's pretty rabidly anti-Smart. SDS, the whole works."

Smart Derangement Syndrome.

"Tread carefully. Dealing with the media is like petting a shark, holding a snake by the midsection, whatever dangerous creature metaphor you want to pick."

"Got it," Zara said, flipping through her phone, looking for Rae's contact information.

On the computer, the algorithms spit out the results of Cassie's likely path, which led to either the Anacostia or Congress Heights Metro.

"Let's start there." Zara pointed.

"Got it. Sending alert now," Wise said. He typed a brief sentence that was digitally transmitted like a text message to all Artemis team members: Patient 17 at Anacostia Metro. K/C.

"Kill or capture?" Zara asked.

"Yes. You have a better idea?"

"Why the capture? What good is she to us? She's already implicated in the assassinations. Alive, she can only hurt us. Dead, she can only help us."

Wise nodded and typed: Correction. Patient 17 at Anacostia Metro. K only.

CHAPTER 17

Mahegan, Owens, Hobart, and Van Dreeves huddled around O'Malley's computer in the CIA safe house near Nationals Park stadium. With all of the new construction, the CIA had wisely purchased an end-unit row house in a mixed-income community that had a two-car garage and a basement.

A designer had appointed the home with Colonial-style furniture. Lots of antiques and hardwoods. Bookcases lined the study, one of which was a trapdoor to the basement. The basement was reinforced with steel plates in the walls, which allowed it to double as a holding cell. Heavy mauve drapes covered the Lexan bulletproof and blast-resistant windows. Biagatti had a Lexan glassed in cell built for purposes of holding detainees off location, should the need ever arise. The 15-by-15-foot cell jutted out from the far right corner about thirty feet from the stairway.

"Look, this might sound wild, but I've been tracking unusual comms traffic in the DC area. I'm able to weed out ninety-nine percent of the normal bullshit, like routine phone calls and texts, and look for new systems or networks. I've got something that looks weird. See these blue dots, about fifteen of them in Southeast DC?"

His finger nearly touched the MacBook screen. There were three blue dots near the Anacostia Metro, with two more closing in, with another two blue dots near the Congress Heights Metro. Not far to the north was a red dot, and there were another eight blue dots scattered elsewhere throughout the city.

"What is it?" Mahegan asked. He thought he might know, but wanted to hear O'Malley's assessment. Also, based upon Cassie's latest communication, he believed that this was some type of force closing in on Cassie.

"Honestly? It looks like Blue Force Tracking. What every army combat unit uses to provide real-time situational awareness."

Mahegan left the study and walked along the hall filled with pictures of famous landmarks around DC. The Washington Monument. Vietnam Veterans Memorial. Lincoln. Jefferson. He entered the family room and pressed the Band-Aid on his mastoid bone behind his ear. An audible beep told him the line was still operational.

"Go," Cassie said. She was breathing heavily.

"You've got five at Alpha and two at Charlie Hotel."

"Roger."

"Need help?"

"Send me their locations."

"Roger. Stand by."

Mahegan walked into the study and said, "Sean, send Cassie the locations on her BLEPS."

O'Malley looked at Mahegan, then turned and entered some commands into the computer. From the rustling sounds, Cassie was apparently digging through her rucksack, looking for her ballistic eye protection, or BLEP. As part of the communications upgrade, Mahegan's team had an advanced form of Google Glass and the heads-up display could be shown through either glasses or contact lenses. Cassie had both, but he guessed that since Cassie was in a combat scenario, she would opt for the clear-plastic eye protection.

As O'Malley was working, Owens said to Mahegan, "Why can't we have Sean just hack it and issue a stand-down order?"

O'Malley overheard and said, "I can probably do that—"

"No, don't," Cassie interrupted. "This is my decision. We need to have them all exposed."

"A lot of risk," Mahegan said.

"And then what? They go in hiding and they'll keep coming after me."

"Stand-down order and go public," Owens said. "Could work."

Hobart and Van Dreeves stood watch from the side of the window and front door, respectively.

"No. Again, this is my decision," Cassie said. "We do this my way. I'm the one taking the risks. Put me on with Sean."

"No need, Cassie," Mahegan said. Then to O'Malley: "Don't give any orders. Just provide the locations."

After a few more seconds, O'Malley turned and looked over his shoulder and said, "Okay, she should have it. Three-D terrain and whatever tracking devices they're using."

"Got it, Cass?"

"Just a sec," she said.

The tension in the room had grown tenfold. All eyes were on Mahegan, thinking about Cassie, the mission, and maybe even their relationship. Cassie was surrounded and on the run. The world believed that she assassinated the president, vice president, and Speaker. The stakes could not have been higher.

"Yes. I've got it. And . . . thanks."

"We need you back. You're the only one who can pin this on Zara and Jamie."

"Love you, too."

"Roger. Be safe."

"Out."

Mahegan didn't like the odds of seven to one, but respected Cassie's intuition. The intel feed should help, but still. She had done well so far, though. Her bruised body and mind had endured chemical torture imposed by Zara at the Valley Trauma Center. The only reason Mahegan and team had not raided the center was the age-old dilemma of developing enough intel to actually know what was happening versus acting too soon and potentially making the wrong call or planning the wrong type of operation. Cassie had actually suggested her infiltration to the Valley Trauma Center when Jake had visited her one day at Walter Reed.

*   *   *

"We're getting intel that Resistance members are training in the Blue Ridge," Mahegan says.

"What kind of training? Where?"

"Reports of firearms training and hand-to-hand combat. Someplace called the Valley Trauma Center. It's part of a conglomerate owned by a billionaire who supported Senator Carter's bid for the presidency."

"Who are they recruiting?"

"Seems that the women are athletic, intelligent, and young, like you."

"And their mission is what?"

"We don't know that yet. Just some chatter about training. We've got voices on signals intelligence. Have matched a few. Moles within the government appear to be working with the Resistance outside the government."

"So it's an attack? What?"

"We're not sure. We need more intel."

Cassie pauses, thinking. "Get me there. If they do brain injury stuff."

"It doesn't work like that. You have to be invited there."

"Jamie Carter is coming to see me tomorrow. Maybe she can help."

"Be careful. Think this through, Cassie."

They had done their best to think through the second- and third-order effects. The plan was simple. Get Cassie into the Valley Trauma Center and let her report out to Mahegan on what she was seeing and hearing. They had not expected the extreme drugging, but it made sense in retrospect. Zara Perro was a psychiatrist who had experimented on a range of post-traumatic stress therapies. Once they had identified her as a central player in the VTC, the end game became clearer: this was going to benefit Jamie Carter, whose campaign Zara had worked for.

Cassie's plan to get into the center had worked, but the ultimate success remained to be seen. She was presently outnumbered seven to one in Southeast DC. Could she continue to flee, drawing out the Resistance fighters? As the rabbit, her mission was to keep running until they made a mistake.

Of course, to keep running, she needed to stay alive.

Mahegan pulled out of his thoughts when O'Malley said, "Look. They have a kill order out on Cassie."

"Who is *they*?"

"I'm pinging the IP address right now. It's pretty well-disguised, but I've found a way in, I think." Then after a brief pause, O'Malley's eyes grew wide. "Holy shit, the mother ship. This is an FBI protocol coming from Zara Perro's apartment less than two miles from here."

"Okay, saddle up, guys. Sean, you and Patch stay here and monitor Cassie. Be prepared to react at my command. She's near the Anacostia Metro. Hobart and VD, you're with me."

"Roger that," they all seemed to say in unison. Finally a mission they could sink their teeth into.

Mahegan made a quick trip upstairs to check on Biagatti. She was in the bedroom, fully clothed, lying on the bed with her hands clasped on her stomach as if she were in a casket.

"Yes?" she said, opening one eye.

"We've got a lead we're going to follow," Mahegan said.

"You sound like Magnum, PI. What's your intel?"

"Zara Perro is operating a command-and-control operation out of her apartment here in DC," Mahegan said.

"What is she commanding and controlling?"

"Looks like about fifteen assassins," he said.

"Let me know how it turns out. I'm resting for now."

"Roger that." Mahegan turned, noticed two cell phones on her nightstand, and departed.

Running back down the steps, he bolted into the garage, where Hobart and Van Dreeves were waiting. They sped out in the Panamera, loaded with weapons and intel.

CHAPTER 18

Cassie stood on a metal ladder and pushed at a manhole cover. She managed to move it to the side. To her front, left, and right was a fence. The manhole cover was next to a public restroom, which was directly behind her. The stink of urine permeated the tunnel, the restroom, and now her clothes.

She thought of Jermaine and how the run-down tenement led to his private tunnel, which connected to this culvert. Jermaine had helped. She looked at him and hoped he was okay.

The reception on her BLEP heads-up display improved dramatically once she popped her head from the tunnel. Immediately, she saw the blue Metro sign lit up like a beacon. Inside her BLEP, the heads up display showed blue images moving in on her location. There was one red image that was stationary. She imagined that was the woman she had killed. The blue moving pieces were trying to box her in. As Jake had told her, there were five dots moving toward the Ana-costia Station and two toward the Congress Heights Station.

As she studied the lens, three of the dots were lined up, one behind another, nearly directly behind her; then they disappeared from the BLEP display.

The assassins were in the tunnel, coming in from behind her. The same way she and Jermaine had fled.

"We've got to move. Do you know your way around?"

"I take the Metro to school some days," Jermaine said.

"The women trying to kill me are in the tunnel be-hind us."

"Let me up. I have an idea," Jermaine said.

Cassie kept her eyes on the field in front of her, knowing that half the threat was in front of them. She climbed out of the hole and slid onto the nasty concrete pad outside of the brick restroom. Cigarette butts, con-doms, and beer cans littered the ground.

Jermaine popped from the tunnel and ran in the op-posite direction, backpack slung over his shoulder. "Be right back," he called.

There were two women walking quickly, almost like Stepford Wives, their heads turning slowly in uni-son, searching . . . hunting. They were about a hundred meters away on the other side of the fence that cor-doned off the park.

A minute later, Jermaine was back with a steel rebar rod and a bike lock.

"This may not fit, but it doubles as a weapon," Jer-maine said. Voices floated upward from the tunnel. They were close. To emphasize that point, the blue dots reappeared on the BLEP, nearly overlapping their position.

They nudged the manhole cover back into place as a shot pinged off the heavy metal.

"Hurry," Cassie said.

More shots peppered the circular shield, feeling like drumbeats. One bullet escaped from the narrowing gap, whizzing past Cassie's arm. The plate set in the rim as Jermaine tried to loop the bike lock through the hasp. He nearly had it when the cover thumped upward and rested above the rim. Two of the attackers below had to be pushing up. Cassie forced the cover back onto the rim against constant pressure from below.

Jermaine slid the lock through the hasp on one side and then the other, snapping it shut. Still, the manhole cover rattled, allowing a gap for pistols to snake through. Cassie kicked at them and then jammed her pistol into the opening, firing five muffled shots that echoed through the tunnel.

The pressure on the cover ebbed. Her BLEPs still showed blue dots. Maybe it took a while for them to turn red or maybe no one was killed. Either way, Cassie pulled Jermaine to the other side of the brick building. Open fields in each direction. She changed magazines, clicking one out and one in with a magician's sleight of hand. A playground with swings and slides was behind them. The women at the Metro had stopped and were pressing their hands to their ears.

Communicating.

"Listen, Jermaine, you've been a huge help. Please go home or wherever is safest for you, because this is about to get really ugly," Cassie said.

"Like that was beautiful?"

If she wasn't out of time, she would have laughed and hugged him, but the women at the Metro snapped their heads up, looked in their direction, and began running.

"Go. Now!" Cassie hissed.

Jermaine saw the women running toward the fence and ran in the opposite direction, toward the playground.

Cassie edged behind the building. If they enveloped her, there would be little chance of surviving. She needed to pick one off at a distance and deal with the other, however she presented herself.

Two of the three blue dots in her heads-up display turned red. One was still alive. With each train entering the station, there was a rumble beneath her feet. Nosing around the brick building, she aimed. One woman was on a knee aiming in her direction, covering the woman climbing the fence. At one hundred meters, it was a low-percentage shot. But Cassie was good and she had refreshed her training at the VTC, moving from ten to twenty-five to fifty and then seventy-five meters. She had scored above 90 percent on those ranges, while the instructors yelled at her.

Cassie waited until the woman had her back exposed to her. The fence climber was about to flip over when her shirt got caught on an exposed twist of chain link. Cassie fired twice and retreated behind the restroom, barely in enough time. Two bullets chipped dusty brick into her face.

Cassie came around the other side to do battle damage assessment. It took her opponent a second to fire two more rounds at her. The shots sang through the night. Would residents consider this another typical DC gunfight or something different? There was a lump at the bottom of the fence. She'd hit her target. But still, the two blue dots remained. If she could hit at one hundred yards with her pistol, then she might as well try it again. She spun behind the building, this time coming back out the same side. The woman had stayed in the same spot on one knee, her pistol through the chain-link diamond.

Cassie popped off another two-round burst and spun behind the building. Three shots sprayed the edge of the restroom. Sirens began to wail in the distance. Apparently, not another typical DC evening. She couldn't continue to trade fire, especially with the one blue dot backing out of the tunnel, and another two blue dots moving quickly down from Congress Heights Metro Station. Four attackers coming at her from three directions.

The one advantage she had was that she could see their positions, yet they ostensibly could not see her location. Thankfully, Rax had helped her remove the chip, which had seemed like a lifetime ago. Her back stung at the thought, the retrieval incision still fresh. With sirens becoming louder, Cassie had limited options. She was pinned from the east, north, and south by women wanting to kill her. The police would be on the scene in minutes, if not seconds.

The manhole cover with the bike lock through it loomed large in front of her. Though the blue dot had faded, the attacker from the north was most likely still in the tunnel. If moving at the same rate Cassie had moved, the woman would be out shortly. She would come out of the ramshackle row houses near the back stoop where Cassie had killed the single attacker who had entered through the stairwell.

Her best play was to reenter the tunnel and back-track through the tenement. She would still have the river to contend with, but night had fallen, making it much easier to blend into the mayhem as she moved through Ward 8. Retrieving her Leatherman, she low-crawled over the stench and detritus to the manhole cover. She snuck a peek at the fence where the shooter had been; Cassie didn't see her. Either she had relocated, or Cassie had scored a hit. One dot near the fence was still blue in her heads-up display, while the one climbing the fence had turned red.

A kill probably registered when the body temperature fell below a specific threshold, Cassie figured. She had the wire cutter function gnawing at the bike lock. She only needed one side free so that she could lift it against the other hasp, which would act like a hinge. There was an audible click when the wire cutters snipped through the bike lock's twisted metal. Looping a finger through the released hasp, she tried to lift, but it barely budged.

She grabbed the rebar, which Jermaine had left behind, and braced it against her thigh to lift the heavy plate. After getting it a few inches off the rim, she slid her backpack under it, dropped the rebar, and pried back the heavy lid until it clanked backward.

The sirens whooped directly across the street. Blue

lights bounced off the glass dome of the Metro, refracting into the sky. Distracted by that and the BLEP appearance of another blue dot directly on top of her location, Cassie hustled into the hole.

"Hey, bitch," a woman said in the darkness.

Cassie pressed her body to the side as four shots sparked off the metal ladder from no more than five feet away. She returned fire, but the woman rushed her, knife at the ready. Cassie ducked, barely escaping the powerful thrust. She tackled the woman with a forward lunge, but not without exposing her back to the hammering knife blade. She felt repeated punches into her backpack until she had the woman on her side and the knife hand was coming at her face.

Parrying the thrust, Cassie grabbed the powerful forearm of the woman. She was close enough now to smell the foul breath and see the clenched teeth. Eyes wild with fury, fueled no doubt by Zara's concoction. Hisses and quick breaths. Claustrophobia closing in. Pain in her back. Blood oozing down and pooling at her waist.

She repeatedly slammed the attacker's knife hand against the dirt wall until it fell to the floor. Cassie quickly slipped her Blackhawk knife from its sheath and sliced upward across the woman's face, then drove it into her heart.

Footsteps above. No time. Blood curling over her hands. She retrieved her knife with a wet sucking sound, collapsed the blade, and slid it back into the sheath. As she stepped over the dying woman, there was a small rucksack tucked against the wall.

Must be this dead assassin's bag.

She grabbed that and lowered into a fast crawl in the opposite direction, away from the manhole cover. Before long, she lost wireless connection through her BLEPs, one rucksack on her back and one in her hands.

She was making decent progress when she noticed a reflection off her BLEPs. The yellow glow of a flashlight glinted off the polycarbonate lens. She was almost at the mouth where she and Jermaine had entered earlier.

"Down here. In this room. She's got to be here somewhere," a woman's voice said.

She stopped, took a sharp breath. The flashlight continued its awkward arc. The voice was louder.

"Somewhere in here. That's where the others went."

The sole person who could expose the conspiracy—had seen it all firsthand and could testify to Zara's and Jamie's crimes—Cassie knew she needed to survive. Both the police and Jamie Carter probably had shoot-to-kill orders on her. She was trapped.

There was only one way out.

She opened the rucksack of the woman she had just killed and scrounged through it, finding used syringes.

"C'mon, damnit," she hissed. A junkie needing a fix. She unzipped an inner pouch padded with foam on either side. "Yes."

She retrieved the remaining two vials of DHT-and-Flakka mix, placing one in her rucksack and using her teeth to pull the protective plastic nose off the other. She retrieved her Maglite, running out of precious seconds, spit out the plastic, and clenched the flashlight in her teeth. She rolled up her sleeve, tightening it around her bicep to make her vein pop, found the vein, and slipped the needle in.

Pushing the plunger with her thumb, she felt the fire spread through her veins. Her mind gained clarity like an evaporating California marine layer suddenly giving way to the stark clarity of the unmitigated sun.

She was going to kill her way out of this tunnel and then, if necessary, kill the president of the United States.

CHAPTER 19

Mahegan exited the vehicle with Hobart and Van Dreeves on his flanks. They boarded an MH-6 Little Bird helicopter with canvas wing seats. He checked his phone and saw that Cassie's icon had disappeared.

Probably in the tunnel.

There were more red dots than blue dots on the app O'Malley had loaded into his phone. He had been able to mirror the communications and tracking data emanating from Zara's condo at the Wharf.

They took off from a soccer field a mile from the safe house. General Savage had repositioned aviation assets last week in preparation for clandestine operations. The blades whispered overhead as they lifted off and flew low along the Washington Channel, the black helicopter blending with the dark water. The musty smell of the water wafted upward as if pulled in by the rotors. Mahegan rode alone on the starboard side, with Hobart and Van Dreeves on port. Their approach to the penthouse apartment would put them on the roof, from which they planned to scale down onto the terrace.

They passed the Nationals baseball stadium and Fort McNair, the general's massive brick mansions lining the riverfront. The helicopter lifted from the river and tilted between two high rises at the Wharf, then powered straight up to the roof of the target building.

"Ready," Mahegan said.

"Roger," Hobart replied.

"Standing by," Van Dreeves said.

They were each wearing the new Band-Aid communications system that allowed them to operate hands free. The helicopter alighted on the roof like a dragonfly on a grass blade. Mahegan and team were off in less than a second, and the helicopter was away into the night.

And, in fact, they *were* on grass blades. The roof was one of those green spaces, a park on top of the building. Kneeling on the grassy rectangle nearly twenty meters long and wide, Mahegan studied the rooftop. Low boxwood shrubs hemmed in the lawn. Beyond that were other squares of grass, punctuated by ventilation stacks, fireplace chimneys, HVAC systems, and a satellite dish. Van Dreeves had a 120-foot nylon rope coiled across his chest. They each carried silenced pistols, Mahegan his trusty Sig Sauer Tribal with suppressor. As they moved, the dirt and grass insulated the sound of their steps.

"Status," O'Malley said into Mahegan's earpiece.

"Green," Mahegan replied, confirming they had made rooftop landing.

On such short notice, they'd had little time to study

the apartment other than a layout from the condominium website. Given Zara Perro's level of preparation for this coup, Mahegan was assuming the floor-to-ceiling windows were bulletproof and that the two-story penthouse condominium had a server room for all of the high-tech computing that O'Malley had discovered.

The terrace was wide and surrounded the condo on three sides. To the right, or south, was the largest section with a Jacuzzi, small infinity pool, and barbecue grill. The east-facing terrace would catch the sun rising over the Potomac River. A sofa framed by two chairs seemed positioned to take advantage of that feature. The north terrace provided a view of Capitol Hill and the Mall. More chairs and a hammock secured between two metal poles dotted the stone inlay decking.

The question had been, do they penetrate as a team at one point, or individually from two or three points? Not knowing what was inside, Mahegan preferred to have mass and brutality of action. He had opted for the brute-force method of mass penetration at a single point. Hobart was the explosives expert in the group and had two blocks of C-4, detonation cord, and blasting caps. He also carried three smoke grenades.

"Check the chimney," Mahegan said.

Hobart walked carefully to the rectangular metal stack, peered over, quickly shone a flashlight down the hole, and took a knee. Looking over his shoulder, he flashed a thumbs-up, which meant the flue was open and they could drop a smoke grenade, if it came to that. He had the pin pulled.

Mahegan considered his options and still preferred the three-on-two odds, provided there were only Zara and her FBI accomplice inside. He didn't like the idea of smoke confusing the situation and providing a slight warning to Zara Perro and whoever was in there with her.

Normally, they would do a recon, but they had operational intelligence and Mahegan knew the information was perishable—that they needed to act now even if it meant not having a fully developed intelligence picture. They had confirmation that the directives were emanating from the condominium directly below them. A quick search of the records had shown Perro Enterprises as the owner of the condo. She either had not thought much about disguising her digital footprint or she had cleverly set a trap.

Either way, they were going in.

"Sean, any change?"

"Steady output of comms from the satellite dish you're standing next to," O'Malley said.

"We're on top of correct unit?"

"Yes," O'Malley said.

The Band-Aid communications devices also doubled as a soldier-monitoring system. Body temperature, location, hydration status, sleep cycle, pulse, and other key information fed to O'Malley's data collection efforts.

Van Dreeves had moved to the lip of the roof that ended just above the north patio. He held up his hand and made a fist: *don't move.*

Voices floated up toward them through an open window or balcony door.

"I can't believe that we've lost that many," Zara

Perro said. Mahegan clearly recognized the lyrical voice with a hint of Hispanic accent.

"All we can do is continue," a man's voice said. He didn't recognize it, but by the cadence of their conversation, they seemed to be the only two in the apartment. There was no *Hey, let's step outside,* or whispering voices. Just normal conversation, as if they were on a Netflix and chill date.

Mahegan held up his fist so that Hobart could see it. He had begun to step and laid his foot softly on the gravel roof, next to the chimney about ten meters from the grass square where Mahegan was standing. The night was still. Revelers from the Wharf twenty-five stories below hooted at something. An airplane circled in for a landing at Reagan National. Cars honked and crept along I-395 in both directions. The lights from the Jefferson Memorial cast an upward glow against the thin layer of clouds that had crept in.

Frozen in time.

Mahegan saw Van Dreeves lower himself and immediately knew why. A man walked to the edge of the balcony. The top of his head was visible. The old Army mantra rolled through Mahegan's mind: *What could be seen could be hit. What could be hit could be killed.*

But there was no confirmation that this man had anything to do with Cassie or the Coup Assassinations.

"I'll tell you what, gorgeous," he said. He could be any man trying to get laid. Using his best lines, being what they were. "You've got a great view up here. This place had to run you, what, five million? I'm wondering if I should have the FBI investigate your financial background."

FBI. We're in the right place.

"Wouldn't do you any good. All of my money comes from the Chinese in the form of bribes for classified information. That wouldn't be of any interest to the chief of counterintelligence, would it?"

"Nope. We pass that stuff up to focus on important things, like presidential elections when one party isn't happy with the result."

Zara laughed. "Well, she should be happy enough tonight."

"She should be, but this thing is far from over. You have to know that."

The man was quick with his pistol. He spun, had it up, and was firing at the rooftop near Van Dreeves. Mahegan rolled forward and pumped two rounds at him, but the man had cleverly run into the dead space beneath the overhang. Zara appeared on the opposite side, pistol up and firing. They were pinned on the roof, a small patch of grass their only safe haven.

"Smoke now!"

Hobart tossed a smoke grenade on either side of them, obscuring their positions, then one down the smokestack. Bullets snapped through the developing fog.

Then Van Dreeves, who never said much, shouted, "I'm hit!"

Mahegan low-crawled to him, the smoke beginning to provide sufficient screen. Hobart returned fire against Zara on the south, while Mahegan fired two blind shots over the lip of the roof to the north. He kept his pistol angled almost at ninety degrees to prevent from firing wildly over the railing into the civilian population that might be on the street twenty-five stories below.

Directly beneath him was the sound of the slider closing. Rustling in the condo. The target possibly getting away. Then next to him was Van Dreeves bleeding on the roof.

"Where?" he asked.

Van Dreeves was lying on his side, eyes wide. "Neck," he said.

The blood was pouring profusely from his trapezoid, not his neck.

"Through and through on your trap, VD. Your neck's fine," Mahegan said.

Van Dreeves nodded and winced as Mahegan applied pressure from a wadded cloth. Hobart brought the aid bag over and patched up Van Dreeves in five seconds, enough time for Zara and her man to escape.

Van Dreeves got to one knee and shook it off, like a wide receiver taking a big hit in a football game. Mahegan and Van Dreeves jumped onto the terrace on the east side. Hobart followed and they had their three-man stack going into the apartment. The automatic blinds were lowering in sync on each side, giving them a diminishing view of Zara grabbing a pistol and running to another part of the condo. The man had turned his back to them and was scooping up a MacBook and stuffing it into a duffel bag. Thick gray smoke was billowing from the fireplace, toward the elevator shaft as Mahegan entered, preventing Zara and her man from finding the gaping doors.

As his team entered the condo from the terrace, shots cut through the haze. Mahegan saw movement toward a bedroom and returned fire. Hobart was to his left, along the south end, the riverside of the apartment. Van Dreeves was to his right, stepping into the kitchen, his wounded trapezoid muscle painting the white gauze red. Mahegan was in the living room, the smoke coming at him like an Iraqi sandstorm. Soon the entire place was a blanket of smoke. It was cutting both ways: blocking Zara's withdrawal, but preventing them from finding good targets in an unfamiliar condominium.

The floor plan they had studied briefly prior to the mission was useful. Mahegan determined that at least Zara was in the master bedroom. There was an escape through the master bath into a back hallway that led to the general-population elevators and a fire escape.

Standing in the fog, Mahegan said, "Check fire." He didn't want any friendlies hurt and at the moment it was difficult to tell where his own team was located.

The sprinklers reacted to the smoke, spraying the condo with water, reminding Mahegan of his jungle training in Panama when he walked through torrential downpours. The water doused the grenade that had kicked from the faux logs onto the floor of the living room. A sofa to his right and two chairs to his left came into view. Like darkness gives way to dawn, the receding smoke began to show the condo in full relief. Mahegan cleared onto the south terrace where there were two oxygen tanks—the ones from the CIA safe house where the president and vice president had met. He knew that Cassie had been here, but this tangible reminder made it all the more real and reminded him of the danger she was in at this very moment.

Van Dreeves, perhaps pumped on adrenaline and pissed off about being shot, fired three quick shots toward the elevator. Mahegan moved toward the hallway adjoining the master bedroom in time to see the doorway slam shut.

Zara was loose in the hallway. Mahegan began to pursue, but her accomplice leapt from the fog bank near the elevator and tackled him. The blind side hit had turned a defendable thrust into something he had to contend with at the moment, disrupting his momentum. Mahegan rolled to his right, found a familiar wrestling position, and used his leverage to flip his attacker on his back in the narrow hallway. He snatched his Blackhawk knife from his ankle, flipped it open, and sliced at the man's arm.

The hallway door opened, and Zara fired two rounds at Mahegan. Instead, she hit his attacker, who stared at Mahegan with wide, dying eyes.

Mahegan shoved the man off him, raced into the hallway to find firefighters and building security coming his way. A haze of smoke lingered in the hallway, partially obscuring him. Zara's footsteps echoed sharply in the fire escape across the hall.

He pressed the Band-Aid pad and said, "Immediate pickup."

Returning to the condo, he found Hobart picking clean the ID, cell phone, and weapons from the man.

"Let's go," Mahegan said. "Rooftop, now."

They filed out of the condo, found the ladder on the south side, and climbed back up to the grassy square. The MH-6 materialized and seemed not to stop as Mahegan and his two men slid seamlessly onto the bench seats. Flying low along the channel, they reversed the process and passed the baseball park before turning into Southeast Washington, DC. They landed on the soccer field and jumped into the Panamera to return to the safe house. During the drive, Mahegan tried the Band-Aid comms with Cassie, but got no response. When they pulled into the garage, Biagatti, O'Malley, and Owens met them at the door.

"Shit show?" Biagatti asked.

"Sort of," Mahegan said. "We surprised them. They surprised us. We were probably clumsier than we should have been, but we got intel. VD needs you to look at his trap, Patch. Any status on Cassie?"

They pushed past Biagatti into the living room adjacent to the study where O'Malley had established his command and control center. Owens, who had always been the team medic, placed a towel on the sofa, nudged Van Dreeves onto it, and then retrieved his aid bag. After a quick inspection of the wound, Owens said, "Shit job fixing it, whoever did it."

"That was me, hero," Hobart said. "Brain surgeon couldn't have done a better job."

"That's because VD doesn't have a brain," Owens said.

"Just clean it and stitch it, Patch" Mahegan said.

"Roger, boss. Honestly, it does look bad," Owens said. "Might want to call a chaplain."

"Oh, fuck you, Patch, just give me some morphine and flush it so I don't get sepsis," Van Dreeves said.

Meanwhile, Biagatti had come into the living room. She stared at Van Dreeves's messy wound and said, "He needs to go to the hospital."

"We've got it, Director. This is what we do."

"I don't care what you think you can do, I'm saying he needs to go to the hospital. Walter Reed is thirty minutes from here. Ten, if you take the Little Bird."

"Okay, we will stabilize him first," Mahegan said.

"Looks stable to me," she said.

"Let us do our job, Director," Mahegan said. "You focus on the big stuff."

Biagatti looked at Jake with a steady gaze and said, "I reserve the right to send him." Then she walked into the kitchen and poured herself a Tito's neat from the freezer. Mahegan turned toward Owens and whispered, "WTF," then shrugged and said, "I'll clean it and stitch it and we can go from there."

"Roger. Thanks," Mahegan said.

"Now that that's settled, we've had no comms with Cassie since you left. What intel do we have?" O'Malley asked.

"This," Hobart said, dumping the wallet, cell phone, FBI badge, and pistol onto the table next to O'Malley's computer array.

O'Malley whistled a long, low-pitched sound. "FBI. The plot thickens."

"We knew there was a chance of this," Mahegan said.

"We did. We have one Sydney Wise, chief of counterterrorism in the FBI. And he was not there to apprehend her?"

"Maybe to have sex is a better guess."

"Where is Mr. Wise now?"

"Dead on the floor. Zara shot him. She had a clean

shot on both of us and she chose him," Mahegan said. His shirt was covered in blood and bits of flesh from the spatter. "I didn't give her a chance for both."

"We've got a dead FBI guy in Zara's apartment. And a major coup under way," O'Malley said. Owens was working on Van Dreeves on the sofa. The blood was flowing, but had slowed. Biagatti watched with silent consent. The furniture could be replaced, Van Dreeves not so much.

"We don't have much time," Biagatti said. "If Syd Wise was killed in Zara Perro's apartment, then the cops have him by now. We need to track what they are doing and saying. The FBI is going to go nuclear over this. I should call Director Clancy."

Melvin Clancy, a former Marine judge advocate general, was the director of the FBI. President Smart had appointed the JAG two-star general after the rampant scandals and cover-ups that ran amok during the end of the previous administration and beginning of the new one.

"Let's hold off on that one, Director," Mahegan said. "I'd rather know who's who in the zoo before we go pulling other people into this." Then to O'Malley, "Run the phone, Sean."

"Roger." O'Malley plugged the Droid into a USB cable that was connected to his computer. He tapped on the keyboard and a program began pulling the calls, texts, e-mails, photos, and other data from the phone. Biagatti floated to the adjacent room behind the sofa, where Owens was operating on Van Dreeves. The iron smell of blood permeated both rooms. Owens's quick hands were flitting about Van Dreeves's shoulder, cleaning, washing, flushing, stitching, and bandaging. Biagatti gazed down with a look that indicated she might be concerned about how they were going to discard the sofa. Hobart was standing toward the back of the room, staring at the array of camera feeds. Always the sentry.

O'Malley looked over his shoulder and then at Mahegan. He began speaking in a low voice so that the others in the room across the hallway might not hear them.

"Okay, Wise's last several days of texts off a secure app were to someone with the username Cardinal. Wise was Lancer. I'll read them to you."

O'Malley read the conversational thread aloud:

> Lancer: Relationship building going well.
> Cardinal: Keep working it. Need to know plan.
> Lancer: Roger.
> Cardinal: And then . . .
> Lancer: Getting fragments.
> Cardinal: Need entire picture.
> Lancer: Working it.
> Cardinal: Work harder. Not much time left.
> Lancer: Mission Accomplished. Congrats.
> Cardinal: Still something off. Can't place it.
> Lancer: The Indian and his team are all over this.
> Cardinal: Kill them then. Team Artemis is up for the challenge.
> Lancer: Roger.
> Cardinal: Cassie is pinned down. Think that's about over.

Lancer: Tough woman. But will redirect Artemis upon BDA.

Cardinal: Won't last much longer now.

"And that was the extent of their communications," O'Malley finished. "Wise is obviously Lancer. The assassins who prosecuted the coup are Team Artemis. But who's Cardinal?"

Mahegan felt a thrum in the back of his mind. He worked through several different combinations of thoughts and memories, then recalled the brooch that Jamie Carter was wearing earlier today.

"What is the state bird of Virginia?" Mahegan asked.

"We're into the flora and fauna now?" O'Malley smirked.

"Look it up. I bet it's the cardinal," Mahegan said.

O'Malley typed in some commands. "You're right. And this means what?"

"The state bird of North Carolina is also the cardinal," Mahegan said.

"Impressive knowledge of state birds, boss," O'Malley said.

"Who is the only senator to ever serve from both Virginia and North Carolina?" Mahegan asked. He was working his way through the problem verbally. "And who was wearing a cardinal pin at the swearing in?"

"Why do we care about that? Besides, it called a brooch," Biagatti said, walking into the study where Mahegan and O'Malley were free-associating their way through the evidence.

O'Malley said, "But, holy shit."

"That's right. Jamie Carter could be Cardinal. Perhaps she's been calling the shots all along. But why did Zara kill Wise?"

Mahegan tapped O'Malley on the shoulder, urging him to play along. They already knew who Cardinal was, but keeping Biagatti engaged was key.

"Because, alive, he could give up her and her boss," O'Malley said.

"Or Wise was clean. Was he undercover as a Counter Terrorism guy?"

Owens came back in, hands bloody.

"Van Dreeves will make it," he said.

"That's unfortunate," O'Malley quipped.

"I'm standing right here, O'Malley," Van Dreeves said from over Owens's shoulder.

"Then you'll be interested in what I have to say," O'Malley said. "We've got two possibilities. First, Wise is a good guy who was man-to-man coverage, so to speak, on Perro. Or he was a bad guy liaising and coordinating with her. Either way, he was communicating with someone with the code name Cardinal, who we think is Jamie Carter."

"She was wearing a cardinal brooch at her inauguration. The cardinal is the state bird of both North Carolina and Virginia, the two states she had been senator from. She is the one to benefit most from a hat trick of killing the top three elected officials in the country."

"A lot of circumstantial evidence. You're talking about the president of the United States now. What you do know is that you saw Zara kill Wise when she had the shot on you. Why would she do that? If there's anyone in all of this mess that stands out as an objective nonpolitical player, Jake, it's you. You seek the truth.

Justice. It has always been your way, according to Bob Savage and what I've seen of you for the past month. If Zara were an enemy of the state, why wouldn't she kill you first, then Wise?"

Mahegan ran through several options, coming up with nothing tangible other than lame thoughts, such as *Zara missed* or *Zara had the better shot on Wise* or *I moved out of the way before Zara could get another shot off.* But none of those rang true. The only two logical paths that were feasible were either Zara needed Wise dead and Mahegan alive so that he could continue to follow whatever clues she had left, for whatever reasons she had, or Wise was part of the Resistance and Zara wasn't.

Zara had run the Valley Trauma Center training camp for the assassins. Cassie was living proof. She had infiltrated that outfit and reported out. Firing ranges. Hand-to-hand combat. Adrenaline-and-testosterone cocktails, making them hyperaggressive and feral. Zara had been inside Jamie Carter's campaign as a close personal advisor and had been photographed at Jamie's estate in New Bern, North Carolina.

"Sorted it out?" Biagatti asked.

"Zara has to be dirty. She's at the center of this," Mahegan said.

"Really?"

"Valley Trauma Center," Mahegan said.

"Do we have any reports that Zara was actually involved in all of that?"

"Yes. And that she shot Broome in the chest," Mahegan said.

Biagatti continued. "Broome, it turns out, was heavily involved in training the assassins, as well as abusing them. Is it possible she is a force for good? She killed Broome—and Wise, who, it turns out, was feeding bullshit information with just enough real information. He leaked the memorandum stating that the secretary of state was also on the list. He's in Asia somewhere. Why would the coup take place with the secretary of state out of the country if he was a target?"

"Perfect place to be, actually," Mahegan said, mulling the possibility over in his mind. It didn't feel right, but it was something to consider.

Ignoring Biagatti's track, Mahegan regained control of the conversation. "Let's focus on what we know. The MacBook in Zara's apartment was commanding and controlling the operation with the assassins. We know that Team Artemis is made up of the women that were trained at the Valley Trauma Center. I trust Cassie's reports."

"She was drugged and suffering from traumatic brain injury," Biagatti said. She looked at Van Dreeves, who was pale and sweating in the leather chair behind them. "But enough of this speculation. Jake, I want Van Dreeves taken to the hospital."

"Patch cleaned him up well enough," Mahegan said. "We've been over this, Director."

"You know I outrank you by about a million levels, right?"

"At least that."

"Then drop the authority issues and have two of your men take him to Walter Reed, where he can be seen," she said. "Now."

"This is a combat environment, Director. A combat medic has treated him. In fact, two combat medics have worked on him. He's going to be fine," Mahegan said.

"Mr. Owens, may I see your medical license," Biagatti said. She held out her hand.

"I'm combat lifesaver qualified, but I don't carry my graduation certificate with me, Director," Owens said.

"Mr. Hobart?" She spun toward Hobart, still holding out her hand.

Hobart looked at Biagatti, then at Mahegan, shrugged, and then looked out the window, always on guard.

"Two take him to the hospital, now. That leaves two here with me, which is my normal protection detail," she said. "And two to stand guard at the hospital."

"These aren't normal times," Mahegan said.

"That's why I've got two with Mr. Van Dreeves."

"It's just Dreeves. His first name is Van," Hobart said as if defending Van Dreeves's honor.

"My apologies. Now, if we're done with the nonsense, get Van Dreeves to Walter Reed Military Hospital, now."

Mahegan stared at her for perhaps a second too long. Fire burned in her eyes and he wasn't sure if it was passion for his men or something entirely else.

"Do I need to drive them myself, Jake?"

Without removing his eyes from Biagatti's, he said, "Hobart, Patch, you take VD to the hospital. I'll keep Sean here to work the intel. I'm good if the doctor stares at him for five seconds and sends you back. Get your asses back here ASAP."

"Little Bird okay?"

"The quicker, the better," Mahegan said.

O'Malley typed in some commands and said, "Five minutes it will land at the soccer field."

Hobart looked at Mahegan, then at Biagatti. He ran his finger along the Band-Aid behind his ear. Mahegan got the message.

"Hurry up, guys," Mahegan said.

Hobart drove with Van Dreeves in the passenger seat and Owens in the rear.

Mahegan returned to find Biagatti standing behind O'Malley as he worked the MacBook.

"Satisfied?" Mahegan said. "You've cut your security by more than half."

"Both of you, look at me," Biagatti said. O'Malley continued to watch the screen.

"I've got blue dots headed this way," O'Malley said.

"Look at me, O'Malley. Now!" Biagatti said. "I need both of you to focus on the mission at hand right now. We've had an attack of an unprecedented nature on our country. Are you up to the challenge? Because if you're not, I'll find new men to provide my security. My team needs to be top notch. The very best. Only those that can cut it in today's intelligence community—"

"We get it, director," Mahegan said. "Just let us do our jobs."

"Do them," she said.

There was a thud on the doorstep, followed by soft footfalls on the roof. O'Malley typed more commands, sending the Team Artemis tracking information into the cloud so that Cassie could continue to maintain situational awareness. He snapped the lid down on his

MacBook and unlatched the window when Biagatti had turned away toward the basement door.

"What do we have?" Mahegan asked.

"Movement outside. Four blue dots around the house, maybe on the roof. This doesn't give relief," O'Malley said. "A few fleeting images on the cameras, as if they know where they are."

"Zombie women from the valley?" Mahegan asked.

"Maybe," O'Malley said.

"Get your stuff and put it in the gun safe. Then stay up here while I get the director downstairs to the safe room."

"Never leave your wingman, boss," O'Malley said.

"I'd feel much better with both of you downstairs with me," Biagatti said.

"Sean can be down in two seconds. Let's go," Mahegan said.

O'Malley nodded and drew his pistol from his hip holster. Mahegan grabbed Biagatti by the arm and escorted her down the steps. She turned and locked the dead bolt of the basement door, saying, "Don't want those bitches getting down here."

"Let's go, Director," Mahegan said.

"Roger, as you would say," Biagatti said.

Muffled pops rang out all around, but the deeper they retreated into the basement, the more distant the shots sounded. Mahegan's job was to protect the director of the CIA during this time of national emergency. He had always been duty bound, and always to a fault. The only competing factor to ever make him waver in choosing between duty and another component of his life had been Cassie, but he trusted Cassie's compe-

tence, and General Savage had given him the mission
to keep the CIA director alive, and so he would.

The moment he stepped onto the concrete floor of
the basement, he knew something was significantly
wrong. The air was cooler than normal, probably from
an open window or back door. After another half step,
Biagatti stepped back, wrenched her arm free of his
firm grip, and retrieved her pistol, aiming it at him.

Hobart's voice sounded through the Band-Aid comms
device: "It's a trap. Four Artemis around the building
now. We circled back. In a firefight."

Mahegan looked at Biagatti.

"Now drop yours," she said, motioning at his Tribal.

A movement to his right told him that they were not
alone in the basement. The only person who could
have opened the steel door or triple-bolted windows
would have been Biagatti. Perhaps she had snuck down
here when they were on the mission at Zara's condo.

Two women emerged from the dark corners. The
metal Lexan container that served as the interrogation
site and holding cell sat in the far right corner. Otherwise, the basement was sparse. Some random yard tools,
such as a hoe, hedge trimmer, and weed eater were hanging from a Peg-Board to the left. An extra washer and
dryer were to the front, and the stairwell to the outside
alley behind the garage was in between the washer/
dryer combo and the holding cell. Its door was triple-
bolted with locks and keypad access. There was a similar door beyond that one, with equally challenging
security.

The Artemis assassins remained in the corner, apparently ceding control of the situation to their leader.

He had three weapons aimed at him, making any kind of artful dodge a near impossibility. He knelt down and placed his Tribal on the concrete.

"Duty always calls, Jake Mahegan," Biagatti said. "The best deception plans use a sliver of the truth, right? Similarly, the best way to deceive someone is to appeal to their basest element. What moves them? What motivates them? Why do they act? What do they do?"

She tossed a pair of handcuffs at him. "Put these on. Then get into the holding cell."

He caught the cuffs. "Double lock, triple hinged? You've put some thought into this, Director."

"Yes. And I'll put a bullet in your head if you don't put those on right now. Three pistols aimed directly at you right now. Make the call, Jake."

Mahegan slipped the cuffs over his wrists and snapped them shut with a click. The woman in the far left corner stepped forward with a vest rigged with C4 and a timer. She slipped that over his shoulders and zipped it all the way up then looped a coil of rope around him, securing everything in place.

The assassin had short black hair, a hard edgy face, full of scars, as if she had been on the Ultimate Fighting Championship circuit or hit in the face with an IED. *That's actually a possibility,* Mahegan thought. She had the lean, bony frame of a hardened soldier. The woman's irises were black as night, either dilated from the Zara drug concoction or a genetic mutation. She smirked with thin lips, the only sign she was actually human, as she cinched the knot and then placed the pistol to his forehead with one hand and then a wiry hand in the small of his back, nudging him toward the holding cell. He stepped toward the open door, contemplating his moves, but a needle slid into his neck.

He felt the liquid seep into his body. His mind swooned. His final stumbling steps were into the holding cell. He was aware enough to realize she had shoved him through the doorway. As the woman was closing the door, he heard Biagatti say, "Find and kill the others if your two partners haven't already."

Then Mahegan's mind went blank.

CHAPTER 20

Cassie surged forward, propelled by the DHT-and-Flakka shot.

She was like a high-powered motocross bike spitting dirt behind her. She emerged from the tunnel, bursting through the hanging gray tarp that Jermaine had led them through earlier. Pistol at the ready, she fired twice at the recognizable woman in the near left corner and then twice at the woman in the far right.

Scoring direct hits on both, she scurried to the nearest woman and fieldstripped her of all intelligence and weapons. A pistol, knife, radio, and two fragmentary grenades. The woman who had been two rooms down from her in the Valley Trauma Center had been an Olympic-quality alpine skier who had suffered a traumatic brain injury when her helmet had come off in a spectacular fall from Jackson Hole's treacherous double-black diamond run. At least that's what she had told Cassie, but after seeing Bergeron at Daingerfield Island, she wasn't so sure anymore. Maybe they were all legends? At this point, it didn't matter other than to figure out that, if Jamie Carter was behind this, why would they let her, Cassie, into the mix? Perhaps it was the "friends close, enemies closer" theory, or maybe it was what Cassie called "snuggle tactics." ISIS and Taliban forces knew that the American military could easily defeat them using stand-off: jets, helicopters, artillery, mortars, or long-range rifles. They adapted, however, and began fighting in close where those systems weren't effective or would risk killing American troops as well.

Maybe Jamie was holding Cassie close to minimize her ability to see the bigger picture. Pull her in and make her go native, get intoxicated by the power and want more.

For all her years of knowing Cassie, Jamie evidently didn't understand her goddaughter very well.

Cassie moved to the woman on the far right, whom she had seen but never met. She made the same haul from her. The women were uniformly outfitted right down to the number of grenades. This one had a cell phone, though, which Cassie pocketed.

Scraping and clicking noises escaped from the tunnel mouth. Whoever was chasing her from that direction was closing in. She quickly cleared the subterranean rooms beyond where she had just killed the two assassins, and returned to take a solid shooter's stance aimed at the mouth of the tunnel.

She saw the tarp flutter with a hand pushing at it, and quickly fired two shots at where the head connected to that hand might be. The movement stopped and Cassie bolted forward to the tunnel mouth, pressed her back to the side, retrieved a hand grenade, and flipped the pin. She heard a similar ping from inside the tunnel. The assassin had her own grenade.

Cassie lifted the tarp and hurled the grenade in like a baseball pitcher with a submarine fastball, getting it as deep as she could. The explosion was loud, but muffled by the earthen tunnel. For good measure, she lifted the tarp and fired two rounds into the lead woman and two more into the trail.

Four dead.

There were more coming her way.

Stepping around the corner was a slight figure.

Emma? My roommate? How the hell did she cave in to the pressure?

"Emma? What the hell?"

"Hi, Cassie." Emma raised a pistol. "You're proving quite difficult to kill."

Emma fired. Cassie dove to the side and returned fire. Everything in Cassie's mind was upside down. Emma, her friend, was now a member of the Resistance. *Did the Resistance place Emma next to me? All this time, Emma was protesting my presence, and she was actually doing the spying?*

Cassie charged her wounded roommate and tackled her wiry body. Emma retrieved a knife and tried to stab Cassie in the neck, but Cassie blocked that effort with her forearm. Emma's wiry body squirmed beneath her. The professional bull rider was expert at holding on and Emma was proving challenging to pin down.

Cassie swiped at her forehead with the butt of her pistol, which glanced off Emma's temple.

"Bitch," Emma grunted.

Voices began floating out of the tunnel behind her.

Emma was delaying her escape. Another straight downward blow with the pistol had more effect. Oddly, she didn't want to kill Emma, who seemed intent on killing her. Emma's eyes rolled backward and she went limp, the knife falling from her hand onto the dirt floor. Cassie didn't discount Emma's deception, though, and remained ready.

"The last ride is never the last ride, and the end is never the end," Emma said. She spun on one knee, ready to rebound. A roundhouse kick to Emma's face made the small woman do an aerial flip and she landed on her back, this time unconscious. The voices in the tunnel became louder and Cassie was moving.

She pressed the Band-Aid communications device, hoping she had reception.

"Jake, Cassie."

No response.

"Jake, over."

Static over the comms line matched the electric charge she felt in her veins. As she knelt next to the brick wall, the BLEPs reconnected, red dots—fourteen in all—appearing near the two locations she had been. However, there were five blue dots concentrated at a location in Southeast Washington, DC, across the Anacostia River.

Knowing she needed to get away from Emma and the others, she hustled through the dilapidated tenement, found a different staircase than the one through which she had entered, and popped out on Morris Road. With the onset of the evening a couple of hours ago, the day's relative tranquility was replaced by cars cruising slowly, dealers hanging on the street corners, and kids on bikes, sentries, reporting intel to their network. Jermaine was nowhere to be found. She hoped he was safe.

The roving drug dealer and territorial patrols provided her some advantage by keeping the assassins on the move or in hiding. She dashed across the street to a wooded, empty lot. There was some elevation to it and she burrowed through the underbrush, climbing the surprisingly steep hill. The trees and foliage gave way to construction equipment and a partially cleared spot at the top. She moved to the far side of the backhoe and knelt.

Why isn't Jake answering me?

All this time, they thought she was the one with the riskier mission, which maybe it was, but that didn't mean that his task was without peril.

"Jake, Cassie, over," she tried again.

"Go," Jake said.

Her breath caught. Surprised at her own reaction, she took a second to compose herself and respond. Still amped. Still pumped. Still fired up. Her veins were burning hot. She'd killed and she was ready to kill some more.

"Status?" she said.

"POW," he whispered.

"Team status?"

"Uncertain."

"Location," she replied without hesitation.

"Sierra Echo Sierra Hotel," he replied. "Study window. Cease comms, out."

Mahegan's words were rushed. She didn't respond. She retrieved the burner phone she'd found on one of the assassins and pulled up the map function, corresponded what she was seeing in her heads-up display to an approximate location on the map. Five assassins in one location would have to be a high-value target for them.

Jake had rattled off the phonetic letters *SESH*. Jake was a surfer and often called his outings sessions, or a "good sesh," but she didn't believe that he would be joking about that, given his predicament.

"Southeast," she whispered. Everything in DC was NW, NE, SW, or SE. So that had to be the first half. He was with the CIA director, who operated typically from safe houses. *Southeast safe house*. While she didn't know where that might be, she looked in her BLEPs and figured she had a pretty good idea.

She wanted to tell Jake that she knew where he was, but if his comms had been compromised, she would be giving away everything, including her ability to help Jake. Still pumped. Still surging. Still electric. She turned her head, scanning for threats, and focused on her path to the river. She moved swiftly, like a running back slicing through a hapless defense, catching the seams, the intervals, the tactical equivalent of hitting every green light on the way to the hospital with a pregnant wife.

Back at her original landing spot from earlier in the day, she was surprised to find the appropriated kayak was still lying on its side. She approached carefully, expecting a trap. Circling wide and then closer, she checked the park buildings, the bridges on I-295 and I-395. Nothing she could see. She darted to the kayak and slid the plastic boat into the water, snatching the paddle with her free hand. She rowed with silent abandon, feeling like a Native American in a hollowed-out canoe paddling to deliver a message that could save her tribe.

In a way, that's exactly who she was. She alone held all of the firsthand information that could expose the coup and who was truly pulling all of the levers. With each stroke of the dual-bladed oar, her hands brushed the surface of the river. The smell was musty, a combination of dead fish and the sewage plant upstream. The water was cool to the touch. Powered by her surging adrenaline, Cassie made landfall near the marina from which she had originally acquired the kayak. No one seemed to be looking for it. She pulled it onto the bank and bolted across Water Street and then followed a bike path across Southeast Freeway. Traffic was heavy, but no one seemed to be concerned about a grungy white chick dodging cars in this part of town. She began following the map in her BLEP toward the row house on Third and K Southeast. That was all she had to go on.

She thought about where she was going. Either she was going to barge in on a meeting of the assassins, or they had descended on a high-value target and were guarding him or her. *Jake? Biagatti? Both?*

She slowed, only to make sure she was moving toward the target, and expected that the assassins would be using an exterior and interior defense array. While she couldn't fathom who might be able to best Jake, Sean, Patch, Hobart, and Van Dreeves, she became concerned that they had somehow become separated. Five of the best operators in the military would be nearly unbeatable.

Unless they were outranked. Jake and his men were

tough, seasoned operators, but they were also patriots who followed orders. *Who could have split them, if that's what happened? Biagatti? Jamie?*

Either one of them could have done it, but were they both in on the coup? She knew that Zara and Syd Wise were the masterminds behind the overthrow of the government. To what extent did Jamie know any of this? Was she simply a beneficiary of massive good fortune?

The wild card had always been Biagatti. General Savage had placed Jake there for a reason. Ostensibly, the reason was to protect the director of the CIA. But did Savage know more? And if he did, why hadn't he said so?

She was two blocks away. Traditional DC row houses, with their blocky, rectangular façades, dotted the streets in every direction. These were newer homes, maybe five to ten years old, built with two-car garages and small front yards the size of two picnic tables. Cute black two-foot-high wrought iron fences outlined the yards, serving decorative purposes only.

If the safe house was the home at the center of the congregation of blue icons, then she was two blocks away. She anticipated guards on the rooftops, so she circled wide toward a soccer field and saw . . . a Little Bird helicopter.

Kneeling over two men on the ground was Hobart. She pressed her Band-Aid and said, "Hobart, Cassie. Status?"

"IED. Two wounded. Evac time now," Hobart said.

"On location. Going in," she said.

"Wait for me. They have Sean and Jake."

As she had feared, the team had been split.

"Roger, meet you at the northeast corner of your location."

"Roger, out."

She moved away from the safe house and circled around the soccer field to the opposite, northeast side. The MH-6 lifted off with two bodies strapped to the bench seats. Owens and Van Dreeves, she presumed, based upon Hobart's report.

Hobart moved silently toward her, a phantom appearing in a different location every five seconds. Suddenly he was next to her.

"You okay?" he asked. A rare show of concern from the robotic warrior.

"I'm good. Ready to go in. What happened?"

"Unimportant. We've got four bogies guarding the house. Two inside and two outside. One of them is on the roof and she's got a sniper rifle. But if you got this far without getting shot, she's probably not much good in close, given the angles and dead space."

"VD and Patch okay?"

"We'll see," Hobart said.

Cassie nodded. "Okay. If you got hit with an IED and there have been shots fired, haven't the police responded?"

"This is DC. I heard all the units were responding to twelve dead bodies across the river."

"Touché," she said. "I've got a plan. You just need to provide overwatch."

"Tell me," he said.

And she did. Then she retrieved another syringe of Zara's juice, rolled up her sleeve, and prepared to pump more of the liquid into her veins.

"I wouldn't do any more of that," Hobart said. "You're pumped enough."

He placed his hand on her arm.

"You haven't seen anything yet."

"You're better without it," he said. "Trust me. Rely on your Ranger skills. Not some juice that bitch gave you."

She nodded, handed him the syringes of the concoction, slapped him on the back and then began running toward the row house complex. She reached the base of the town house row, one block east of the safe house, and knelt, leaning in the dark shadows of the end unit. Above her were two magnolia trees that stood barely over twenty feet high, but they still provided decent concealment.

Cassie thought about what Hobart had just said. He was right. She was better than needing some drug to perform at her best. She hadn't needed drugs to get through Ranger School or combat in Iraq, Afghanistan, or Iran. She had relied on her instinct and intuition, her mettle and personal fortitude. She gutted it out on the long runs and ruck marches. She had escaped from the infamous Serbian special operations soldier Dax Stasovich, not once but twice, as he chased her across Jordan.

Taking a deep breath and exhaling slowly, Cassie regained focus and clarity. Zara's entire purpose had been to disable her. And if that was true about Zara and potentially Jamie, then Biagatti had to be doing the same thing with Jake. Holding him close, keeping an eye on him, preventing him from having freedom of maneuver to see the big picture, which was what he did best.

She was a block away from the man she loved. Cassie shamed herself for ever doubting him, not that she had fully run with the concept that he could be aimed against her. She was certain the recordings that Jamie and Cassie had played for her were doctored. There were software programs that could mimic anyone's voice nowadays. Terrorists the world over were using the app to filter their voices to avoid intelligence community voice match technology. It wasn't a stretch that Jamie would have access to the tapes with her service on the Senate Armed Services Committee.

Safe house. An oxymoron if she ever heard one.

With renewed conviction and sense of purpose, Cassie stood and readied herself for the fight that she was sure she would join at the safe house.

CHAPTER 21

Zara Perro stepped into the basement of the CIA safe house and looked at CIA Director Carmen Biagatti, who was talking to two of Zara's assassins.

"Shoot anyone who tries to get in here, and shoot him if he tries to get out." Biagatti pointed at Mahegan, who was secured in the Lexan-paneled container. The sheets of bulletproof glass were anchored by plate steel at the top and bottom, with large bolts secured into the ceiling and floor.

"We've caged the beast," Zara said.

"But we lost Syd. He was a good man."

"I had to kill him. He knew everything," Zara said. "And I had no shot on Mahegan."

"IED got half the team. Not sure where O'Malley is. There was a fight at the front door. I imagine he's in the wind, but he doesn't know for a fact what is happening. He may suspect, but he doesn't know."

Zara walked over, tugged on the heavy metal hasp, and locked eyes with Mahegan. She blew an air kiss to the big man with the hard eyes. She found it impossible to hold his gaze for more than a few seconds. The intensity of Mahegan's eyes was penetrating. Instead of being the proverbial windows into *his* soul, his eyes were long, piercing daggers digging into *your* soul. She had heard this about him. Always on the attack. Never stopping.

Well, he was stopped now. Locked in a cage, where he belonged.

She turned to Biagatti. "Shall we go?"

"We've got two upstairs and two down here. I saved your best team to hold Mahegan. It seems Cassie got the best of several," Biagatti said.

"I recognize them all. They were good trainees."

Standing in the corner was Sarah Blackstone, whose legend was that of a rock climber from Colorado. Really, she had been in Leavenworth for three counts of murdering her children and husband. Beneath her black polypropylene shirt and cargo pants was a lithe, wiry frame. She wore her black hair cut short around her ears. Thin lips were pressed together beneath her slender nose and ice-blue eyes, which were staring at Mahegan. A zoo visitor admiring a rare species. Sarah had taken a beating in prison. Many had not expected her to live, but she was a fighter and the Valley Trauma Center had nursed her back to health, on one condition.

In the opposite corner with her pistol drawn was Emily Delouise, who actually was a former defense attorney and amateur skydiver. When one of her criminal clients didn't appreciate the fact that she had lost his case and threatened her, she had methodically planned and executed the murder of Johnny Ray Smith. Charged and convicted of murder with the special circumstance of Lying in Wait, she had been serving time in Bedford Hills Correctional Facility for New York. Wise's subtle outreach program had eventually landed her in the assassin training wing as well.

Syd Wise had employed FBI software to sift through the legions of female inmates around the country who had been convicted of murder or other first degree felonies. Biagatti had directed the effort, telling Zara and Wise that they needed twenty-five assassins to carry out the plan. Ever thorough, Wise had accounted for attrition and provided thirty-five. Zara had put the overage to good use by staging an attack on Biagatti's house as a ruse. The assassins were, by definition, expendable. Each team had a purpose. Kill the president and vice president. Kill the Speaker. Create a ruse. Kill Cassie Bagwell. Contain Jake Mahegan and his team.

All were intended to open Jamie Carter's path to the presidency, and they had succeeded.

"Emily, Sarah, you've got the mission here. I've been called to meet with the president," Biagatti said.

The two assassins nodded.

Zara escorted Biagatti up the steps, where they reiterated instructions to the two assassins on the main floor. Both acknowledged their duties as they entered the garage and stepped into Zara's BMW 5 Series.

"I know this is a step-down from your normal ride, but in a few minutes, you'll have a motorcade all your own," Zara said.

"Not soon enough," Biagatti said.

They wound through the Capitol Hill East area and parked near the Russell Senate Office Building. Given the around-the-clock coverage of the coup, it didn't matter that the time was approaching midnight. Television anchors were lined along the sidewalk, each with their own spotlights and camera crews shining on their live stand-up, reporting with the de facto White House in the background.

Because Jamie Carter was operating out of her office, the press was able to get much closer than they normally would to the White House. As they walked toward the building, they had to navigate a cordon of reporters that had formed.

"Director Biagatti! Any trace of Captain Bagwell? Is she responsible for the coup murders?"

Zara tried to pull her through the throng, but Biagatti stopped and said, "You'd have to ask the FBI, but the evidence certainly seems to indicate that."

Sensing someone willing to answer questions, no less than fifty journalists packed around Biagatti. Zara suddenly was worried that they had not properly prepared to navigate the massive horde of protestors, conspiracy theorists, journalists, and basic curious citizens. But she couldn't risk breaking away any of the four remaining assassins. They needed Mahegan to lure Cassie, and they needed Cassie to hold up as the traitor who had engineered the coup. Wise had already fabricated thousands of e-mails between Cassie and the thirty-five assassins date-time stamped from the day she entered the Valley Trauma Center. The physical evidence placed Cassie at each of the assassination locations. The electronic evidence, meticulously crafted, supported the entire scenario that painted Cassie as the lead conspirator. They even had Hootsuite loaded to ignite social media pages for Cassie proclaiming her pride in dismantling the Smart administration.

"Are you being considered for a cabinet position?" another reporter asked. The throng was like a mosh pit at a concert, swaying as one. Two Capitol Police officers fought their way in and began to push the crowd outward, giving Biagatti room to maneuver toward the door.

"I'm here to brief the president on threats to our nation. They are both foreign and domestic," Biagatti said.

Zara knew that had nothing to do with why they were visiting with Jamie, but Biagatti sounded authentic. Zara paused when she saw a recognizable military figure walk into the door of the Russell Senate Office Building. She nudged Biagatti, who looked up. They had effectively served as an unintentional diversion for General Bob Savage to sneak through the mass undetected.

What the hell is he doing here? Zara wondered. Savage was Jake Mahegan's, and now Cassie's, mentor and boss. The commander of the Joint Special Operations Command could only mean trouble for their plan.

She broke Biagatti free from the crowd and followed in the evaporating wake of General Savage. As they entered the outer chambers of Senator, now President, Carter's office, Jamie noticed them and waved them both into her office. She seemed to be buzzing with energy.

"Director. Zara. Come in, please," Jamie said.

They sat in the same seating area where they had been earlier in the day with Jake Mahegan and Cassie Bagwell, before everything blew up.

"Have you met General Bob Savage?" Jamie asked.

"We've met briefly," Biagatti said stiffly.

Savage was dressed in a gray business suit, with a solid red tie against a white button-collared shirt. His steel-gray buzz cut offset his diamond-gray eyes. He had a ruddy complexion from years of hard fighting. His face was stern, giving no tell.

"And this is Zara Perro, my strategic advisor."

He nodded at both women without saying a word.

"I've got a press conference in fifteen minutes. That's why the crowd is so large outside. Not that it has been much smaller," Jamie said.

Zara thought that she seemed positively energized. Perhaps she would make a good president. Rising from the ashes of this tragedy, Jamie seemed poised and ready to take on the world.

"What sort of announcement?" Zara asked.

"I'm naming Carmen here my vice president and General Savage my FBI director," she said. Zara nodded. Jamie naming Biagatti as vice president was always part of the plan. But Savage? Where did that come from?

Slack-jawed, Biagatti said, "Does the general have the requisite experience to serve at such a high level?"

"I could ask the same question about you," Savage said. His first words spoken were a burn on the serving director of the CIA.

"Seriously," Biagatti continued. "Is this a position you would even want?" She directed her question at Savage.

"Director, I know it is your profession to pretend to know everyone else's business and that you are a master at spycraft. Your clumsy questions toward me point to a lack of political skill and, frankly, manners. It's no fucking business of yours what I want," Savage said.

"Jamie?" Biagatti protested.

"That would be Madam President to you," Savage countered. "The first thing about chain of command is knowing where you are in it. You have a boss. Act like it."

"He's quite right, Carmen. I'm all set to make you my vice president, but I must say, if out of the starting block you question my decisions like this, then I might reconsider my decision."

"My apologies, Madam President," Biagatti said. "My concern is only for your administration. I'm sure I'll quickly learn to work with General Savage as the FBI Director."

"He's from North Carolina, my new home state, and will represent the state and the nation well. I appreciate your support, Carmen. Now, are we ready, or do we have more concerns?"

"I'm solid," Savage said. He stood. A strong man, over six feet tall, Savage wore the suit well, Zara thought. If Jamie was truly making him the director of the FBI, the man would be able to pull it off based on his gravitas alone. While Jamie had not consulted her on this move, she couldn't say she had a good reason to oppose the selection. It was entirely possible that she had chosen him in the vein of *The Godfather Part II*'s reminder: "Keep your friends close, and your enemies closer."

"Let me just do a quick change," Zara said. She was still wearing the clothes she had on when she had put two bullets into Syd Wise's spinal column. She excused herself, found a white shirt, navy blazer, and black heels that would work with the pants she was wearing. In less than five minutes, she had freshened up in the same bathroom through which Cassie had escaped earlier. She reentered the office, joined the group, and they walked through the masses lining the hallways. A page led them into one of the hearing rooms that the Senate staff had transformed into a quasi–White House Press Room.

"Zara, I've fired the White House press secretary. I thought she was utterly incompetent and a liar, so I'd like for you to make these introductory remarks," Jamie said.

Zara took the piece of paper from Jamie's hand as they entered a small room off to the side of the hearing room. It was outfitted with low blue sofas and wooden chairs. There were three coffeepots filled to different levels of what was certainly cold swill. She sat and glanced over the words Jamie had asked her to read, digested them, and then got into her CNN media mindset. Focus, have three talking points to which she can pivot:

This is a terrible time for the nation.
Stability is critical.
Jamie Carter will lead us through this.

"Ready?" Jamie asked. Zara nodded and she walked through a back door into the conference room, following a page onto the floor in front of the dais. A large podium with a broad wooden base was centered in the room. Zara circled wide, almost stepping on the cameramen who were seated cross-legged on the floor. On the front of the podium, she saw the Seal of the President of the United States.

It was happening.

As Jamie, Biagatti, and Savage entered the room, a loud murmur rippled through the crowd. Camera shutters flickered loudly, long arms held smartphones high to video the first official press conference since the swearing in a few hours ago.

Zara felt the rush of excitement boil in her stomach. She smoothed her blazer and stepped to the microphone, tapped it; a muffled, amplified echo sounded throughout the room, and she began speaking.

"My name is Zara Perro and I am President Carter's new press secretary," she began. A roar rumbled through the crowd then quieted. "The president understands that this is a terrible time for the country, and we mourn the loss of our nation's three highest-elected officials. President Carter will speak in a moment, but first wanted me to let you know that she has spent the entire day conferring with the National Command Authority, several allied heads of state, and some of the cabinet. In that vein, she would like for me to officially announce that CIA Director Carmen Biagatti will begin service as the vice president of the United States, effective immediately."

The group erupted with unintelligible shouts and rumblings. Zara let the moment pass for about thirty seconds and then continued. She choked out the next line.

"Also, effective immediately, Major General Bob Savage, a soldier with four decades of public service, will serve as the director of the FBI."

Another loud eruption, with several high-pitched questions of "Who is he?"

Savage was a discreet warrior by his nature. It made sense that not many people would know who he was.

"And now, I'll turn over the microphone to President Carter."

Zara stepped away to the left and Jamie walked into the room, nodded at Zara, Biagatti, and General Savage, then stepped to the microphone, adjusted it—Jamie was six feet tall in heels—and began speaking.

"My heart goes out to the families of our fallen president, vice president, and Speaker of the House, as well as the many who died in their service. This has been a uniquely tragic day for America. Not since John Wilkes Booth entered the president's box in Ford's Theater, not even a mile from here, has the country seen such a nefarious conspiracy against our institutions of government. The president is dead. The vice president is dead. The Speaker of the House is dead. As the sitting Senate pro tem, I reluctantly accept this mantle of responsibility. But do not let my reluctance be mistaken for weakness. Do not let our vulnerabilities as a nation be mistaken for frailty. Do not let this moment of crisis in our country be mistaken for the norm. Rather, it is the exception that proves the rule of our democracy. We are strong and we will demonstrate strength. We will find and bring to justice those that committed these atrocities upon our nation and our institutions. And we will move forward out of these divisions together and unify as one nation focused on our collective future of prosperity. We have endured over two hundred and forty years of growing pains, and we will not let this day of outrage define us as a nation in the short term or the long term. Tomorrow I will occupy the White House and begin daily operations. Tonight, I'll take a couple of questions, but it's well past midnight and we all need to focus on repairing the damage."

The crowd erupted with a thousand questions.

Jamie coolly pointed at a well-known CNN reporter in the first row.

"Yes, Jim," she said.

"Madam President, let me be the first to congratulate you on your ascendancy to the presidency. There are many, many people in the country right now that are actually supportive of the events of the last twenty-four hours. How would you respond to them?"

"There is nothing to congratulate here. I was simply in the right place at the wrong time. And no one should be supportive of the assassination of three of our nation's leaders. I condemn it wholly and without equivocation. Regardless of whether you agree with our elected officials, they are elected by us. There is no room in this country or my administration for this type of thinking. Next question."

"Yes, John," Jamie said, pointing at a longtime Fox News correspondent.

"Given that you recently won a special election for senator in North Carolina and subsequent appointment by your peers as the Senate Pro Tem, one could argue that you had the most to gain from the murders of the top two in the succession line ahead of you. Can you give us a statement reassuring the people of the United States that you had nothing to do with this, and that any investigation into these murders will not lead back to you?"

"I can and I will. I had nothing to do with these murders and I understand the rumors, theories, and suspicions that I might. I moved to North Carolina because it's a beautiful state. I had no idea that my good friend Senator Hite would be murdered. Think of the blood trail here. It's a fiendish plot, and I had nothing to do with it, I can assure you. That said, I intend to fully investigate each of these murders, including that of Senator Hite, where it all seems to have begun."

She called on a third reporter, this one from CBS.

"My sources tell me, Madam President, that there are multiple armed women who have been killed and that they have been found by the DC Metro Police Department. Several were in Anacostia and others throughout the city, and even in Northern Virginia. The police are saying that they suspect these women are the assassins. And the lead assassin is a captain in the United States Army named Cassie Bagwell. I have documentation of logistical and coordination e-mails between Captain Bagwell and the assassins. What do you know of this?"

"I've known Cassie all of her life. I find it hard to believe that she would be involved in any of this. It's rather shocking, but I have seen the same reports you have. As I said, I will fully investigate this," Jamie said. "Now, it has been a long twenty-four hours. Good night and may God bless our United States of America."

Jamie stepped away from the podium and began walking to the door through which they had entered. The crowd erupted again with another unintelligible volley of questions. They exited through a basement walkway onto a loading dock, where security was waiting. As they were climbing into the Suburban, Zara let General Savage climb into the rear seat. She flipped it back, essentially locking him in place, and then let Biagatti climb in on the same side, while Jamie was on the other side. The chase car was behind them. The Suburban driver was to her left. Suddenly Zara said, "Oh my God, I forgot something. Just a second."

Zara closed the door, with Biagatti shouting, "Hey!"

Slipping behind the loading dock's metal door, she moved along the interior loading bays, found a stairwell going down, and popped out in the underground tunnel that went to the Capitol. She hooked a right, away from the Capitol Building and toward Union Station, and found a way out on the opposite side of the building.

Zara jogged to Union Station, then hailed a cab and gave the address for the CIA safe house where Mahegan was being held.

CHAPTER 22

Cassie pressed the band-aid pad and said, "Savage has the package, but Zara escaped."

Hobart replied, "Roger."

She was kneeling behind a low brick wall that was a block from the target house. In her BLEPs, she could only see four blue dots on location. The fifth blue dot was on Capitol Hill, moving west along Pennsylvania Avenue.

"Sniper on the roof. Northeast. Looking at you."

Hobart replied, "Roger."

Hobart had been able to retrieve from the trunk of the Panamera an SR-25 7.62 mm sniper rifle, with Leupold scope and muzzle suppressor.

"Fire when ready."

"Ready."

There was a metallic ratcheting from across the soccer field, but no loud muzzle blast. She held up the night vision goggle to her eye and saw the sniper jerk. A small black spray exploded from the sniper's head.

One down, three to go. As the Delta Force saying went: *Hobart never missed.*

"I'm guessing one in the front door and two in the basement," Cassie said.

"Movement on roof. Go," Hobart said.

Another ratcheting sound served as a starter gun for her. She didn't wait to see the result. *Again, Hobart never missed.* She darted around the street corner and then hurdled a series of low black fences as if she were an Olympic sprinter, each gallop perfectly timed. Amped. Juiced. Wired. Cassie was on the move.

She pushed on the near window, but it didn't budge, so she moved across the doorstep and pushed up what must have been the study window, the one Jake had mentioned. Stepping into the room, she visualized Jake and the team in these chairs and on the sofa discussing how to save her. She scanned the room from left to right. Front door. Open hallway, with adjoining living room. Stairwell heading upstairs. Bookshelves to the ceiling in the study.

She trundled up the stairs, found the rooftop terrace, and confirmed two dead bodies.

Hobart never missed.

She cleared the rooms upstairs. Two bedrooms and a small gymnasium. As she moved back down the steps, her BLEPs showed two red dots on the roof and two blue dots in the basement.

"Rear door, give me some C-four," she said.

"Poet who don't know it," Hobart muttered. "Two minutes out."

She slid silently down the stairs and took up position directly outside the door to the basement stairwell, with her back pressed firmly against the wall.

Footfalls creaked up the steps. One of the platforms squeaked about midway up, and whoever was ascending, stopped. Cassie's breathing was steady, focused. She visualized her movements.

Wait for Hobart to detonate the back door.

Their focus will be aimed away from the steps. Put two bullets in the lock and bust her way into the stairway, diverting their attention from Hobart. Both will be distracted for a second, which was all Hobart would need to get off one shot.

"Ready," Hobart said.

"Go," she whispered.

The explosion pushed a heat wave all the way against the wall, warming her back. She spun and fired two rounds into the dead bolt, which shattered in a fine spray of miniature shrapnel into the air, some clicking off her BLEPs. She pushed through the door with her pistol up, just as she had visualized.

The assassin's head was turning back toward the door, away from the explosion. Smoke was boiling up the narrow stairway. Cassie recognized this woman, had seen her assaulted by the guards at the Valley Trauma Center. Had connected with her on some level at that time, their eyes making contact, passing an unspoken message: *help me.*

When their eyes connected again, Cassie didn't hesitate to give her a third one in the middle of her forehead. The pistol rocked in her hand and the woman fell backward. Cassie double-tapped her in the chest for good measure. Noticing the key chain on the woman's belt, Cassie snatched it loose and palmed the loop as she bound down the steps, three at a time, pistol at the ready. Landing on the floor of the basement, she saw

Mahegan standing in the Lexan detention cell. He was handcuffed and looked thicker, bulkier than usual. *Why?* Hobart was crawling through the hole the blast had created in the rear door. The second assassin was wounded, but not dead.

Cassie aimed and then stopped. In the assassin's hand was a key fob. Cassie froze. Mahegan's bulkiness. Suicide vest.

The assassins had strapped a suicide vest on him. What Cassie didn't know was whether it was a pressure-release or pressure-applied device. If the assassin was holding the clip, like a hand grenade spoon, or lever, when released it would detonate, killing Jake. Only if she had to press and release the fob to detonate, did they have a chance.

"We've got you, bitch. I press this thing, your boyfriend dies," the assassin said.

Press. Pressure applied will detonate.

Hobart fired a shot through the woman's head.

"Sorry I didn't kill her the first time," Hobart said, scrambling to his feet. His SR-25 had smoke wafting from the bore. Cassie rushed to the dead woman and carefully removed the fob from her hand.

"Hang on to this," she said, handing him the black plastic device.

Jake was saying something through the soundproof glass, motioning with his manacled hands. He looked drugged. Eyes were half-lidded. Movements lumbering and slow. He shuffled toward the door, using his hands to try and point at his chest.

Then she saw it. An LED device was on his abdomen, counting down from fifty-nine seconds. She fumbled with the keys to unlock his cell, trying each one, focused on sliding them into the heavy-gauge padlock. Finally the fourth one worked. She opened the lock, removed the chain, and flung the door open at the same time there were footfalls from the floor above.

"Twenty-five seconds," Jake said. His voice was steady. Calm. Words measured and paced. No fear.

She found the key to the double-lock handcuffs as she pulled him toward the door. Hobart was on him, unzipping the vest. The footfalls had made it to the stairway, but all that mattered was getting this vest off Jake.

"Ten seconds," Jake said.

The second key was stuck. Cassie said, "Fuck it," and removed her Leatherman to snip through the chain that was also looped through a metal D-ring on the suicide vest. The noise at the top of the steps was now moving down the stairway. Someone was coming to the basement.

"Five," Jake said.

Hobart slid behind Jake and yanked the vest from his big arms. Cassie pulled him from the glassed-in room, still holding the handcuffs. Hobart flung the vest against the far wall, following Jake and Cassie out.

Cassie wheeled Jake and Hobart in her direction, toward the near corner and up against the Lexan glass. She pressed Jake and Hobart behind her as she held the door with both hands.

The vest exploded, fire and shrapnel finding the open portal and following the path of least resistance.

The Lexan glass held, but the door blew off the hinges, nearly ripping her shoulders out of socket. She flew backward as the door shot like a missile across the room.

Someone had stepped onto the concrete floor, but rapidly leapt into the more protective stairwell. As the fire licked out and then receded, Cassie pinned her body against Jake and Hobart, who were holding on to her.

Cassie checked herself the same way she would do after an airborne drop. Everything was intact. *Good to go.*

Jake and Hobart were both on one knee, behind Cassie. The Lexan had held and funneled all of the explosives in the direction of the stairwell. Cassie bolted forward and collided with Zara, whose black hair was singed into jagged edges. She aimed a pistol at Cassie, who spun and kicked the weapon away. Zara followed suit and tackled her, negating the use of her own pistol. Cassie whipped a sharp elbow into Zara's face, making blood and saliva fly from Zara's mouth. Cassie clasped the back of Zara's head with laced fingers and drove her knee into Zara's nose. A loud cracking sound erupted, and blood sprayed in every direction.

Zara reached her hand into her pocket as Cassie stepped back to deliver a finishing kick to the woman's throat.

"Cassie!" Jake shouted as he dove toward them.

Zara's hand held a syringe, its needle glistening with liquid that was driving toward Cassie's leg. A shot rang out. Zara's hand exploded. The syringe flipped into the air. Cassie's boot heel pulverized Zara's throat. Jake slid behind Zara, not wanting to interrupt Cassie's momentum or get in the way of a second shot from Hobart.

Cassie realized she was still holding the handcuffs, which whipped across Zara's face once, twice, three times. Blood sprayed from her nose and the gashes the hard metal created. Cassie then slid behind Zara, who was crumbling into the concrete floor, and put the handcuff chain across her throat, pulling in opposite directions like she was using a fancy new workout machine.

"Don't need your juice, bitch," Cassie spat.

Jake and Hobart pulled her away, but she fought them. Just a few more seconds and Zara would choke out.

"Stop, Cass, we need her alive," Jake said.

His voice had always been reassuring to her. She eased her flex and Zara spat, gasping for air. Tossing the cuffs to Hobart, she said, "Lock this bitch up."

Surveying the room, she thought forward. What was the next step? They were so close to accomplishing the mission to find out who exactly was in charge of the Resistance. She looked at Jake.

"We've got to get to Savage. He has the package," Cassie said.

"Roger," Jake said.

Cassie led them up the steps and back to the soccer field, where the MH-6 waited. Hobart jogged past her, smirked, and said, "See? Better without the juice."

Cassie nodded, still feeling a mixture of emotions and thoughts tumbling through her mind. Loading the bench seats, she strapped Zara onto her side, while Jake and Hobart sat on the opposite side. She pressed her Band-Aid comms device and asked the pilots, "Status on VD and Patch?"

"Touch and go," the pilot said.

"Roger. You know where to go."

The MH-6 lifted and nosed over, passing through restricted airspace, heading west.

CHAPTER 23

The MH-6 landed on the lawn of the CIA safe house where she had placed cyanide tanks in the SCIF circulation unit yesterday. While Zara believed that she had been an unwitting participant in the scheme, Cassie had known what was in those tanks, had known everything all along. Operation Double Crossfire, the objective of which was to smoke out the highest-level Resistance operatives in the government, had produced Syd Wise and Carmen Biagatti, the masterminds.

They already knew that Zara was complicit, but it had been unclear the level to which the Resistance penetrated the whole of government. There were others, for sure, but the goal was to cut the head off the snake so that the body would die. No form of government could fully operate with opposition gumming the gears from within. Nor could the administration move its agenda forward with active opposition blocking the way.

Cassie jumped off the wing seat, followed by Jake

and Hobart, who were dragging Zara along. Cassie led the way into the house and took a left through the kitchen and a right into the long hallway leading to the SCIF. The hallway had white chalk outlines and plastic numbered evidence markers dotting throughout. The door had buckled but held, and the wall was riddled with pock marks. Someone had sealed the few areas of penetration using epoxy and resin.

Tugging at the warped door, she saw Jamie, Biagatti, and General Savage sitting around a six-seat table, one at the end and each of the other two on either side. Jake and Hobart waited in the hallway.

"About time you got here," Savage said. "Can't handle all this estrogen."

"Well, you've got more coming your way," Cassie said.

"What is going on?" Biagatti squawked. "Why are we even here? This is a crime scene and I'm vice president of the United States."

"Carmen, we've still got to sign the paperwork and swear you in and all the stuff that actually makes that happen," Jamie said. She turned to Cassie and asked, "Is it done?"

Cassie nodded. "We've got Zara and we've got all of her private, back-channel communications."

Jake dragged Zara into the SCIF and sat her in a chair next to Biagatti.

"What is this?" Biagatti spat.

"If Syd Wise were still alive, he'd be here, too," Cassie said.

"And? Is that my concern?" Biagatti shrugged.

"Ask Zara," Cassie said. Cassie was still focused and could feel the drug filter receding. Otherwise, she might have pummeled Carmen Biagatti for all the damage she had done to the country.

"You're deranged," Biagatti said to Cassie. "This woman can't even talk. You've beaten her so badly. She looks like she's been in a CIA black site."

Cassie said nothing, but a grin formed at the corner of her mouth. Jamie Carter got up and left the room with Savage.

"She's all yours," Savage said.

"Where are you going, Jamie Carter?" Biagatti spat. "What the hell is going on?"

Jamie stopped at the door and said, "Carmen, I may be disappointed I didn't win the presidency, but I'm not a traitor." With that, she followed Savage from the SCIF into the hallway. They closed the door behind them, and now it was just Cassie, Jake, and Hobart with Biagatti and Zara.

"You said the magic words," Cassie said. *"Black site."* She grinned and sat across from the two women. She pushed a piece of paper and pen across the conference table to each woman. "You're going to write on these pieces of paper the names of every Resistance member you've worked with."

"You really think this is productive?" Biagatti asked.

"Probably not," Cassie said. "We can be more productive if that's what you want." She pointed at Hobart, who stepped out and then came back in with a half sheet of plywood, a garden hose, and Jake, who had a burlap sack with some weight to it.

"Really? Waterboarding?" Biagatti said. "This scares me?"

"Worth a shot," Cassie said.

"What else you got?" Biagatti scoffed. "Bitch."

"Oh, I don't know, but it sure is getting stuffy in here. How about some *oxygen*?"

Biagatti went silent, her eyes flitting up to the vents. Cassie walked over to the control panels, opened the compartment, and placed her finger on the CIRCULATION button.

"Jake, Hobart, ProMasks, please."

Cassie put her finger on the button that would ignite the system that pulled compressed air from the tanks positioned on the racks outside.

"Not so cocky anymore, are we? Zara, want to remind us what's in those tanks out there?"

Through broken teeth and split lips, Zara jerked her shoulder toward Biagatti and said, "She knows." The woman was defeated physically and mentally.

"I know, because she told you to do it," Cassie said.

Cassie slipped on her mask and sealed it. Hobart and Jake did the same. Her finger began to press on the button. Biagatti flinched and shouted, "Okay!"

"First question," Cassie said, looking at Zara. "Which app did you use to mimic Jake's voice on that altered tape?"

"What?" Jake said. Cassie held up her hand at him signaling that she had control while keeping her eyes locked on Zara, looking for the tell.

Zara looked at Jake and then down at the table.

"Lyrebird," Zara muttered.

"Should have killed you," Cassie said. "Now both of you give us the names of the Resistance and the remaining assassins."

Zara picked up the pen and started writing. Biagatti did the same. For an hour, they filled five pages of names.

Government workers in the CIA, FBI, DoD, NSA, office of the DNI, and all of the other three-letter agencies.

When they were done, Cassie collected the papers, removed her protective mask, pressed the button, and watched the mist begin pouring from the vents.

"What are you doing? We did what you asked!" Biagatti said.

"Oh, it's just compressed oxygen. The same people who fixed the SCIF switched out the tanks."

Crestfallen, Biagatti dropped her head into her hands.

"Shall we?" Cassie asked Jake and Hobart.

They stood and stepped outside of the SCIF, which had a fresh hasp placed on the outside. It was now a holding cell when Cassie clipped a large Master lock through the bolt. Jake led the way into the kitchen and then into the family room, where Jamie and Savage were sitting.

"Done?"

"Yes," Cassie said, handing the papers to Savage. "They confessed. It's all on video. And here is a list of names. I'm sure this isn't all of them, but it's a start."

"Well, you know your next mission, then," Savage said. "Take a short break, heal up, and prep for the next level. Ferret out these weasels until they're gone or can be loyal to this country."

Cassie nodded. Jake stood behind her, giving her the presence she deserved with Savage, the recognition that she had sacrificed and done well enough. Maybe not perfect, but she had represented and accomplished the mission.

"Here's the letter the president signed saying that he

is, and has been, capable of serving," Savage said. He passed it to Jamie. "You're good with this? Everything we've done? You've done?"

"Do I have a choice? I made my decision when you first talked to me a few weeks ago."

"Doubtful, but give it a shot," Savage said.

"Are you now going to finally tell me how you knew?" Jamie asked Savage.

"We never reveal sources and methods, but I can tell you it was purely by luck," Savage said.

"Whose luck?"

"Not yours, that's for sure."

As Cassie listened, she recalled Jake telling her about a JSOC training exercise in an abandoned building complex along the Neuse River near New Bern, North Carolina. The operators had brought back a string of unintentionally intercepted communications. In light of the recent combat in Iran, which involved significant cyber warfare, Savage was testing a new cell phone jammer and interceptor to be used for combat overseas.

The results were significantly better than they had anticipated. So much so that they not only intercepted faux "enemy" communications, but they picked up local traffic as well. While not entirely legal, she knew that Savage didn't care, especially when he saw the text string:

> Cardinal: Patient status?
> Lancer: Full recovery but TBI
> Cardinal: Will she do?
> Lancer: We need her. Op starts soon. Think so
> Cardinal: I'm going to see her tomorrow

Lancer: Which makes her perfect
Cardinal: Be careful
Lancer: Will do

When Jake had shown Cassie the transcript, she committed to infiltrating the Valley Trauma Center. There was no doubt that Cardinal was Jamie Carter, her godmother. Savage then had O'Malley work the deep web links to all the previous communications where they were able to trace the links to Syd Wise's personal computer. Of the same ilk and no smarter than the FBI cesspool of co-conspirators involved in the Crossfire Hurricane scandal, Wise operated under the arrogant assumption that he was smarter than everyone else. He wasn't.

Cassie wasn't sure how General Savage had convinced the president and vice president to go along with the scenario, but the fact that all pretense of objectivity in the media had been lost certainly contributed to their decision. No matter what President Smart did, the media continued to go for the jugular. So, why not expose the entire lot?

Turning Jamie Carter had been the key.

"If nothing else, working with the president to lance this Resistance boil, and to try to bring the country back together just a bit, may help," Jamie continued.

"Some good lawyers might be able to keep you out of jail, Jamie, but we've got enough evidence to show your participation early on," Savage said.

"I've got good lawyers," Jamie said. "The possibility of any future is better than being dead, I guess. The only thing I really feel bad about is the Speaker," Jamie said. "He's dead and we can't change that."

"He was as deep into the conspiracy as Biagatti," Savage said. "As you."

"Maybe so, but that doesn't make his death any easier."

"Well, deal with it," Savage said. "Just remember we've got an insurance policy. This coup was originally your idea, it seems."

"Will I ever be able to escape your noose, Bob?"

"Doubtful. Too many great Americans have put in too much blood, sweat, and tears to let weasel politicians destroy it from within."

"Seems I've made a deal with the devil," Jamie said.

"At least it's the devil you know."

"Indeed."

"And you owe an apology to Cassie," Savage said.

"Why?"

"You used software to manufacture that conversation where it appeared Jake was leaving Cassie behind," Mahgean said. "O'Malley already has your computer and is shredding through it."

"I never doubted you, Jake," Cassie said.

"That's not the issue, Cass. She's crossed all kind of lines, but for me, that's a personal line. How about it, Senator?"

Jamie looked at Jake, then at Cassie and nodded.

"Yes. That was mostly Zara, but yes. I was part of it. I apologize, Cassie. As your godmother, I should never have considered such a thing."

"How about as a human being?" Jake shot.

"Jake," Cassie said, placing her hand on his arm. "Jamie, I can't accept what you've done or your apology. When I'm called to testify, you'll learn just how pissed off I am. Right now, I'm glad the country is secure and that you're going to be ushered off to prison."

Jake departed briefly and returned with the medical cooler and opened it in the kitchen, where Cassie joined him. Inside were more communications Band-Aids and a syringe filled with liquid.

"Is this what I think it is?" Jake asked.

"Yes. It supposedly reverses the DHT-and-Flakka mix," Cassie said. "Zara gave it to me once and it took me in the other direction. I had two shots of DHT in the last twenty-four hours. I'm coming down, but that could be helpful right now."

Mahegan retrieved the cool plastic syringe and handed it to Cassie, who walked across the room near the fireplace, and tossed it into the yellow flames. The syringe melted and the liquid evaporated, erasing any vestige of Zara's influence on Cassie's life.

"Better?" Jake asked.

"Better," she said.

Jake nodded and smiled, a rare moment of happiness in the last few months.

The roar of helicopter blades thundered above as an MH-47 passed overhead and landed in the front yard, where it had landed yesterday to evacuate the wounded.

Cassie and Jake walked down the steps with Hobart providing overwatch.

Vance was first off the back ramp, followed by President Smart and Vice President Grainger.

"Welcome back, Mr. President, Vice President," Cassie said above the din of the rotors.

The president smiled, patted Cassie on the shoulder,

and said, "Damn, you're good. Watched the entire thing from some bunker in the Blue Ridge Mountains. Now let's get this show on the road."

He pulled out his phone and began banging out a tweet:

@realjacksmart: To all the haters who were happy I was gone, I'm back from the dead! Resistance crushed. I knew Biagatti was dirty the whole time but now we have proof. Life in jail for her or anyone else who tries to take us down!

EPILOGUE

As morning broke, Jake said to Cassie, "Ready?" Cassie nodded. They walked from the parking lot of the Valley Trauma Center into what had been Broome's office. Where it had all begun. Jake removed the crime scene tape that crisscrossed the door as they stepped through. The police had investigated Broome's murder, but evidently the Valley Trauma Center had still been functioning until authorities could figure out what to do with the patients.

The sun was glaring through the windows as Cassie waved a fob in front of the keypad for the retracting circular doors. She had always wondered about why Broome had needed the security.

"Broome died right there," Cassie said. She pointed at the chair. The bloodstains were still present.

Cassie walked him through the closet and narrow hallway that led to the back of the kitchen.

"What makes you think this is the place?" Mahegan asked.

"Just something she said," Cassie replied. "Zara's list shows just one remaining Artemis assassin. I know I only saw one blue dot remaining in my BLEP, but it went blank somewhere near Charlottesville. Whoever it might be was probably on her way here and most likely had the GPS tracker removed."

Mahegan pulled his Sig Sauer Tribal from his clip-on holster. The operations tempo had been intense and their mission to stay inside Zara and Biagatti's decision cycle had them all running on fumes.

She still had Broome's fob card and used it to gain access to the residential hallway where she and Emma had bunked for two weeks. The building was eerily quiet. Spooky. She remembered the random sounds of the guards' keychains, women shouting, and Emma's rapid-fire voice.

There was none of that now. Just dead silence.

They walked past the first room and saw a woman huddled in the corner, wild eyes searching them. *Friend or foe? Who knows nowadays what those terms even meant?*

Cassie took a deep breath, bracing herself, as she looked through the window of her room. She didn't see Emma, but written in red letters—perhaps blood—was Emma's saying:

The last ride is never the last ride, and the end is never the end.

A chill shot up her spine.

The end is never the end.

"Cassie," Jake said.

"Yeah," she muttered, distracted. Then she turned and saw why Jake had nudged her.

Emma was standing twenty yards away at the end of the long hallway. Her hair was matted with blood and sweat. She held a pistol in one hand and a knife in the other.

Behind her stood ten other women, all armed with knives, and lying in wait. Without warning, they ran toward Jake and Cassie.

Keep reading for a special excerpt of
DARK WINTER by Anthony J. Tata.

DARK WINTER
A JAKE MAHEGAN NOVEL

The world order is being hacked to pieces . . .
By the time anyone realizes what's happening, it is
too late. A dark network of hackers has infiltrated the
computers of the U.S. military, unleashing chaos
across the globe. U.S. missiles strike the wrong
targets. Defense systems fail. Power grids shut down.
Within hours, America's enemies move in. Russian
tanks plow through northern Europe. Iranian troops
invade Iraq. North Korea destroys Seoul and fires
missiles at Japan.

Phase 1 of ComWar is complete.
Enter Jake Mahegan and his team. Their mission:
Locate the nerve center of ComWar—aka Computer
Optimized Warfare—and shut down the operation by
any means necessary. There are three ComWar headquarters, each hidden deep underground in Russia,
Iran, and North Korea. Each contains a human
biometric nuclear key that the team must capture to
shut down the imminent nuclear strikes. Splitting up
the team is Mahegan's only chance to prevent the next
wave of cyberattacks. But even that won't stop the
sleeper cell agents—here in the United States . . .

When Phase 2 ends, World War III begins.

Look for* DARK WINTER, *on sale now.

CHAPTER 1

Jake Mahegan kissed the scar on Captain Cassie Bagwell's back as the sheer curtains fluttered inward from the southwest sea breeze on Bald Head Island, North Carolina. He ran a hand from her bare shoulder along the taut contours of her back, heard a slight moan escape her lips, and continued running his fingertips along her hip and leg.

"Been a week," she whispered, her head turned toward the open patio sliding door. "No phone calls."

Mahegan concentrated on the task at hand, which was pleasing Cassie. Plus, phones didn't ring when they were turned off. Ignoring her comment, he brought his hand back up and firmly traced the muscles on either side of her spine, starting just below her clipped blond hair near her shoulders. He found a few knots and worked the kinks out. He'd learned that she carried her stress between the scapula bones. He rubbed the lateral muscle of each for a few minutes, feeling her body let go of a little more anxiety.

Every day had been the same. Make love. Rest. Sleep.

Eat. Make love some more. Walk on the beach, which was just over the dunes beyond the fluttering curtains. Swim in the Atlantic Ocean. He furrowed his brow as he recalled the worry on Cassie's face yesterday when he had swum a mile out to sea and a mile back. An easy swim for him. Something he had been doing most of his life, especially during his rehab from his combat wound.

He had grinned walking up the beach, spotting her cut body in the flimsy bikini. His smile slowly faded, though, as he noticed the concern etched in her countenance. Fixed gaze, doubting look, full but straight lips, arms crossed.

"Don't do that again, Jake," she warned.

"I just swam, like I always do," he replied.

"You were . . . gone. I couldn't see you—" She stopped, covering her mouth. A full tear slid from her eyes. "I'm sorry."

He had hugged her and pulled her tight, his feet on either side of hers in the sand. She had slowly relented and wrapped her toned arms around his large mass. Mahegan was nearly six and a half feet tall and a former high school heavyweight wrestler. All muscle, no fat, Cassie was five feet ten inches. She rested her head on his chest and shoulder. He felt the tears continue to flow.

He had asked himself, *isn't this what you've always wanted? A good woman to love and to love you?*

At that moment, he realized Cassie was precisely who he wanted. Never considering himself fortunate enough to find his person, she'd suddenly become a fixture in his life.

Now, this morning, he looked from Cassie's bare

back to the sun rising over the dunes and said, "I won't."

Cassie turned her head on the pillow slightly and then rolled toward him, pulling him toward her.

"You won't what?" she asked.

She had a dreamy smile on her face as if Mahegan had spent the last hour finding every spot of pain and pleasure on her body, which was exactly what had transpired.

"I won't do that again," Mahegan said.

The smile faded and then grew into something more deep and meaningful. Her eyes opened a bit, green irises radiant as blazing emeralds. A tear fell off her cheek, the first of the day.

"I've been trying to hold back, protect myself from being hurt, but I can't any longer, Jake," she whispered. "Loving you is worth the risk."

Mahegan said nothing. He let his heart receive her love, something that perhaps he had been incapable of doing before. Ever self-reliant, Mahegan had enjoyed the company of other women, for sure, but the mission always seemed to come along and nip any budding relationship before it had a chance to bloom. Still, the others had been different. Maybe it had been fate just clearing the way for Cassie. She was unique. And they'd shared dangerous combat action together, not in the sandbox of Afghanistan, Iraq, or Syria—though they had both served in those locations—but in North Carolina.

"Are you just going to stare at me with your blue eyes and square jaw?" Cassie asked. She ran a hand along the fresh shaved sides of his head. Two days ago, he had gone to the town barber, a former Marine from

Camp Lejeune just up the coast, who convinced Mahegan he needed a Ranger high and tight. Ten bucks later, he looked good as new.

"Pretty much," Mahegan said. "View of a lifetime right here."

More tears. Her fist pounded his shoulder.

"Don't you dare do this, Jake Mahegan. Don't make me love you," Cassie said.

Mahegan frowned but understood. They had all been through too much combat, too much loss to ever risk the pain of having this connection and losing it. Dull and muted emotions were more manageable than the highs and lows of plumbing the depths of love. Solitude enhanced decision making. There were no other factors to consider. He could die a hero instead of growing old—as the Croatan saying went—without the worry of hurting someone else. The ultimate selfless sacrifice: don't love, don't hurt, don't feel. Pure execution. In thirty years of life, he had lost his mother, father, and best friend in the worst possible ways. What good was love if it was just going to be snatched away from you?

"Don't give me that puppy dog look, damnit," Cassie said, sobbing.

He kissed her forehead and then her lips. She kissed him back, opening her mouth, pulling him deep.

"Don't *let* me love you, damnit," Cassie said, pulling away briefly and then diving back in for more.

Mahegan let his actions do the talking, taking them both for another physical and emotional ride that ended on the floor, the sheets wrapped around them like a shroud. A rectangle of sunlight spotlighted them. The end table lamp lay askew on the floor and two pillows were scattered around them.

"Oh my God," Cassie said, laying her arms flat on the floor. She looked outside and then back up at Mahegan. "I just hope you can keep up."

Mahegan smiled. He was beginning to wonder, as well. Cassie was relentless in bed. At first, he'd chalked it up to her working out aggression or past issues, but now he believed something different.

She loved him. No question. And she was giving herself to him. Every bit.

The helicopter blades chopped in the distance. Mahegan reared his head like a German shepherd sentry. His instincts had been muted, lost in the moment. This was what love did.

He rolled off Cassie, placing himself between her and the patio window, protecting what he held dear. Then there was a loud pounding on the front door, like a battering ram.

"My gun," Mahegan said, turning his head.

But he never had time to retrieve it.

CHAPTER 2

Luiz Yamashita smelled North Korean president Park Un Jun's morning fish breath, thinking *I can't believe I'm this close.*

Jun had just finished his breakfast and now leaned in close to Yamashita, whose only job was to interview the president. Jun was small and seemed less of a caricature in real life than the thousands of pictures and cartoons Yamashita had seen. They sat across from each other on the man's favorite balcony adjacent to his palatial living quarters. Sloped and tiled roofs overlapped above them. The courtyard was well secured with heavyset armed guards at every possible entrance. The security personnel were heavily armed with Uzis and were wearing special glasses that provided situational awareness.

A U.S. based global technology company called Manaslu had provided the glasses. Yamashita knew this because Manaslu had hired him to conduct this interview about Manaslu's new corporate facility being constructed north of Pyongyang as part of an economic development initiative. The glasses were just one of many products the hegemonic tech giant had developed. Word had it that Jun was enamored with Manaslu and its enigmatic leader, Ian Gorham.

Yamashita was a Japanese reporter living in Vancouver, Canada. While he enjoyed the rainy days and the excellent coffee, he was ready for his big break. When a mysterious man named Shayne had reached out to him to conduct the interview, he'd leapt at the opportunity. He had visions of his article appearing in the *Atlantic, Washington Post, New York Times, Huffington Post, Breitbart,* and other highly read news sources. Appearances on CNN and Fox News would follow.

He could see it now: *Luiz Yamashita, the man on the ground in North Korea, forging peace through economic development with Manaslu's enigmatic leader, Ian Gorham.* Gorham was viewed as the young new visionary. Bigger, more badass, and better than Elon Musk, Mark Zuckerberg, Jeff Bezos, and Tim Cook combined.

Shayne had provided him the documents, the questions, the access, the $100,000 advance—one hundred thousand dollars!—an unbelievable amount, and the unrestricted travel budget. Claiming to be a senior official with Manaslu, Shayne looked more like a young hipster than a corporate chief technology officer.

"Mr. Yamashita," Jun began. "A Japanese reporter in North Korea. I am opening North Korea to many new experiences, aren't I?"

"Yes, Supreme Leader. You are forging a new path for North Korea," Yamashita said.

Jun nodded and smiled. "I know you will be asking

the questions in a minute, but I want to make sure you get me on the record as thanking Mr. Gorham for allowing North Korean workers and materials to build his Manaslu factory in North Korea."

"Yes, Supreme Leader, I agree that Mister Gorham's generosity is unprecedented. But it is the strength and will of the good people of the Democratic People's Republic of Korea that have built this facility."

Jun nodded and smiled. "I'm glad you understand."

Out of the corner of his eye, Yamashita noticed several guards moving to his two o'clock, a far corner about ten yards away.

"Do not worry about my security detail," Jun said. "They are the best."

"I am not worried about anything in your presence, Supreme Leader," Yamashita said, though the entire security detail had converged to one spot and their faces, all covered in sunglasses, were peering up at the morning sky. The tall ivy-covered walls provided only a small opening of fresh air. The sun peeked through the firs angling off the steep mountain slopes overlooking the presidential redoubt.

Concern creeping into his subconscious, Yamashita hurried with the interview. "What is it you are most excited about, Supreme Leader, when it comes to the opportunities that the deal with Manaslu will provide to the good citizens of the DPRK?"

"I am thankful that UN negotiations have provided for this opportunity," Jun said. "As you know, the legacy of the Eternal President, my grandfather, is Military. The legacy of the Chairman, my father, is Self-Reliance. My legacy will be Economic Development while I continue the legacies of my mentors and family."

"All great legacies, Supreme Leader. Do the people of the DPRK believe that hosting a Manaslu factory will offset the halt in nuclear weapons production you agreed to as part of the Beijing Accords?"

Jun smiled. His lips pulled back against his teeth, making him look like a Gila Monster. His oily black hair was swept back in a youthful swatch. The jowls on his cherubic face were beet red in the cool morning air. "Next question."

Yamashita wondered, *Was he not going to comply with the accords? Of course not. No one expected him to.*

"What excites you about the Manaslu factory?" Yamashita pressed ahead. "You've said you will allow for the distribution of products but not the social media or search aspects of the Manaslu platform."

"We have twenty-five million citizens who need the same products people everywhere need. They get their information from Korean Central Television. This is the only satellite and Internet we need. We are one people."

Avoiding the topic of information and social connectivity, two of the most important and profitable platforms of Manaslu, Yamashita dove into the essence of the production and warehousing of products that Jun had agreed to perform. "What is your vision for Manaslu, an American company, in the DPRK?"

Before Jun could answer a question that truly had no answer—Yamashita believed Jun's cooperation to be a ruse—he saw a drone hovering high overhead. It was a standard quad copter, though bigger than the ones he'd seen previously. Its four whirring blades held the unmanned system in a perfectly stabilized orbit over their heads.

While it was disrespectful to break eye contact with the Supreme Leader, Yamashita's self-preservation instinct took over.

"Relax, Mister Yamashita. This is my security. We have gone high tech," Jun said. He laughed a feminine, high pitched chortle.

"Then why is there an artillery shell inside the cargo claws?" Yamashita asked.

His question was too late. The shell dropped.

Luiz Yamashita's last thought before dying was that perhaps there was more to Manaslu's overture after all.

The explosion created a fireball that incinerated everything and everyone in the courtyard.

At exactly the same time Luiz Yamashita was watching a bomb drop from a plastic hover copter in North Korea, Janis Kruklis huddled in the bushes only four hundred meters from the mighty Eighty-second Airborne Division's basecamp along the Estonian border with Russia. While Kruklis had been unable to kill any of the famed paratroopers when he was serving as an ISIS mujahedeen, he was glad that someone had recognized his skills as a mortar man. He pushed the 81mm mortar baseplate into the ground, leveled it, and covered it with dirt. Then he inserted the tip of the mortar tube base into the opening on the baseplate, twisting it to secure it in place. Screwing the mortar sight onto the frame of the weapon, he began adjusting the angle and deflection of the weapon based upon the numbers he had received this morning by coded and encrypted e-mail.

He wasn't sure why he was shooting at the Russian army, but if it would result in killing American soldiers, then he was just fine with that.

One of many ISIS fighters to flow into Europe as the quasi-caliphate in Raqqa crumbled, Kruklis had returned to Latvia forlorn. His friends had wondered where he had gone, but he never told anyone, though he imagined if someone were good enough they could monitor the chat rooms he had visited as he had prepped for war in Syria. A former sniper and mortar man with the French Foreign Legion, Kruklis missed the combat and had turned progressively against the West based upon the atrocities he saw his peers commit in the Central African Republic.

Over the past week, he had used a flat bottom boat to transport his forty rounds of 81mm mortar ammunition to his hide location less than a kilometer north of Latvia. He had good cover and concealment and hoped that he could fire all forty rounds, race to his boat, and escape to Latvia before the counterfire became too intense.

In the cool October evening, Kruklis checked his phone one last time, confirmed the elevation and azimuth of his settings, and waited for the prompt, which came almost immediately. Kneeling in the damp ground, he sighed, his breath turning to vapor. He lifted the first bomb, which looked more like a nerf football with fins than a weapon.

He lowered the fins into the tube, released the body of the projectile, and then turned away. The mortar made a loud *thunk!*

Loud enough to hear a mile away, he thought. Knowing that while the round would be in the air almost a minute, Russian and American radars had already detected it. He raced to get as many rounds into the tube as he could, one right after the other.

Thunk! Thunk! Thunk!

He heard the explosions that were some three or four miles away in Russia, thunder reverberating back toward him.

He was over halfway through his pile of ammunition when he heard Humvees along the road leading from the American paratrooper base. Machine-gun fire whipped over his head. They didn't know exactly where he was, couldn't see. They may have had the grid coordinate, but it would take them another minute to find him. That was at least ten more rounds.

He shot all but three mortar rounds before American soldiers surrounded him.

"Cease fire!" one soldier wearing night vision goggles shouted.

As Kruklis raised his hands, he heard the familiar whistle of artillery rounds screaming overhead. Russian counter battery fire. He smiled. He would kill some American paratroopers after all.

The heavy artillery tossed him into the air, along with the Americans. It was incessant and unrelenting.

His last thought was that these were big bombs, not the little ones he had been shooting at the Russians. As he lay there dying, he stared at the open eyes of a dead paratrooper and smiled again.

* * *

Ian Gorham, the CEO and founder of Manaslu, Inc., the conglomerate that had overtaken Facebook, Amazon, and Google in the social media, retail distribution, and advertising marketplace, sat in the back of his chauffeur driven Tesla S70. He stared at the information being piped to his iPad via Manaslu's microsatellite constellation he called ManaSat.

He had four such satellite constellations in the atmosphere as he prepared for his mission. Gorham viewed himself as a bona-fide genius. A Mensa member at an early age. Trouble understanding and relating to others as a child. His lineage was of average education—rural farmers and manufacturers. He had somehow hit the jackpot in the brains department. A one in a million chance. An odd mutation that combined the best of everything from both lineages—separated wheat from chaff—and distilled into his cerebral cortex.

Algorithms and code were a first language, English a second. Rapidly acquired wealth led to newly interested parties—women, men, transgenders—in his late teens. It was all so confusing.

In his early twenties—a few years ago—he'd read about the Jungian study of deep psychotherapy and realized he needed to unpack his brain so he could understand it better. With his wealth, he'd hired the best deep psychiatrist in the world. Given his exploration of the Deep Web, he'd thought it was fitting that he was going through therapy with an expert of deep psychology.

As the Tesla idled, exhaust plumes rose like fog. The bar was the target. It had a sign that read MOTOWN MIXER. Actually, a cook in the bar was the real target.

In a few seconds, Gorham had a complete dossier on the bar and its owner, Roxy Bolivar, who was no longer alive. She had bequeathed the bar to her son, who ran the place. He was gay and had the beginning stages of pancreatic cancer. His medications had just started, but the doctors didn't believe there was much hope.

He had mined this information through the Mana-Web, Manaslu's own private domain within the Deep Web, where algorithms and machine learning matched information and automatically continued to dig and match until a complete profile had been developed . . . within seconds.

During his search, he had profiled everyone associated with the bar. One profile frustrated him. The apparent cook, reported for duty at six pm, had hacked the ManaWeb. This person had penetrated the domain Gorham thought was impossible . . . and improper. It was like penetrating his own psyche without permission.

In response, Gorham had launched a delivery drone with a spy camera to the Internet Protocol address location. It had followed someone wearing a hoodie pulled over the head and face, a chef's white shirt hanging beneath the hoodie, and black pants. The cook went into the back of the Motown Mixer. The drone had attempted to gain facial recognition, but the hacker's hoodie was like a tunnel hiding the face way back in a cave.

On the brink of executing his elaborate plan, Gorham could ill afford a minor issue. The hacker was an issue. Gorham's considerable business experience taught him that minor issues often became major problems. And this hacker was an issue. He began to spin, cycling faster and faster, thinking of possible outcomes, some not so good, others very bad.

With a shaky hand, he looped his Bluetooth ear-piece around his right ear and pressed a number from the RECENT selection in his phone.

"Yes, Ian," the voice said. Part melody, part syrup, part Eastern Europe. She always gave him pause.

"Doctor Draganova," Gorham said. "Spin cycle, again."

"Please. As always, I must remind you, it's Belina," she said.

There was noise in the background. Banging, as if she were in a construction zone or kitchen somewhere.

He couldn't call her Belina. She was as beautiful as the name. He stared at the picture on his phone. Long black hair. Light blue eyes. High cheekbones. Full lips constantly pursed. Fashion model collarbones. Long neck. Slim hips.

No, he had to call her Doctor Draganova. He couldn't think of her as an object of desire *and* a therapist. It was counterproductive. "I'm spiraling a bit," he said.

"This is not a regular session, Ian. You pay me well, but we schedule our sessions. I'm almost always available, but right now I have little time."

"It's . . . okay. Just soothe me. I'm about to do something . . . high stress. I know my motives. You've helped me understand them. I know the purpose of my genius. I'm bringing all of that together. We've unpacked my mind, layer by layer. Now I need to bring it back together so I can execute."

Depth psychology focused on understanding the

motives behind particular mental conditions in order to better resolve them. Draganova had been focusing Gorham on discovering the catalyst for his actions whether they be conscious, unconscious, or semiconscious. All the big names in psychology had contributed to this field of study: Jung, Blueler, Freud, and so on.

"It's . . . it's not that simple, Ian."

Was she worried? Ian thought she sounded concerned. Her soothing voice took him back to that place he didn't want to be—viewing her as an object of desire instead of the mechanic of his mind.

More noises in the background. Some shouting. She was busy doing something. It never occurred to him that she may have a personal life. Perhaps she was entertaining guests and preparing a big meal or just in a noisy restaurant with friends . . . which made him a little bit jealous.

"I know," he whispered. "It's been a month since I've seen you."

"We've talked on the phone since. Sixteen times. We've even used ManaChat," she said. Manaslu's equivalent of FaceTime or Skype.

"What are you doing?" He realized his question sounded too familiar, and said, "I mean, what are those noises?"

"Ian, we can talk tomorrow. You know your drills. Please do them. Good-bye."

The silence in his ears was a screwdriver through the brain. Just like a Ferrari needed the world's best mechanic, his mind needed Dr. Draganova. Regardless, no matter how much he tried, he couldn't unpack his drive and desire for her. She had become shorter and shorter with him on their phone sessions. In person—always in a neutral place to which they both had flown at his expense—her clothing had been more and more provocative. Was she teasing him or challenging him to focus? Like Tiger Woods' father rattling change when he was a kid practicing putting. Perhaps that was her technique for getting him to focus on the matter at hand.

But she had helped scramble his mind, unpack it completely to its core. The drive and ambition to create a dominant global tech conglomerate came with personality traits that he needed to understand. Draganova had helped him reach in his mind and more objectively observe his mania, his fears. Obsessed with success and power, Gorham was relentless, but to his credit he wanted to know more about himself. Or was that just more megalomania coming out? He didn't have time to think about all that now.

He was at the moment where he needed to be able to synchronize a global operation. He could do it, of course. It would just be harder. Require more thinking. More individual construction of his mental faculties. Put everything back together himself instead of with her help. And he needed to do it right now.

You know your drills.

He did a few body meditation drills, working his hands into his quadriceps and hamstrings, massaging and pulling. Then he pulled at his face, stretching it in every direction, relieving the tension. Dax Stasovich, his faithful bodyguard, was outside pacing, impatient.

After a few minutes, Gorham felt well enough. He

needed to move now. The car with his commandos came rolling around the corner, parking two blocks away. Stasovich looked at him through the car window and shrugged.

It was go time.

Gorham stepped out of the car, tugged the Tigers cap down low over his face, thinking, *get your shit together, Ian*. He was one of the most recognizable men in the world. Bezos, Zuckerberg, Brin, Page, and all the other brilliant entrepreneurs were equally recognizable. In the last two years, though, he had become the hot property. He had to be careful.

He pulled the ball cap bill low over his forehead. Stasovich, a giant of a man, walked in front of him about ten yards. The man's legs pushed out and forward with every step. His bulk swayed. His arms barely moved. The man was nearly seven feet tall. Hard not to notice. That was part of the drill. Like a magic trick. Everyone look at this freak of nature friend, not the normal looking curly haired guy walking behind him.

They entered the bar and Gorham grabbed a booth. There was a slight crowd. He immediately noticed a good-looking short-haired blonde sitting at the bar. Next to her was a big man with a Mohawk haircut. He wasn't as big as Stasovich, but close. What did she see in him?

He looked at his ManaWatch, what he called his equivalent of the Apple Watch. The ManaWatch used the ManaSats and was therefore encrypted. Two messages popped up from Shayne with little green check marks next to them.

Estonia

NoKo

The plan was in motion. He glanced at Stasovich, a bull scraping his hoof looking at a red cape.

Gorham typed a message and hit SEND. "Go."

CHAPTER 3

Mahegan stared in the mirror, which reflected a man in a baseball cap across the room hunched over his beer in a booth on the far wall near the entrance.

The cap's bill was curved enough so that the man's eyes were hidden. It was a Detroit Tigers baseball cap. The man didn't look like a baseball player, didn't have the build. Wisps of light brown hair curled up onto the blue material. Not that curly brown hair disqualified a man from the major leagues, but Mahegan thought he looked too slight. Maybe he was one of those skinny middle relievers that went a few innings. Or a lanky first basemen. But Mahegan didn't think so. The man looked more like a fan, if that.

But still, that face. He was trying to place it when Cassie elbowed him in the ribs.

"Don't stare," she said.

"I'm looking directly at three bottles of tequila," Mahegan countered.

They were in downtown Detroit because Mahegan's teammate Sean O'Malley had found a nugget of information in the Deep Web indicating an attack would begin in this musty bar. The purpose of the pending raid was unclear, but was supposedly related to something much larger. That was all O'Malley knew. Something big. So, they watched and waited.

It had been O'Malley pounding on their door on Bald Head Island and Patch Owens who had been in the back of the helicopter to pick them up.

Something big had already happened, though. Hours ago, news of the death of the North Korean leader had cycled through the top-secret information circles. Mahegan was surprised that after a few hours the news programs were not covering the story. News of a provocation in Estonia was just leaking out. Apparently the Eighty-second Airborne show of force in Estonia had gotten into an artillery mix up with the Russians. Not good. Something big.

Mahegan and Cassie sat on barstools in the Motown Mixer, a trendy, hipster place intended to look like a seedy bar. The bartender had placed in front of him a tap poured Pabst Blue Ribbon. It was his first beer of the night and he had only taken a sip, which was mostly foam still settling from the pour. It was all for show. Not that he didn't want a beer. He could use one. But he had bigger urges to satisfy than drinking a beer. Stopping a raid. Getting the intelligence. And then moving to the next level of unraveling whatever it was that O'Malley had discovered.

Cool October wind rushed in every time someone opened the front door to Mahegan's eight o'clock. A sticky dark wood bar with a vertical hinged opening at the far end ran the length of the establishment. A dozen different taps shouted the names of popular draft beers, the bartender working the levers like a slot machine. An ancient color television was set to a cable news program in the corner. A reporter was speaking from a windswept field in Europe somewhere. The crawl at the bottom of the program read *Russian artillery causes casualties in Eighty-second Airborne Division deterrent force.*

"At least we had a week," Cassie said.

"Roger. Time to focus," Mahegan replied.

Cassie nodded.

"Paratroopers got hit with artillery," Mahegan said. He showed her his phone, which had practically blown up when he finally turned it on after O'Malley rushed them onto the helicopter this morning.

"Saw that. Any chance it's connected?" Cassie asked.

"Anything is possible." Mahegan scanned the growing crowd, not sure what they expected to find. "But we've got to have something to connect it to."

Earlier, when the place was nearly empty except an old guy hunched over his whiskey, Mahegan counted exactly ten bar stools, each one stained and sticky from years of beer spills and marginal maintenance. Five booths lined the wall and six tables occupied the floor.

An old time circular battery powered clock showed it was seven o'clock in the evening, which explained why the place was packed with hipsters, prepsters, college students acting twenty-one, and older men trying to pick up younger women.

Two had already tried to hit on Cassie, his "date." She was dressed in hip-hugging blue jeans, a loose, untucked button down shirt, and sharp toed leather cowboy boots. Mahegan was wearing his standard olive cargo pants, tight fitting black pullover, black leather jacket, and Doc Martens boots. With his hair looking something like a Mohawk down the middle, Mahegan, a Croatan Indian from the Outer Banks of North Carolina, was feeling the kinship with his ancestors.

He was also feeling the mission the way someone with a bum knee senses a low-pressure system. "Notice baseball hat guy?"

Cassie didn't look at the throng of people drifting through the bar, but replied, "Roger. You were staring at him. Seems twitchy. Think that's him?"

"Not sure, but he keeps looking at his watch. Pressing it, like he's reading e-mails on an Apple watch. Looks familiar, too. Can't place him, but I'm guessing his Bumble date either stood him up or we're moving any moment now," Mahegan said.

"I've got back door," Cassie replied.

"Gotta be quick."

"Roger that." Cassie scanned the room casually and said, "Use the mirrors above the bar. See shaved head guy in the corner? Like he's watching a tennis match. Us. Then baseball hat guy. Then us again. He's huge. Out of place. Like you."

In the mirror behind the whiskey and tequila bottles Mahegan studied what Cassie mentioned. It was likely the large, bulky man with the shaved head was protection for the guy in the baseball hat, their possible target. Turning back to Baseball Hat, it was impossible to discern his age. From across the room, he looked average in every way.

Was he the target?

The front door slammed open. Cool air rushed in again. A man stood with an assault rifle assessing the throng. The surreal moment hung there suspended in air. The patrons continued their revelry until someone saw the rifle, but even then, the slack-jawed observer could only open her mouth; no words came out.

Mahegan pushed away from the bar, picking a line to the rifleman the way a running back finds the gap in a defensive formation. As he found his own opening, he realized there were two ways into the pub, the front door and the kitchen door in the rear. Mahegan wasn't sure, but by the look on the face of the man with the assault rifle, the potential assailant was studying, looking for a specific person . . . and probably had an accomplice coming in the back way.

That meant Cassie would have a target. As an army intelligence officer and the first female ranger school graduate, she could hold her own.

The man at the front door was wearing all black with what looked like an outer tactical vest. He was short with Asian facial features and black hair cut to a crew. The intel had predicted assault rifles, not suicide bombers, but they couldn't be sure.

The lights went out and all hell broke loose.

As Cassie chose her line to the back door, he retrieved his Sig Sauer Tribal, sliding seamlessly through the throng, most of them seeing the look in his eyes, or the pistol, and stepping out of the way. But with the lights out, half the crowd was whooping it up as if the darkness was their newfound friend.

Enough ambient light came from outside to guide

Mahegan to the front door. As he approached, the man raised his assault rifle to fire. Mahegan kicked the weapon to the side as the attacker popped off several rounds.

Mahegan shot the man in the leg, snatched the assault rifle, and quickly inspected him for other weapons, yielding a Makarov pistol and bowie knife. He kicked the man in the head and ran toward the back door where another man had entered through the kitchen. Flashlights crisscrossed like lasers. By now, Mahegan had his night vision goggle on his head. In the green haze of the NVG, this attacker appeared stocky and white, wearing basically the same black uniform. There was a glint of an insignia on the tactical vest.

Cassie used the light of the gas flame to take aim at the man's legs and squeezed off two rounds. The man spun around, the AK-47 spitting 7.62 bullets into the kitchen hood. Smoke poured everywhere, like steam hissing from a pipe. Cassie was on top of the man, knocking him unconscious with a rap of her cowboy boots.

A third man, this one dark skinned, almost Arabic or Persian in appearance, caromed into the kitchen and shot the cook, who was wearing Backbeat Pro earphones, most likely with rock music cranked at full volume. In fairness to the cook, only five seconds had passed since the action at the front door.

Mahegan fired two center mass shots at the black clad intruder and realized he was wearing body armor. Quickly closing the distance, Mahegan leapt over Cassie, who was kneeling and making sure her target was incapacitated and tackled the third intruder. Mahegan carried him to the floor using an inside trip, an old wrestling move he'd learned in high school.

Using the butt of his pistol, he struck the man with his entire force, everything his six and a half foot, two-hundred-and-thirty-pound frame could put into it. The man's head lolled to the side and Mahegan immediately stepped behind him and dragged him through the door into the back parking lot.

Patch Owens, one of Mahegan's closest friends and a former Delta Force teammate drove up in a black SUV with shaded windows. He stopped and was quickly out the door and opening the back hatch where the front-door attacker was lying prostate. Another close friend and former teammate, Sean O'Malley, was leaning over the captive, checking his pulse. With the lights from the vehicles pumping into the kitchen, Mahegan removed and stowed his NVGs in his side pocket. He hustled outside.

"Still alive," O'Malley said.

"Cook's shot in there," Mahegan said. "Got to be the target."

"I'll grab him. What about baseball hat guy?" Cassie said as she darted back into the kitchen after dumping her prey at the rear of the SUV like a cat drops a mouse on the steps.

"No time," Mahegan said to Cassie. Then to Owens and O'Malley, "One more than we expected."

"Let's load, man," Owens said, nervous.

They loaded the other two men, O'Malley standing watch from the back seat. Cassie returned with the cook, a disheveled person wearing a white T-shirt, who was bleeding from his left arm.

"Damn, dude. WTF?" the cook said. The voice pitch was higher than Mahegan anticipated. Forced. Softer, too.

"Do what you need to do, Cassie," Mahegan said. Cassie simultaneously shoved the cook into the SUV and placed a rag filled with chloroform over the cook's nose. She removed a bottle of Betadyne and some gauze from an aid kit in the vehicle, flushed the wound, and wrapped the cook's upper arm tightly. More than a flesh wound, but nothing serious.

"Sean, grab their vehicle," Mahegan directed.

"Already got the keys," O'Malley said. He had rummaged through their captive's gear until he found the keys to a Buick Crossover.

He leapt out and flicked the key fob until lights flashed at the far end of the parking lot. He ran, jumped in, started the car, and pulled up behind Mahegan and team in the black SUV.

What had started as four teammates on a mission to capture two insurgents and an unknown hacker was in progress with four friendlies, three enemies, one wounded civilian, and two vehicles leaving the parking lot. The patrons spilled out of the bar and watched with shocked, curious eyes, perhaps notions of the Las Vegas massacre ringing in their ears.

Mahegan saw the stares and the cell phones to their ears, all calling 911. Some were using their phones to record.

"JackRabbitt okay?" Mahegan asked. The JackRabbit was a cell phone jammer that was blocking all calls from the immediate vicinity.

"Roger, but something got past it to shut down the grid. Look around. Nothing's on," Owens replied. He had both hands on the steering wheel as he pushed the SUV to ninety miles per hour.

Once Owens had the SUV a mile away, he slowed to just above the speed limit, turned onto the interstate, and raced toward their safe house in Ann Arbor. Everything they passed was completely blacked out.

"This guy stinks," Cassie said. "Smells like onions."

"Suck it up, Ranger," Mahegan said. "Wound okay?"

"More than a scrape. Less than anything serious," she said.

Mahegan nodded. He looked in the rearview mirror and saw O'Malley tracking close behind them. He noticed and gave Mahegan a thumbs up signal. They drove in silence after that, smelling the grease of the unconscious cook and the acrid aftermath of fired weapons.

Reaching the farm, Owens turned onto the dirt road and traveled all the way to the barn. Mahegan jumped out and opened the doors then closed them after Owens pulled the SUV into the brightly lit cavern. O'Malley kept the Buick outside initially.

"Patch, help Sean check the Buick for IEDs," Mahegan directed. Then to Cassie, "Lock the cook in the friendlies cage."

His charges executed their missions and returned in quick order.

"Vehicle's clean. Found a briefcase with some electronics. No explosives. Sean's going to pull it apart.

He's pulling the car in now," Owens said. The barn doors opened, O'Malley pulled in, and then the doors closed.

The barn consisted of a high-tech command pod with satellite connections and a ten terabyte Internet drop, providing Mahegan and his team instant access to everything going on in the world and any information they needed. O'Malley, their team's resident tech genius, had been instrumental in building out the barn to a disguised server farm. Owens had used his construction skills to build five prison cells from two by fours, iron rebar, and bricks. Each was completely soundproof if the door was sealed shut. O'Malley had added avatar and music capabilities to the interior of each ten foot by ten foot cell to enhance interrogation of the prisoners they expected to capture. He had outfitted each cell differently. One had a "window" that looked out onto the skyline of Moscow, Russia. Another had the minarets of mosques and the red tiled roofs of Tehran. The third had the drab office buildings of Pyongyang. And two others had Washington, DC and Tel Aviv backgrounds, respectively. The walls of the cells acted in the same fashion as the blue screen for the weather man. O'Malley could make each chamber look like anywhere in the world or even someone's worst nightmare.

Originally an operating base used by the Drug Enforcement Administration to monitor trafficking from Canada, JSOC had assumed control of the property for training purposes, mostly. Because the special mission units' training was so realistic, the facility was basically combat ready.

Mahegan opened the back to the Suburban. The three attackers they had subdued were lined up like freshly caught fish in a livewell.

"Get them to talk," he said to Cassie. "Figure out their nationality."

O'Malley and Owens tugged at the boots of the obviously white, European looking man.

She lightly tapped him on the face. "Water?"

The man nodded, then said, "Da."

"Russian," she said. Not rocket science.

O'Malley and Owens lifted the Russian by his feet and shoulders and hefted him to the Russian cell.

Looking at the man with olive skin and black hair, Cassie said to Mahegan, "Unconscious, but my guess is Iranian."

Mahegan agreed. O'Malley and Owens returned and took the man to the next structure in the barn.

The man that Mahegan had shot and kicked in the head was still alive, but barely.

"Looks Korean. Probably going to die."

"I'll try to patch up that chest wound long enough so we can talk to him," O'Malley said. He and Owens dragged the man to the farthest cell and broke out an aid bag.

The barn was nearly half a football field long and wide. Each of the cells was in a different corner with the fifth, the American cell, along the middle of the far wall from the command center. The barn sat on the back side of 120 acres of heavily wooded timber and farmland purchased several years ago by the U.S. government. Towering hardwoods fronted the property, which eventually gave way to a cleared fifty acres where about twenty cattle grazed. They were live, but props.

Mahegan gathered his team on the floor of the elevated command post and typed into the keyboard. Secure.

The response was immediate. Charlie Mike. Continue the mission.

There was no immediate need to communicate that they had an extra prisoner. While the intel intercept had come from O'Malley pinging around the Dark Web, they had either rescued the cook or properly detained him, the definition dependent upon what unfolded next. And just like they'd been uncertain of the specific number of attackers, they'd needed the attack to unfold to determine the real target of the raid. The cook had special skills, apparently.

"Okay, team. Now the fun starts," Mahegan said.

He retrieved his Blackhawk knife from its sheath on his riser belt and walked to the cell in which they had placed the cook. Before opening the door to the enclosed room, he nodded at Cassie, who shut the lights in the barn from the command center.

Opening the door, he stepped through the threshold into an anteroom, like an oxygen chamber in a submarine, closed the exterior door, locked it, and then opened the door to the cell. The cook was huddled in the corner of a room that gave the appearance of looking onto the capitol dome in Washington, DC. The hologram effect made it seem as though they were inside an office building, looking through a window onto Grant's statue and the capitol building. O'Malley had done good work. Cars drove by in real time. Pedestrians waited at street corners. An airplane banked to the south, landing at Reagan National.

"You guys FBI?"

Mahegan said nothing. He processed his surroundings and waited, even though he knew that they had no time to spare. The higher pitch in the voice seemed off-key. Forced European accent or perhaps as if the cook was trying to sound more masculine. Blood streaked across the cook's face. The prickly scalp was shiny with sweat. The huddled body, not small, maybe even lanky, but slender. The white apron was splattered with hamburger grease, as were the white T-shirt and black pants. Black Keds high-top canvas sneakers on the feet. Cassie's bandage job expert.

"Come on, man, say something."

Forced vernacular, Mahegan thought. *A woman trying to sound like a man? A man trying to be a woman?* Who knew nowadays?

The cook was shivering, perhaps needing a dose of meds.

"Why were they coming for you?" Mahegan finally asked.

"What? Who?"

"We don't have time for your bullshit. Something major is happening and you know what it is. You found it."

A moment of recognition flashed on the cook's face and in the eyes, recognizing trouble. Mahegan also recognized that this was a woman. She was forcing the octaves of her voice down, like trying to stuff too many clothes in a suitcase. It didn't work. Had the opposite effect. Regardless—man or woman—this person supposedly held the key to murder of the President of North Korea and the Russian attack on U.S. forces in Estonia, at a minimum.

"Look, man. I want a lawyer," the cook said.

"First, quit forcing your voice. I know you're a woman. It doesn't matter. And, no, you really don't. That's not how this works. You tripped over something in the Deep Web and we followed you until we couldn't follow you anymore. I'm done talking with you unless you give me something to work with. I've convinced them that you'll talk. I see it in your face." Mahegan switched his knife to his left hand and then rested his right-hand palm on the gritty grip of his Sig Sauer Tribal pistol.

A long pause ensued. The cook watched the traffic outside, seemed to consider something, and then looked at Mahegan. "How did I get from Detroit to Washington, DC?"

"And here I thought I was asking the questions." Mahegan closed his hand around the pistol grip and inched it slightly from its holster.

"Total combat," the cook said.

Mahegan stopped his motion, stared at the woman, and let the thought sink in. "Go on."

"I call it RINK. Russia, Iran, and North Korea. They're like Japan, Germany, and Italy in World War II. They're attacking asap. Everywhere. Total chaos. Total combat. Computer optimized warfare."

"Why?

"Because they can," the cook said. Eyes averted. Hands shaking like an alcoholic needing a drink.

"Who are you?" Mahegan asked.

"Just a fry cook." The words were quick, tumbling together. Rehearsed but lacking veracity.

Mahegan's hand tightened around the pistol and he removed it from the holster. To the cook, he must have looked menacing. Six and a half feet tall. Native American. Form fitting black stretch shirt. Ranger haircut. Razor sharp knife in one hand and lethal Tribal in the other.

He knelt in front of the cook. "What made you a target?"

Another long pause. Mahegan saw the cook assess him, perhaps seeing everything that Chayton "Jake" Mahegan was meant to be—The Hawk Wolfe. Named by his Croatan Indian father, Mahegan carried the instincts of both predators.

"I know who's running the show."

"Who might that be?"

"This is where we trade," the cook said.

Mahegan leveled a fierce gaze on the woman, who was now kneeling, hands on the walls, feeling the glass partition that O'Malley had built into the cell. Like a room within a room, the glass was six inches from the HD screens upon which the illusion played out.

"The trade is for your life, you understand, right? You tell us what we need, you live. You don't, you don't."

"Where am I?"

"Washington, DC," Mahegan said. "Now, you've wasted a question." He lifted the knife, blade glistening against the backdrop of a Washington, DC night. "Tell me something useful."

The cook's eyes flitted from Mahegan's menacing face to the sharp combat knife to the pistol. Mahegan stepped toward her, worked the knife in his hand, rolled his wrist, working for the best angle. Keeping the cook off balance.

Knife or pistol, which would it be?

"Phase one is conventional. Phase II is nukes."

Mahegan stopped. "When does it start?"

"What do I get for cooperation? Immunity?"

"You want immunity go get a flu shot. Like I said, your life," Mahegan growled. "If what you're saying is true, that is. Now, what's happening?"

"As I said, Computer Optimized Warfare. ComWar. Like those algorithms that figure your buying habits and show in your Facebook feed what you like to get on Amazon. This thing is fine-tuned. Shuts down power grids. Drops cyber bombs. Closes every Wi-Fi hotspot. Electromagnetic pulse. Directed Energy. All combined. Followed by artillery launches. Tanks attack. Infantry rolls through. Computerized blitzkrieg. Then it assesses how effective a particular attack was, makes the necessary algorithmic changes in seconds, updates the programming in all of the weapons and communications systems, and keeps attacking. Does it all in stride. Artificial intelligence and machine learning blitzkrieg. That's ComWar."

"ComWar? When's it start?"

"Dude. It's already started. And there's nothing that can stop it. Well, one thing."

Dude. Mahegan let it slip because he was getting somewhere with the cook. "What's the one thing?"

"Biometric keys. Humans. Russia, Iran, and North Korea each have one person that is the biometric key. It's the lowest tech that supports the highest tech. Brilliant really."

"The keys do what?"

"They unlock the nuclear arsenal. Anything is hackable nowadays. Why would nuclear codes be any different?"

"Where are these people?"

"In their countries, of course."

"Like next to the decision maker?"

"Something like that. Protected. Available until needed."

"Who's behind it?"

"And for that, you have nothing worth trading, my friend. Because you saw they were going to kill me. So, it's either you or them and as scary as you look, I'll take you over what I saw in their Dark Web planning site."

Still, something hung in the back of his mind. *Nothing that can stop it?* That was what people said about actual blitzkrieg when the Germans rolled through Europe during World War II. While he wasn't a computer genius, Mahegan did know that in general, nothing was perfect. Nothing was completely unstoppable. Something may be *hard* to stop, but that didn't make it unstoppable. He thought of an army maxim. *If you can be seen, you can be hit.*

"You're a computer genius. You probably either built this or found it. If you can find it in the Web, you can stop it."

The woman opened her eyes and locked on with Mahegan's flat stare. She had wide oval eyes, brown irises, but those could be contact lenses. She had gone to some length to hide her appearance and her person.

Part actress, part computer nerd, she was something more.

"There's only one thing that can stop it. You've got three days or we're all toast. And when you're ready to trade, I'll tell you exactly what's happening."

"The biometric keys?"

"Not saying anything else until we've got a deal."

"What kind of deal?"

"Let me go. I want to live."

"As long as you're with us, you'll live. It's out there that's more dangerous."

"Maybe. Depends on where you are. Stuff is happening fast."

Mahegan nodded. Felt the sense of urgency.

He walked out of the cell and into the barn where he gathered O'Malley, Owens, and Cassie. "If this cook is right, this is World War Three. And we've got seventy-two hours to stop it."

Visit our website at
KensingtonBooks.com
to sign up for our newsletters, read
more from your favorite authors, see
books by series, view reading group
guides, and more!

BOOK CLUB

BETWEEN THE CHAPTERS

Become a Part of Our
Between the Chapters Book Club
Community and Join the Conversation

Betweenthechapters.net